Stavewood

A novel
By
Nanette Kinslow

2013 Lighthouse Publishing
Copyright © 2008 by Nanette Kinslow
ISBN-13: 978-0615808147
ISBN-10: 061580814X

lighthousepublishing@comcast.net

First Lighthouse Group publishing April 2013
Second Lighthouse Group publishing June 2013

Published in the United States by Lighthouse Publishing Group
Cover design by Patrick Warn

To my wonderful husband Patrick who fulfilled all of my fantasies and taught me the meaning of unconditional love, my daughter Jessica for her support and enthusiasm
And
To
Faye

Fairy Tales are born from our need for love and without romance the world is bitter.
With love in your heart the world is always sweet.
~ Nanette

Chapter One

*A*nother stitch dropped. Rebecca fumbled with her needles trying to get back into her rhythm. She wished she could blame her mistake on the constant jostling of the rattling train car, or the worn and bent condition of her bone needles, but, as usual, her efforts to distract herself failed as miserably as her knitting.

She deposited her handiwork into the folds of her lap and instead tried to peer out into the mist beyond the window. The rain drove in sheets across the plains, relentless, as it had been for nearly two days. Dampness had overtaken her skirts and her stockings clung in uncomfortable stickiness to her slender ankles.

Rebecca pulled the watch from her pocket and checked the time. Caught between wishing her trip was finally over and yet terrified of arriving at her destination, she turned back to the window pane and saw only her own reflection. The blanket of pouring rain ran in steady drivels and left a dreary view, her face gray in dampness and wearily etched with exhaustion. She surrendered any attempt to make out the surroundings outside of the train and attempted to return to her knitting.

Even to the casual onlooker Rebecca was something out of the ordinary. One might notice that her clothing, though finely made, was threadbare, or detect the air of dignity with which she carried herself. Perhaps they would see her elusive manner of being, which spoke either of great strength or perfect fragility, since in some it is very hard to identify the difference. Noticeable also would be her age. At nearly eighteen Rebecca certainly was a young lady blossoming into womanhood. But, however you perceived her clothing or age or mannerisms, Rebecca undeniably possessed exceptional beauty. Her pale complexion, creamy as porcelain against her dark sable hair, and her delicately arched brows gave her the look of a fine China doll. Rebecca was indeed hardly bigger than a doll, even in the best of health. These days found her thinner than usual and her fair skin showed darkening circles beneath bright emerald eyes. Her unusually long hair was knotted to the nape of her neck and the collar of her worn cape fell open at her pale throat.

"This is madness," her cousin Emma had warned her. "You're a mail order bride? That's what you're doing Rebecca. You're selling yourself out as a mail order bride!"

Since David's death Rebecca had tried to hold her head up everywhere in her society. How could he have left her so shamed, penniless and outcast? She blamed herself for her foolishness. She had given up blaming him. He was dead now, and she was certain she had learned from her mistake. This time it would be different. There would be a new life, a new world, and a stranger for whom she cared nothing. This time it was going to be under her control. She steadied herself on the wooden seat and inserted the old bone needle into a dropped stitch with determination.

Wife wanted. Widower. Large farm owner. 12-

year-old son. Marriage within one year. T. Elgerson, Billington City, Minn.

She thought the ad perfect in its simplicity. No frilly words or even promises, except of course the arrangement of marriage taking place within one year. This wasn't going to be a man fraught with embellishments and flourishes of promises. No David this man, no indeed. This man would be very different. Other ads were so often filled with fancy pledges and guarantees of prosperity, all of the this-and-that Rebecca was sure were likely lies. Handsome? Humph! Why, many of the ads had horrendous spelling errors, frightful grammar and some made little sense at all! No elaborate lies indeed from Mr. T. Elgerson.

Rebecca had studied those ads all so carefully since coming across the publication in the kitchen dustbin. How funny she had thought it, that anyone would choose such a method to find a wife. She often entertained herself for hours over the ads, so many and so many so very funny. She read them often to Emmy at tea and they would laugh naively at the silliness of it all. David regarded it as petty and foolish to find such amusement with something made use of by the help, but he would wave his fine hand and tell her that if it kept her occupied, what did he care? Rebecca thought it silly but harmless as well once. David didn't really care, she knew, but she never imagined at the time that he was satisfied as long as she was occupied with anything at all and did not suspect or interfere with his gambling and infidelities.

Rebecca checked the watch again, frustrated that

only a few minutes had passed. She put aside her knitting and pulled a carefully folded bundle from her bag, gently untying the satin ribbon and then methodically spreading the tattered contents across her cloaked lap. She carelessly lifted a stray strand of hair from across her slender cheek and tucked it back behind her ear. She set aside the stub to her train ticket assuring her passage from New York to St. Peter with irritation. Rebecca was certain that Mr. T. Elgerson had intended her trip to take place on the first class Pullman car and never planned her to suffer here in third class. Although she had to admit that the ticket spelled this out she couldn't help feeling that clearly the porter was somehow responsible for the mistake. It never occurred to her that things would be any other way, so Rebecca had never bothered to read the ticket while in England. The telegram, after all, said it all:

May 10, 1895
Passage arranged
Rendezvous Coach in St. Peter
West Hotel
September 1
T. Elgerson

Rebecca had been so thrilled the day it had arrived. The poor delivery boy surely must have thought she had taken leave of her senses when she hugged him unashamedly in her excitement. Nearly every cent had gone toward paying the photographer who had taken her picture to be sent with her reply to the ad. Rebecca hadn't realized until the telegram arrived that she had been so tense with anticipation for weeks.

"It's here! It's from him!" she nearly sang while dancing about the foyer and hugging the confused boy. Her flowing skirt swept around the both of them and she spun in her exhilaration. Rebecca shoved a meager coin into the bewildered lad's palm, and, gathering up her billowing skirts, she dispatched him eagerly. She held the telegram to her bosom in relief and expectancy.

The bell rang a second time and Rebecca flung open the portal, still swept up in the excitement of the moment.

"Goodness gracious, Becky!" Emmy exclaimed. "You're all rosy and flushed… what on earth?"

Rebecca took Emmy by the hand and excitedly towed her into the parlor. In an animated production Rebecca described her design for her future, reading aloud a copy of the letter she had sent in reply to the ad.

"Oh Emmy, it was so perfect," she splashed on excitedly. "I was very careful to not let on anything about David and all that. I wrote back just like he had posted in his advert. You know, that I was a widow and seeking a new life. Not much more than that. Then I enclosed the picture. A very serious picture since I'm sure he's a sober type of man." She attempted, suppressing her exuberance, to duplicate the pose, illustrating her portrayed attitude for the picture. "Well, you get the idea," she declared when her attempt at an unsmiling stance failed her. "And then today, just now," she rattled on, "I get the telegram! Rendezvous… that's what it says," she bubbled. "Isn't it wonderful?"

Emma had only stared at her in disbelief.

"Why did I even tell her?" she asked herself as the train took another unnerving jolt. Emma would never understand. How could she? Spoiled and living without want she would never appreciate any of it, Rebecca thought. Emma knew nothing about debts, about losing her home, her property. Nothing about nothing. Rebecca had just that when David had died, nothing. Emma never knew how an afternoon invitation to tea and cakes would be Rebecca's only meal that day. She never saw that patched petticoat was done up out of necessity and that Rebecca had no means to replace it. Emma had made it sound so dirty, so humiliating… mail order bride… "Picture bride", she had said. Rebecca shuddered at the thought.

It could sound that way, yes, and Rebecca had had those same thoughts once, until the debt collectors had visited so many times. Until the day that shameless piece of trash had appeared at her door without even having the decency to disguise her obvious condition claiming that she was carrying David's child and expecting to be included in the trust! It didn't matter that the trust no longer existed. It did, however, matter that this hussy had visited the lawyers and David's family before approaching Rebecca's door and that, over the next few weeks, she was merely one of several others in similar situations.

The day Rebecca saw the tiny ad from Mr. Elgerson she knew it would all change. It *would* change and Rebecca knew that this would be how.

She'd answer the ad and it would change everything.

Emma's wrong, Rebecca told herself. This was the answer. In a year she would be remarried, far from home, far from prying opinions and debts and those poor illegitimate babies and free to do as she pleased. In a year she would invite Emma to a fine wedding with a rich landowner and Emma would see the light. *That* Emma would understand. After all, every beau her cousin had considered marrying herself had title, and marrying for love was something Emma would never do. This time I won't either, she reaffirmed. Not this time.

She shivered in the stuffy train car and tried to shake off the memories, again checking her pocket watch in apprehension and anticipation. The scent of weary travelers spoiled the air and the sounds of snores and whimpering children hung as an intrusive backdrop to her thoughts. Steam clung and dripped along the tiny window and the train pressed on as Rebecca fought with her resolve, pressing her doubts and fears deeper into herself.

Rebecca leaned her petite head back against the hard seat and daydreamed of the open acres of land that awaited her, a sweet smile curving on her slender lips. Romping horses dotted the horizon as she imagined herself knitting on the veranda instead of this stifling train car. She would feel the warmth of the sunshine and would plan her wedding in her newly planted rose garden. If only the rain would cease she was sure her dream would spread out before her.

A hard jolt of the train jerked her back to reality, the piercing whistle signaling yet another in what seemed like endless stops.

"Ticket please, Miss," the porter requested once again. Rebecca carefully unfolded her precious bundle and searched for her rite of passage. Sure she had had the ticket moments ago, she fumbled through her few personal belongings, rummaging around while the porter hung patiently over her. Finding the stub, she pressed it into to his hand impatiently, lifting a fine brow to show her disdain for his chosen profession.

"Sir," she said, in her most condescending tone, "after all of the wretched miles I have traveled in this horrid contraption, and the innumerable times you have asked for that ticket has it not occurred to you sir, that I do indeed possess a ticket? Or perhaps it is something you are incapable of recalling?"

"No, Ma'am." He turned away from her and began to approach the passenger seated behind her.

"Sir?" Rebecca readdressed him, more frustrated than ever and thoroughly dissatisfied with his response. "I have not yet finished speaking to you!"

The porter turned briefly towards her and then returned to his duties.

"Humph!" Rebecca sighed. "Heathens!" she thought. How rude these people were, but soon that would all change and they would all recognize her for what she really was.

Suddenly she hung her head in realization. "Who am I really?" she thought. "I'm seated in this third class seat with my patched petticoat and unwashed hair, wretched to the very core of my being." She hoped the hotel in town near her new home would afford her the opportunity to freshen up, and a chance to change into the one appropriate piece of clothing she had carefully packed into her trunk. The satin visiting dress, carefully remade from her mourning attire, in the smart black and white that showed off her trim figure would be perfect, she thought, for her first meeting with Mr. Elgerson. Of course, a hot bath would renew her spirits, and then everyone, especially her newly intended husband, would see that she was indeed a lady. The watch ticked on, bringing her closer to her destination and her uncertain future.

The steady click of the train wheels coaxed her back into her daydream, and the wash of the rain continued to splash dully against the car. Rebecca's past fell further and further behind her as she pressed on towards the realization of her new dreams.

"Mail order bride," she thought. "We'll see who's ordering whom." Rebecca drifted off to thoughts of warm sunshine, fine foods, lovely gowns and poor Mr. Elgerson at her beck and call. She could imagine him now, fussing over her. She felt sure the initial T. must stand for something very distinguished. Thurston possibly, or maybe Talbot, or perhaps, since this was America, Thomas. Yes. "Thomas".

"Thomas dear, bring me my wrap," as she lounged around the parlor fire.

"Of course, darling, straight away!" And off the man would go.

"Yes," Rebecca smiled. "That's exactly how it will be."

A clamor rose up around her tearing her from her

blissful musings as passengers bumped and bustled about in the crowded car.

"Haaaawk Bennnnnd Staaaaaatiooooonn," the dreadful porter intoned loudly.

Rebecca gathered her things close to her. She hated these endless interruptions. Hundreds of them it seemed. These pointless delays, although sometimes called "rest stops" by other passengers, gave her no rest. She watched the pitiful girl across the aisle bundle up an infant in one arm and then pull a toddler by the hand through the commotion towards the end of the car. No one anywhere on this awful machine, that she could see, had anything in common with her. Each of them seemed more horrid than the last. All were sad, dirty and exhausted common folk. Their attire was unflattering and mundane. Even those not wearing homemade clothes seemed to have chosen only the most ill-fitting and poorly made garments.

At least these people were a step up from the wretched lot on the ship. Rebecca tried to be thankful that she did not suffer her sea voyage in steerage, although her passage had been far worse than she ever imagined possible. Rebecca's stomach churned at the memory, reminding her that she had not eaten since morning.

Electing not to abandon her torturous bench to fight the crowd toward fresher air, she peeled open her oil stained paper parcel and extracted a small slice of bread and a sliver of dried meat. The beef was as tough as shoe leather and she bit off the smallest taste disdainfully and chewed it slowly. The small chunk of bread went down more easily although she knew that, by the following day, what remained in the package would not be edible. The tiny apple she tried next was much more satisfying and still held a hint of its sweet original flavor.

"There surely will be an orchard," she whispered to herself. Rebecca could almost hear the warble of birds happily flitting through her future orchards and feel the sun streaming through the trees. She'd go there, she vowed, and gather the magic of it into her lungs.

The woman across the aisle climbed back to her seat and the filthy toddler peered sadly towards Rebecca while she delicately sampled her apple.

"Why doesn't she feed that child?" she thought. "Over two days I have not seen her put a single bit of food before him. What kind of people are these?" She pulled the remainder of the bread from her meager collection and offered it to the waif. The child waddled across the aisle precariously and put out his tiny hand.

"Thank ya, Ma'am. That's right kindly o'ya. Where ya travl'n to?" the emaciated mother asked.

"St. Peter," Rebecca replied under her breath, uncomfortable with conversing with the female. "Then to Billington." Rebecca turned away towards the window hoping her reply would sufficiently satisfy the woman's curiosity.

"Fine country there ya s'pose?" The young mother asked. "Home to ya, is it?"

"No. Well, yes." Rebecca looked straight ahead.

"'Scuse me?"

"I'm going there to marry." Rebecca bit her lip. "Why on earth did I even reply?" she asked herself. "It's not her business where I live or don't."

"Pit'ure bride are ya?" The woman pried on.

"Pardon me?" Rebecca gasped

"Y're one of them pit'ure brides! They's men there lookin'. That's why I'm headed out this way m'self!"

Rebecca's face turned ashen and she steadied herself on the wooden bench. She felt her chest tighten and a cold chill of perspiration began running between her breasts and into her corset. She pushed her bundle frantically into her satchel and rose to exit the car.

"This waif," she thought to herself. "Why this girl couldn't be more than fifteen, and two children in tow as well?" Rebecca scrambled to leave the car, her heart pounding loudly in her head.

"Excuse me, Ma'am." The porter planted himself in Rebecca's path and took her arm. Rebecca felt the world around her reel and her legs go limp beneath her.

"Are you alright, Ma'am?" The porter steadied her and eased her back into her seat.

"I need to get off this train," Rebecca whispered. Her mouth had turned dry and she felt her lips tingling. How could this be? A picture bride? "Oh, God, please," she whispered.

"You want off the train? The train's about to leave the station," the porter urged.

"No!" Rebecca gasped. "Please let me off now!"

Rebecca felt herself being lifted down the aisle by two of the male passengers, one under each arm, her skirts dragging on the splinters of the rough floorboards. The dread was consuming her too rapidly for her to feel the embarrassment she would

Rebecca surrendered to his pleas, certain he'd give her no peace until she entered his desolate station. What if the man had intentions? She didn't want to think about it. What did it matter anyway? She decided he was a bit simpleminded, but likely harmless.

"Now Miss, where ya bound for then?" The man stood, obviously proud to have lured Rebecca inside as she shuffled into the station building and plunked down onto a hard wooden seat.

"St. Peter," she replied dejectedly.

"Why ya're not far from there at all!" he beamed triumphantly. "Too bad ya got off the train. Ya'd about be there by now!"

Rebecca shot the man a glaring look. Why did he insist on deepening her misery? Be there by now? Then what? Rebecca shuddered, soaked through and chilled to the bone

"I suppose ya left your luggage on the train. I'll telegraph ahead and they can leave it at the station there."

Rebecca again burst into tears, unable to imagine what it would be like to finally arrive in St. Peter. She knew that there would be a carriage there to take her to Billington, but until now it had never occurred to her that no arrangement had been made in the event that she did not arrive promptly in St. Peter. The only things she now owned were her boat and train tickets. No money, no hotel fare. "What a fool I've been," Rebecca thought. "That poor girl on the train was no better off than me, but she had the sense to stay on the train and arrive at her destination on time." Rebecca groaned miserably.

"Another train'll be along soon, Miss." The man began wringing his fur hat in his hands while trying desperately to sooth the sobbing girl. He unscrewed a battered flask and poured a dark liquid into a misshapen tin cup. He slunk his bulk down onto a bench facing her and offered up the cup.

The warmth of the hot metal mug and the curiously pungent liquid calmed Rebecca and, although the beverage was unfamiliar to her, it was strangely cordial to her broken spirit. After a time she felt some of the chill pass and she found herself feeling unexpectedly comfortable, alone in the isolated station with only the simple man.

"Finn's the name, Ma'am." He tipped his fur cap to Rebecca as gallantly as if it were a silk top hat. It painted an odd picture to Rebecca who studied the man's huge calloused hands and soiled garb.

"Rebecca Fagan," she replied. "I'm off to St. Peter and then to Billington to be married!" Rebecca giggled at her bold announcement. "Yes married," she hiccupped, "To a man I know nothing about."

"Why ya're one of the brides!" Finn looked at her excitedly. "Ya're such a pretty thing I ought to get me a bride from the papers too!" Finn blushed deeply and Rebecca radiated.

"Thank you, sir!" Rebecca replied.

Rebecca couldn't make sense of her feelings. She was terrified of her situation, yet strangely she didn't care so much now. She felt warm and somehow cozy and Finn's kindness made everything seem different somehow.

"Could I have more?" she asked, offering the cup to the man.

ordinarily have experienced at any other time from such rough handling.

Chapter Two

$\mathcal{T}$he men deposited her onto a log bench beside a small, closed station and she heard the call of "Alllll aboooooooard!" The engine hissed and creaked as the train tugged away.

Rebecca buried her face in her hands and sobbed violently.

"What have I done?" she cried. "I don't know where I am and my trunk is on the train." Rebecca's body rocked with agony.

"If that girl is going where I'm going and she answered an ad and she's one of the girls who…" She couldn't bear to think about it.

Rebecca pulled her satchel against her chest and rocked like a child. What did it matter that her skirts pulled rain from the puddles beneath her like a lantern wick? Nothing mattered to her now. Her life at home was over even before she had left, but now there was no future, no promise for tomorrow, nothing. Rebecca angrily kicked her foot sending a spray from her skirts and cloak into the doorway of the little station.

"Whoa there, Missy!" a voice bellowed from inside. "If you want to set out there and get yourself soaked to the skin go right ahead, but keep it outside with ya!"

The pitiful young woman sobbed uncontrollably, gasping deeply as the voice revealed itself to be a stocky man wearing a fur cap and oiled apron as he stood in the open doorway. The timber frame outlined his solid structure and made him look like a natural addition to the coarse log building.

"Now, now, Miss, it can't possibly be all that bad. Come on in out of the rain there and we'll set ya right."

Rebecca looked up at the man through soaked lashes and sniffed softly.

"I'm off the train," she sighed. "I can't go on and I can't go home. Leave me be."

"Why, ya can always go on, Miss," the attendant replied. "No matter what, ya can always go on. No problem that ya're off the train. Folks leave the train all the time and wander off, but ya can get right back on the next one and show ya're ticket and you're back on ya're way. No problem." He smiled at Rebecca with such simple promise and warmth in his round face that she was only more convinced that he had no idea of her misery and she began to cry uncontrollably again.

Unsure of exactly how to deal with the pitiful girl suffering on the bench, he approached her and stood wringing his hands before her.

"Well, at least come inside, Ma'am. I can't leave ya out here gettin' soaked and I don't fancy being soaked much myself."

Rebecca gazed around the solid structure and found she had to struggle to focus in an attempt make out her surroundings more clearly. The rough walls were hewn from solid, straight logs, giving the building a weighty feeling, the solidness of it making her feel safe and protected. A small iron stove sat centered in the room and she held her feet close enough to bring a light steam from her soaked skirts. There were several solid benches and a small partial wall on one side that she supposed was some kind of ticket booth. A huge moose head adorned one wall and upon peering around the corner she spied a sagging cot against the wall in a small adjoining room.

"Do you live here?" Rebecca queried, rising on her feet and tipping back a bit on the bench. Her tongue felt thick and heavy as she spoke and she caught the edge of the bench in a slight wobble.

"Suppose that'd be enough," Finn replied. "Who's the man to be?"

"Oh my," Rebecca gasped at a hiccup. "What man?"

"Yar groom Miss, who ya marrying?"

"Mr. T. Elgerson," Rebecca smiled boldly. "He's my man!" She lifted her arm as though to cheer.

Rebecca was aware of the room slipping quickly to one side, although she could not imagine how that would be possible.

Chapter Three

Rebecca woke to the sound of a harsh woman's voice in the other room.

"You gave her brandy, Finn? Before or after she told you she was the one ordered for Elgerson? You're a damned fool, Finn. Nuthin' but a damned fool!"

"She was soaked to the skin and they put her off the train. I couldn't jus' leave her out there to freeze to death." Rebecca recognized Finn's deep coarse voice. "I didn't know nuthin' about her comin' for Elgerson until after."

"Well, we can't just put her back on the train. I suppose we need to find some other way to send her on her way," the woman huffed.

Rebecca had prayed for sun throughout most of her trip, but the blasted, bright beams assaulting her as she looked around the unfamiliar room brought her no pleasure.

She was suddenly awake on a narrow cot and unable to fathom how she came to be there. Her head felt twice its normal size and her eyes ached painfully as she attempted to assess her situation. Where were her clothes? She wrapped the rough flannel sheets around herself in embarrassment and tried to free herself of the sagging cot to make her way towards the doorway. Rebecca knew she was in a bad situation, but she felt compelled to find out where she was. The girl was frantic with confusion. Her head pounded as she rose and a disturbing uneasiness roiled in her stomach.

Stumbling across the room, she caught the sheet in a large splinter protruding from a small table and a lantern hit the wooden planked floor with a loud crash.

"Well, well, her highness lives!" Feet firmly in the doorway there stood a huge mass of a woman. "So, you've decided to get up I see!" The female was dressed in men's dungarees and appeared to be papered in a mammoth plaid shirt. Her hair was piled on the back of her head in a careless fashion, the red tones of it ranging from carrot to the bright color of barley straw framing a ruddy, round, weathered face.

Rebecca heard heavy footsteps as the woman advanced threateningly towards her. She grabbed Rebecca's arm roughly and sat her squarely on the cot where she had been sleeping.

"Who are you?" the woman demanded.

"Rebecca Fagan," the girl replied softly. "What happened to my clothing?" Rebecca tried to sound bold through her fear and misery.

"Worthless," the woman declared. "Can't wear them anymore. I'll get you others. Finn said you're a picture bride for Elgerson. That true girl?"

"Yes," Rebecca replied timidly, unable to find any resolve in her quivering voice.

"When was the last time you heard from him?"

"When he wired me my travel arrangements." Rebecca shuddered and pulled the flannel closer to her petite frame. "You know him?" Rebecca ventured.

"Everyone knows Elgerson 'round here I suppose."

Rebecca was suddenly encouraged. Someone who knew him could help! She could find out so many things she wanted to know about the man even before she saw him!

"Oh, please," she tried sounding friendly and kind to the gruff woman. "Please tell me what kind of man he is!"

The woman rubbed her chin thoughtfully.

"Oh, a fine elderly man," she responded.

"Elderly?" Rebecca gasped to herself. She shook off her disappointment, certain the woman must be wrong, but tried inserting an older, but distinguished gentleman into her vision.

"I see," Rebecca responded with distress.

The woman smiled down to Rebecca in a crooked fashion and left the room, promising to return with suitable clothing.

She returned with a stack of items in her arms and Rebecca ventured another question.

"Are you the one who undressed me?" Rebecca blushed in shame.

"Who else?" the woman coarsely replied.

Rebecca stuttered, "W-well I remember Finn and then…" Her voice trailed off.

"Finn? Finn can't hardly dress himself. Get those clothes on and I'll take you to Billington myself."

Rebecca apprehensively took the clothing and turned her back to the woman.

"Call when you're finished… Bedra!" the big

woman exclaimed and left the room.

"Bedra?" Rebecca whispered to herself, assuming it had to be the woman's name. She tried to convince herself that the woman's rough mannerisms were non-threatening and began to look through the clothing. Her disappointment forced her to plunk down on the cot. Men's clothing, how unheard of! It hadn't occurred to her that this outfit seemed suitable clothing to the huge woman.

Rebecca pulled the first item of clothing from the stack and found it to be a course and thinly worn pair of men's britches. She slipped her slender foot into the garment and realized that she could fit completely into one leg of the baggy pants. The textile was so threadbare that she was certain the awful article of clothing, if it could be considered that, offered no decency whatever to her trim backside. She relaxed, somewhat, upon donning the roomy shirt, since it fell to her ankles, but, without her camisole beneath it, the fabric felt rough against her delicate breasts. The oversized jacket offered a bit more decency, but the cap she found as the last item in the stack made the entire ensemble all the more ridiculous.

Rebecca sat on the bed with the tattered cap in her pale hands and considered her predicament. It was impossible for her to consider going anywhere in this outlandish garb. The thought of meeting anyone, especially Mr. Elgerson, clad in such an outrageous costume was unthinkable to her. The fog in her head began to clear a bit and she tried to remember where exactly she was.

What was the last train stop? She rubbed her aching head and tried to remember what the porter had called out before stopping here. Rebecca groaned. She knew it would do her no good whatsoever since she had never bothered to look at the schedule of stops and even a recollection of the porter's calls would give her no clue as to her location.

"My trunk!" Rebecca gasped.

Finn had said he would be able to wire ahead to the train and recover the trunk. "That would solve so many problems!" she whispered to herself. If she could simply recover her belongings she could rid herself of this peculiar outfit and resume her travels on the next train as Finn had assured her. Once in St. Peter, dressed decently, she could decide a course of action. Perhaps she could ask around about Mr. Elgerson and he would fetch her as she had planned. Or perhaps she could wire Emmy.

Rebecca shook her head. "No," she told herself. Asking Emmy to bail her out was impossible. She decided that getting her trunk and going on and meeting Mr. Elgerson was her only alternative.

She gathered her lengthy hair, twisted it into a coil, stuffed it under the cap and then shoved it firmly onto her head. She took a deep breath and stepped towards the doorway.

Peeking into the room, she recognized with relief that she was still at the same train station she had arrived at the previous evening. She discovered that she was situated in a room behind the ticketing desk. Behind the counter the huge female was precariously perched upon a small stool, the main bulk of her broad backside spilling generously to either side of the straining seat.

Rebecca stepped boldly into the room, determined

to recoup her belongings and be on her way as quickly as possible.

"I'm ready," Rebecca spoke up.

Bedra leapt from the stool, unbalancing the piece of furniture and ignoring it as it fell and toppled to the floor. She hurriedly stuffed several slips of paper into a small pile while glaring at Rebecca sternly.

"I told you to call me from there when you had dressed!" the woman bellowed, her ruddy face flushed and agitated.

"Where's Finn?" Rebecca stepped forward swallowing hard.

"What's your concern with Finn?" the woman snarled.

Rebecca cleared her throat delicately in an attempt to keep her voice from cracking.

"Finn assured me I could catch the next train without complication and that he would be able to retrieve my trunk by wiring ahead to the next station. I would like to know if he has done so." Rebecca folded her arms in an attempt to appear determined, despite her apprehension. She began tapping her tiny foot, regarding the woman openly, while trying to look unwavering in her request.

The massive woman looked over Rebecca from head to toe and gave the girl a disapproving glare.

"That's impossible now," the woman informed Rebecca while stuffing papers into her back pocket. "The train is not running so your desires must go unfulfilled," she chuckled gruffly. "I'll take you to town myself," she announced, waving her hand toward Rebecca and straightening the stool.

Rebecca's face fell and her chest tightened in

dread and disappointment.

"B-but I can't possibly go like this…" Rebecca stammered.

"It's no bother," the woman grunted back oblivious to Rebecca's predicament.

"No, I mean…" Rebecca's voice trailed off.

"Go bring the buggy 'round from the back and I'll get you to town."

Rebecca stood hesitating and uncertain as the woman turned impatiently towards her.

"What are you waiting for?" the giant woman queried gruffly.

"Well," Rebecca began, "I just…" Her voice trailed off once again.

Rebecca peered cautiously through the doorway toward the tracks. No one was about to witness her outfit. Once she was sure there would be no onlookers, she tiptoed outside.

The day was awash in brilliant sunlight and the dazzling brightness assaulted Rebecca's vision, intensifying the ever-present pounding of her head. Beyond the tracks she saw a seared hillside, blackened and ghostly, with tall tree trunks bare and scorched. The image was foreboding and disturbing, showing no signs of life anywhere. A damp mist hung along the ground, dissipating into the sunlight. The eerie picture seemed fitting somehow, as though the sun had deceived her, hiding for days behind the rain to reveal the land's true nature only now. Rebecca saw it all as the perfect cruel joke. This was the reality of her vision, all a nightmare she would never wake from. Rebecca blinked back a single tear and rubbed her nose with a rough sleeve.

"Mother, that fool horse has pulled the buggy right onto the tracks. He's going to kill himself and take the buggy with him!"

Rebecca winced and returned to the tangle of laces.

"Hush!" Bedra touched her lips with her index finger and her tone was suddenly low and guarded. She gestured to the door and the two women stepped outside onto the platform, leaving Rebecca inside to put on the boots.

Chapter Four

*I*n the light of the morning sun, Bedra looked fondly at her daughter, Octavia. The younger woman stood over six feet tall, a strapping, solid young female with wild red hair and a completely freckled complexion. It was readily apparent to others that Octavia would someday become her mother's image. Someone else would also see that, although younger by nearly twenty-five years and not yet possessing Bedra's full girth, Octavia could not be considered attractive.

Not so in Bedra's eyes. Bedra's vision of her daughter was that of a healthy, strong girl from hearty stock. Bedra was rarely stern with her, but this situation called for it.

"Where is she, mother? Uncle Finn told me Elgerson has ordered a picture bride and she got off the train here last night." Octavia's voice was just above a whisper, yet she still stomped her foot in agitation.

"She's inside and you want nothing to do with her," her mother replied.

"I want to see her! How dare he think of doing such a thing after all these months! Why, I never!" Octavia folded her arms across her ample bust and stomped her foot again.

"Now calm down child." Bedra tried soothing the big girl in a sweet tone.

"There's nothing to look at," she went on. "The girl is no more than a child, perhaps sixteen at most and skinny as a bean pole at that! If Elgerson were to lay eyes on her he'd see in a heartbeat that she'd never survive. She'll be just another to go the way of all those other homesteader's wives. And simple? Why the girl can't even speak properly and has the backbone of a worm. Now quit your fussin' and let me handle this. You have no more concern over her. You go on as you have been with Elgerson and he'll see what talents you have soon enough! Like I said, if he can pick out fine work animals like he always does, he'll see that anyone like that nit of a girl in there is a waste of his time and that *you* are what the man really needs."

"But Mother, I want to see her! And what if…"

"There'll be no 'what if'," Bedra assured her. "He'll never lay eyes on her anyway. Now head off and wait for me at home."

Octavia turned, rebuffed and disappointed, and mounted her carriage reluctantly. Her dress was a dreary gray, although fashioned from a top quality silk. The bodice was cut so deeply that it barely contained her massive bust and she pulled herself upright sturdily in the seat. She tugged at her skirts, pulling them coarsely into the vehicle and turned the carriage around.

"You'll take care of it then?" Octavia asked reassurance from her mother.

"You go on now," her tone was comforting. The mother waved after her fondly as the younger woman bounced away. There was nothing in the world she wouldn't do to keep her only child happy. Nothing. Cursing herself for failing to have dealt with Rebecca in a swifter manner she returned to the inside of the station determined.

Bedra filled the doorway. "We'll be going now," she announced to Rebecca.

Rebecca hobbled out to the buggy in the awkwardly knotted boots and climbed self-consciously into the seat. She hung on tightly, trying not to lose her balance while Bedra climbed aboard and the contraption swayed violently.

"Are we going to St. Peter or Billington?" Rebecca ventured as the woman snapped the whip sharply and the buggy lurched forward.

"No," she grunted back. "I'll be taking you straight away to Elgerson's. Road's washed out. It's better this way."

Rebecca clung terrified to the bouncing vehicle. The rough jostling of the ride was miserable and unnerving. She dreaded the thought of meeting her intended husband in these conditions and the painful pounding of the ride brought Rebecca to tears. She sat as balanced as possible on the rickety old transport and tried to look straight ahead, clamping her jaws together in agonizing resolve and an attempt to save her teeth. Rebecca had been raised to behave like a lady, always taught that, no matter her situation, if she maintained her dignity she would uphold her self-respect. The girl never imagined that her pride and self-preservation would be put to such a test.

After a few torturous miles Rebecca could not help but take in the passing countryside. In the brilliant sunshine her new world was glaringly illustrated as it spread out around her. The rutted, muddy road was hardly more than a cart path and on either side the hillside appeared scorched and fire ravaged. After a time she questioned the woman beside her cautiously.

"Everything is black. Was there a fire?"

The woman glared towards her and her only reply was a gruff, "What do you think?"

Rebecca kept to herself for what seemed like an eternity.

"Yep, big one last year," the woman replied eventually. She had taken so long to reply to Rebecca's question that for a moment the girl had no idea as to what the woman was referring. She was so relieved by the woman's response she began to bubble with questions, still hoping the woman's gruff manner was nothing personal towards her.

"How sad and awful!' Rebecca observed. "Everything looks so distressing and dismal. Did the fire burn a lot of land? There must have been so many homes destroyed, what did people do?"

Again she received no answer to her queries and kept the remaining hundreds of questions that sprung into her mind to herself. The seared timberland gave way to a considerable tangle of forest that began to close in around them thickly.

In the late afternoon the woman announced that they had nearly reached their destination and Rebecca was sadly disappointed and thoroughly confused. There were no homes that she could see and although they had ridden out of the desiccation they had passed through earlier, the land was rough and foreign to her. Tall, straight pines lined the passage, enclosed on either side by impenetrable forest. Rebecca tried peering into the depths of forest intently, but could see only a few feet. The path that they traveled had become overgrown and appeared to be rarely used by any travelers on carriages or horseback. Rebecca clung to the buggy staring ahead expectantly in fervent hope that the forest would spread open and reveal a settlement, or perhaps a small village. The looming darkness of the thick woodland felt threatening and sinister making her more and more uneasy. Rebecca could not recall when she had eaten last and, had her stomach held any contents, she was certain they would not have remained inside her.

The huge woman pulled the cart sharply into a stand of birches along a muddy path that seemed no more than a section of forest that had washed out, leaving exposed roots and rocky gulches.

When the powerful woman pulled her contrivance up before a crumbling shack, Rebecca could take no more. She sat shaking violently in the rickety buggy unable to compose herself.

Lumbering down from the buggy the woman quickly circled to Rebecca's side.

"Get out!" she bellowed.

Rebecca quaked in fear and misery.

"Is this Mr. Elgerson's?" her voice trailed off trembling.

"Yep," Bedra declared, taking Rebecca violently by both arms and plunking her to the ground.

Rebecca felt her knees buckle beneath her and violent shivering overtook her.

"Elgerson's out I suspect. I'll get you inside and you can wait there for him until he returns."

The woman led the suffering girl to the shack doorway and pushed in the patched door with her massive foot. The hovel was dim and dusty and held a musty smell. Cobwebs consumed the rough walls of the hut and it was apparent that there had been no one living inside in the extended past. The big woman pulled Rebecca into the cabin and tossed her roughly onto the dirt floor. Rebecca felt her stomach retch and she curled into a tight ball, gagging and shaking. Quickly binding Rebecca's wrists and ankles with a rough cord, she lifted the girl and easily deposited her onto a makeshift cot against one wall.

Rebecca began to wrestle in her captivity, sick with fear and confusion.

"You can wait here for your Mr. Elgerson!" The woman barked and laughed loudly before kicking Rebecca hard in the stomach and hitting her hard with a piece of broken board.

Rebecca's dark world faded to black, closing in

around her from all sides. She tried to cry out, but no sound emerged and she fell limp on the dusty cot.

Chapter Five

*T*he seam of the feedbag gave way, caught against the loose nail on the buckboard bed. Elgerson cursed under his breath, deftly catching the opening and standing the bag on its end beside the vehicle. His patience was worn thin by the sulking of the boy and, with the meeting time fast approaching, he had no time to devote to gathering up the feed.

"This bag's unraveled," he rumbled to the youth. "I haven't time to repair it. Now you go on and stack these bags in the shed. I'll be back, it can't be helped."

The boy hung his head dejectedly, nodding.

"Yes, sir," he responded dully.

"Enough!" Elgerson sighed. "You'll be fine! We'll get up to the house when I return. Keep to your chores and mind those chickens. I'll be back before you know it."

The youth nodded again, unconvinced at the reassurance. Every trip it was the same. Every time would be the last he'd be here alone. He set to hauling the bags towards the shed never turning to watch the impatient man pull the buckboard away.

Timothy Elgerson stood a strapping six feet four in stocking feet, though he himself could not recall the last time he'd been out of his boots. He was obviously a capable man, tanned and rugged from a lifetime of logging and hard labor. Beneath the thick mane of golden hair and substantial beard, his bronzed face was serious and his eyes a warm soft brown with sharp intelligence. His frame was solid and broad shouldered with a trim waist and powerful thighs, undeniably displaying his Scandinavian heritage. His healthy outdoorsman stance gave him a commanding presence in any situation, often making men step back and women take notice. Yet, something of Timothy Elgerson gave evidence that he was set apart from the common logger. There was the manner of a gentleman to him that often made many, who upon first meeting him, wonder about his background. His reputation was that of a fair-minded man, if somewhat blunt in manner. In recent years, however, there were those who questioned his reasoning.

Elgerson drove his horse hard in an attempt to make up for lost time and reach his meeting in a timely manner. He had single-mindedly spent the last months of his life negotiating land deals for substantial purchases. He found he was good at it and the trades kept his mind occupied most of the time. There were periods when the bargaining didn't distract him and late nights alone and long rides to meetings were two examples.

The man's mind drifted to the boy and the lad's dejected ride to the logging cabin. Since the death of the boy's mother, Timothy Elgerson found the main house depressing and haunted with memories. Once he had decided to spend more time at the isolated logging cabin it had evolved into something of a small farm. The boy had spent so much time alone there that Timothy had brought up the dog as company for him. Then, when the chickens went uncared for at the main house, a makeshift coop was built at the cabin as well. Eventually there was so much to keep up that the boy was needed more at the cabin than at the main house.

At twelve, Mark was capable and hardworking, but his depression was more than Elgerson could bear. Caught in what should have been a magical age for the lad, somewhere between childhood and the responsibilities of manhood, he was awkward and shy. The boy held the promise of stalwart good looks, his dark hair disheveled and his eyes unusually dark and intent. He hovered in anticipation of adulthood with an obvious self-conscious manner that frustrated Elgerson and tested the man's patience relentlessly.

In the two years since the death of his mother, Mark, instead of enjoying the freedom of adolescence, had seemed to become more withdrawn. The lack of a mother's support and encouragement had overshadowed his enthusiasm and left him moody and sullen. Timothy was certain that the boy felt somehow responsible for the death of his mother.

Despite fervently trying to contemplate his

upcoming land deal, Elgerson couldn't shake his worry about the lad. The boy's misery seemed to be spiraling and Elgerson was at a loss as to how to bring him around. Where constant occupation and distraction helped the man himself adjust to the loss of his wife, Mark seemed to only slip further and further away. It wasn't just that the boy was not Elgerson's blood child. He had been young when he came to live with the man. Timothy loved him as his own and their relationship could not have been closer had they been natural father and son. The man was capable in his business dealings and progressed though his life fearlessly and without hesitation, but the moods of the boy and the loss of his wife left him emotional and distracted, feelings he feared he himself would never get a handle on.

Elgerson hoped his plan to put a woman into the boy's life would ease his melancholy. Once he signed his land deal he'd meet the woman he'd arranged for in Billington and move her and the youngster up to the big house. He'd keep himself at the cabin and go about his business from there.

The female who responded to his ad seemed capable and had replied in a clear, businesslike way to his carefully worded ad. The photo included was serious, dignified and ordinary which suited Elgerson's needs sufficiently. He had arranged for her journey as quickly as possible through the train companies and expected her to arrive as agreed.

He'd consent to marriage since he believed that most women who responded to such ads were simply in search of support and housing and Elgerson knew he was capable of doing that much. He also felt that many of these women did not seek romantic involvement or such entanglements. Who would expect that from such an arrangement? He had no intention of falling in love. Love was something Mr. Elgerson would not succumb to again.

The main house would suit any capable woman well, he was certain. Finely built and skillfully crafted it would house her and the boy easily. When Timothy Elgerson had built his home he had poured himself into it like a man possessed, planning a large family and a grand life for himself and a wife. Though it stood now barely functioning as a home, it was still a fine house and perhaps a woman about the place could bring some functionality back into it for the boy.

Timothy Elgerson checked the location of the sun and turned his buckboard down the steep decline toward Billington and his arranged meeting.

Chapter Six

$\mathcal{F}$inishing their business, the portly financier rose to shake Timothy Elgerson's hand. "What are you planning to do with all of that land, Tim?"

"Own the whole territory," Elgerson joked, "and then I'll run you all back east!"

"Well, my Missus would thank you for that," the banker replied. "Good luck to you Tim. Don't run off too many of us though. You might need a few of the boys about to keep up your mills."

"You're good with a saw then, James?" Elgerson teased. "Perhaps instead of sending you east I ought to put an axe in your hands?"

"I don't believe I'd be able to swing it past this," the gentleman replied, patting his generous abdomen.

"That wouldn't be there for long," Tim remarked, gathering up his packet of deeds. "A week or two of good hard swinging would set that right."

"If I didn't take it off with an axe first!"

Elgerson chuckled warmly to the man and pulled open the bank door.

"Take care, Tim!" The banker shook with laughter.

"Same to you," Elgerson replied. He closed the door behind him and studied the coach stop across the muddied road.

It hadn't occurred to him before this moment that he might be in any way nervous about picking up a bride.

"Bride," he thought. A funny word for such a situation. It sounded romantic, even hopeful. Elgerson's only hope was to get retrieving the woman over with, and he strode out into the street towards the small receiving office.

"Why, my dear Mr. Elgerson! What on earth brings you to town today?"

Timothy turned in response to the sound of his

name and moaned softly to himself at the sight of Octavia Weintraub lumbering towards him up the walkway, the bulk of her weight bringing up a creaking complaint from each plank she stepped upon.

Clad in her odd attire, a colorless piece of clothing straining beneath a dangerously revealing neckline, Octavia more rolled to Elgerson's side than strode.

"How pleasant a surprise to find you here today and so convenient as well, Mr. Elgerson!" Octavia purred as she slipped her generous wrist inside of Elgerson's arm.

"How's that?" Elgerson asked, preferring not to hear her reply.

"Why, I'm nearly faint with starvation and I can't imagine anything more delicious than partaking of a meal with you, sir!" Octavia exclaimed while vainly attempting to bat her thin lashes.

"Miss Weintraub," Elgerson studied the massive girl. "A strapping girl like you, starving?" Timothy could not resist the comment.

"I'm healthy and capable for anything that'd please you, sir," she giggled.

Elgerson suppressed a shudder. "And where would your mother be on this fine day?" He knew when Octavia was around her doting mother would not be far away.

"Mother's off on an errand." Octavia bit her lip absentmindedly. Wherever her mother was, it had better be getting rid of that picture bride!

Octavia knew precisely why her intended gentleman was hanging around the carriage stop. She dared not let on, but the thought of his disappointment at not finding his child bride was practically unbearable in its pleasure.

"So, Mr. Elgerson," she hummed. "Why was it again you are in town today?"

"I just closed my final land deal, Octavia," he replied distractedly.

The woman found herself flustered that his answer was only partially the truth and pressed on.

"Why then, we simply must celebrate! You will be having a party of course, to announce your acquisition. Oh please, when?" Octavia studied Timothy's face searching for any sign of excitement.

Elgerson looked at her squarely and felt his blood rising. Octavia was a master at putting those around her into compromising positions. Timothy could never let her know that his property transfer was not the entire reason for his being in town. It could be a perfect distraction for the woman to think he planned to celebrate the land purchase.

"I've been so busy with the procurement, Octavia, I just didn't think about it." Elgerson attempted an excuse.

"That's not a problem!" Octavia waved her hand triumphantly. "I'll pop up to your place tomorrow with my girl and put together a celebration straight away. Mother will be delighted to help, I'm sure, and that lazy staff of mine could use a good celebration to get them moving. We'd all enjoy a bit of a ball anyway what with everything being so dismal with all the merciless rain!

"I'll plan the menu straight away and the invitations will have to go right out..." Octavia began to wave wildly to an approaching passerby.

"Amanda, you know Mr. Elgerson, of course. Why he's just made the most huge purchase of land and we'll be throwing a celebration. You and Roger must attend, I'm sure it will be so grand!"

Elgerson stuttered and cleared his throat.

"W-well, Octavia I really don't think that…" he choked, realizing that the woman had taken the idea to this extreme.

"Don't be silly, dear!" The big woman ignored his protests and continued her invitations. "We'll see you and Roger of course, Amanda, and please do bring your darling brother and his wife." Octavia quickly moved on to a couple approaching from across the street.

Railroaded again, Elgerson thought. Well, he sighed, what harm would it do? As he watched the buxom woman toddle across the street, excitedly inviting anyone and everyone in her sight, Timothy slipped unnoticed into the tiny carriage stop and approached the desk. At least he'd be free of dining with the woman and in her preoccupation he could see about the bride's arrival privately.

"No, sir. No one from St. Peter today," the clerk responded. "Expecting anyone special?" he asked.

"No one special," Elgerson replied, more disappointed than he imagined he'd be. Perhaps she could have been held up with the rain. He felt agitated that he'd have no one to bring home to the boy and he'd need to return to the stop in the morrow to attempt to retrieve her again. He slipped around to the back of the building in order to avoid Octavia and her shouting to the entire town and headed for the saloon.

Madam Rival turned from the customer she was

charming and watched Timothy Elgerson enter the saloon. Through the thundering loud environment she watched as he clapped several men on the back, exchanging vigorous handshakes and warm greetings. Holding back for the time being, and returning to her gentleman, she knew it would do her no good to approach the man until he was well into his cups. In a few hours he'd be willing and would pour his heart out to her in her private room upstairs. He'd rebuffed her once before while sober. His rejection was something she did not want to experience again.

Rival's Saloon was infamous all through the territory for its hearty brews, earnest gamblers and women of every possible description. The girls were clean and for the most part attractive and, although the Madam was just past her prime, she was energetic and still beautiful with her deep copper penny hair and voluptuous figure. It was considered by many of the men a compliment to visit her personal quarters.

Bess Rival moved with ease through her business, mingling openly and joking with the men. There were a few couples among the patrons, since she tried her best to run a reputable establishment, but the girls tramping blatantly with customers up the stairs kept her from being within acceptable limits to many. Women often openly shunned her as she shopped in town and the men behaved as if they had no recognition of her, even though almost the entire territory's male populous had been in her place at one time or another.

Timothy Elgerson, however, was another story.

One particularly brew-inspired evening he had stayed long after most of the patrons had left for the night. When she had approached him with the pretense of sending him on his way he had warmed up to her and found himself facing the following morning in an embarrassing situation, although they both knew nothing intimate had transpired between them. Elgerson came to regard Bess Rival as something of a mistake, but Bess was still hopeful that would change. Like many who had fallen into her profession, she still held onto the hope that possibly one day she'd be married properly and Timothy was exactly what she wanted. She surveyed him from across the room, the deep timbre of his voice drifting towards her through the bustling crowd and she studied his reserved smile as he visited among the men. He was a fine specimen, she thought to herself and cursed the differences in their ages with Timothy not even thirty and herself denying the accumulating years.

He moved with a grace uncommon in most men of his height and size and was ever the gentleman. She could barely wait for the evening to wind down to the time where Mr. Elgerson would bury his head in his hands, intoxicated and weary, and ask for her opinion. She'd seen him once in town with his boy, a handsome lad with the promise of his mother's good looks and a shy air about him. Elgerson had not turned away, but instead introduced her to the adolescent in a very matter-of-fact way as, "the woman who owned the saloon up the way." Bess was sure the boy blushed slightly, giving away the fact that her business reputation had preceded her, but Timothy had simply tipped his hat and continued on his way. It had occurred to her later that possibly the introduction to the boy was an omen in her favor. Bess liked children and had often wished she had a living child of her own.

"Elgerson, you're no fool taking in all that land after the big fire," one gentleman commented. "But throwing a party with Octavia Weintraub might make you otherwise!"

The men around the table laughed heartily.

"Somethin' you're not telling us, Tim?" the man teased.

"Hardly!" Elgerson bellowed, putting up his powerfully built hands in a gesture of denial. "That girl will stop at nothing to involve me in her shenanigans!"

"I doubt that's all she'll be wanting to involve you in, Tim!" another man from across the table interjected.

Elgerson chased down his shot with a deep gulp of his beer as the men around the table burst into laughter.

"With all the woman around these parts clamoring to get at you, Tim, you ought to think about taking another wife just to quiet down your life," someone seated beside Timothy threw in thoughtlessly.

The mood changed suddenly as Timothy Elgerson gathered his pint and moved to the bar. It was widely known by most that he hadn't fared well after his wife passed on, and Timothy Elgerson was just not the same. Over time he'd come into the saloon on occasion to raise a few glasses to drown his sorrow and attempt to put away his memories, but a melancholy lingered that most knew never passed. Mr. Elgerson sat alone, ordering another shot at the bar. His relocation in the establishment did not go unnoticed by Bess Rival.

More than a few shots, and several hours later, as the last of the patrons shuffled out and the barkeeper stacked his washed glasses for another day, the madam pulled up a stool beside Timothy Elgerson. The deep masculine scent of him teased her senses and she snuggled a bit closer.

"Evening, Tim," she spoke softly.

"Bess," was his one word response.

"Let's take that last mug of beer upstairs and finish it off up there," she proposed.

Elgerson stumbled off of the stool and followed her silently up the staircase.

Once in Bess's opulent room he sunk into an oversized velvet chair and leaned his head back against the frame.

"What happened tonight? Looks like someone took the wind out of you," Bess asked cautiously.

"Woman never showed," Elgerson lamented. "Never came in."

"That girl you sent for to care for your boy?" Bess was concerned about Elgerson's secretive posting of his ad. Timothy had assured her that he'd only placed the ad to find a mother for his son, but the madam had enough competition in Billington for Timothy's attention and sending for a girl was too risky. Bess had studied Tim's ad, the girl's reply, and scrutinized the photograph but there was so much unanswered. The response was so brief, too tight and lacking any real information and the correspondent had merely given her first initial as "R". The picture had been so damaged in transport it was impossible to put together an idea of who this woman might be. Elgerson's belief that these girls only wanted stability and steady meals was grossly unfounded and Bess Rival knew otherwise. Many of her girls had arrived as mail order brides, either coming to the St. Peter area or just passing through. Most were impoverished and helpless, but nearly all were filled with romantic notions. Any girl who had thrown in with the lot and found Timothy Elgerson at the end of her venture couldn't help but consider herself blessed in her fortune.

"Yes, she wasn't at the carriage stop," he groaned.

"Most never make it to their destination, Tim." She went on.

"Do you think something happened to her?" Elgerson sat upright and weaved slightly in the big chair.

"No, no," Bess reciprocated. "I mean many of them find something else along the way. In a day or two if she doesn't arrive you should just put it away. Why, there's women right here in Billington who'd make a fine mother for your son. I even took a liking to the boy myself." Bess Rival had decided she was tired of playing the role of a confidant and dropped her hint boldly. If the woman should not arrive in the next few days Bess thought it was time she got moving into Elgerson's life a bit more seriously before he ordered another, or worse.

"You're a good woman Bess," Timothy stated kindly, blearily peering into the madam's face.

"That's sweet of you to say. You've got a good heart and you've been a fine friend. I'll find a way to settle the boy down." The man rose unsteadily to his feet.

Bess cursed under her breath. This is one damned handsome man, she thought to herself, but bull headed as an ox. Deciding to take it one step further she took hold of Elgerson's arm, steadied him and tried gently to lure him towards the back of her apartment.

"I'll be going now. I appreciate you, Bess, really." Timothy looked kindly into her eyes. "But I don't expect I'll be back. Thank you," he said tactfully, and headed slowly towards the door. He turned back to face her and regarded her sadly. "You've been good to me, Bess, a real friend and I thank you. You take care now. I hope you find what you're looking for, but Bess…" Timothy Elgerson's words trailed off and he closed the door behind him.

Bess Rival stood alone in her lavish dwelling and counted each footstep as Timothy descended the stairs. She knew she was far from her youth, but the sob that wretched from her throat was something she had not experienced since she was a child.

Timothy Elgerson staggered to the stable, retrieving his horse and buggy and slowly rode out of town.

Chapter Seven

Mark mumbled to himself, "He'll not be back today." After piling the sacks neatly inside the stable as his father instructed, he took off into the woods towards the clearing where he spent much of his solitary time. He supposed he could do his chores and gather the eggs just as well tomorrow and his father wouldn't discover any drop-off in the laying so it didn't matter when he did it. In the isolated meadow he searched beside a clump of roots and extracted his bundle of traps.

Weasels were nasty animals. Mark didn't much care for them and, although his father had specifically forbidden his trapping them, Mark liked to try to ensnare one now and again for fun. He'd only actually caught one thus far, but since the disturbing feeling that he had experienced finding the last mangled animal had passed, Mark was ready to try his hand at it a second time.

His friends trapped all sorts of animals, often bragging and exchanging pelts when they traveled into town for events. Most of the men at the logging camps trapped some on the side and Mark could see no real harm in it. The boy was certain that his father had only forbidden it to make Mark more miserable than he already was.

The youth was left out of everything, he thought, with his Pa running off on some land deal or another and not returning when he said he would. The last stay at the house had lasted for only two nights and there was no one for miles for him to talk to, not even the cook to bother. It was as if his father couldn't stand the main house now. Mark missed the time when the residence was bustling with visitors and meals, a well-fed pig in a pit roasting on a summer's day. There were friends and cousins and rides on the back of the buckboard in the warm evening. His Pa would take him out fishing nearly every week and out for a good hunt at least a few times a year. These days he couldn't even recall where the fishing poles were, or a good number of the rifles for that matter. The boy inspected the three traps and took them into the dense forest.

He pulled a leather pouch from his bulging pocket and selected a strip of dried rabbit, placing it in the trap and setting it carefully in the center of three rocks he had found situated beside a large pine. Unsure that it would be discovered by his intended prey, h decided instead to set it further from the tree in ; open area of pine needles and then ran off to set t remaining pair. Mark was determined to have a r clutch of pelts before his father returned. I conceal them under the buggy boards to get home and have something to be proud of the time they traveled to the logging camp.

Once he had accomplished his stealthy r he decided to return to the cabin and go ab gather the eggs. The job would be f entertaining with the distraction of imagin the animals that were being snared while I As he splashed along the creek he was c heard a horse and cart off in the distance, returned to the cabin he found no evidence of anyone passing through or his father's return.

Timothy Elgerson slowly pulled into the drive of the main house in the crescent moonlight. The soft croak of the last of the season's frogs hung on the mist as if to enhance the desolation of the homestead. The promise of the approaching autumn waited in anticipation, a chill in the air whispering softly along the tops of the tall pines.

The his shoulders slumped in misery as he entered he silent building and stood before the soaring ircase. Once he would have gazed in appreciation beamed with pride for the accomplishment of ଃ fashioned the spectacular flight. The wide ɘ of stairs opened before him hauntingly in the As if lost in another world, he wandered up se and staggered slowly down the upper is back against the wall, he slid down in ne desolated corridor and deep cries olid frame. The ritual had occurred st two years. Mr. Elgerson could not ry, and no amount of land titles or chase the demon away. In a ried out. Like an animal left to wished he would merely slip he pistol at his side while of his boy's suffering, the boy had been the only may have failed as well. eside him on the floor.

Chapter Eight

$\mathcal{R}$ebecca struggled for breath. Was she drowning, suffocating? Encased in total darkness and hearing only her heartbeat against her throbbing skull, the girl writhed and whimpered. There was something warm and sticky against her cheek and after several minutes of squirming she figured out that a snug hood was somehow glued to her face and that both of her wrists and ankles were tightly bound.

The diminutive captive fell from the cot with a sickening thud to the dirt floor, but her ineffective struggling only tightened her bondage and consumed the little air inside the black hood. As the time passed she began to recall her trip to Elgerson's shack and the vision of it, but little more.

Once again composed, she considered that the wad she had chewed in the cloth had pulled it forward some and she began to turn her head to one side and tugged at a different section of the material. After her fourth attempt at the plan the sack slipped suddenly and, by turning her head against the dirt floor quickly from side to side, the terrifying contraption slid free.

Rebecca was perspiring earnestly as she lay in the dusky darkness surveying her surroundings. The shack was no bigger than a large horse stall and had been pieced together from broken planks and rotted timber. A door of sorts, now wedged closed, hung from what appeared to be leather shoe soles used as hinges and the entire structure had a haphazard design, which attested to the fact that it had been hastily thrown together. The hard packed floor was uneven and cluttered with bits of pinecones and needles. In one corner it appeared as if an animal had taken residence and the abandoned nest was laced across with a huge spider's web. Rebecca could not be sure, but she feared that the pile in the opposite corner was bits of gnawed bones and she began to cry uncontrollably, terrified at the thought that perhaps they could be bones of another person who had been left there previously. Rebecca kicked violently, her tiny ankles rubbing the insides of the clubby leather boots.

She had laced the boots tightly in an attempt to keep the monstrous hoppers on her narrow feet but she suspected that if she squirmed enough, the laces might loosen and, with the rope predominately encasing the boots, she might be able to pull at least one foot free.

Rebecca struggled for hours, fighting with determination until she lay exhausted for a time. She then gathered herself up again and writhed furiously against her bondage. Her lips were pale from fatigue and the lack of nourishment. Her breasts heaved hard against the rough clothing as she tried to breathe and maintain her battle.

When one ankle finally pulled free, the girl was so exhausted she lost consciousness against the ground, damp now from tears and perspiration.

Sunlight poured through a large crack in the timber wall streaming along the floor and illuminated the dusty interior of the dilapidated shack in a bright haze. Rebecca whimpered quietly and attempted to lift her head. Her stomach churned and she struggled to focus on a rustling sound within the tiny enclosure. A shadow came towards her slowly and as it merged from the darkness into the dim light Rebecca could make out the outline of a massive rodent. Its face was white against a huge gray body, the nose a bright pink and the creature peered at her inches from the girls face with mammoth black eyes, its menacing grin exposing razor sharp teeth.

Rebecca screamed deafeningly, sending the startled creature scurrying into a smooth tunnel beneath the cot. Giving no thought to discovery by her captors, Rebecca continued shrilly, terrified that the beast might return should she stop her earsplitting wailing.

With indignation Mark had forsaken his responsibilities at the cabin and, after a restless night, decided that he could no longer wait to check out his venture at trapping. He knew that his intended victims were nocturnal beasts and if he were successful, it would be in the hours of darkness.

When he heard the shriek of a living thing he froze. Suddenly regretting his disobedience he stumbled and tumbled to the ground tripping over the forest floor and dropping to his knees. The wail of the animal's terrifying cries tore at his conscience and he pressed his palms against his ears. He swore to himself out loud that he would never again defy his father's wishes. He would behave ever after and never question the authority of the man. He would accept and obey all rules. Mark's mind screamed out in contrition, promising to do anything to be good if the animal would only stop.

Yet the being continued with a terrified screeching and Mark scrambled to his feet. Against his better judgment and overwhelming fear, he ran towards the sound.

Coming abruptly upon the shack nestled deep in a stand of trees, Mark was perplexed. The boy knew the surrounding forest as well as any tracker, but he had never come across this before. He took quick stock of the immediate area and was certain the structure had been constructed only recently, at least in the past summer months. He ran up to the makeshift door and caught his breath. Whatever was inside was not a beast caught in his trap, but he was not relieved. He pulled at the leather binding that held the entry closed and threw open the door.

Rebecca saw the silhouette in the bright doorway, caught her breath and began to repeat her wails. The person simply stood there framed in the vivid dusty light with arms hanging limply at their sides. Her captor was a huge woman, too tall and immense to fit easily through the opening. The figure brightly outlined before her now had not nearly half the bulk of her enslaver and Rebecca stopped screaming abruptly and tried to wriggle under the cot. The recollection of encountering the huge rat and its route of flight stopped her suddenly and she lay quiet, trapped and unable to escape.

The boy dropped to one knee in the doorway struggling to comprehend what he was witnessing. On the muddy floor lay a bundled human being, perhaps a young boy, bathed in dirt and blood and crying softly.

"Hello?" Mark offered cautiously, unsure as to exactly how he might handle someone properly in such a situation.

Rebecca sobbed deeply. "Who are you?"

"Mark," the boy replied and ventured closer. He quickly realized that his original identification of the captive was mistaken. This was instead a young girl, perhaps not too far from his own age and she was tied up in heavy ropes, a dark ooze covering one side of her face. The sight of blood conquered his fear and he ran up to the girl and attempted to free her.

Rebecca fought him, confident that he meant her more harm.

"Easy there," the boy tried to calm her. She looked like a terrified colt and Mark had handled injured animals many times in the past.

Rebecca was not assured and demanded to know who he was.

"Like I said. Mark," he replied leaning back onto one knee. "What happened to you?"

"She brought me here and tied me up," Rebecca poured out. "And she left me to die. Please don't hurt me!"

"I'm going help you if you will lay still."

"Please," Rebecca pleaded, looking into the youth's eyes for a promise of safety. He was much better-spoken than the people she had met on the train, and she found comfort in his voice.

Mark tugged at the heavy ropes, and, after resorting to his pocketknife to free the girl, he helped her to her feet.

Rebecca lost her legs underneath her and fell to the cot. Then, in an awkward attempt to leap from the bed for fear of the rat, fell squarely into the boy.

"Relax!" The lad stood up and dusted himself off. This girl was certainly pitiful, but kind of silly he thought.

"There's a giant rat living under there, this big!" Rebecca held up her hands in illustration of the beast's size.

"A rat? I've never seen a rat that big! Out here?"

Rebecca wanted to be free of the shack, concerned that the woman might return, and in no mood to argue with the boy, she tried again to get to her feet.

Mark steadied her and led her into the sunlight.

"I have to get away from here," Rebecca looked around apprehensively. "If she comes back she'll kill me, I'm sure."

"Who?" The boy searched the surroundings, suddenly aware that whoever had captured the girl might take him as well.

"She said her name was Bedra." Rebecca felt as if a horse had trodden upon her.

"This way," the boy led her deeply into the woods. "Never heard the name before. Who are you and where did you come from? You sound foreign or something."

"Rebecca," she replied. "Let's just get away from

here!"

The lad led her away a good distance. stopping frequently along the way while the girl struggled in pain and exhaustion. When they reached his cabin he helped her inside and deposited her onto a freshly made bed.

The building was cozy and rustic, constructed from peeled logs notched expertly together at the corners. Although this house had been more masterfully constructed than the train station, Rebecca wondered why the Americans built so many things out of logs. Didn't they have the means to cut lumber? There were windows here, which she appreciated for their civility and the bed bore a soft downy tick that felt like a cloud after weeks of hard travel on wooden seats and her night on the dirt floor.

"We'll need to deal with that cut," he told her and the boy pulled up a bench beside the bed and placed a fine pitcher and bowl upon it. Rebecca looked down at her filthy hands and was horrified that they were both covered in blood.

"Oh my heavens," she gasped. "I'm bleeding?"

"It'll be alright I think," the boy remarked. "We won't know until we clean it up." He took a small hand mirror from the dresser, handed it to Rebecca and left the room.

The girl was overcome when she looked into the glass. The image reflected was not recognizable to her, it couldn't be! Her face was gray with mud and a dark stain ran down one cheek covering the side of her face from the hairline. Her lips, a pure white, quivered beneath her flaming red eyes. She reached up to touch the gash on her head and fell back in a faint against the yielding mattress.

When Mark returned, sloshing the hot water he had gone to heat, he rushed to her side, afraid she was dead. He watched her for a moment and heard her soft breathing. Once assured that she was still alive he decided it might be best if she slept through his doctoring, unsure of how much pain he'd need to inflict to clean and dress the wound properly.

As he applied the warm compresses he began to wipe the mud from Rebecca's pale features while he waited for the warm liquid to soften the dried blood. He lifted her slightly to try to situate her in a more comfortable position on the bed.

Chapter Nine

$\mathcal{M}$ark nearly dropped the girl in shock. With her face nearly cleaned up and her clothing lying against her he realized that Rebecca was not a child like him, but instead a grown woman. The boy was certain that even as filthy as she was, he did not recognize her. Mark knew almost everyone around the area and he was sure he would have remembered her, her features as fine and delicate as a doll.

Studying her face he reflected that she looked a little like his grandmother. Her coloring was probably not the same, though it was hard to tell since this lady was whiter than a sun bleached bone. Her hair was dark too, he thought, but there was something in her fine face and tiny upturned nose that felt familiar and comfortable to him.

Instantly he thought of his father. What would his father say? Mark thought of the possibilities. He'd brought a woman here that he'd saved from a shack that wasn't there before, but was now. His thoughts were a jumble. His Pa would want to find out who she was and who had done this, but Mark had no idea when he would return and what would the boy do with her in the meantime? He could take her by horseback down the mountain, but what if whoever was after her saw them, or came here looking for her? And as pale as she was, he wasn't even sure she'd survive the trip. When he cared for his sick animals he knew that poor color was not a good sign.

The boy paced the room in a panic, ran to the front of the cabin, and peered out of the door cautiously. He'd have to hide her, he thought, just in case. That way if anyone came looking for her she might be safe. He began to gather blankets and a bedroll and decided to transport her to the old stable up the hill. She'd be safer there and he'd tend to her as he could.

He crept up the hill several times, setting up a makeshift bed in the abandoned stable and returned, slipping silently back into the house intending to move the woman at once.

While thinking about lifting and carrying her to the hideaway, Mark lost his resolve standing beside the bed. She was taller than him, and if he couldn't carry her well enough she could get hurt. She wasn't big though, he thought, mostly just in big clothes. He moved aside the bowl on the bench and sat watching her.

The afternoon's ordeal had exhausted him and his nerves were frazzled. He just couldn't think of a way to address the whole situation and wished, as he had many times before, that his father would arrive. His Pa would know exactly what to do, and no one messed with his Pa. Ever. They'd be safe and he'd make everything right.

As he watched the woman sleep silently, he too, soon grew drowsy. Mark moved to the big chair in the corner and drifted off.

At nightfall he woke suddenly and cursed himself for falling asleep. Something in his memory tugged at him, recalling an event that had happened a few summers ago. One of the loggers had gotten hit on the head and there was something about not letting him sleep too long or he'd never wake up. Mark decided he had better wake the woman just in case, he was kind of hungry and she might be hungry too. Anyway, it might be nice to have someone share his supper. He leaned over the girl and touched her arm carefully, whispering her name softly.

Rebecca opened her eyes wearily, and although she was paler than ever, she seemed somewhat coherent.

"Hungry?" Mark asked.

"Oh yes," the woman whispered hoarsely.

Mark left to heat a stew and Rebecca tried to sit up on the soft bed. Every muscle of her body cried out in cruel pain and her head pounded mercilessly. She wanted to slip into a deep long sleep but something kept her on the edge and she began to imagine that she was home at her dining table with a fine meal spread out before her.

"I made this for us," the boy interrupted her dream.

Rebecca pried open her aching eyes and saw Mark squatting before her, a huge steaming bowl in his awkward hands. She knew she could barely move, but the smell of the food was so enticing.

"Could you help me sit up?" she whispered weakly. Setting aside the bowl, Mark arranged the bed and tried to hand Rebecca the bowl but she seemed too confused to hold it herself. Instead he spooned the soup into her carefully and after she seemed to be unable to accept any more he shifted her down onto the mattress and let her continue to sleep.

"How old are you?" he whispered. She looked really young, but he remembered when he was little and Grandmother was really sick she looked a lot like this, frail and helpless like a tiny bird. Maybe she was much older than he thought. Maybe she had a son of her own somewhere and she'd want someone to look after him. The boy was disappointed that she couldn't talk to him while he ate, but he filled himself a bowl of stew and sat in the big chair he'd pulled up beside her and watched her. He decided he'd spend the night close to the front door, just in case, and make sure the rifle was close at hand should anyone come after his patient.

Morning arrived without incident and Mark stretched beside the front door where he had spent the night. He'd gotten up several times in the night to check his new responsibility and found her sleeping, but not so soundly that she wouldn't respond if he spoke her name.

He mixed up a large batch of porridge in the hopes she'd have more appetite and be better company and took it in to his guest.

Rebecca responded much more lucidly this time, able to sit up with support and could even lift a few spoonfuls to her mouth on her own. Her drowsiness lingered and it took the boy a full day of spooning food into her and hauling her out to the outhouse before it seemed that she might improve. He'd cleaned her wound as best he could and since it didn't fester he was sure that it would heal alright, but it would most certainly leave a scar. He didn't mind scars much himself, sometimes they were fun to brag over, but he didn't imagine a lady like her would care much to have one right on her head where her hair was. It was too early to tell though. The gash was still bloody and looked ragged.

Pa always told him that when a sick animal began to get feisty they were healing well and Rebecca was becoming just that. She started asking the boy every time he approached her if there were any way she could get a bath. He offered her some of his own clothes and she accepted them very sweetly but the only way she might get into a bath would be either to wash with a bucket or go down to the stream like he did. He was sure the trip to the stream would be impossible, and he feared taking the girl out, but he did eventually devise an idea for a bath.

He rolled in an old split keg that they sometimes used to collect rain water. He scrubbed it out thoroughly in the yard with buckets full of water he had hauled up and left it in the sun to dry. When he rolled it into the room he announced to Rebecca that it was a bathtub just her size.

The young woman was thrilled with any container that might hold her and some water as well and thanked the boy profusely in her usual manner. Mark spent most of the afternoon heating water for her bath and, once the tub was filled with the steaming liquid, Rebecca's excitement was engaging. The boy sat her in a chair beside the keg, concerned she might fall and handed her a cowbell to ring periodically so he'd know if she drowned. Rebecca thought it hysterical, yet delightfully thoughtful, and shooed him away from her chair beside the tub. Mark gathered the blankets he had pulled from the bed, finished replacing them with fresh ones and slipped out of the room timidly.

Rebecca carefully pulled the filthy, mud encrusted clothing from her aching legs. Although she had been convalescing for days she was shocked to see that she was deeply scratched and bruised. One ankle had what looked like a nasty burn and both of her knees were nearly black with discoloration. Her abdomen was swollen and distended on one side and her arms were spotted with blotches.

"Are you alright in there?" Mark called through the heavy door.

"Oh yes, fine," Rebecca replied weakly. "I'm sorry I forgot the bell." She had to laugh in spite of the ache in her side and her dismal discovery of her condition. The swelling in her side alarmed her most of all, sending a shiver up her spine.

She rang the cowbell loudly and could hear the boy's chuckle outside. Lifting her weight carefully and slowly she lowered herself into the keg and slid into the steaming water. Her head began to pound instantly and she realized she still had much healing to do before a bath, even one in a rough old keg, would be at all enjoyable. She rang the bell again and painfully lathered herself with the soft soap the boy had given her. After several excruciating attempts to wash her hair well and much ringing of the cow bell she decided she had done enough when she could barely focus as she watched a thin trickle of blood drip into the hot water from her forehead. Fearful she might need to call out to the boy for assistance should she linger much longer, she pulled herself painfully from the keg and wrapped the blanket he had left for her around herself. Dressing in clean clothes would have to wait as Rebecca fell to the mattress.

No longer hearing the bell Mark called out to her.

"I'm alright," she whimpered back.

Mark was alarmed at the tone of her voice and announced that he was coming in. Before Rebecca could protest he burst into the room and found her faint and bleeding on the bed. Throwing another blanket over her bare legs he arranged her as carefully as possible and pressed a clean cloth to her head.

Rebecca shivered violently and it was clear she was feverish. The boy cursed at how the bath may not have been a good idea and contemplated, as he had several times since finding the woman, riding down the mountain for help. No one would come looking for her he hoped, but if he left her alone and someone did, he would never forgive himself.

"Damn it, Pa," he cursed aloud. "Why aren't you back yet?"

Rebecca whispered a weak thank you for the wonderful bath and drifted off to sleep. When Mark was sure she slept peacefully and that the bleeding had stopped on her forehead he stepped outside the cabin to catch his breath.

He thought he heard the hooves of an approaching horse for a moment, but it passed quickly. He listened tensely for several minutes to the wind in the trees. He'd spent every night beside the door and concluded that he could not leave the woman alone. He would have to wait until his father returned.

Chapter Ten

Once her fever broke Rebecca regained her strength quickly, joining the boy guardedly outdoors.

When Mark's father did not return as promised, the boy reminded himself that his late arrival was not unusual and did his best to help Rebecca heal quickly.

She followed him out to feed the chickens in the afternoon.

"What would happen if you didn't take their eggs away?" Rebecca asked as she helped Mark gather the eggs.

"They'd grow chicks," he informed her, perplexed that the woman knew practically nothing about keeping fowl or any animal at all.

"I would expect that," she replied in her funny proper way.

"Then we'd have no breakfast and a bunch of chickens!" Mark laughed.

Rebecca scowled. She wasn't a fool, she thought that there was something to taking away the warm eggs daily that she didn't quite understand, but the boy found her ignorance so entertaining she held her tongue. His attitude towards her was improving though, she thought. She told him the best way to weed the garden while the soil was soft and damp, but not too muddy and he taught her not to be afraid of the chickens. She overdid, lying in pain at night, but she didn't want the boy to see her as fragile and incapable of doing all the things a child could do.

Both of them remained watchful, not venturing far from the cabin. Rebecca avoided the boy's questioning about her as much as possible, preferring not to explain her reasons for leaving the train, or why she had come to America, and Mark spoke about his relationship with his father only when pressed, being as evasive as possible.

Some books were left for Mark to study, but his father had stopped checking his progress over time and Rebecca helped him catch up. When they talked he'd ask her about England, never tiring of teasing her about her accent or what he called her "proper ways", often mimicking her and laughing heartily at how different their descriptions were of the same things.

Mark began to talk more and more about his mother and how desperately both he and his father had missed her. It concerned Rebecca that, although very capable of caring for himself, so young a child was left unattended for such a long period of time. She didn't think much of Mark's father for his neglect of the boy, even in the light of explanations of the man's business dealings and grief over his lost wife.

Rebecca did not put much thought into the man during her early convalescence. But now his return began to concern her. She stood in front of the mirror and tried to see herself through the eyes of a stranger. The boy's clothing was clean and decent she supposed, but she could not adjust to wearing pants instead of a skirt. The huge scab that had formed on her hairline was healing well, but still looked ghastly to her so she took to wearing a felt cap much of the time, stuffing her hair up into it to keep the waist-long mass out of her way. The clothing, though small, still fit her badly so she wore a large jacket over it most of the time. It occurred to her that the boy may have spent so much time laughing at her, not simply because she was a "foreigner", as he called her, but perhaps because she looked so utterly ridiculous. She tried removing the cap, removing the jacket, replacing the cap without the jacket. Rebecca gave up hopelessly.

It worried her that anyone might encounter her in such a state and she tried to devise a way she might find acceptable clothing. She was handy with a needle and she knit quite well. She mentioned that to Mark one day and it seemed to surprise him that she could be handy, even in a feminine way. Contrary to what her dead husband had once said to her about such things being best left to the peasants, as he often referred to the help, she enjoyed them and missed her tatting and the hours spent before the fire working on her bobbin lace. There was no way however that she could do anything about clothing herself in a suitable manner now. Rebecca began to wonder if perhaps she and Mark should leave the cabin and set out to find someone to care for the boy and possibly some kind of employment for herself, although she knew she possessed few marketable skills.

"Mark," she ventured one day. "I'm worried about your father. We really need to consider leaving. How would you know if something happened to him? I can't just live here forever."

"We could ride back to the main house I suppose," he responded to her suggestion. "I did it once before when he was gone for a while. He wasn't too happy though." Mark hadn't forgotten his promise to always behave. He didn't want to leave without his father knowing and he himself had begun to have concerns over explaining the woman. He did not want to admit to Rebecca that he had been worried now for quite some time about his father and where to go from here. He decided to be forthright with her and admit his concerns.

"I'm not sure what Pa'll say about you being here. I had a friend ride up here once and he didn't care for it much. Like I said, since Ma passed he's been, well…, he's sorta short sometimes. Maybe I could send you down alone you think? No one's come looking for you and maybe you could find a way to get back home."

Rebecca thought the boy's father completely unreasonable if he were unable to see that her being at the cabin was unavoidable. She was also terrified of leaving alone, and what would she do if she actually made it to anywhere? Dressed this way no one would listen to her, even if she did attempt to explain. How would she get home? She had no money and the only people who knew her were Mark… and Bedra.

What if Bedra were to find her? Rebecca trembled at the thought. She tried to explain her reservations to the boy without sounding too fragile.

"I could give you money!" he volunteered. "Once you get down to the bottom of the mountain you could set the horse free and she'll come back on her own. I know a lady friend of my mother's that might take you in and give you some regular clothes to wear!" Mark had become animated with excitement at his plan.

Rebecca pondered, frightened over the idea, and then decided there was no alternative except to venture down on her own and try to improve the situation. She went over possible problems with the boy, even trying to get him to at least go part of the way down with her. She wished the boy wasn't so fearful of his father and would simply come with her.

She had become so concerned over the boy being alone that she promised that if she did make it down safely she would quickly inform his mother's friend of the boy's isolation.

"I'm fine," he assured her. "He'll be back, he always is. Must'a got sidetracked is all. I'll be just fine."

Mark hung an unusual hand beaded bag from the saddle horn on the morning she decided to leave.

"There's some money for you."

Rebecca pulled the cap far down on her head, fearing that she'd run into Bedra, and hoping if she did she would not be recognized.

"You'll be fine," the boy assured her. "My Ma used to ride that horse everywhere, if she could do it you can, too! I'll look for you when Pa's back up. You remember all the directions I told you right?" he asked as he helped her onto the horse.

"I think so." Rebecca winced at the continuing pain in her side and fought back tears of uncertainty.

Mark gave the horse a sharp slap and the chestnut mare started in a slow pace down the mountain, still unfamiliar with Rebecca's tentative form in the saddle. The young woman looked back at the boy and worried he'd be alright, but his open smile put her a little more at ease and she focused on the path before her.

Standing before the cabin, overwhelmed with emotion, Mark watched the girl ride down the path. When she turned back once or twice he waved openly to her. She looked very different than the day he had found her all beaten up in the abandoned shack. The sun drenched autumn days had put color in her cheeks and regular meals had filled her out some. Her help with the chores around the cabin had made her stronger and built her confidence. Mark wondered how he ever thought she was a boy like himself. Even dressed in the boy's clothing she was definitely a woman and she carried herself on the back of the horse in a very ladylike manner. The boy thought again of his mother and how she sat upright so similarly whenever she was nervous.

Despite his assurances to Rebecca he'd become unusually concerned about his father, and now he had grown attached to this woman and she had taken the horse. When the animal returned he thought it might be long enough to think about heading back to the main house. He wasn't too worried about the woman, she did have some curious ways and there were many things the boy knew she needed to learn to live easily in his world, but he felt confident she'd find her way alright if she didn't run into those folks who had waylaid her.

He knew if he did go down in a few days there'd be some things he have to take care of and with Rebecca there he had never picked up those blasted traps. He set out into the woods to find the snares and get rid of them.

Chapter Eleven

Timothy Elgerson awoke with a stiff neck and an aching back, his pistol still beside him and his head pounding like thundering horses.

He cursed himself and staggered downstairs to the study where he pulled a bottle of brandy from the immense desk. He sloshed a generous amount into the snifter and took a hard pull at the rich liquor.

"To another blasted day!" he toasted to himself and dropped into the chair behind the desk.

After several hours of sleeping off his stunning hangover, he took to roaming the house moodily. Every board, each piece of furniture and ornament bore the thumbprint of the man. He loved the house immensely and with every project to refine the home he'd stood beside Corissa enthusiastically displaying his latest creation.

"Do you like it?" he'd ask his wife, wanting nothing more than her approval. "I want it to be built perfectly, and I hope the woodwork is to your liking." Her smile faded in his memory.

The huge Victorian style home boasted the finest design from the deeply polished floors to the delicate crystal chandeliers. Its grand expanse opened at the entry with a wide central staircase and solid oak doors that fit perfectly into pocket enclosures leading into the grand parlor to the left, a cozy study situated to the right.

Timothy had once thrived within the walls of the

vast home and the spectacular landscape surrounded by stands of strapping white pines. He had loved the excitement of friends at gatherings and often filled the home with bustling visitors, the sounds of a lively band filling the evening air.

He cringed at the thought of allowing Octavia the opportunity of bringing guests into the house once again. A party was one of the things he had avoided with determination since his wife's death and he planned to make himself as scarce as possible.

His musings were interrupted by the sound of a commotion in the back kitchen and he passed the staircase towards the rear of the house to investigate the disturbance. A limited staff did oversee the residence but the uproar sounded like a larger group than the few lingering employees.

"Ah, sir!" Simmons, the butler ushered Timothy into the kitchen as soon as Elgerson had stepped towards the door. "It's good you're here sir, we didn't hear you come up the drive," the butler carried on in a rushed tone. "There's been some trouble with the train, sir, most unfortunate!"

Several of his neighbors occupied the space, jumbling about with a number of the staff as well as the newly appointed deputy sheriff from Billington.

"Seems there's been some sort of robbery," Deputy Albertson interjected. "Looks like a pair of men hid out on the express with some dynamite and it's pandemonium up at the bend there just past the bridge. We're riding out now to make sure everyone's alright. I'd sure like to see you join us, Tim. We could certainly use your help."

Timothy Elgerson took the stairs two at a time,

donned a clean change of clothes and gathered a few provisions before meeting the deputy and four other men in the stable. The group set out at a gallop through the pines towards the bridge that bordered the south end of Elgerson's property.

It was the second time a robbery had been attempted in the region, but the close proximity to his home made Elgerson nervous.

When the team of men reached the river they could hear the voices of frantic passengers and railroad employees raised in panic. Several of the travelers stood in groups at either end of the short bridge, and the engineer and conductors were frantically describing the raid to the Billington sheriff. Elgerson slid down from his horse and surveyed the damage.

"Well, the only thing I can figure is that they must have boarded at Hawk Bend on the early train," fretted the engineer, pacing and wringing his rough hands. "They had to have hidden out in the blind baggage because I never saw them on board and neither did any of the conductors." Three uniformed conductors nodded their heads vigorously in agreement.

"Then, right before we hit the bridge the express car just blew up! Damndest thing, she opened up just like a tin can!" The engineer threw apart his hands. "Didn't do enough damage to stop the train and it didn't appear that anyone was hurt badly. They didn't get much, but the car's awfully damaged. Those fellas got right at the safe they'd blown up and headed off into the woods that way." He gestured towards a narrow break in a thick stand of pine.

"I've got men up there now," the sheriff began. "Appears they had horses hidden back up there waiting. They must have left them there earlier, got on the train somehow and figured they'd blow it here on the bridge, maybe take the bridge out and get away clean. We're putting together a group of riders to see if we can track them. Sure could use your skill with that rifle, Tim," the sheriff went on.

"I'm none too pleased with how close this is getting to home these days, Ben," Elgerson replied. "Where are the men?"

"Up past the old mill road, Tim. I'm sure you can find them. I'm obliged to you."

Elgerson caught up with the small posse after taking stock of the clearing where the robbers had obviously been hiding their horses. The old maple stained with tobacco spittle and a small covered heap of ashes gave evidence that the men had most likely spent the night before riding down to board the train at the station in the early morning hours.

The posse was made up of a group of men Elgerson knew well, an honest capable bunch made up of neighbors as well as his former foreman, Roland Vancouver. The men greeted him as he approached and he fell into their ranks easily. They rode the woods in the most direct path, all noting evidence of previous riders towards the Hawk Bend station.

"They either know the area well, or at least took time to go through here a couple of times," James Evens commented.

"It does appear that they knew how to get right to where they wanted," Roland remarked.

Elgerson had the same thought himself. Although the path through the backwoods was something he'd walked or ridden many times the trail wasn't obvious to anyone unfamiliar with the woodland. Where it led into the area ravaged by the previous year's fire the men searched the black mud for prints. Whoever had put together this plan knew this property well. Elgerson felt uneasy.

The men scouted the area around the station and cut through the forest attempting to pick up the trail of the robbers. At a small clearing they dismounted and uncovered a small camp area, but after careful inspection they decided that the thieves had not lingered there, at least on this occasion and the men continued on their way.

They spent time discussing evidence and they all agreed that there were only two riders, and somewhere at this point they must have separated. One heavy horse bearing a large rider appeared to head toward Billington. The other, a finer and probably swifter animal had cut out across a narrow plain and likely through the gulch along the river. The men had met here often themselves for mornings of fishing with their youngsters and knew the passage well.

Elgerson was not far from the cabin where Mark was waiting and considered a detour to check the lad. He decided against it for now, opting instead to remain on the trail of the bandits. Feeling confident that the boy was capable, he turned to a discussion with his associates.

"Emmett and I will head back towards Billington and see if any strangers passed through town, Tim," Roland decided. "Why don't you and Nils see what's going on up the gulch?"

Having agreed on a plan of action, they parted ways. Nils Evens and Timothy Elgerson were well known to be two of the best marksmen in the territory. Not far from Billington the men who headed back were not likely to encounter any problems. The gulch that these men headed into however, afforded several good locations with cover and, if one of the thieves were waiting, the more accomplished Elgerson and Evens were the better choice in a possible exchange of gunfire.

Timothy was the more accomplished of the two at tracking and took the lead as they followed along the trail. At nightfall they set up camp, confident they were close on the trail of their man.

"How's your boy these days?" Nils asked, watching Elgerson peer indolently into the small fire.

"Fine," Timothy replied. "Still down in the mouth, but I'm hoping it'll work itself out alright."

Nils Evens had known Tim Elgerson since they were children together. With so many acres lost in the previous year's devastating fire, so soon after the loss of his wife, Nils wondered how Tim and the boy had ever made it through.

Evens had been witness to Elgerson's struggles getting to know his stepson on countless camping trips they had taken with Nils' boy along. Tim possessed a warm heart and good common sense, but his mannerisms could be easily misunderstood and

Nils had watched the boy struggle to reach an understanding with the man. Elgerson could seem curt and impatient in his forthright ways and Nils felt that it wasn't until they had shared the loss of Corissa that Tim and the boy began to appreciate one another. Evens lamented that it was unfortunate she never saw them growing close while she was alive.

The men had a long built and easy understanding between them and Evens knew better than to question Elgerson further. He unpacked his bedroll and called it a night.

The sharp crack of gunshots shattered the morning mist sending both men into the woods scrambling for cover.

"Are you alright, Nils?" Tim called out through the forest.

"Yeah," Nils called back. "I've been hit, but I'm alright!"

Elgerson called to Nils to stay where he was and wove his way swiftly through the thick trees. When he reached Evens his concern mounted. Nils sat, his back against a pine, bleeding profusely from the thigh.

"Damn it, Tim, did you see him?" Nils attempted to keep his composure.

"No, but he can't be far. How are you feeling?" Elgerson pulled off his belt and began to wrap it tightly around the injured man's groin. It became quickly apparent that the wound was serious and Elgerson pulled the belt tighter.

"I got on my feet alright, but he hit me while I

was running. I think he set himself in the thicket towards the east there. Whoever's shooting might be afraid to cut through that old Indian cemetery. He fired three times before he hit me. I think he just got lucky. If you could help me up I think I might be able to get at him from the other side." Evens looked pale.

"No, you just relax. I heard him take off into the woods," Elgerson lied. "We'll be fine, let's just see what we can do about that leg."

Timothy circled around behind the man and headed for the horses. He slipped stealthily through the trees hoping not to be spotted by the sniper and that Evens wouldn't notice his caution. He knew the wounded man should not be moved. Evens was not one to sit there if there was a threat and Elgerson had to keep him quiet.

He retrieved his horse and led it back as silently as he could to Nils. The bleeding had slowed with the pressure from the tourniquet and Elgerson loosened the belt and packed the wound with a poultice from his pack. The herbal concoction might keep the injury from festering until he found a way to get the man down the mountain.

Tim did his best to make the wounded man comfortable, while keeping his eyes closely fixed into the half-lit woodland and listening intently for any signs of movement. Just before sunrise he had heard the shooter's horse snort softly and move off in the distance. Without fear of another attack he began to devise a plan to take Evens to safety. He scouted the woods for a distance, but could not find Nils' stallion and considered now that both men would have to ride back on Timothy's own mount.

Any movement of the man opened the wound and Elgerson decided that the only hope would be to leave Evens and go for help. Nils remained coherent, despite a great loss of blood and Elgerson reminded him that the belt had to be loosened at regular intervals. He made sure his friend was wrapped warmly and fed him well before preparing for his journey.

"I'll be fine Tim, really," Nils reassured him. "If it weren't for this damned leg I'd hop right beside you there and we'd go for a nice ride together. All those years I've known you I always wanted to share a horse like that night when we were kids and we raided that melon patch."

Timothy chuckled at the memory and appreciated the humorous remark.

"I never had a sweeter melon than that night, or a sweeter ride," he laughed. He knew it would be a full day before he could return and feared for his companion's life. Even pulling the wounded man behind him on a makeshift travois would be an undertaking through dense wood he could not accomplish alone.

"I'm going to need help getting you down the mountain, Nils. You hang in there and I'll be back with help as soon as I can." Elgerson mounted his horse.

He rode hard all day, and into the next, crisscrossing through the trees and stopped only once for water and to relieve himself.

As the afternoon shifted towards dusk he heard voices down the mountain and brought the horse around to a thicket and listened. The relief from recognition of the friendly conversation spurred him to a brisk gallop in the direction of the party ascending the hill below his position.

"Timothy?" the men called, pulling their horses around and watching Elgerson rush through the brush towards them. Deftly guiding the horse downward through the tangle of roots they waited for the big man, his mass of golden hair flying behind him as he bent over his driving beast.

"Evens is up past the gorge near the old burial ground with a bullet in his thigh. I couldn't move him alone and I left him in a tourniquet. He's in a bad way. I'm going to need to get him down as quickly as possible. It doesn't look good." His last remark was directed to the sheriff.

"We'll take care of him, Tim," the lawman replied. "What happened? There's nothing going on in town, but it looks as though someone doubled back towards the north and we lost their trail about halfway up."

"My boy's staying up at the cabin," Elgerson panted.

"We never got up that far, Tim." Sheriff Carson could not conceal his concern. "We'll take care of finding Evens. You can check on your boy."

"Go ahead, Tim," Vancouver remarked in a tone too discouraging to ignore.

Elgerson turned his mount and faced the men. He knew it was likely that Nils had lost consciousness by now. If he couldn't respond to the men when they called out for him they might never find him. He led the men of the posse up the mountainside toward the old cemetery, hoping to find Evens still alive and vowing to return to his son as quickly as possible.

Chapter Twelve

*T*imothy Elgerson rode desperately towards the cabin, frantic with worry over the boy. He was certain that Evens would not survive the gunshot wound despite the fact that they had finally found him unconscious but alive. The man drove his exhausted mount in the most direct route possible through the thick forest.

Had he stopped and checked the boy when the opportunity arose he knew that the lad would have joined their pursuit. With the boy's skill with a rifle, things might have gone differently. Evens might never have been shot and he would not be running to save the boy from a similar fate. A million possibilities raced through the man's mind.

Elgerson's head pounded from exhaustion and he had the look of a demon as he rode frantically, insane with worry and the stress of the previous week's events. His knuckles white and tearing into the reins, he kicked the foam covered animal beneath him. He rode on for hours, giving himself and the huge black

Arabian no reprieve from his single-minded mission.

When he reached the ridge below the cabin he pulled the animal to a sudden halt, hunkered down low against the horse's back and circled a small clearing while he and the exhausted stallion tried to regulate their breathing. The Arabian was coughing hard and Timothy stroked the tortured beast as calmly as he could, trying to quiet the horse's strangled breathing. If there were someone besides the boy at the cabin, he hoped to ride up undetected until he could assess the situation. Timothy hoped vainly that perhaps Mark was alone and if all were well he would not frighten the boy. His heart was bursting from the panic and overwhelming fear for the lad, admitting to himself that losing the boy was more than he could ever bear.

After several minutes the big horse walked quietly once again beneath him and blew softly as Timothy Elgerson quietly directed him towards the edge of the thin trail that led to the cabin less than a quarter of a mile away.

He could make out a soft stomping approaching slowly along the trail and Elgerson turned his mount about in a tight circle, steadying the dark beast behind a vine-covered stand of rotting stumps. He sat tensely in a hunter's stance anticipating the rider's appearance through the trees.

Coming into Elgerson's view, the rider paused cautiously for a moment, revealing to Timothy that the animal headed down the trail was his own, a spirited chestnut once purchased for his wife. From the saddle hung the beaded bag that Corissa had received as a gift and had kept at the cabin filled with currency for an emergency. Elgerson's Arabian could feel the man's muscles tense and steadied his limbs in anticipation of the man's attack.

Elgerson kicked the stallion into action and the beast bounded from their hiding place clearing the stumps and bursting onto the path. The chestnut ran frantically in terror down the trail, cutting into the wood in a panic, fleeing from the unanticipated assault and attempting to upset its unfamiliar passenger. The alarmed animal sprinted through the trees, its inexperienced passenger clinging cruelly to the mare's neck in horror.

Elgerson's stallion kept pace with the terrified chestnut nipping sharply at her rump and bounding forward to overtake the horrified mare.

Rebecca clung to the horse tightly, certain that if she lost hold of the chestnut she would fall to her death and be trampled.

"They've found me and they'll take me back to the shack and kill me this time!" she gasped in horror. Outpacing her pursuer while still remaining on the horse seemed her only hope for escape. The horror-struck girl leaned forward against the animal's rigid neck and the chestnut lunged forward.

Elgerson urged his Arabian ahead, pulled alongside of the thief and leapt from the stallion onto the mare, unseating the fleeing girl. The two riders tumbled violently to the rugged forest floor with Elgerson's steel grip encircling his prey.

Rebecca fought her attacker with every bit of her strength, writhing and kicking in panic and fear.

Elgerson struggled to maintain his hold on the terrified prisoner, caught tight in his mighty grip and fighting like a wild animal. Pinning his captive beneath him, he pressed the thief to the earth, straddling both legs and pushing both shoulders hard to the ground.

Rebecca thrashed fiercely and, as Elgerson raised his fist to silence her, she let out a shrill "Pleeeeeeeaaaaase!"

Her petite face and her tiny frame beneath him made Timothy Elgerson stop abruptly in mid-swing. In confusion he studied his captive quickly and restrained himself from bludgeoning his victim.

A woman? None of this made sense.

"Who are you?" he demanded loudly.

Rebecca wailed and pleaded, but Elgerson held fast.

"Who the hell are you?" he persisted.

Realizing that this attacker was one she had not encountered before, Rebecca began to plead with the man to unhand her.

"If you and your gang of thieves have done anything to my son I swear I'll kill you all!" Elgerson blared into the girl's face.

"I've done nothing!" Rebecca fought. "Get off of me right now!"

"We'll see about that!" Elgerson bellowed, rising to his feet and hauling his tiny victim up with him. He whistled for the stallion and Rebecca bit into the man's hand solidly.

"Stop!" the he commanded, tearing Rebecca's sleeve. "You're coming with me!"

"I will not!" Rebecca kicked the man squarely between his cast-iron thighs.

Elgerson lost his grip on the girl as his legs began

to buckle beneath him and he was overtaken with retching nausea.

Rebecca pulled free, scrambling to her feet and running towards the man's steed. The Arabian towered over her and she struggled in a panic as she tried to pull herself onto the animal's back. The agitated beast stepped aside and Rebecca fell flat to the ground.

"Oh no you don't!" Elgerson grabbed her by the collar and, standing bent beside her, held her clear of the ground and himself.

"Let me go!"

"No, now stop! You're coming with me now!" Elgerson glowered into the girl's face threatening.

"I will not!" Rebecca spat.

Elgerson staggered upright uneasily and called the horse. The animal paced nervously until Elgerson snapped a command and then cautiously approached his master.

Holding Rebecca firmly by her slender waist he threw her over the large leather saddle and mounted behind her. Rebecca tried to shift her weight to her legs in an attempt to slide from the huge black beast and the he grabbed her pants roughly, slapped her on the backside, and set her firmly across the saddle.

"If you don't stop I'll tie you up!" he threatened huskily.

The girl squirmed in pain and indignation.

Elgerson kicked the horse to a gallop with Rebecca clinging terrified to the jostling saddle, Elgerson holding her fast by her waistband.

When they reached the clearing at the cabin Rebecca lifted her head as the horse slowed and began to scream in warning to Mark. Elgerson dismounted, hauled the girl from the horse and tried to drag her into the cabin.

Rebecca twisted in his grip and reached out to claw at his face, catching a handful of his hair and pulling it viciously. Elgerson reached up and captured her wrist in a vice-like grip and Rebecca twisted to free herself.

Mark ran towards the cabin, bursting from the forest to witness the violent struggle. Rebecca and his father fought like animals, the girl kicking and screaming while his father struggled in an attempt to contain the girl.

"Pa!" he shouted as he ran towards them. "Stop!"

"Run, Mark! He's going to kill us both! Run!" Rebecca screamed shrilly.

"Mark!" Elgerson exclaimed. "Thank God you're alright! I caught this thief riding down the…" Elgerson's voice trailed off in confusion.

"She's not a thief, Pa!" Mark ran to the girl's side.

Rebecca fell to the ground and sobbed uncontrollably as Elgerson loosened his grip and hung his head as he dropped to his knees.

"What the hell is going on here?" he raised his flushed face and barked at his son.

Rebecca's incessant sobbing made explanations impossible and Elgerson finally instructed the boy to take the exasperating female into the cabin and hush her up since it was clear that the boy knew the crazed girl.

"She's not a thief, Pa. I found her," the boy called back, leading Rebecca into the doorway.

Mark settled her into the bed, as he had the day he

first discovered her and Rebecca curled into a tiny ball and wept quietly. When he returned he found his father beside the fireplace with his head in his hands, exhaustion clearly displayed in his demeanor.

The boy silently set about preparing coffee for the depleted man, deciding to wait for his father to question him before venturing any explanations.

Timothy Elgerson sat running his hands through his hair and pulling at his bearded chin until the boy filled the man's big hands with a steaming cup of coffee.

Elgerson peered at the boy curiously and took a swig of the dark fluid.

Mark appeared contrite as he stood before his father wishing the man would say something. He didn't even care any longer what he might face as long as the man spoke.

"Alright," Elgerson finally announced. "You want to explain to me what that wildcat was doing on your Mother's horse running off with our money?"

Mark pulled around a chair to face his angered father and began to relate the events surrounding his discovery of Rebecca, even venturing to confess why he had gone into the woods to begin with.

Elgerson studied his son carefully, barely able to believe the boy's description, except that the facts were too amazing for even the most vivid child's imagination. He knew that the boy might select omission on occasion, but rarely made up a story to avoid ramifications. He wondered about the shack the boy talked about and speculated to himself that maybe the robbers had constructed a hideout not too far away.

However implausible the story might be. Elgerson had to admit the boy had to have been seriously tested caring for the gravely injured girl and he listened to the boy's story intently.

When Mark concluded his tale he finished with a serious look directly into his father's tortured face.

"I'm sorry, Pa. I know I'm not supposed to have anyone else up here while you're away and I swear I'll never trap again. I just didn't know what else to do with her and she was so hurt and I guess it just kinda happened. Then I couldn't keep her up here for too much longer and I didn't know when you'd be back." Mark cut himself short, careful not to shift the blame onto his father's late arrival.

"It's alright," Elgerson told the boy. "There was some trouble with the train. I'll explain it all to you later."

Relieved that his father showed no sign of the outburst he had convinced himself he would, and hoping to head off any possibility that he might still be upset, Mark attempted to distract him with questions about the train.

"Not right now, boy, I haven't slept in days. After I get some rest we'll talk some more. You have seen no one else?"

"No, sir," the boy replied.

Elgerson struggled wearily to his feet and made his way towards the sleeping quarters.

"Pa…" The boy was certain he'd forgotten the sleeping woman occupied the bedroom.

Elgerson stood in the doorway, took one look at

the girl's tiny, curled up figure and thought better of tangling with her again. He left the cabin to find rest in the stable and Mark decided he had better check on the woman.

Rebecca was covered with mud once again, and her arm was scraped and beginning to bruise in her torn sleeve.

"I heard," she whispered, sniffling. "Thank you."

Mark left her weeping in the bed and decided he was ready to try some coffee himself.

Chapter Thirteen

*E*lgerson concluded his story of the last few days to his son. "If that shack is a hideout then we should take a look at it. I can't rest easy knowing there's someone in the area that might try coming here. I need you to stay here and keep an eye on the place just long enough for me to get an idea where the shack is. Once I get a bearing on it we'll ride down and I'll get some men up here to try and flush the thieves out. Where exactly did you say it was?"

Mark struggled with a clear direction and then suggested that Rebecca might help find the location where the building stood and she could show his father.

Elgerson groaned at the thought of encountering the girl at all, but finally agreed that he'd take her along as long as she behaved, just to scout the place out. He was growing concerned over who the girl was and where her family might be and thought he'd best take her down the mountain into town as well, and try to find her folks. Mark had described her as a woman in his explanations of her, but to Elgerson she couldn't be more than a child and he expected that Mark was just too young to be able to distinguish between a woman and a girl.

In his forthright way he headed into the bedroom and informed the girl she would be riding with him.

Rebecca scrambled to the opposite end of the bed and flatly refused.

"You're taking me off somewhere and I will no longer tolerate your abuse."

Elgerson thought her accent and attitude probably made her appear older than she certainly was, fairly swimming in oversized clothing, further evidence that the boy was mistaken about her age.

Rebecca held the torn shirt against her chest and glared at the outlandish beard and massive tangle of hair. His eyes were red and frightening and the memory of his rough handling of her was more than she could bear.

Mark pleaded with her that she would be perfectly safe and that his father was no lunatic, as she insisted. Eventually Rebecca surrendered, once the boy convinced her that after she took a ride with his Pa they could go down the mountain to town. Rebecca believed that if she could only rid herself of the current situation there might be some hope for her and she ventured up to the giant.

"I'll go," she announced boldly, her hands clasping her tattered attire. "But you will not lay a hand on me!"

Elgerson agreed, glaring at the girl, and again Rebecca protested when Mark offered to lift her in front of his father to mount the very beast he had used to drag her here.

After intense prodding, Rebecca plopped down in the saddle in front of the him and the pair finally set out on their mission.

"I'll take you to town and get you back to your family as soon as we finish this up." Elgerson remarked gruffly as they rode towards the shack.

"I have no family here," Rebecca remarked flatly.

"Where do you plan on going?" The sooner he was rid of her the better, he thought.

Rebecca choked back a sob and he decided to let it drop.

Elgerson felt her tiny form slip to one side in the saddle and he caught her deftly with one hand as they rode through the deep forest.

Rebecca gasped at the placement of his hand and Elgerson sat upright in shock. Clad in baggy boy's clothing as she was, he was shaken and stunned that the handful he had captured righting the girl in the saddle was not the thin ribcage of a young girl, but instead the full breast of a grown woman.

Rebecca huffed in embarrassment and blushed deeply with the insult of such handling by this horrid beast.

Elgerson blushed as well and shifted in the saddle, increasingly uncomfortable with the woman's close proximity.

When they spotted the shack, Rebecca began to shake uncontrollably and her fear brought the realization of her situation clearly to Elgerson. The frail girl turned and buried her face in his chest and he cleared his throat, turning the horse back towards the cabin.

"It's alright, Rebecca. Right?" He was at a loss as to how to calm her shaking. He talked to her in a soft voice assuring her that she'd be fine and thanking her for showing him the place. He had hoped to get a look inside but the girl was plainly terrified and Mark's description of her experience in the shack and her condition when he found her, made Elgerson begin to understand her fears.

Rebecca lay against the man's solid chest, more terrified at the sight of the shack than she was of him. His heartbeat calmed her fears and she snuggled against his warmth.

Elgerson shifted his position. The girl pressing into him left him nervous and self-conscious. He was uncomfortable but greatly relieved when they finally returned to the cabin and he lowered Rebecca from the horse. Her tiny face, encased in the massive wool cap, looked up at him briefly and Elgerson dismounted the animal from the opposite side. The chestnut stood near the side of the cabin, kicking the dust and snorting a greeting to the Arabian and Elgerson gathered both animals by the reins.

The three packed their bags carefully in preparation for their descent and Elgerson avoided the girl guardedly. From the doorway he watched her and Mark pack the last of the belongings, witnessing their easy camaraderie and saw Rebecca tussle the boy's hair the way Corissa had done once. Uneasily he announced that it was time to leave.

"Rebecca can ride with me, Pa," Mark suggested.

"Let her ride alone, Mark. We'll ride together," Timothy stated impatiently.

Rebecca blushed as Elgerson pulled the boy up behind him.

They descended slowly down the mountain, Elgerson becoming increasingly aware that Rebecca did not ride well and when the boy dozed off behind him Elgerson pulled his horse up beside the chestnut, fearful that Rebecca would slip from her saddle.

"You need to settle into the saddle more," he instructed. "If you tense up like that the horse gets skittish and she might unseat you. Feel her movement and ease into her."

Rebecca tried relaxing into the saddle.

Elgerson studied the girl curiously and Rebecca felt embarrassed by his searching gaze.

"Of course, she may upset you no matter how well you ride, just from the look of that hat you've got on there." Elgerson looked straight ahead and chuckled.

Rebecca, at first mortified, began to laugh herself.

"Does that hat have a purpose?" he asked still

chuckling. "I mean other than to scare horses?"

"There's an awfully bad cut there." Rebecca indicated her forehead with embarrassment.

"Well, I can't imagine that even a split skull could be more frightening than that hat." Elgerson's hearty laughter was contagious and Rebecca began giggling, in spite of her self-consciousness.

Rebecca pulled the cap from her head briskly and gave her head a shake dropping the length of her hair onto her shoulders and tumbling down her back. She sat upright, turned towards him, grinned pleasantly, and remarked, "Is that better?"

He gasped and felt his breath catch in his throat as her hair fell free about her and he saw her smile for the first time. He saw her petite nose, touched with freckles, wrinkling slightly as she turned away. Elgerson steadied himself and stared at her in disbelief. The young woman's beauty was striking and startling and very disconcerting. Thoughts of having wrestled her suddenly came back to him and he pulled his eyes away from her and stared down at his hands.

Rebecca thought that the wound on her forehead must look as awful as she feared and she tried to steady herself on the mare while attempting awkwardly to replace the hat, stuffing her hair up inside with one hand.

"What is your name?" she asked nervously, hoping to cover the scar without further embarrassment. "I only know you as 'Pa' and I don't suppose that will do." Rebecca wished her remark might return the man to his friendly mood.

"Timothy," he replied uneasily.

"Timothy," Rebecca repeated as the man pulled his horse ahead of her.

Rebecca was mortified. The man had tried to help her, was even being friendly and she had upset him. She considered apologizing but decided not to embarrass either of them further. The shock on his face had been quite clear and a warm tear rolled down her cheek and she studied the figure before her.

The man was solidly built, broad in the shoulders upon which tumbled his golden hair. Not quite the giant she first feared, she could see he was trim and distinguished for a man of his height and he rode with an easy grace and perfect posture. The young boy riding easy against his father's back, dozing in complete trust, which Rebecca had enjoyed herself. She recalled how warm and safe she had felt against him as they rode from the hideout and she blushed, and attempted to focus on the road ahead of her instead of the figure of the man before her.

They rode in silence until the boy awoke and began a steady stream of cheerful chatter in anticipation of returning home. He talked about cousins and friends and attempted to engage both adults in his excitement. Puzzled by Rebecca's mood, he finally took to whistling a silly polka, unable to contain his enthusiasm.

Rebecca's thoughts teetered between concern over what would happen when they actually arrived in town and how ridiculous Timothy thought she looked. She pulled at the torn sleeve and held the cuff closed against the reins.

Elgerson noticed the girl's subtle arrangement of the cuff, along with her boyish attire and decided it was something he'd have to address soon. He was not entirely comfortable with the prospect of seeing her dressed like a woman instead of the disguise she now wore, her current outfit being far easier to handle than her feminine display earlier, but she could not travel in such an ensemble. Timothy recalled her disarming smile and swallowed hard. He was certain that the girl was uncomfortable and he felt somehow responsible for her tattered state. Elgerson decided to resolve the problem as soon as they got into town. Once things were sorted out he'd send her on, but wherever that might be, she could plainly not travel in her current state.

He'd need to find out about Nils, Elgerson thought. There'd be news of him and maybe of the hunt for the robbers as well. Then there was Octavia. Timothy groaned to himself. In all of the excitement he had completely forgotten that his home would soon be overrun by Octavia, most likely her mother and certainly almost everyone in town. His hopes for a peaceful return home were suddenly dashed and Timothy's mood darkened.

In the evening gloom they rode into town quietly. Elgerson arranged a night's lodging, leaving Rebecca and Mark to tie up the horses. Rebecca held her head down hoping no one would take notice of her standing beside the boy and kicking the dirt in the same way he did. Timothy had decided to spend the night in town before continuing on to the house and Rebecca hoped maybe she could find a posting somewhere from someone seeking help. She thought of asking Mark where she might find such postings as Elgerson returned and led them across the street.

"Mark, I want you to wait here while I take Rebecca into the shop."

Rebecca was already admiring the gowns in the shop window and read the sign overhead, *La Longue Robe Shop - Ladies Clothier and Millenary*. She considered the ramifications of entering the shop, her current clothing, her lack of coin and she did not want to owe Timothy in any way. He shuffled her into the doorway as she opened her mouth in protest and Octavia Weintraub nearly toppled into them.

"Why, Timothy, wherever have you been?" Octavia gasped.

"Evening, Miss Weintraub," Elgerson nodded hesitatingly.

"I have so much to tell you, but it will all have to wait until the party!" Octavia waved a meaty hand. "I can hardly wait! I'm just picking up my gown and mother is in a hurry."

"Oh," she remarked as she brushed past them. "I see you have your boy with you. Hello Mick!" Octavia patted Rebecca firmly on the head as she exited the shop.

Something about the woman made Rebecca uneasy and, although she could not recall ever having laid eyes on her before, the girl felt certain that she might have met her somewhere. She decided that she probably was just irritated by the awful woman thumping her head along with her rude mannerisms.

An elderly female pulled aside the heavy curtain towards the rear of the shop and rushed to them.

"Why ,Tim, what a pleasure!" she exclaimed. "It's been so very long and I have missed seeing you so!" The tiny dumpling of a woman peered over her low glasses at Rebecca. The shop owner was bouncy and full figured with a cushion stuffed with pins on her left wrist and a warm smile on her face. Thin strands of her silvery hair were caught in a tight bun balanced on top of her perfectly spherical head, while the remaining wisps framed her face in a soft halo of curls.

"And who might this be?" The woman approached Rebecca boldly and began to spin her around slowly.

"My dear!" the seamstress exclaimed. "Where did you come up with such an outfit?" She plucked curiously at Rebecca's garb and whisked the hat from her head.

Rebecca tried to pull her hair across her forehead and wandered away towards the back of the shop as Elgerson avoided the view of the girl and attempted an explanation to the shopkeeper.

"She's from out of town and has had some trouble and has lost her belongings. If possible could you perhaps supply her with something of a proper wardrobe and possibly a suitable gown for the party?"

"Oh yes, yes, the gathering! All of the ladies in town have been to visit me looking for gowns for your gathering. It is good that you are having the parties again. It's always so good for the business you know!" The woman's eyes twinkled at Timothy. Such a handsome example of a man she thought, and always so generous as well. "But of course, I cannot supply a full wardrobe today, but I can outfit her appropriately for the time being. Is that acceptable to you?" The woman tittered with excitement.

"That would be perfect," Timothy replied.

"Rebecca, I'll pick you up when I've finished my errands," the man announced.

Rebecca hastened to catch him as he left the shop. "I cannot possibly pay for this and I cannot…"

"Just go with Anja, Rebecca. She's a good friend and very discreet. Trust me. I think it would be best if you were more suitably attired. We can make arrangements that suit us both at another time."

Timothy bowed slightly to the tiny shop owner and left the store, always uncomfortable with spending time in the tiny dressmaker's and the sight of Rebecca with her hair tumbling free still making him even more uneasy.

The seamstress shuffled the young woman into a tiny, cluttered back room strewn with pins and bits of fabric and began to help her disrobe.

"The dressing rooms, they are prepared for fitting appointments, we are okay here, no? Oh my, you have lost your undergarments as well! Not to worry." She quickly recovered from her shock. "I have just the thing!" Shuffling through a stack of boxes in the corner she returned with a lacy armload and continued removing the boy's clothing from the young woman.

"Ahhh," she turned her head to the side examining Rebecca's naked form carefully. "Poor Miss," she sighed. Then, looking Rebecca unflinchingly in the eyes, unable to ignore the welt from a large handprint on the girl's pale derriere and several bruises, "Such terrible marks, and on such a lovely girl. Do not be concerned, my dear. I will have my girls make you such a gown that shows only your beauty and makes all of 'dis easily forgotten! You'll see. It will be much better." Her eyes were open and sympathetic and Rebecca sighed deeply, comfortable in the women's kindness and understanding.

The little woman was a flurry of activity, measuring and commenting to herself. Rebecca stood silent in mortification, not uttering a word while the lady helped her step into a lacy pair of silk bloomers and slipped a beautifully adorned camisole over her head.

"These you take now, though such a shame I cannot do more until tomorrow."

Rebecca felt the delicate silk against her body and sighed. She had always appreciated fine lingerie and these lacy pieces were of a quality she never had been able to afford. She groaned at the thought of how she might pay for such finery.

"Tomorrow I will have your corsets ready and enough petticoats for any gown you might choose." Pulling heavy bolts of cloth from the shelving on the wall the woman tried to balance them on a nearby chair.

"Oh, let me help you!" Rebecca exclaimed, afraid the tiny woman might be buried in the yards of cloth.

"Why, child, you're British! My late husband and I traveled to England once, many years ago. How delightful!" The dressmaker was bursting with questions about Rebecca and how she had come to be in the company of dear Timothy. She had hoped that the girl was not a relative of the man, believing that it was time he found another wife. The petite girl was so very beautiful and they would make such a fine looking couple, the girl with her dark hair and delicate green eyes, and Timothy so fair and rugged.

"I have just the thing for the party gown," Anja announced, unfurling a rich emerald velvet across Rebecca's chest. "Also there is a piece one of my girls has designed, such a clever girl she is, with embroidery I'm sure you'll be pleased with! I'll get my girls to work up some others as well for your wardrobe, a bright clover perhaps and maybe a lovely shade of claret as well. I'm sure you will not be disappointed. Colors are so lovely for gowns, no?"

"Of course you will need bonnets and you must have gloves for fall as well," the dressmaker bubbled on. "And I'll get Gustov to measure you for suitable footwear, oh stockings, yes, plenty of stockings. I promise you will be very pleased."

Rebecca stammered, but she could not bring herself to complain or offer up resistance. The fabrics were all so fine and the woman was so sweet and her work so beautiful. There was also mention of a party. Rebecca's head swam.

"I'm sure everything will be very beautiful," she acquiesced. The young woman felt so much more civilized for having something, even the lingerie to wear. She dreaded slipping back into the boy's clothing, but after a long expanse of time while the woman prattled on and draped her in an endless secession of fabrics, Rebecca began to hope for Timothy's return.

Chapter Fourteen

$\mathcal{T}$imothy Elgerson gathered the horses and he and the boy set out for the Evens house situated just on the edge of town. Elgerson worried that he may be confronted with a grieving widow and although he did not enjoy the thought, he knew at least he would need to pay his respects to Nils' dear wife.

To Timothy's shock and relief, Catherine Evens met his knock at the door warmly and beckoned him and Mark inside.

"How wonderful to see you, Mr. Elgerson, and you as well, Mark! How can I possibly thank you?" Mrs. Evens held Timothy's arm affectionately.

"I take it Nils has survived his ordeal. How is he?"

"Oh, he's doing so well! Please come see for yourself!" She led Timothy up the stairs while announcing his presence and showed him into a room bathed in the sunshine of the late afternoon.

Nils Evens sat partially upright on a mountain of white and buttercup yellow blankets, pale, but clearly alive.

"Tim!" Evens beckoned from the bed. "So good to see you're back and looking well. Did you ever find that shack? Please, have a seat. Cathy, bring us something to drink!"

Catherine Evens gave her husband a stern look but then smiled warmly, rolling her eyes for Timothy and set off for refreshments.

Timothy Elgerson pulled a chair up beside the bed and gestured to Mark to do the same. The boy had known Nils Evens since his mother's marriage to Elgerson and he was thrilled to see the man alive, as well as being asked to join in the men's conversation.

"It's so good to see you well," Elgerson took his friend's hand and pressed it briefly, both men knowing how badly their ordeal could have ended.

Mark watched the two men's interaction and noticed a gentleness he had not seen his father display in a long while.

"Oh, I told you I was fine, Tim!" Evens laughed stiffly. "The boys got me down the mountain alright. I don't remember most of it actually, probably just as well. Doc pulled that bullet right out, says I'll be good as new!

"Never did get the fella though. Damn shame I got hit, we would have had him by now you and I." Evens shifted carefully on the big bed. "But, like I said, I'll be up and around pretty soon and let me tell you Tim…" Evens leaned towards Elgerson and whispered, "Could have been a lot worse you know. Another couple of inches and the Missus would be pretty disappointed."

The two men laughed and Mark blushed, pleased and embarrassed to have been allowed to hear the man's remark.

Catherine appeared in the doorway bearing a tray of three snifters, two generously filled with a rich brandy and one filled nearly to the brim with a dark grape juice. The boy held his beverage carefully between his upturned fingers and toasted proudly with the men.

Elgerson thanked Catherine as they were leaving, Evens having grown tired with the excitement of the visit.

"Take care of him, Catherine," Timothy spoke softly. "I feared when I left him up there he wouldn't be here now."

"I know," Catherine replied pensively. "He was so bad when they brought him down the doctor suggested I say my goodbyes. But, you know Nils, he'd hear nothing of it!"

"You take care of yourself, too." Elgerson stepped out onto the porch.

"Thank you," she waved. "And Mark, you make sure your Pa brings you around again!"

"I will," the boy called back as he and his father mounted their horses and set out to the office of the sheriff.

"Good seeing you, Tim, and you too, Mark!" Deputy Albertson exclaimed with relief as Elgerson strode into the headquarters, the boy at his side.

"Ben's up north and is headed back. I don't expect him until later this evening. How'd you make out at your cabin? Everything all right?" The deputy continued.

"There's some kind of shack up there and I'd like to get a few men together to check it out. I brought both horses down. There are only a couple of chickens are up there now that I'll get later. Shack is just north of my cabin. It looks like it was thrown together and built in a hurry. I never got inside of it so I can't be sure what it was being used for." Timothy decided to leave the girl out of his story until he talked to Carson personally. "The boy never saw anyone headed up that trail, but he may have heard them. I'd feel a lot more comfortable heading back up there with the boys, just in case."

"Well, you've got that party at your place tomorrow. I know Ben's planning on being there, along with half the territory. Could be a good opportunity to get a group together and flush out the whole area up there, and back south of your place too. It's one of the few places to hide out after the fire. I'm sure you could raise a good band of men then."

Elgerson should have had the thought himself. In the recent events he'd had too much on his mind to come up with such an obvious notion and he thanked Albertson for the suggestion. The gathering was the perfect chance not only to flush out the woods near the cabin, as well as the house, but a good excuse to make himself scarce at the party. He'd much prefer spending the evening planning a search party than fighting off Octavia's advances and playing host. He bid his farewells to the deputy and he and Mark headed back towards the hotel and the tiny dressmaker's.

When he strode back into the overcrowded little shop, Rebecca was standing inside of the shop window, pale and exhausted, still clad in the boyish clothing. Anja Zweig was scolding her staff in brisk tones in the back of the store and rushed out at the sound of the bell.

"It is so unfortunate that I can't put a dress on the girl tonight," she apologized to Timothy profusely. "The girl is so petite, but by late morning tomorrow I will have made adjustments to several pieces and I will have plenty to fit her then. Please forgive me. There is nothing I can do more quickly! My girls are working up her gown now and I'm sure it will be perfect for the party!"

Elgerson was disappointed that the woman could not dress the girl more appropriately, but thought it was just as well that she remained in her current clothing until he got her home. He knew he had asked Anja to perform a miracle with so little time and assured her that her having clothing ready by late morning was more than he expected. He wasn't sure exactly what to do with the girl, hoping to get suggestions from the sheriff who would certainly want to question Rebecca. He was glad that he had considered the possibility that the girl might be at his place the following night and that he had thought to procure her a suitable gown.

The hiss of the gas streetlamps in the evening air made Rebecca shiver as Timothy led her and Mark to the nearby hotel.

"I fear that the dressmaker is going to great extremes," Rebecca ventured, as they walked along the shop fronts. "I have no coin, sir, and I…"

"Let it be." Timothy pointed to the hotel. "Here we are."

The tall, three story structure, one of the largest on the main street, featured clean federal lines of red brick and stone, with sizeable, warmly lit windows.

Rebecca studied it as they crossed the street, relieved at the promise of sleeping in a room with flat walls. She hoped she'd never spend another night within the dark confines of rough-hewn logs.

Mark followed Rebecca to the corner, and stood beside her in the lobby, as far as possible from the front desk, where she chose to linger discreetly while Elgerson checked them into their rooms. She could see from her safe distance that he was greeted warmly by the staff and, after a brief visit, he collected their room keys and gestured for her and the boy to accompany him on the stairs. Rebecca stole across the open room and Timothy thought her furtive steps were more obvious than her unusual clothing. To an uninterested party she might look like a friend of the boy's until he caught sight of the edge of her lacy camisole beneath the back of her shirt. Elgerson shuffled her and the boy quickly up the stairs, no longer certain that others would make the same mistake as he had, not recognizing her as a woman. He led the pair quietly up the hall toward their rooms.

"I think it would be a good idea if we talked to the sheriff tomorrow," Timothy remarked as he showed Rebecca the door to her room. "If you come up to the house, we can do it there and then arrange for whatever travel you require."

Rebecca nodded silently, unsure of how she should respond. She expected there would be questions, and, knowing she had nowhere else to go, slipped into the room without comment.

She stood with her back against the door in relief once deposited in the room. The space was opulent and open with heavy, wine velvet drapes over delicate white lace. A large mahogany four-poster bed, covered in thick quilts, stood invitingly against one long wall and the room radiated with warmth. At the foot of the bed an enormous chest held a crystal vase overflowing with wildflowers and a bowl of fresh fruit. Rebecca rushed to grab an immense apple and bit into it hungrily. She thought the accommodations heavenly, and was overcome with joy when she looked through an open doorway and discovered that the room had an indoor bath.

She stomped around in eager anticipation of a bona fide hot soak and spent several minutes turning the faucet off and then on again in her excitement. As she kicked off her boots she heard a tap at the door and stood frozen for a moment, afraid of who might be on the other side.

"Rebecca?" Timothy called as he knocked again.

She opened the door a sliver and peeked out.

"Mark and I are going down to the dining room for supper, maybe you'd like to join us?" Elgerson didn't expect the girl would accept their invitation, but if she was nearly as hungry as he was, he hoped she might put her embarrassment aside in order to eat.

Rebecca considered his invitation carefully, opening the door wider. The apple was delicious, but not enough to fill her and a hot meal was wonderfully tempting. Of course, so was the promise of a hot bath. Rebecca hesitated with indecision.

"If anyone sees me like this, but I'm so hungry. There's a lovely bath here you know…" she thought aloud.

Timothy understood her dilemma, and though disappointed, suggested that it might be better to have her supper sent up to her room. She agreed with the man, though a little disappointed herself. The thought of a fine meal in a proper dining room sounded so elegantly delicious.

Thanking him for the invitation, and feeling a bit ashamed at refusing his generosity, she returned to filling the bath, but her excitement at the discovery of indoor plumbing had dissipated.

As she lounged in the glow of her warm bath she thought about the man and puzzled over who he really was. Mark was clearly respectful of his father, not quite fearful, but certainly unsure over how he might react sometimes. There was no question the man could seem like a monster, his attack of her clearly illustrating that he was not someone to be trifled with. Rebecca understood however, that his mauling of her was provoked by his concern that thieves had injured his boy. He seemed moody sometimes for reasons she didn't quite understand, yet he was so attentive to notice her apprehension over her appearance. Custom clothing, or even a limited wardrobe from the fancy dress shop would be very costly and Rebecca grew nervous thinking about the man's possible intentions.

She imagined talking to the sheriff. Timothy obviously knew everyone here. If he found out she was a mail order bride… she pushed the thought from her mind. A party, he had mentioned she needed a gown for a party. It was all more than Rebecca could think about and she slid down under the water in the large bath.

The young woman felt guilty and apprehensive. The man was being so kind and she should have at least accepted his dinner invitation. If he were not embarrassed to take her into the dining room then she should have accepted graciously, tolerated her outfit and gone along. And Mark! He had tried so hard to care for her. She might have died without his help had he not rescued her.

"I should have joined them, even if just for the boy," she sighed.

Rebecca groaned to herself and slipped out of the steaming bath. She continued to scold herself even as she slipped into the silky robe provided by the hotel and combed out her hair with a quill from a feather she found in a vase.

When she heard a soft tap on the door she let in the porter with her meal. He rolled in a silver cart piled high with food, more food than Rebecca could possibly eat in a week! She was astonished at the presentation as the porter set the table swiftly, pulling out her chair gallantly and offering champagne.

Rebecca felt spoiled and refined as she sent the boy on his way and began to devour the sumptuous meal. She imagined herself in a fine dining room, giggling charmingly as she delicately tasted the delectable cuisine. Remorse overtook her again as she thought of Mark and his father rebuffed by her pettiness and she finished eating gloomily. When the lad returned to collect the remains of her meal Rebecca was sure that, even though she had eaten past her fill, more food remained on the table than she had been able to consume.

Climbing into the warmth of comfort of the lofty down bed, she promised herself that, in the morning, she would apologize to Timothy and Mark and show much more appreciation for their kindness.

She slipped into a deep exhausted slumber, memories of the past weeks drifting in and out of her head.

"Rebecca is going to have her supper in her room," Elgerson informed his son somewhat briskly as he returned to his room to gather the boy.

Mark's face showed obvious disappointment. The boy was looking forward to having her join them, certain that Rebecca would appreciate a meal in the fancy dining room. Mother always loved being in town and looked so pretty in the candlelight, her face glowing with pleasure.

The boy's mood frustrated Elgerson, having seen Mark's attitude so obviously improved by the girl's company. He had planned to visit the carriage stop, and the telegraph office to see if there was any word on the woman he had sent for. An inquiry at the hotel desk assured that the woman had not checked in. Perhaps Bess had been correct and the woman would not make it. The memory of Rebecca's obvious fondness for the boy made him sure that the boy needed a woman's attention, perhaps more than that of a father. Elgerson decided that maybe he should think about a woman among those that he knew. If he were willing to marry someone purely for the benefit of his son and not for love it might be worth considering. A picture of Octavia Weintraub popped into his mind and his mood darkened.

The two began their dinner quietly, Timothy

telling himself that the girl had the right to eat where she pleased. Certainly, once she was situated and had spoken to the sheriff, she would continue on her journey.

Mark was eager to get home and excited that Rebecca was joining them. He began to devise a plan to approach his father with the suggestion that Rebecca stay with them, although he had not figured out just what the woman might do. She could cook a bit, but they had a cook already, a talented woman of whom his father was fond. Mark decided that he had better come up with something else the woman might do. Suddenly he had the perfect idea! Rebecca could tutor him! She had studied with him at the cabin and it seemed like a wonderful plan. Unable to contain himself and his brilliant plan he poured the idea out to his father.

"Pa!" the boy blurted out excitedly. "Rebecca can live with us!"

"What?" Timothy was pulled away from his reverie. "Rebecca doesn't need to live with us, Mark. I'm sure she has her own family somewhere who are worried about her and she'll want to get home as soon as possible."

Rebecca had spoken so little about her own home and family it hadn't struck Mark that the woman had anywhere to go before now. He just figured she'd stick around there. He had stopped thinking about her possibly going anywhere else. He had wondered when he first found her where she had come from, but, since she seemed to avoid the topic whenever he had asked, he'd given up questioning her. Now his father's words made sense and Mark began to realize that Rebecca might move on. He knew she had no money and thought that if she were able to afford transportation she would undoubtedly want to go to her own family and home now. His father would surely give her whatever she needed as soon as she asked. Mark grew silent in the devastating realization that Rebecca would be leaving.

"She's going up to the house with us tomorrow though, right?" he asked hopefully after careful thought.

"Yes, and in the morning we'll pick up the clothing we ordered before we head up. We'll take her home and she'll meet with the sheriff and once he is finished we'll look into arranging her trip home." Although he had imagined from the beginning that this would be the plan, Elgerson found he was a little disappointed at the thought of the girl leaving himself, and not only for the boy's sake.

Something about the unusual woman made him uneasy, yet he found she was almost constantly on his mind. Soon she'd be gone, he thought to himself, and no longer his concern.

Timothy watched the boy pushing food about on his plate listlessly and cursed to himself.

Chapter Fifteen

$\mathcal{R}$ebecca sat in her coach in the late night fog, wrapping her cloak tightly around her shoulders and listening to her driver curse the cracked wheel. London's shops were long closed and the street lay damp and deserted. In the mist a fine black carriage approached, its door opening to her.

"Come in, I'll get you home," a masculine voice beckoned.

She could not see the face of the man, but was sure she recognized the voice and felt safe as she took his extended hand and climbed inside of the rich vehicle. He pulled her in, close to him and held her warmly, driving out the night's chill and quickening her heartbeat. She turned her face to him, surrendering to his warmth.

"It's alright," the deep baritone of the man's voice was smooth and comforting and Rebecca felt him pressing his lips hot against her own. He held her tightly and she hungered for his touch as she slipped her hands around his neck and yielded to him. His golden hair felt silky through her fingers as she ran her digits through it eagerly, devouring his kisses as she felt his hand cupping her breast.

His face was so familiar and she tried to make out his features, writhing in hunger and ecstasy as he stroked her breast and whispered to her.

"Timothy," she whispered.

"Timothy!" the man bellowed. "Timothy?"

Rebecca pulled away abruptly and recognized David's angry face inches from her own.

"You bloody bitch!" he spat at her. "How dare

you accuse me of infidelity while you come to me using another man's name!"

Rebecca fought to free herself from her husband screaming at him in return. "You drunken sot! How dare you! All of those women! If you had given any thought to me, if I had any value to you, you would have never wasted everything on them and the gambling tables! You gave away everything and drank our marriage away. You left me! You left me with nothing but your wretched corpse to identify! Did you ever think that when you owed so much that those men wouldn't kill you? Did it ever occur to you that I was waiting all those months, all those nights, watching for you sick with worry, knowing you'd stumble in, stinking of alcohol and lying to my face? How could you, David? You were my husband, my partner. How could you humiliate me so horribly?"

David pulled at her dress and exposed her shoulder with a loud rip. She turned to fend him off and met the glaring face of Timothy, his eyes crazed with anger.

"What kind of person are you, Rebecca? You picture bride!" he roared.

Timothy Elgerson rose at sunrise and hurried through a morning bath. He woke his sleeping son, rushed through breakfast and headed out to run his errands in hopes of reaching home before noon. Leaving the boy outside, he checked the carriage stop and found no news of the woman he had sent for by mail order. Stopping by the hardware store, he placed a large order while the boy examined the bins of nails and fiddled with the tools. High above the long expanse of counters was a gleaming black bicycle. The cycles had gained popularity in prosperous Billington and Mark even had the chance to sit upon one once, but never one of his own. Elgersor finished his order with the clerk at the counter, arranged for a wagon at the store and towed Mark off to his next errand.

After placing a grocery order he rushed to Anja's shop and he and the boy gathered the armful of parcels and packets and carried them back to the waiting buckboard.

When they approached the wagon Mark gasped in surprise at the sight of the gleaming bicycle among the parcels and barrels.

"Oh, Pa!" The boy was overcome with pleasure. "Thank you!" He hugged the man tightly around the waist.

Timothy was pleased at the boy's reaction, excited himself in the brisk fall morning for the first time in years to be headed home.

"You deserve it, boy." The father looked down at the boy's wide grin. "I'm sorry I left you at the cabin for such a long time. It won't happen again."

"It's alright, Pa. It couldn't be helped. Can I ride it after we unload at the house? I think I know how."

"There'll be plenty to do at the house before the gathering tonight, but if you have time, I suppose so."

Mark tried to hurry his father along the street, eager to gather up Rebecca and get home.

Rebecca woke, her silk robe drenched through and her delicate lingerie clinging to her skin. She covered her face in fear, crying bitterly and she rubbed her eyes hard trying to shake off the terrifying nightmare. For months after David's murder she had dreamt of him, arguing with him in her sleep in a way they had never done when he was alive. Her anger and frustration had revealed themselves to her in her sleep. Rebecca tried her best to be a loving and accepting wife to him, never speaking about her suspicion of her husband's disloyalty, even to herself.

In the time she had spent at the cabin with Mark, the nightmares had disappeared. Evil things had her waking and screaming in the night in terror, always portraying David as a monster, insulting and abusive to her. Rebecca had been sure that the day she had identified her husband's battered and bloody body that somehow she was responsible for his death. In her attempt to fulfill her responsibilities as a loving wife she tried to ignore all of the evidence. As she looked at David in death she believed she had killed him herself by not loving him enough to protect him from his vices.

Their match had been so unlikely, David nearly twenty years her senior and given to such boisterous ways, and Rebecca so young, reserved and inexperienced. Her family had loved David and his charming posture and, when her parents had died, he'd asked her to marry him and she had agreed. Youthful and devastated, with no family, it had not occurred to her that David had really fallen in love with her inheritance. Rebecca had been flattered at his proposal and he was the answer to her fears of living alone. She had agreed and they were married immediately. Rebecca's denial of David's infidelities had begun straight away when, on her honeymoon, he left their bed and did not return for three days. Almost immediately he showed no interest in intimacy with her and Rebecca blamed herself, believing she was skinny and unappealing and a miserable failure as a wife and lover.

She could not understand Timothy's part in her vivid dream and was immensely embarrassed when she recalled him fondling her in her fantasy. How bold of her imagination to conjure up such a thing as making love to the man, but she knew exactly what his insult at her waking moment meant and she vowed to tell no one how she had come to be in the territory. Should anyone ask she was simply passing through when taken by Bedra, on her way to somewhere else, anywhere else, to make a new life. Rebecca shivered in the covers. Soaked with resolve, she heard a soft tap at the door.

Mark did not wait for her reply but began to call to her announcing that they were ready to travel home.

Rebecca wrapped herself in the coverlet and opened the door to the keyed up boy.

"Oh, Rebecca, hurry and get dressed! We're ready to go home, and wait until you see what Pa has!" The boy bounced around the big room excitedly. "We got you a dress and all that stuff and guess what?"

Rebecca chuckled and peered out into the hall in

search of the boy's father. "What?" she asked absently.

"Look, Rebecca! Pa got me a bicycle!"

"How exciting, Mark!" Rebecca turned her attention to the lively child and rubbed the sides of his head briskly.

"I'll hurry and dress. Where's your father now?"

"He's waiting downstairs. He's got the wagon loaded up and he's checking us out of our rooms now. Hurry! We're going home!" The boy pushed the petite woman towards the bathroom handing her the neatly folded boy's clothing from the nearby chair.

Rebecca dressed hastily as she thought about Timothy, still wrestling with the vivid memory of her dream. She tried to fill out the details of the story she had decided to tell, hoping that careful planning would make her lie seem more believable. Rolling her moist lingerie carefully in a bundle, the delicate pieces being too damp to wear, she grabbed a handful of fruit from the bowl, filled her pockets, stuffed her hair into the felt cap and followed Mark down the hall.

Rebecca was seized by the boy's excitement, and her relief at devising her lie. No one had to know why she came and she felt set free by the thought. She was no longer a 'picture bride'. She was simply a young woman who had met with a terrible accident on the way to another world.

Mark ran around the corner of the hall towards the stairs and Rebecca bounded after him. She landed with a thud against the solid chest of Timothy Elgerson and he caught her by both arms as she bounced off of him from the sudden impact, nearly losing her footing.

"Good morning!" he grinned, standing Rebecca up in front of him.

Rebecca felt her face flush as she faced the man and his deep voice brought her back to her dream. She stood for a moment looking into his eyes and Timothy froze in her gaze.

"Hurry up!" Mark called from the bottom of the stairs and Rebecca broke off her exchange with the towering male and tried to compose herself as she headed down the stairs.

Outside Mark was chattering on about his gift, attempting to pull Rebecca up into the seat of the old buckboard, while the girl seemed to unable to get good footing in her boots. Hesitant as exactly how to help the girl, Timothy offered his hand, resisting the temptation to grab and lift her from around her waist. Rebecca looked briefly into his face and placed her tiny hand into his firm palm delicately. Her touch unnerved Elgerson and, as she stepped up to the vehicle's bench, Rebecca's boot slipped and she fell back against his chest. With no alternative in the girl's awkward position, he was forced to grab her by her slender hips and deposit her into the seat.

Rebecca brushed herself off absently and settled into the seat quite properly as Timothy stood watching. Even in her laughable clothing and the comical hat, the strange girl behaved as if she were some kind of royalty and he shook his head and circled behind the backboard, checking the tethers of his two horses behind the buggy. He was sure he'd never fathom the young woman.

As Timothy lifted her into the seat, Rebecca

thought how strange it was that the man had her feeling so on edge one moment, and so at ease the next. Tall as an oak in his stacked leather boots and wearing a well-traveled oilcloth duster he was an imposing figure, but Rebecca thought it was more than his tall stature that made her feel so flustered. For all of his impressive size he seemed warm hearted, if puzzling, in his mannerisms. Although she had seen him at his most violent she thought that he was probably not easily angered and his fondness and patience with his son was often apparent.

Both adults rode in silence, Elgerson going over his plans for meeting with Sheriff Ben Carson and bracing himself for the evening's gathering. He glanced sidelong at Rebecca occasionally as she perched upright studying every detail of the landscape.

Mark chattered on, pleased over his new bike and anxious to at last be going home.

Watching the countryside expectantly, Rebecca marveled at the dazzling blue skies and towering pines. They passed rivers blocked expertly by beaver dams and she often caught sight of the tiny white tails of deer fleeing into the forest. The woodland opened to a wide meadow, exposing a vast lake, hectic with the honking of trumpeter swans, pure white and glistening in the morning sun.

Timothy gestured towards the sky in the distance as an enormous eagle circled overhead and Rebecca pulled the brisk air into her lungs and sighed. For the first time in this rugged land she felt the exhilaration of the beautiful landscape and virgin wilderness and she began to look ahead expectantly to Mark and

Timothy's home. She felt that even if they lived inside of logs it might be acceptable in the astounding surroundings.

Mark began to squirm excitedly as they entered a dark road leading into deep woods, announcing that they were nearly there and tugging impatiently at Rebecca's arm. His exuberance was so engaging and the girl so expectant that Timothy Elgerson, too, began to feel excitement, seeing his home for the first time through the eyes of a stranger, as he pulled the buckboard around a tight bend toward his property.

Towering rows of black maple bordered the road, spreading dense branches, which arched above their heads. As the road widened broadly before them, it seemed to Rebecca as if something, somehow was anticipating their approach. A vibrant red cardinal flew across the back of the horses chirping sharply and disappearing into the trees. Leaves drifted down upon the riders from the thick canopy of vivid foliage of bright greens, vivid oranges and deep reds.

Chapter Sixteen

$\mathcal{T}$he magnificent Queen Anne stood proudly on the hilltop, her majestic turret piercing the dazzling blue sky. Leaded glass windows glittered brilliantly, each facet reflecting the surrounding white pine and deciduous forest, as if the glorious spectacle existed entirely to frame the regal home.

With a pentagon shape at the main structure, the sprawling structure featured two side extensions, giving the home a welcoming feeling, as if beckoning with open arms. A porch of turned rails led to a wide, friendly entranceway.

Each wall was paneled in sections of oak framing, surrounding the vast expanses of windows and enclosed porches. The turret, rising from the structure contained an open landing beneath a lofty roof, topped with a golden spire.

Deep in the center of the wild and wonderful land that she found herself within, Rebecca approached a home so beautiful and perfect amid open, unspoiled surroundings that it made her feel as if she had always belonged there. For the moment it didn't matter that it was not her home, only that it beckoned her to share its magnificent, tranquil world.

Rebecca gasped and held her hands to her throat where she choked back a lump as she rose unconsciously from the buckboard's seat. Mark and Timothy turned to her proudly, pleased that she found the home as beautiful as they thought it was.

Timothy watched the girl, the reflection of his beloved home in her deep emerald eyes and the expression of recognition on her delicate face. He knew that she understood what he had done, that she saw the home the way he had always envisioned it should be seen.

"Welcome to Stavewood, Rebecca." Timothy Elgerson swallowed hard.

Rebecca looked down at the boy smiling and then locked eyes with Timothy, her own eyes glistening with tears, and she squeezed the boy's hand.

"Oh, Tim," she whispered across to him. "This is the home you built?"

Rebecca was sure she was in a dream, sure that they would ride past the beautiful stately building on route to their log cabin, but the beaming smiles of the two beside her showed such pride, that now she understood why Mark had been so anxious to return and why Timothy's heart broke every time he visited the home he had constructed for his lost wife.

Rebecca knew that the sight of the beautiful home would remain in her memory until her dying day and she clung to the bouncing bench as Timothy kicked the horses to a soft trot.

Standing behind the home were magnificent towering stave oaks and stands of soaring Norway pine. The wide lawn extended rich and green. A massive sprawling oak stood tall and strong, spreading its leafy branches across the yard.

Timothy pulled the buckboard along the side of the house towards the pantry entrance, and fought hard to swallow the lump in his throat. Still fighting the emotions of being near the home he was now overcome with Rebecca's reaction. She looked at him and understood his pain. Timothy Elgerson pulled the buggy to a stop in the large drive and circled around to lift Rebecca from her seat.

Mark was so glad to be home he had bounded across Rebecca's lap before the vehicle had reached a full stop and ran through the large double back doors of his home, announcing his arrival loudly.

Timothy lifted Rebecca lightly from the bench, not even considering how inappropriate his grasp of her might be and, as he set her to stand in the driveway, she thanked him demurely and looked once again with understanding, deep into his warm brown eyes.

Feigning concern over how much there was to carry into the house, she broke off by asking if he would need any assistance unloading the buggy.

"No, Ma'am," he took her by the elbow cautiously. "I think it would be best to introduce you to my household. The men will unload the cart."

Suddenly aware of her strange apparel, she adjusted her cap slightly, thinking better about removing it, tugged at her jacket in a gentlemanly manner and cleared her throat.

"I'm ready," she announced firmly.

Timothy chuckled and led the petite girl into his home.

The kitchen was in chaos and Timothy was instantly assaulted by a rotund and frantic cook, two gentlemen who Rebecca thought might be butlers, and several young girls in starched, white aprons. Mark was hugging the cook and grinning broadly and, although the woman was obviously quite distracted, she held her arm about his shoulder in an affectionate manner while firing objections at Timothy feverishly.

Overwhelmed by the onslaught, the girl tried to

She fell easily into instructing the staff amid the chaos. Having been brought up in an affluent household arranging a large gathering fell comfortably into the skills that she possessed. She delegated tasks without hesitation and her natural command in the midst of the disorder was readily accepted and appreciated by the overwhelmed employees.

When Timothy returned from unloading the buggy he sent two maids upstairs with armloads of wrapped bundles. He found his kitchen buzzing with organized activity, and left for a quick ride to the sheriff's home. Content and relieved that the household had somehow overcome whatever their emergency was, he felt free to continue his errands.

He never saw Rebecca and wondered where she had gotten to, assuming she had found a place to make herself scarce while she waited for him to send up her packages of clothing. He returned to the house, instructed one of the maids to prepare a room for the girl and help her in whatever she needed and rode out.

Rebecca had discarded her cap and piled her hair onto her head. Then, donning an apron, she stood in the corner of the colossal kitchen instructing the cook which herbs she'd like used to crust the rack of lamb for part of the main course. She saw Timothy come into the kitchen twice, speak briefly to the maids and leave quickly, relieved that he did not see her with her hair disheveled and covered in the herb rub.

The counters of the gleaming kitchen soon were filled with steaming tureens of wild boar soup and platters of smoked trout. Crisped onions encircled the cold goose liver platter and the crusted rack of lamb was roasting nicely amid mounds of golden potatoes.

For dessert, Rebecca had instructed the cook to prepare a chestnut moose with a rum scented chocolate sauce. The two women readily exchanged ideas and experience openly, while discussing how to best prepare and present each dish.

Although many of the foods were unusual to Rebecca, she reasoned that taking a basic approach and combining it with her knowledge and love of cooking, each recipe should be enjoyable to the guests. Refined by the accomplished experience and suggestions of Birget, the menu was varied and generous, and Rebecca was pleased with their combined planning.

Chapter Seventeen

*B*y shortly past six, the prepared food began to emerge from huge ovens, filling the house with an appetizing aroma. The staff buzzed with excitement, proud in their accomplishments and Rebecca went to check on Mark and the butler's arrangement of the long serving tables. The boy had convinced the men to pull out the decorations the family had kept stored and they had adorned the stairway and overhead chandeliers with garlands and ribbons. She set the two young maids to laying out the delicate lace table linens she discovered in the butler's pantry and asked Mark where she might find a place to clean up.

Mark led her up the grand oak staircase to a cozy room upstairs, saying it was hers and leaving the girl to dress for the party.

Rebecca surveyed the lovely room, its rich woodwork and enclosed fireplace radiating warmth into the surroundings. The setting sun cast soft, filtered light through the lace curtains and Rebecca admired the fine, solid furniture and thickly padded carpets. Piled on the bed was a generous collection of carefully wrapped parcels and boxes, one of which the young woman hoped was her gown for the evening. She began to carefully inspect the contents of the packages. The smaller of the packages was filled with the finest lingerie, lace-trimmed camisoles and fine, silk stockings. There were corsets and petticoats of delicate, rustling silk. Larger bundles contained gowns and day dresses, delicate footwear emerged from boxes as well as a deliciously feathered bonnet. Rebecca was overcome with the beauty, quality and amount of clothing.

It was apparent from his generosity that Timothy was a very successful man, but she had never expected, or was sure she even wanted such an extravagant collection of clothing. When she opened the largest of the bundles Rebecca gasped in awe. The emerald gown was the finest piece she had ever seen.

With mutton sleeves at the upper arms and a fitted

bodice that dipped at the waist in a deep point to a full gathered skirt, the fine velvet shimmered in the sunlight. The bodice was embroidered with a gentle, raised leaf pattern, as were the lower, fitted sections of the sleeves. A deeper, emerald braiding adorned the edges of the sleeves and trimmed the neckline, which was cut to curve gently across the bust. Braiding secured the bodice in a crisscross of lacing, parting slightly to reveal a slim opening. The heavy fabric was draped luxuriously across the bed as Rebecca laid out the dress, overcome with emotion.

A soft tapping at the door pulled her away from the overwhelming collection and she opened it to find a young girl in a smart, black uniform.

"Pardon me, Miss," the girl bowed slightly, a bit surprised at Rebecca's appearance. "I've been instructed to help you dress."

Rebecca was thrilled to hear the girl's gracious offer, and was thrilled for a female's assistance. She quickly beckoned the girl into the room.

"Hello!" Rebecca took her hand excitedly. "How relieved I am to have your help!"

Rebecca showed the girl the beautiful garments and the young maid helped her by running a bath and gathering the articles Rebecca would require for her preparation. She left briefly but returned with a hairbrush, hairpins, and colognes. She hung the gowns in the large wardrobe and filled the drawers of the bureau with lingerie, while Rebecca languished in the generous bath.

When Rebecca had finished her bath, the young maid brushed out her hair and deftly arranged it in a soft twist, fashioned high against Rebecca's head.

The girl had gathered flowers from a centerpiece while collecting the bath articles and suggested that the delicate leaves and tiny, white flowers might adorn Rebecca's hair nicely. She wove the stems in stylishly, the soft flowers beautifully contrasting with Rebecca's dark, sable hair.

Rebecca slipped into the sheer undergarments and tried to ignore the continuing ache in her side while the maid laced her corset.

As she fashioned the back of Rebecca's gown the young woman gasped.

"Oh, Miss! How beautiful you look!"

Rebecca studied her reflection in the tall mirror, astounded by her own image. Helping the boy at the cabin had given her a healthy appetite, and hearty meals had filled out her figure. Her bust swelled against the well-fitted bodice provocatively, the narrow opening of the lacing divulging an enticing view of her cleavage. Her slim waist, encased securely in her corset, set off her softly rounded hips, the full gathering of the skirt accentuating her curved derriere. Clear skies and bright sunlight had given her complexion a warm blush and her hair, sleek and shining encircled her delicate features elegantly and softly swept across her forehead, entirely concealing her fading scar.

Rebecca took a deep breath, suddenly apprehensive over the large group of people expected to attend the gathering. Although sure that her appearance was more than acceptable, and actually quite pleasing to her, she knew that someone would inquire as to her identity and she worried over how believable her story would be.

The young maid excused herself, complimenting Rebecca profusely and assuring her that she would be the most beautiful woman at the party. Rebecca took one last look at herself in the tall mirror, placing a touch of the delicious, lavender cologne behind each ear, before going downstairs to make a final check on the dinner preparations.

The delicate, new slippers on her slender feet were a drastic change from the heavy boots she had become accustomed to and she tiptoed along the hall carefully. Stepping onto the first step on the long staircase, she descended with care, familiarizing herself with the dainty footwear. Rebecca looked up as the front door opened abruptly and Timothy burst into the foyer hurriedly.

Timothy Elgerson stopped briskly in his rush to dress at the late hour and stared, astonished, at Rebecca on the stairs. At first he did not recognize the stunning woman. This vision he thought, must be a guest that had arrived early. He was sure he had never laid eyes on her before, but then, as Rebecca stepped closer and he met her eyes, they filled with warmth and appreciation. In a rush of recognition he froze.

Rebecca's emerald eyes locked with his own, her look tentative and engaging, and he saw a transformation he found unbelievable. Her astounding beauty unsettled him as his mind raced with a rush of memories of his dealings with the girl. Rebecca was most definitely no child and, as she stood before him eye to eye near the bottom of the steps, Timothy felt his heart pounding in his chest.

The deep green of her familiar stare penetrated his and he examined the girl slowly, drinking in the view of her. Her slender outline stood in anticipation before him, her full breasts rising and falling slowly as Rebecca tensely awaited a reaction from the man. Compelled to approach her and react impulsively to his overwhelming desire to take her into his arms, Elgerson cleared his throat hoarsely and attempted to gather his senses.

"Rebecca," was the only word that escaped his lips.

"Timothy, how can I possibly thank you? The gown, everything… it is all so beautiful!" Her smile was warm and genuine as she stood anxiously, studying his face openly.

Birget bounded from the doorway in search of Rebecca and stood between the two of them looking appreciatively at the young woman.

"Why Miss, you look most beautiful!" she grinned.

Elgerson pulled his hat from his head, twisting the brim in his big hands with a slow nod.

"You had better change, sir," the ample-bodied cook suggested. "The guests will be arriving shortly and you'll need to dress!" She chuckled. "We can't go about the place looking like that with the young Miss being so beautiful, now can we?" She toddled off, smiling to herself and returning to her bustling kitchen.

"Rebecca, you look very beautiful, very beautiful indeed," Timothy blushed. He walked slowly past the girl and ascended the steps briskly.

Rebecca puzzled at the man's reaction, uncertain about the stunned look upon his face. She wanted to thank him profusely, but didn't seem to be able to find the right words. She felt that she must find a way to thank him for his generosity. She turned towards the dining room vowing to find the means to show him.

Timothy rushed into his room and threw his hat and duster onto the chair. He hurried through a bath, lathering his thick hair briskly and then combing it smoothly down against his head. He contemplated trimming back his beard, noticing that it had become more unruly than he had realized and then decided a full shave might be more appropriate. He cut into the mass with sharp scissors and began to lather up his chin.

Mark called from the doorway and, once beckoned into the room, was thrilled to find the man preparing to shave. He thought better about bringing up the fact that he had not seen his father clean shaven since his mother's death, choosing instead to ask if his choice of clothing was appropriate and how late he may be allowed to remain at the party.

Timothy accepted that the boy could stay up much later this time than the normal hour and sent Mark downstairs to keep an eye out for Octavia.

Elgerson finished trimming his remaining moustache and chose a fitted, black velvet jacket over a silk shirt with a crisp, high collar. His dark slacks fit his narrow waist fashionably and he set aside his high stacked boots for a low, black leather dress shoe. He rummaged through his drawer impatiently for the wide black ribbon he once used to contain his long mass of hair, as he heard the guests beginning to arrive. He tied up his hair quickly and checked his appearance in the mirror, surprised at how much younger his shaven face appeared, and how thin he had become since last taking time to study his own reflection.

Satisfied with the transformation, he headed down the hall to begin greeting his guests. He listened to the voices in the foyer, but did not hear that of Octavia and wondered where the woman could be.

Chapter Eighteen

$\mathcal{R}$ebecca had done a final check of the dinner preparations, pleased with the tantalizing spread and well-organized presentation by the staff but uncertain where she should go. The sounds of the four piece band tuning in the far ballroom increased her indecision and she returned to the foyer to wait for Timothy, hoping he might tell her where she ought to be when guests began to arrive.

Gebhard began opening the wide oak door,

bowing and collecting coats and capes and greeting the guests efficiently. Rebecca stood at the bottom of the stairs, smiling nervously, attempting to appear gracious and introducing herself as a friend of Timothy's while trying to avoid the guests' questions. She began to adjust to her situation easily in the crowd of first arrivals, amiably welcoming them and directing Gebhard confidently.

When Timothy arrived at the landing he had Mark beside him and watched Rebecca for a moment as she welcomed guests into the home. The boy was anxious and eyed his father curiously as Timothy watched Rebecca unseen from the upper corridor.

Moving gracefully amid the steady stream of arriving guests, Rebecca greeted each one warmly, complimenting both the men and women genuinely. Her stylish gown swayed along the smooth oak floors, complimenting her stunning beauty. She glided elegantly in the midst of the partiers and the highly appreciative glances of the arriving men were not overlooked during Timothy's observation of the girl.

The foyer emptied, momentarily, as the newly arrived guests milled towards the sounds of music on the night air and the enticing aromas wafting from the main dining room. Rebecca took an obvious deep breath and looked up, composing herself for the next onslaught of callers.

The bell rang again, the door pulled open by the butler and the foyer again filled with guests.

Mark pulled anxiously at his father's sleeve and Timothy advanced to the stairs. The upturned faces of the group announced his appearance and Rebecca turned to see Timothy Elgerson descending the massive staircase.

Rebecca knew him more by instinct than by immediate recognition. She knew those fine shoulders, straight and broad beneath his freshly shaved neck, his face sober and handsomely masculine, and his warm brown eyes meeting her briefly in a deliberate glance. As he stepped to her side she felt her breath quicken, her diminutive height affording the man a provocative view of her décolletage, and he stood stiffly and straightened his fitted jacket.

"Timothy," Rebecca whispered discreetly, as he gave her a side long look, "it would appear that underneath all of that hair you have been concealing a very handsome man."

A bit flustered by the girl's obvious pleasure, he smiled. "Perhaps, Madam, we have both had much we have been hiding."

He stepped forward, attempting to put his attention into greeting his guests and avoiding the enticing view of her creamy cleavage. The scent of her delicate perfume teased his senses and he struggled to ignore the distraction of her occasional gentle touches on his firm arm.

Rebecca was keenly aware of the man's presence beside her as she greeted the arrivals and smiled warmly. Without the tall boots his height was less overwhelming and, although a solid man, without the huge beard Timothy was not nearly the hulking giant she had at one time feared. She looked up to him intermittently and caught him studying her oddly and became certain that somehow she was making her handsome host uncomfortable.

Nearly all of the guests had arrived and Timothy asked the young woman beside him if she had seen Octavia arrive. Unsure as to what the woman's arrival meant to the man, she assured him that Octavia was not yet in attendance. Timothy cursed under his breath and turned towards the dining room. The front door burst open and Octavia pushed through the portal, flinging her heavy woolen cape aside towards the butler and rushing to Elgerson.

"Oh my dear, Timothy," she crooned. "Do forgive me for being so very late. Mother was off on an errand and I had to dress on my own. I so wanted to look especially beautiful tonight. What do you think of my gown?"

Octavia twirled away from him, spreading her ample arms and displaying her frock. Although finely made, the evening dress, a dull shade of brown, strained dangerously at the seams. It appeared that Octavia had either filled out since the garment had been fashioned or was generous with the lacing of her corset since the dress appeared to be several sizes too small. Her ample breasts swelled, overflowing her bodice perilously and her strawberry red hair was piled haphazardly upon her head. She had rouged her plump cheeks lavishly and her lips were painted in a vivid shade of bright red. As she spun about in her display she caught sight of Rebecca standing quietly beside Timothy and stopped suddenly in the middle of her show.

"Who are you?" she questioned the petite woman rudely.

"This is Rebecca, Octavia." Timothy took a half

step protectively between the two women and attempted to lead Octavia towards the dining room.

"Please excuse us," he said to Rebecca.

"Who is she?" Octavia demanded as Timothy steered her away from Rebecca by the arm.

"Rebecca is a visitor. Would you like something to eat?"

Since most of the guests had arrived, Rebecca slipped away to the kitchen to assess the serving of the food. Something about the woman irritated her, rather beyond just Octavia's appearance, and Rebecca tried to shake off her uneasiness as she spoke to the cook.

When Timothy and Octavia reached the dining room they were greeted by a tide of compliments regarding the evening's fare.

"The finest lamb I've ever tasted, Tim!" one man called out.

"The trout is heavenly!" a tiny woman commented.

"I suppose your compliments ought to go to Octavia," Timothy announced to the crowd as Rebecca entered the room. "It's my understanding that the menu planning was all her doing!"

The compliments continued, several people taking Octavia by her gloved hand and praising her choices.

At first perturbed with Timothy's assumption, Rebecca thought about how she owed him so much and, since Octavia was obviously a close friend of the man, decided to let the mistaken assumption pass. She took pride and comfort in the fact that the meal was so greatly enjoyed by all and decided to find the ballroom and listen to some music while letting her frustration and unease with Octavia unwind.

The ballroom was magnificent. The floor gleamed flawlessly with wide planks of oak and twinkling, crystal chandeliers softly lit the room. Encased in rows of leaded glass windows, the sprawling expanse led to a massive doorway opening to a large veranda outside.

Rebecca stood just inside the entrance to the room and tapped her tiny foot to the strains of the music. Elegant couples danced vivaciously across the floor enjoying a lively reel. Mark approached her excitedly and asked her if she wanted to dance, concerned that the woman looked so beautiful and no one seemed to be entertaining her.

Rebecca looked at the young man and smiled sweetly. A well-dressed man had been watching Rebecca from across the room and her beguiling smile made him decide that it was time to make his move. Rebecca placed her hand delicately into Mark's palm and allowed him to lead her to the floor. As the boy was lifting his arms to begin the dance, graciously taking the girl's left hand, the man intercepted him.

"Go play outside, Mark," the man brushed the boy aside. "I'm sure this heavenly creature would much prefer to dance with a grown man."

"I'm sorry, sir," Rebecca addressed the man in her sweetest voice. "I believe I would first enjoy dancing with this gentleman who has just asked. I don't believe you and I have been introduced."

"This is Mr. Thomas," the boy scowled. "Mr. Thomas, this is my friend Rebecca."

"Your friend you say?" Thomas remarked, never taking his eyes from Rebecca. "Now where on earth would you make a friend like this?" He rubbed the sides of his moustache conceitedly. "I am honored," he whispered to Rebecca, much more closely than she felt was appropriate.

"Very nice to meet you," Rebecca replied, unsmiling. "Please excuse me, but I have promised Mark a dance."

Rebecca took the boy's hand and Mark led her to the center of the dance floor. She couldn't be sure, but she thought she caught a glimpse of the boy sticking his tongue out at the man. However, she decided she would not reprimand him since she was sorely moved to do the same. Thomas reminded Rebecca of her husband David and she hoped he would not approach her again.

Mark danced sweetly, if awkwardly, and Rebecca gathered her skirts delicately in one hand to help the boy avoid his unerring propensity to step onto it. He spun her around the floor a bit too quickly for the music and Rebecca giggled as she followed the young man in his dizzying ballet.

Timothy found Rebecca immediately as he entered the softly lit room. She laughed delightedly as his son tried valiantly to pull her around the floor. Rebecca was light on her feet and scrambled effectively to keep up with the boy. After running the young woman too close to several of the more serious dancers, Timothy decided he had better intercede.

Informing the boy graciously that it was his turn, he took Rebecca by the hand and bowed deeply. "If I may cut in, Madam?" he asked, and winked at the boy. Mark ran off grinning broadly.

Rebecca placed her hand on the man's firm shoulder and he began to lead her in a waltz. He moved confidently around the floor in an easy manner and Rebecca tried to keep from meeting his eyes while blushing at his closeness.

The evening's guests had all wondered who the mysterious young woman might be and several of them gathered to watch the couple and whisper questions among themselves.

Rebecca felt as if she were gliding, the man's perfect lead was so in step with her own natural way of dancing. She looked up at him and he fixed his eyes on hers, smiling handsomely. His fine features captivated her and she was unable to pull herself from his gaze. She studied the depth of his penetrating look and felt his warmth as he slid her effortlessly through the waltz.

The stunning beauty and her handsome friend moved magically in beautiful unison among the dancing couples and one woman remarked that a woman worthy of Mr. Elgerson might have arrived at last.

Chapter Nineteen

Octavia, overhearing the remark, decided it was a good time to take over the stage and make an announcement to the crowd. Pulling herself onto the platform, she pushed the violinist aside and yelled out to the crowd.

"Good evening ladies and gentlemen!"

Timothy and Rebecca interrupted their dance to watch Octavia bellowing from the stage.

"Timothy and I want to thank you all for coming tonight. Timothy, why don't you join me?" she called out.

Elgerson groaned deeply and Rebecca smiled at him encouragingly. "Good luck," she whispered as he stepped away and then turned back to her, rolling his eyes before advancing towards the stage.

Mark stepped up beside Rebecca and whispered something under his breath.

"Excuse me?" Rebecca was not sure she liked what she had heard. "It's not nice to say you hate anyone."

"I know," the boy scuffed his feet. "She's so fat."

"Mark! That's a terrible thing to say. I'll not listen to you if you stand here and make such rude remarks about your father's friends!"

"She always calls me Mick," the boy grunted.

Rebecca recalled the woman patting her on the head in the dress shop and thought that she didn't care much for the woman herself. Timothy seemed to know Octavia so well and she herself was an outsider, but in a way she had to agree with the boy.

Hoping to avoid the presumptuous Mr. Thomas, watching her boldly from a few feet away, Rebecca slipped behind the crowd and found a quiet corner where she could see the stage.

"It's been a long time since we had a good celebration and Tim's been so gracious to throw a party for us all I have to thank him." Octavia grabbed the man roughly and planted a generous kiss onto his cheek. "Oh, look at that," she exclaimed. "The man even decided to shave! I hadn't even noticed!"

The crowd burst into laughter.

Rebecca watched Timothy scowl uncomfortably beside Octavia and thought it odd that anyone could miss the incredible transformation of the man having removed the massive beard. Before, he looked menacing and huge, she thought. Now, one could see that he was slender and well-built, and appeared quite the gentleman. Possibly he had grown the beard only recently and Octavia was just accustomed to seeing the man without it.

"Of course we must mention the reason we have gathered here tonight is to celebrate Timothy's acquisition of three thousand more acres of land," Octavia continued.

Rebecca gasped. She could not imagine how far one would have to travel to survey that much property and suddenly felt plain and diminutive. These odd Americans with their rough ways were no simple farmers. Rebecca began to study the couples around the room. Although their styles were very different from what she had been accustomed to in her own country, she realized that she stood with a large group of rich landowners. They had all seemed so coarse to her with their ordinary sounding accents, but now she saw that, although their clothing was far different than that of the more well-to-do in England, they were all finely dressed in their own fashion. If only her fate had gone differently she could be here with one of the men in the crowd, being introduced as a future bride. Though at first the thought seemed appealing, she now realized that everyone would know how she came to be here, as an intended bride, and she felt ashamed. The realization made her begin to perspire and Rebecca decided she needed a breath of the night air.

Timothy watched the petite woman exit the side door, looking pensive, from his vantage point on the stage.

Rebecca stepped out of the doorway onto the veranda and took a deep breath, reassuring herself that no one here knew her and could possibly suspect how she came to this place. An inviting garden beckoned her from across the lawn and she made her way to the gazebo among the roses. The scent of the blooms drifted around her as she stood inside the large structure contemplating her future.

"Where will I go now?" she asked herself. "I can't possibly ask Timothy for anything more." The thought of Timothy's apparent wealth made him seem even more unapproachable to her and for the first time she realized that she had imposed on his generosity much more than she thought. Every event of the past few weeks, the food, the cabin, the hotel, the baths, the clothing… all came back to her mind in a rush.

Rebecca stood alone in the night air and worried over her fate. She had no family and no one to turn to except her cousin in England. She decided that she would need to accept her failure and wire Emma for help. Not so long ago such a thing would have been unthinkable, but Rebecca's experiences were teaching her that there were more terrible things in the world than swallowing her pride.

"How wonderful, that I should find you out here!"

Rebecca turned to the approaching voice of Mr. Thomas, and felt uneasy.

"I was just getting a breath of fresh air," Rebecca replied while heading back towards the house.

"Oh, please stay," he remarked smoothly. "It's a lovely night and I certainly would like to get to know you better."

"Thank you," Rebecca replied curtly. "I'd rather go back inside."

The brazen man grabbed Rebecca tightly by the wrist and persisted in his attempt to keep her outdoors. "Tell me about yourself, please." His voice was smooth and polished and he again stroked his moustache in a manner that Rebecca found unnerving.

The young woman pulled her wrist away from the insistent man and stepped from the structure onto the grass. He took her roughly by the arm and she could smell the stench of alcohol on his breath. He wrapped his arms around her tightly insisting he now wanted to know her more intimately.

Timothy finished accepting his guests' handshakes and congratulations and made his way towards the side door as soon as he saw Jude Thomas slip outside. He knew the man's techniques well, and that Rebecca was likely in the garden alone. He considered leaving the girl to her own defenses, knowing full well she could disable the man should she choose to. Perhaps Rebecca liked Jude's type, after all, what did he really know about her? He felt a bit beguiled by her himself, but her beauty would attract all types. He wondered for a moment what her type might be.

As he approached the gazebo he heard Rebecca's soft pleas and made his presence apparent.

"Timothy!" Rebecca exclaimed, freeing herself from the drunken pursuer and standing firmly bedside the tall man.

"Jude," Timothy nodded to the man.

"Evening Tim, I suppose congratulations are in order. You've bought up half the country and looks like you get this tasty bit of fluff in the bargain. You always were a lucky bastard."

Jude Thomas found the solid fist of Timothy Elgerson squarely across his jaw and he stumbled into the night.

"Thank you," Rebecca whispered softly, rubbing her arms with her hands and suddenly feeling chilled.

"That's not the first time I've run off that fool. He's got nerve coming back here again. Octavia must have invited him. He's a cousin of hers."

Timothy took Rebecca by the elbow to lead her back to the house should Jude recuperate and attempt to approach the girl again. It was apparent by her reaction to seeing the him that she was not enjoying Jude's attentions and Timothy was relieved.

"Timothy," Rebecca turned to the man. "Thank you."

"Not a problem. Like I said, I've had problems with Jude before."

"Not just for that," Rebecca faced the man, looking him frankly in the eyes. "For everything. I've wanted to say something since I refused your invitation for dinner at the hotel. I was wrong, regardless of my attire. You and Mark have been so wonderful to me. I can't begin to thank you enough." Rebecca began choking on the words.

Timothy looked down at her and was moved by her emotional, intent look. He felt curiously protective of the girl and as he watched her delicate, earnest face he could not believe that she was careless and would give herself to any stranger. Yet, what did he know about her, really? Timothy looked into Rebecca's eyes with growing concern for the effect the girl was having on him.

"There you are!" Octavia bounded across the lawn.

Rebecca pulled away, embarrassed, and tried to compose herself.

"Octavia," Timothy groaned.

"You must dance with me, hurry!" Octavia grabbed the man's arm and pulled him across the lawn.

Rebecca followed the couple into the house and slipped through the hall into the kitchen.

"That woman is so ridiculous!" the cook announced to Rebecca as soon as she entered the kitchen. "Octavia's telling everyone she is responsible for that fine meal. Preposterous! I will tell Timothy how untrue that is and set him straight!"

"No please," Rebecca begged. "This is their party together and he doesn't need to know. Please let it be, Birget. Everything was so perfect. I just think that we should not bring it up in the middle of this fine evening." Rebecca felt overwhelmed and emotional.

She should have allowed, in fact, even encouraged Timothy to kiss her, but she had no right. She was not a rich landowner like these people here. In fact, she had fewer belongings of her own than the staff at Stavewood. Timothy was a rich and generous man. How could she imagine a life with such a man when she was nothing more than a mail order bride? His intense gaze and her undeniable attraction to the man had her nervous and distracted. Rebecca fought off tears and decided she should help the staff clean up from the party and went to the dining room to gather the empty platters.

Birget admonished the girl soundly as she entered the kitchen, her arms piled high with empty plates.

"Madam, you should not be doing such a thing. You'll ruin that beautiful gown!"

Realizing the gown would eventually have to be returned, Rebecca decided she would finish out the evening as best she could, if only out of appreciation for the family who had taken her in, and she returned to the ballroom.

She chatted with a few of the guests and watched Timothy dancing with nearly every female guest, young and old, while Octavia demanded his attention at every opportunity. Rebecca danced with a gallant older gentleman, who reminded her of her father, and spoke briefly with him and his wife before finding a spot along the wall where she could observe the festivities unnoticed.

"So, what is it exactly you are doing here?" Rebecca turned from watching Timothy gliding smoothly across the dance floor, to Octavia tapping her foot impatiently.

"Miss Octavia," Rebecca smiled.

"Timothy has told me nothing about you. Why are you here?" the big woman asked pointedly.

"To enjoy the party, of course," Rebecca replied cautiously.

"Humph," Octavia grunted loudly. "That's not what I was asking."

"I'm sorry," Rebecca turned to Octavia and squared her shoulders. "I must have misunderstood your question." Uncomfortable with the woman's inquisition she chose to face her head on.

"Why are you here at Timothy's?" Octavia showed her impatience.

"I'm visiting with him and his son briefly. I won't be here long." She thought she'd address Octavia's real concern.

"I see," the woman replied and Timothy crossed the room in long strides towards them.

"No, Timothy, don't spend all of your energy dancing with the old women. You must save more dances for me!" Octavia exclaimed and Rebecca could not help but notice that her entire demeanor had changed as the woman slipped her arm into Timothy's possessively.

The man seemed uncomfortable and Rebecca was

sure it had something to do with her. She tried to excuse herself politely, but found it nearly impossible to speak without interrupting Octavia's endless complimenting of the man and his numerous charms and assets. Octavia stood between Rebecca and Timothy chatting on without so much as catching her breath and when her gossip turned to talking about the dancers on the floor, Rebecca was positive she could stay no longer. Timothy seemed to become tenser every moment, glancing towards her several times and she wanted to leave the couple alone.

"And of all the things, the fool man had the audacity to attend with one of those horrid picture brides, why, I never in all my life would have imagined such a thing!" Octavia blurted out.

Timothy choked on his merlot, struggling not to spill the wine and turned to Octavia. Behind the babbling woman the color drained from Rebecca's face. As her legs began to give way beneath her, he stepped quickly past Octavia to catch the fainting girl capably in his arm.

Everyone was concerned with the beautiful stranger's condition, alarmed as they watched the big man carry the helplessly limp girl hurriedly up the stairs, calling for the maids.

When Rebecca revived, Timothy was dabbing her face with a cool cloth while Octavia stood over him, her arms folded across her generous chest.

"Ah, you're awake." Timothy looked down at her, his face pale with concern.

Rebecca saw the glaring look on Octavia's face.

"I guess I had too much wine," Rebecca lied.

It seemed to Timothy that the girl neither ate nor drank all evening. "You should eat something. Fetch her something from the kitchen." Timothy sent the maid scurrying, certain that Rebecca's fainting was not a result of alcohol.

"She looks fine to me," Octavia declared. "We must return downstairs, Tim. We have a house full of people. Surely you can't spend the evening fussing over this girl."

At Rebecca's insistence Timothy returned to his guests reluctantly, concerned over what exactly had upset the young woman and irritated with Octavia's thoughtless remark over the guest's new bride. Had things gone differently he might have a woman of his own in attendance at the blasted party and whoever she may have been, she did not deserve to be talked about in such a cruel way.

The party wound down, Timothy stopping every maid he could find and inquiring about the girl's condition. His guests, pleased with a fine meal and whispering with curiosity over Rebecca and her condition, waved farewell to Elgerson and Octavia and departed in their carriages.

Timothy was exhausted and worried about the girl and it seemed forever before he ushered Octavia into her waiting coach. Her breath smelled strongly of wine and her slurred advances were now embarrassingly forward. He watched with resignation as she rode into the night.

He ran upstairs briskly and tapped on Rebecca's door where he had instructed the maid not to leave her side.

The servant appeared at the door, informing him that Rebecca was sleeping and Timothy went to his room preferring to have seen her.

Without a moment's reprieve from Octavia all evening he had been unable to put his attention to getting the men together he needed to inspect the shack. He had only taken the time to arrange a visit from the sheriff late the next morning so that he could get the information he'd need from Rebecca. With the girl ill, he wondered in frustration if the meeting should wait. Timothy had never had the opportunity to inform Rebecca of the appointment and decided he'd have to wait until the light of day to see about the meeting.

He removed his dress clothing slowly in exhaustion and laid on the bed staring into the darkness. Timothy Elgerson drifted off to sleep with the thought of the girl's perfect face in the moonlight thanking him for the little he had done. He asked himself who the girl might be, suddenly aware that he had more questions than answers about Rebecca.

Chapter Twenty

$\mathcal{R}$ebecca lay awake in the bright morning sunlight watching the poor servant soundly sleeping upright in the big upholstered chair. She hated the burden she had become to everyone and finally rose and gently woke the girl.

"I'm fine, please go get some sleep," she pleaded, insisting that the promise to stay at her side had been fulfilled.

The maid rose reluctantly, unsure that she ought to abandon her post, but, with gentle persuasion, Rebecca finally sent her on her way. She returned to her bed too depressed to face the day. When she had first awoken in the dark hours before dawn she resolved to ask Timothy if it would be possible to post a letter. She hated to ask the man for any further favors, but this one could not be avoided. She had ruined the man's party. She must write Emmy at once.

As soon as it could be arranged she would return home, obtain some sort of employment and find a way to repay Mark and Timothy for their kindness. She rose from the bed and donned a soft satin robe that had come with the other clothing, feeling the rich cloth and overwhelmed by the man's kindness. It was best that she leave as soon as possible and in the meantime she would do her best to avoid the man and not increase her indebtedness to him. Rebecca cried bitterly, feeling trapped by the generosity of others.

When a maid arrived to ask her to join Timothy for breakfast she declined, deciding she'd skip some meals, not even bothering to dry her eyes. Within minutes she heard a knock on the door and asked the returning servant to leave her be.

"Rebecca?" Timothy stood outside of the bedroom door, sick with worry over the girl.

"How can I possibly face him?" she thought, fighting her tears.

"Would you like me to call you a doctor?"

"No," she thought. "I cannot put the man out further."

"I'm perfectly fine," she replied. "A bit under the weather from the wine I believe. I'm sure I'll be just fine." She had learned from watching David that a morning after too much alcohol left you exhausted and ill.

"Rebecca, I really must speak to you," Timothy insisted.

She wiped her eyes quickly and called for the man to enter. She turned her face away in shame and fear of looking at him as he walked into the room and stood over the bed.

"Rebecca, I don't believe for a minute that you are hung over. What's wrong?"

Bursting into tears at the discovery of her lie she sobbed wretchedly and the man's frustration increased in his confusion. The girl was behaving so strangely and he needed to know if something was seriously wrong with her.

"Are you or are you not ill, Rebecca? I need to know."

Rebecca decided that her outburst was only succeeding in making the man more suspicious and decided to try a different approach.

"I'm sorry," she whispered. "No, I am not ill. I'm just exhausted from the party and everything. I will be down to eat shortly."

"Then why did you try to tell me you were hung over? What's wrong?" Timothy sat in the chair beside her bed. "Look at me, Rebecca," he said firmly.

The girl looked up at him, her eyes red from crying and the hopelessness of her situation obvious on her face. Her color appeared fine, but something in her expression spoke of a torment she had chosen not to voice.

Timothy was confounded by the girl and suddenly regretted his harsh tone with her.

"Rebecca." He tried to sound patient with the girl. "Tell me what's bothering you. Maybe I can help."

"I don't want to take any more of your help. Don't you see that? You've already done so much and I can't ask for anything more. Please," she begged. "Please understand."

"No, Rebecca, I don't. You needed clothing and I dressed you. Would you prefer to be running about in Mark's clothing? I think not!" Timothy was completely exasperated. "If you think I've done too much for you, then do something for me. Get up if you are not ill and come down to breakfast. The sheriff is coming in an hour and he needs to talk to you about the people who took you captive. You do that and we'll call it even." Timothy Elgerson rose and left the room, closing the door behind him.

How could he possibly reason with her? She's so unfathomable, he thought. He descended the stairs in frustration, certain that the girl made no sense and that informing her of the meeting with the sheriff had gone nothing like he had hoped. His growing discomfort and distraction with the young woman made him uneasy and tested his disposition.

Rebecca threw back the covers as the man left, completely aggravated with herself for her display. She splashed cold water on her reddened face and chose her clothing carefully. One day she would repay him for everything, but until then she would have no choice. She knew something about her unnerved the man and she wished she could avoid him in any way possible.

When the young woman entered the cozy family dining room for breakfast, her hair was carefully brushed, pulled back from her face and tumbling freely down her back, a soft lock across her forehead. She had chosen a crisp, organdy dress with a raised pattern in a clear, crystal blue, her full petticoat rustling as she entered the room. The dress featured a high collar, trimmed in delicate, white lace and the bodice fit her perfectly.

Timothy studied her carefully, noting that her cheeks were a bit rosy from her earlier outburst. He watched her sit down in a chair and arrange her napkin neatly on her lap. He told himself that he would not be distracted from his mission of understanding the girl by her disarming beauty. She looked so fetching in her fitted dress, an appropriate choice for her meeting and Timothy found himself admiring her trim figure and the soft spill of her gleaming hair down the length of her back.

"Rebecca." His voice was sharper than he intended.

Rebecca bit her lip and nodded.

Mark watched the two adults, sure that something was amiss. His father had gone up to check on the woman a bit earlier and Mark thought that he was concerned about her, yet he had returned angry and silent. Now it appeared that Rebecca had been crying and both adults were behaving strangely. The boy had watched the two dancing together the previous evening and Mark thought that his father was starting to like the woman. In fact, he thought they might be falling in love or something, but now he was worried. He had hoped he would like her enough to ask her to live at Stavewood, but he knew his father, and, if Rebecca angered him, things would not go well.

The adults ate in silence while Mark tried to devise a way to make his father accept the lady. He thought he might talk to Rebecca later and tell her what kind of things he knew the man liked.

Rebecca tried to avoid Timothy's gaze as he stopped eating several times and studied the girl. He wondered why she had to be so sullen. It was a perfectly beautiful day and she had been so cheerful the day before, what could possibly have gotten into her?

Gebhard brought the sheriff into the room as soon as he had arrived and Timothy offered the lawman breakfast.

"Ben, this is Rebecca," he introduced the girl tersely. "If you'll excuse me I want to ride out and speak to a few of the men. Mark, why don't you take a ride with me?" Timothy suggested.

The boy bounded from the table and he and

Timothy exited through the kitchen.

Rebecca took a deep breath and ventured a look at the lawman. She was relieved to see that he was a kindly, if rugged looking, older man, and she hoped he would not pry too deeply into why she had arrived in his territory, preferring only to discuss the events of her captivity.

"Why don't we take a walk outside and talk?" he suggested.

She sent a girl up to her room to gather a wrap, and then she and the sheriff walked out into the bright fall day. There was a crisp nip in the air and the threat of an approaching frost chilled the surrounding woodland. He led her out past the gazebo to a path along the trees and commenced with his questioning.

"Tell me how it all began, Rebecca."

Rebecca started by telling him that she had felt ill on the train and gotten off, but could not recall the name of the stop. The man there had told her she could catch the next train and she was hoping to do that, but had fallen ill and he had left. Rebecca omitted the part about the strange drink the man had given her, ashamed that she had lost consciousness and also her clothing. She went on to say that a large woman had taken her to the woods and she woke up in a filthy, broken down shack where Mark had untied her.

"That's all, Sheriff." Rebecca hoped that her brief summation of the events would satisfy him.

"The man at the station, did he have a name?"

"Finn. He said his name was Finn. He was rather pleasant actually."

"Finn Morgan?" the sheriff seemed surprised.

"He never mentioned his last name as I recall, but I doubt he had anything to do with my abduction. I never saw him again after I…" Rebecca paused, "after I fell ill." She felt panicked that the man recognized the name, and decided she had regrettably supplied him with too much information.

The sheriff studied Rebecca carefully. "And the woman, did she give you a name as well?"

"Bedra," Rebecca replied hesitantly, confident that he knew Finn's name and would recognize the woman's as well. She sighed hopelessly, pleading silently to herself that the man had enough information to complete his investigation and cease his questioning of her.

"Bedra? Are you sure?"

"Yes, positive," Rebecca assured him. "I will never forget it. Do you know her as well?" Rebecca felt a lump in her throat. If the sheriff knew the woman he might arrest her and she might talk about what might have happened while Rebecca was sleeping and, worse yet, tell the sheriff how she had come to be on the train as well.

Rebecca began to shiver with fear and became increasingly pale.

The sheriff could tell that he had probed the girl enough for the time being and kept his remaining questions as short as possible.

"Rebecca, could you describe the woman to me?"

Rebecca began to shake, announced that she couldn't answer any more questions and dashed back to the house.

The sheriff stood at the edge of the lawn, puzzled by the girl's responses. He could understand that she might be quite upset by her ordeal. Elgerson had filled him in on a few details he had gotten from the boy. If Finn was there he knew where Rebecca had left the train. But the part that baffled him most was who was this Bedra?

Chapter Twenty-One

*T*he sheriff rode off to the prearranged meeting place to catch up with Elgerson and they planned to gather a few men and start out at first light the next day towards the shack. He wrestled with the information the girl had given him, hoping to come up with some possible reason Finn Morgan might be involved.

When he caught up with Elgerson he asked the man's opinion.

"Finn Morgan? Are you sure it was Morgan?" Timothy asked, as surprised as the sheriff. The two men rode side by side toward the home of the next man who was joining their posse to check the shack.

"She said he told her his name was Finn and that he was at the train station," the sheriff confirmed.

"Finn Morgan keeps the Hawk Bend Station alright and it's not terribly far from your cabin and that shack we're going to check out," the lawman continued.

"But Finn's not much brighter than a child, Ben." Elgerson reasoned. "How and why would he possibly want to hurt Rebecca? The man's got no history of bothering any woman that I know of."

"That's what I can't figure, Tim. She talked about a woman up there, too. She said her name was Bedra."

"Bedra? That's even odder. Are you sure that's right?" Elgerson asked.

"Girl says she'll never forget the name. Just the mention of it seemed to upset her so much that she took off into the house, white as a ghost, before I could get a description out of her."

"Was she alright?" Elgerson was concerned that Rebecca had behaved so oddly. Maybe the visit from the sheriff was too much for her. He tried to remember her ordeal and thought he probably had been too hard on her. He thought he had better finish up his business and check on her.

"I expect so, just upset was all. I sure would like to question her again though. If I knew what train she was on we might be able to pinpoint the time better. From what your boy said, she's not even sure herself how long she was in the shack. Maybe next time I talk to her it'd be a better idea if you and the boy were there. She seemed fond enough of you on the dance floor last night, Tim," the sheriff smiled slyly.

Elgerson thought that however Rebecca had behaved while dancing wasn't her demeanor now. He hoped that by the time he returned, her mood would have improved.

The men and the boy finished their round up of the men for the following day's investigation and Ben left Elgerson and Mark and headed into town to ask around about Finn Morgan. Maybe there was something someone knew about the man he was unaware of.

Elgerson stabled the horses while Mark played in the yard with his bicycle and then headed inside, unsure of what awaited him. Birget said she had last seen Rebecca in the rose garden inspecting the flowers. Timothy returned to the yard in search of the girl.

"Your roses have aphids," Rebecca informed him as he approached her slowly.

"They have what?" he thought it best to ease into the topic he needed to discuss with her.

"Aphids. Look." Timothy squatted down beside her and inspected the rosebud. Seeing nothing but a bud and some fuzzy green leaves, he looked at her, puzzled.

"Aphids, these tiny green bugs." Rebecca rubbed the tip of her finger against the blossom and brought the microscopic creature up to his face. She laughed quietly as the man nearly crossed his eyes trying to focus on the tiny insects.

"What can those little things possibly do?" he really wasn't terribly concerned with the bugs.

"They'll kill the roses," Rebecca informed him. "If you don't mind I could make a spray from some red pepper that might get rid of them."

Elgerson couldn't imagine why on earth she felt

she needed his permission for something so simple. To his way of thinking the girl was welcome to anything she liked.

"Rebecca, if you want to spray the roses you certainly don't need to ask me. Maybe you can just get a gardener to deal with them. If you'd like to spray them yourself you're free to go right ahead. You certainly don't need permission from me."

"They're not my roses, Timothy," she replied quietly.

The man scratched his head beneath his hat. He didn't care much about the roses anyway. The only attachment he had to the fussy flowers was that his wife had felt that they made the property seem 'more civilized'. He considered that possibly Rebecca had a particular love for roses, but that still didn't explain her preoccupation with the plants. He'd never thought that the roses really 'belonged' to anyone except possibly Corissa.

"My wife had them put in, Rebecca," he remarked. Memories of his late wife rushed back to him. So many summer nights he'd stand in the garden watching over the hill for her return and he often was reminded of her if he caught the scent of a rose, even now.

Rebecca watched Timothy's face darken and cursed herself for upsetting him again. She decided to try to explain to him more calmly than she had been able to in their conversation of the morning.

"Timothy, please try to understand. You have been so sweet to me. You've given me so much, you and Mark. Your boy saved my life and took me in. He fed me your food and gave me his own clothes. I was so vain and complained about them so horribly that you spent a fortune having a wardrobe made for me."

Timothy studied the girl's face in the soft light of the afternoon sun.

Rebecca watched him listening to her closely and struggled to continue.

"You included me in your party and I behaved horribly by making a spectacle of myself and from what Birget told me you took me upstairs and made that poor girl sleep in the chair all night to watch over me. You've fed me and put me up in the hotel. I have nothing, Timothy, no means of repaying you. I'm trapped here with nothing to do but rely on your support. Please understand."

Timothy took exception with her last remark, struggling with her reasoning.

"Rebecca, I never expected anything from you. If you think you're trapped here then why didn't you ask me to send you on while we were in town?"

The man's remark only seemed to make everything worse.

"Don't you see?" she replied again. "I don't want to ask you for anything."

"Then maybe you should," the man replied. "It was never my intention to trap you at all."

"No." Rebecca was frustrated. "You haven't trapped me, circumstance has. Your home is the most beautiful thing I have ever seen, Tim. Stavewood is like heaven, you must know that. I'm honored that you have brought me here, but I cannot ask you to let me stay here. I'll only be in your way." Rebecca thought of how the man seemed so uncomfortable with her in Octavia's presence. Maybe he belonged with the big girl, although Rebecca could not see how. It was not her choice to make.

Timothy sighed and considered the girl's point of view.

"Rebecca," he began. "I brought you here because…" he searched for the right words, relieved that the girl had not burst into tears. "Because you had no place to go that I knew of. You had no clothing and no money and I couldn't very well just send you off."

"I don't want your pity, Timothy. I'm so sorry." Rebecca stood up and headed for the house.

Timothy caught her by the arm, unwilling to let her walk away until he could make her understand.

"Rebecca, it is not out of pity, certainly. You needed help and I helped you. It's just that simple. If you wish to leave you are welcome to at any time. If you want to stay you are welcome to that as well. Mark is so taken with you and I…" his voice trailed off. He fought for the right words, realizing that he wasn't sure himself exactly what it was he felt for her. "I have no problem with you being here."

Rebecca was disappointed, although she told herself that she should not expect more from the man. That was the whole problem with the situation. She decided to let the subject drop.

"Then I will spray your roses tomorrow." She stood before him, not wanting to leave and unsure if she should stay.

Timothy decided he had better broach the subject and explain why he had come looking for her.

"Rebecca, I spoke to the sheriff this morning and he's still got a few questions for you."

Rebecca sighed.

"I know that the ordeal was terrible for you and it's upsetting for you to remember what happened." Timothy tried to choose his words carefully.

Rebecca wished that was the only problem.

"Something just doesn't make sense," he continued.

Rebecca braced herself, wanting to face the man and not run off childishly.

"I know Finn Morgan and I can't see him having any part of this."

"I'm not sure that he did, Tim." The girl swallowed hard.

"And the woman. I thought I knew everyone who lives in the area. Maybe she was just passing through, or she might have something to do with the robberies. It's just puzzling. We're headed up at daybreak to check out the shack and then Mark and I will bring the chickens down. We'll probably close up the cabin, too, at least for the season."

"You're going up there?" Rebecca was apprehensive. She didn't know how many beside Bedra were involved and she was suddenly worried for the man.

"We've got to check it out and find out who the woman is that took you up there. What if she were to take someone else? She could have gone after Mark up there. Mine isn't the only place of its kind. There are families living back in those woods."

Rebecca had been so concerned that her secret would be discovered that she hadn't even considered that others might be at risk. The thought of anyone else lying hurt in the shack terrified her and the emotion of the thought showed clearly on her face.

"I understand why you have to go up there Tim. I don't want anyone else to be hurt, that's all."

Timothy was certain there was something the girl was not telling him. He decided that her color did not look good and they should continue the discussion of the abduction after his return.

"It'll be fine," he tried to drop the subject. "If I were too concerned I wouldn't take Mark up with me to bring back the chickens." He refrained from mentioning that he planned to leave the boy and an armed man at his cabin while the rest of the posse investigated the shack.

"Timothy?" Rebecca asked in a quiet voice.

"Yeah?" He could see that the girl seemed somehow resigned. Maybe there was something she had decided to tell him after all.

"Why do you have to collect eggs every day?"

"Pardon me?" He was sure he could not fathom the girl's mind.

"The eggs. They have to be collected every morning. Why? Mark said it is because there'd be too many chickens and no breakfast, but I'm sure there's something more."

Timothy smiled at her strange question. Her rendition of the boy's explanation was amusing, if not entirely correct.

Rebecca studied his face intently, pleased that she detected a smile.

"If you leave the eggs, Rebecca, it's true many would hatch. But if you don't take them away the chickens will stop laying. Most fowl will keep trying to have chicks and so, if you remove the eggs you'll keep getting more eggs."

Satisfied that the mystery of the eggs was solved with Timothy's reasonable explanation, Rebecca smiled sweetly at the man.

"I'm not sure what that has to do with aphids though," Timothy quipped and Rebecca giggled softly.

"You know, Tim, neither do I." Timothy and Rebecca walked back towards the house as Mark watched them from the yard. They walked in an easy manner and he decided that they must have resolved their differences and called out to them so they could watch his demonstration of the bicycle.

Chapter Twenty-Two

*M*ark coaxed the woman onto the bicycle. "It's fun!"

Rebecca had watched the boy ride the bicycle easily around the yard, but Timothy looked so silly on the thing she announced that she was afraid of the contraption and would likely kill herself if she tried.

"Pa can hold it for you so you don't fall. It's easy!

Pa just is so uncoordinated."

"I beg your pardon, boy!" He folded his arms across his chest, taking exception with the boy's remark. "I can ride a horse or a log for that matter, better than any man in the territory. No coordination, bah!"

"No, wait!" Rebecca put her open palm up in front of her. "If your father has no coordination as you claim, then how could I possibly trust that he won't let me fall?"

Timothy growled at the girl. "Get on!" he thundered, "and we'll see who has no coordination!"

Rebecca was enjoying Mark and Timothy playing with the bicycle so immensely that she elected not to mention that she had a friend that had owned one. One afternoon they had spent hours as he taught her how to balance herself and how to tuck her skirt up beneath her to keep it clear of the pedals. Once she found the secret she had ridden the contraption about the yard for hours. It had been a while since that day, but Rebecca was sure she could easily do it again.

The girl decided it was time to stop feigning ignorance and show what she could do.

She stepped over the frame carefully and pretended she didn't know what to do with her skirt. Mark conjectured that maybe there was some way that she might try tying her skirt to one side. Rebecca pretended to be inspired by his suggestion and pulled up the center of her skirt between her legs as she had done with her friend, tucking it beneath her against the seat. Timothy raised his eyebrows, and the display of her trim ankles did not go unnoticed as he stood waiting for Rebecca to finish her elaborate preparations, and enjoyed the show. He smiled as he waited to be called to hold the bike upright. She had laughed so heartily at his own attempt that he was seriously looking forward to repaying her for her teasing.

When she finally appeared to be ready, Mark signaled to his father that it was his turn to hold the bike and Tim took hold of the seat firmly.

Rebecca put a foot on one pedal, then the other and teetered on the vehicle for a foot or two, then pedaled feverously, riding swiftly away from the boy and his nearly stumbling father.

"You're right, Mark," she yelled as she rode off. "It's really very easy!"

Timothy was dumbfounded. The girl had taken right off on the thing and pedaled back expeditiously, her hair flying out behind her. Then she pulled the vehicle up, sliding in the dust with her cheeks bright pink, panting softly and giggling hard.

He told her to get off the machine and straddled it himself, but at every attempt to straighten out the bike the wheel began to wobble back and forth violently and he had to keep putting down his feet to keep from toppling over. Mark and Rebecca nearly rolled in the dirt, hysterical with laughter as he turned the device around and tried to ride it back, only increasing the amusement for the pair as they fell into one another laughing uncontrollably.

Birget walked out into the yard to announce supper and found Mark and Rebecca convulsing with such violent laughter they could not explain what had taken place. Timothy parked the bicycle in the stable and stomped across the yard into the house. Rebecca and the boy staggered into the dining room, unable to contain themselves, still falling into one another and wiping their eyes.

"Enough!" Timothy bellowed. "I'll not be ridiculed by the two of you any further!"

The tearful pair tried to compose themselves and sat at the table unable to look at the man for fear they could not contain their laughter.

He'd watch them both attempt to keep a straight face and peer at them sternly while trying to enjoy his supper with some degree of dignity. Eventually the two surrendered to his stern looks and settled into their meals.

After supper they retired to the study and sat beside the fire while Rebecca read to Mark from the recently published *Pudd'nhead Wilson.* The boy had squeezed into the wide chair beside her, the two of them whispering and giggling occasionally in Timothy's direction.

Once Timothy had sent the boy off to bed, Rebecca paced the room, touching the curtains absently, and idly pulling books from the shelves. Timothy looked up from his papers, distracted by the girl, attempting to ignore her restlessness.

When she gasped loudly he dropped the documents onto his lap, trying to figure out what she was up to now. Rebecca had discovered a long forgotten box in the corner of the room that had once belonged to Mark's grandmother. Rebecca stood peering into it, holding her face, as if it contained some mysterious terror. Timothy was compelled to leave the comfort of his chair and see what the fuss was all about.

He saw nothing in the huge old box except a few balls of yarn and some needles.

"Is there a mouse?" He could not see what was so startling within the box.

"Did this belong to your wife?" she asked cautiously.

"No, I believe it was her mother's. No one's touched it in years. I'd completely forgotten it was here or I would have disposed of it."

"Disposed of it? Oh, Timothy, please no!"

"It's just some yarn and other bits of things. You're welcome to them if you like." It seemed silly to him. Relieved that she had not uncovered some ravenous vermin, he returned to the warmth of his chair.

Unable to figure out the girl's fascination and concentration having become impossible, he watched her over his papers as she lifted each item out of the box as though it were rare and priceless.

Rebecca ran her fingertip along each of the knitting needles. There were two sets fashioned of fine quality whalebone and a third of highly polished mahogany. In a small, lacy bag was a pair of delicately carved bone tatting shuttles, equal in size, but each distinct, bearing intricate scrimshaw designs. One featured the image of a wild rose, the other a delicate bouquet of violets. Rebecca inspected them carefully, holding them up to the light, and squinting at them through one eye, delighted to find that the tips met perfectly, with no space for fine thread to unwind too quickly.

Timothy watched Rebecca's reverent examination of the box's contents. He had seen women with their knitting before, although he had never watched it closely. He could not imagine why anyone could find it as fascinating as Rebecca obviously did now. He suspected there were other boxes about the place, likely in the attic, which Rebecca might find just as entertaining.

"Rebecca if that old box is so fascinating to you, have one of the girls take you up to the attic tomorrow. There's probably more of that kind of thing up there. You're welcome to all of it if it pleases you."

Rebecca set the shuttles back into the box and leapt across the room, grabbing his neck from behind the chair and kissing him on the cheek. Timothy was shocked and embarrassed by her display.

She stepped around to face him and balanced herself against the edge of the table.

"The pieces are beautiful! I'd lost my knitting at the train station and I have missed it so." She threw her hands up to his neck and planted herself boldly on his lap. "Oh, Timothy, you can't imagine! I've been so lost without it and if I could just get out my needlework I'd feel so much better! Thank you so much!" She kissed his cheek again.

Timothy was quite uncomfortable with the girl planted so intimately upon his lap. Her cheeks were glowing with excitement and her engaging pleasure at the discovery had certainly made her excited enough to forget herself. Timothy was confident that if the girl did not remove herself quickly he would undoubtedly be forced to remove her himself for fear of embarrassing the both of them.

She gazed into his eyes with gratitude as Timothy

let his forgotten papers fall to the floor, fighting off the profound effect the girl was having on his self-control. He attempted to shift his legs underneath her, wondering how she could not notice his intense discomfort and, as his restraint was overcome, he stood up suddenly, setting the girl to her feet and turning away from her. He stood with his back to her, certain that his display of interest would be all too apparent and announced that he was going to bed.

"Good night, Timothy," she whispered, ashamed at having been so bold in her excitement.

The ache of being overcome with his natural desire for the young woman, and his many years without the company of a woman sent him stiffly walking up the long flight of stairs.

Chapter Twenty-Three

$\mathcal{R}$ebecca watched the man ascend the stairs in obvious discomfort, his shoulders hunched and legs rigid. She was sure his posture illustrated his displeasure with her behavior. She stood watching long after he had disappeared from her view, chastising herself for being so bold once again with the man. He was friendly and very kind to her, but it was obvious to Rebecca that he did not feel comfortable if she were too physically close to him and she swore that she would try very hard not to be in the man's way again. Rebecca retrieved Timothy's discarded papers and placed them in a neat stack on the enormous desk.

She returned to her inspection of the wooden box, but her overwhelming excitement of discovering the needlework had dimmed, and it was nearly an hour before Rebecca could stop thinking about how badly she had behaved. She refilled the box and took it into the kitchen for a good cleaning.

Timothy lay awake in the bed, tossing and restless from his encounter with the girl. Although he had not searched out the company of a woman since his wife's death, he began to struggle with the self-control he had taken great pride in. Alone in the dark room he felt frustrated and embarrassed, hoping intently that she had been unaware of his reaction to her. He tried to assure himself that she was likely oblivious, since he had removed her from his shifting lap as swiftly as possible before his excitement became evident. Eventually he drifted off, attempting to focus instead on his commitments to the fast approaching morning and putting aside his experience with the girl.

Rebecca searched the cupboard for a light oil or soft wax to clean and polish the knitting box. After finding something she felt had the aroma and consistency she thought would work, she gathered a few soft cloths and took to vigorously rubbing down the old wood. To her delight she discovered that the box was intricately carved, the large round top adorned with a firmly packed surface of superior leather. She polished the equipment inside as well, buffing the needles and shuttles to a clean smooth surface.

The work soothed her, and eased her mood somewhat, and, as she prepared to organize the contents neatly into the box, the cook appeared on the back stairs wearing a billowing nightdress.

"Why, Miss, what on earth are you doing up at this hour here all alone?" The cook saw that Rebecca had brought out cleaning supplies and was fussing with the old knitting chest. "Ah, I see you found that old box. I thought it had been packed away years ago. I had forgotten how lovely it was."

"Timothy said I might keep it, if that's alright with you." Rebecca asked, concerned that if Birget recognized the box she might like it herself.

"Alright with me? The box belonged to the Old Miss, I have no need for it. When the girls in my home were fussing with such things, I was wantin' to be at the stove. I suppose you could empty it out and fill it with trinkets and such."

"Oh, no Birget," Rebecca exclaimed. "What's inside is the best part! Look!" Rebecca opened the box and showed the cook the contents.

"Ah, a hand-worker you are then. My own mother had a fine hand with such things. In fact I don't recall that she traveled anywhere without her knitting provisions. And that old pillow she kept, the one filled with the pins and the straw, she said it went back generations."

Birget thought the girl sweet and old fashioned and hoped she would remain in the big house. She thought that her employer might be a bit taken with the girl and that the change in his mood and appearance had something to do with Rebecca's presence in the house. Birget had begun to worry that the man had become increasingly despondent, but, as she had watched from the kitchen window and seen them laughing in the yard over the new contraption, she hoped fervently that the man was overcoming his grief.

"Timothy said there might be more things in the attic and possibly tomorrow someone could take me up to find them."

"That box is certainly large enough to hold a bit more. I'll have one of the girls take you up in the morning. I expect you can keep your own knitting things in there as well." Birget knew that the girl had arrived empty handed and from what she had seen with her keen eyes the girl possessed nothing of her own. If Rebecca was so interested in the craft she most definitely had needles of her own, somewhere, she deduced as the girl reacted to her evocative remark.

"I lost all of my belongings while traveling," Rebecca replied, obviously distressed at the memory.

Almost everyone in the household knew the girl had been hostage somewhere near the old cabin, but many details were lacking. Birget thought the girl seemed to know no one and perhaps could benefit from a good ear.

"Birget," Rebecca ventured. "Tell me about Corissa. I have so many questions and I don't know who else I might ask."

"Ah yes, Corissa." Birget began. "The place surely has not been the same since her passing." The woman filled a large cast teapot and asked Rebecca if she would like tea.

Rebecca nodded and sat down at the table listening to the cook.

"I came to work for the Old Miss when Corissa was just a child. When she married Timothy she had lost her husband in an accident on the river and she already had the boy. Timothy was so good to her and gave her so much, building Stavewood almost singlehandedly as his wedding gift to her. He brought the Old Miss and me up here once, just to show us the place. It was nearly finished then and not so much of the land had been cleared. He told the old woman that he was going to ask Corissa to marry him, hoping that the home would persuade her and she might accept his proposal."

"Persuade her?" Rebecca didn't understand.

"Corissa never got over the loss of her husband, Rebecca. Don't misunderstand, she was very fond of Timothy, and he tried so awfully hard to please her, but love… I just don't know.

"When he brought her up to Stavewood on their wedding night, things began to change. The Old Miss and I came up here to live and we loved the place so, and Timothy, he is such a good man, if strange in his ways sometimes.

"Corissa thought the place was too isolated for her taste. The man kept clearing out more trees, putting the rose garden out back for her and leveling out the yard. I'd see him out there days on end felling the trees with his own hand and wearing out those poor horses pulling the stumps. Corissa still found the place out-of-the-way and confining and often took her horse and went into town alone, sometimes for days."

Rebecca recalled the look on Timothy's face when she told him she felt trapped at Stavewood and choked back tears.

"She'd leave the boy up here, but for a long time the man was not quite sure how to deal with a child. The Old Miss and I took over most of the responsibility of the child, while Timothy tried to find his way with him. Yet, Corissa continually reminded him in many ways that the boy had a father already. If not for that I think he may have thought of the boy as if he were his own. Corissa constantly interfered with that while she was alive."

Rebecca insisted that she pour the tea herself, allowing the cook to continue her narrative.

"A few years back, when the Old Miss died, Corissa spent less and less time around the place. Her mother was always at the girl about being away from here so much, and, without her reminders, Corissa chose to be in town most of the time. Timothy would ride out to find her, but often times he came back alone."

The woman stirred cream into her tea absent-mindedly, and continued her story.

"When she'd been away for nearly a month, I guess he had had enough and the two of them got into a dreadful fight. We could all hear them from the upstairs arguing out in the garden. He kept asking her if she was so unhappy here, why did she marry him? She called Stavewood a 'backwoods burden' and she told him she had only stayed because it was someplace to be for the time being. Corissa accused him of trying and failing to build her a proper home so far away from civilization and that, no matter how grand he made the place, even if he were to build her a castle, it would be no more than a glorified outhouse stuck in the woods far away from the city.

"He kept telling her that the place was nothing of the sort and that she could have told him long before that she felt that way. He had built the home out of love, never to be an obligation."

Rebecca sniffled silently, remembering her first look at the magnificent home, perched so gloriously on the hill. She recalled her own conversation with the man in the garden, and could understand now that he was just naturally so generous. It became clear to her why he had told her that he had not brought her to Stavewood out of pity. He just brought her to his home because she had nothing and nowhere to go. Timothy never expected any more than her simple appreciation for any of it. She remembered how he smiled so proudly, yet with something more, when she first had reacted to the wonderful home. Rebecca was convinced that there were many things she did not understand about the man.

"But the house is so very beautiful." She pulled her handkerchief from her pocket and rubbed her nose. "When we first arrived I could not believe the vision of it, as if it were alive."

"Yes, I know, child," Birget sighed. She felt the same emotions every time she approached the beautiful Queen Anne.

"Corissa just didn't see it that way," she went on.

"Oh I'm sure she was fond of the man when she first met him, and he was and is again considered to be the finest catch in the territory. But Corissa didn't see it that way. It wasn't in her nature to be away from the city life. She was widowed, with a young child, and Timothy was no pauper. I think she just thought he'd make her comfortable and care for her son. No one could possibly imagine he would have built Stavewood. What ordinary man would do such thing?"

"No," Rebecca smiled sadly. "Timothy is certainly no ordinary man."

The cook touched the girl's hand.

"The night they fought she took that poor chestnut mare and the next day the sheriff rode out and found her fallen beside the lane, not far from here. She had barely left the place. Timothy placed his wife in her family's plot in the city where she had wanted to be all along. That poor horse came limping back with a bad leg when they buried Corissa the following day. We all watched him in the yard when the mare staggered back that afternoon with his gun in his hand. We thought he had to destroy the poor beast and that she would never walk again. He put down the rifle and spent weeks working with that animal. They told him to finish the horse, but he'd have none of it. As long as that creature seemed to keep trying he kept working on her. The day she trotted out from the stables bearing weight on that leg and he didn't have to care for her any more he started traveling about, buying up all that burned out land. He had named the mare *Love*, a gift on their first Valentine's Day. He never called that horse by her name again."

Birget took a sip of her tea.

"And that fire, awful thing it was. So many died and had it not been for the trains we might all have perished. The poor man was still so overcome with grief he nearly died saving all of us, setting break fires around the place and all along the tracks. They called it one of the worst fires in the history of Minnesota, they did. Burned over 250,000 acres. First those two years of terrible drought and then it all went up in flames. Blazes got so hot they fused the tracks right to the train cars. The Hinkley fire, I'll never forget it. If Timothy had not nearly worked himself to death, Stavewood and many of the local residents might not be here today. Sometimes we thought he believed that if he kept the place standing Corissa might come to her senses and come home."

Rebecca was overcome with emotion. She had no idea what their lives had been like. She sobbed silently.

"Don't cry, Miss." Birget gulped at her tea. "Things are much better now. You've seen him with the boy, I know. And the man himself, I've not seen him so relaxed since Corissa's death. Maybe you have something to do with that, eh?"

Rebecca was certain that if she had done anything, it was to upset the man.

"Tell me what she looked like, please?" she asked, her original thoughts and images of Corissa now had vastly changed.

"A big girl she was, tall and upright as any man. Her coloring was light and she had a determined way about her as if she never stood long in one place."

"Like Octavia?" Rebecca questioned, sure there

was something between Timothy and the big woman.

"Oh, heavens!" The cook exclaimed. "If you took two of me and stacked me up I would still not be the size of Miss Octavia!"

Rebecca giggled through her brimming tears, yet it made perfect sense to her. Timothy had thrown the party with Octavia and seemed worried about her late arrival. The woman he had loved so deeply was a robust girl, perhaps not as large as Octavia, but not the thin and pitiful thing she thought herself to be. Whatever she might have imagined was interest in her was just his kind way. Octavia was part of Timothy's world, a world Rebecca thought she would never understand.

"Thank you, Birget." Rebecca hugged the woman briefly and gathered the box, excusing herself and walking towards the stairs to prepare for bed.

"Miss?" Birget spoke softly. "If possible could you consider looking over the menus in the morning? I must admit I can turn out a fine meal, but I expect that I fall into a routine. I very much enjoyed planning the party."

Rebecca turned to her and smiled. "I would like to very much."

Chapter Twenty-Four

$\mathcal{T}$he cook sat alone in the empty expanse of the warm kitchen and considered the girl. Although she could not say why exactly, Rebecca had brought something to the place that perhaps had always been there beneath the surface.

It was as if the magnificent mistress of Stavewood had been built for something that had not happened yet within her walls. Timothy had put his back and his heart into building her, but something had remained missing. Maybe somehow Rebecca had the answer.

After her late conversation with Birget the night before, and several hours of being unable to sleep as she went over the woman's story, Rebecca rose unusually late and hurried to dress. She knew that it was long past sunrise, but she hoped there was a possibility that Timothy and the boy had gotten a late start and had not left yet.

Rebecca's room seemed unusually close and stuffy and she threw open the drapes, allowing a warm rush of wind into the room. The heat would certainly be much worse in the kitchen and the attic, prompting Rebecca to choose the lightest of the new dresses and electing to forgo her stiff corset for the day. She knew little about the local climate, but was sure the day's heat was unusual.

Her dress was softly draped cotton in a bright shade of gloxinia, adorned with tiny, pearl buttons which fastened at the bodice. She chose the sheerest of bloomers and a light petticoat.

Rebecca gathered her hair softly to the top of her head, one section at a time, pinning it into a knot that allowed the sides to fall loose around her head, soft tendrils framing her face and tumbling down her neck. She arranged a wisp to camouflage the still lingering scar and descended the stairs.

Finding no one in the family dining room, she checked the kitchen.

"Good morning, Miss!" Birget greeted her brightly. "Such a beautiful day!"

Rebecca thought that the temperature was much too warm for her liking and asked if it was normal for such weather in October.

"It won't stay this warm," the cook assured her. "Just a bit of Indian summer I would think. Enjoy it while it lasts, the snow will fall soon enough."

Snow, Rebecca thought. How fun!

"I suppose I have missed Timothy and the boy?" the girl asked.

"Ah, yes, left before sunrise. I don't expect them back before late afternoon or evening. I'll bring you out breakfast."

"Thank you Birget, if possible I'd like to eat in here if you don't mind."

The cook smiled. The cozy table was a favorite spot for Timothy to eat with his tendency to rise early before the rest of the household. Birget thought this further evidence that there was something about this girl.

She served Rebecca a breakfast of fried tomatoes, potatoes and a stack of griddlecakes with sausages in black maple syrup. Rebecca declined her further offer of biscuits and honey, insisting that she would be challenged to finish the food the cook had already laid out before her.

"Birget," Rebecca asked. "This syrup is so sweet and unusual. Where did you get this?"

"From the trees," the cook exclaimed. "In the spring the men drain the sap from the trees and gather it in buckets. They boil it down at the mill for syrup. Mark loves tapping the trees, I'm sure he'll show you how it's done."

Syrup from trees, Rebecca thought it wonderful. She wondered how far away spring might be and decided to begin her day writing her letter to Emmy.

Birget chuckled at the girl. "When you've finished eating, one of the girls will take you up to look for those knitting things if you like. I don't need her much today with all the hands headed out to look at that shack."

Rebecca decided to take the opportunity to see the attic and she could write her letter just as well in the afternoon. She had noticed that the house seemed oddly quiet. Lately, increasing numbers of workmen seemed to be appearing about the place and she suspected that there were more buildings on the property than she knew about. But today, even the yard seemed unusually deserted.

"The men I've seen headed up that road there, where are they coming from?" She decided to ask Birget.

"There's the mill up about a mile beyond the hill. They cut lumber there when it's running. If you head out towards the west the barns are there, and the gardens and such."

Rebecca thought she would like to see more of the

property and decided she might ask Mark to take her riding one afternoon.

"What do they keep in the barns?" Rebecca pushed the last bit of the sausage around on her plate in the sticky syrup trying to force down one final bite of the delicious, rich food.

"Cows mostly, and some sheep. There are chickens usually, and the farm horses. Since Corissa's been gone he let most of the workers and the animals go, but he'll be bringing back the chickens today and he just put in a couple of cows I hear. It'll be good to have fresh milk and eggs again." Birget cleared Rebecca's plates and returned to kneading her bread.

Rebecca gathered a maid to help in her search of the attic and, as she was led up to the third floor, she noticed a door leading out to the turret.

"Could we go out there?" she asked the maid curiously. The third floor was stuffy and unused and Rebecca wondered why this section of the house seemed so abandoned.

The two tiny women pulled at the great oak doors and it felt as if the house sighed when the doors gave way and fresh, warm air filled the hall.

The women stood inside the open turret and Rebecca was astounded at the spectacle.

Perched on the hill, the soaring Queen Anne afforded a breathtaking view of the beautiful landscape. The trees were ablaze in autumn splendor, while the deep green of the Norway pines reached, towering towards the vivid blue sky. Rebecca could clearly see the lake they had passed on their journey to the home, and the maid pointed out that on a day as clear as this you could see the tall tower of the big clock in Billington, far in the distance.

"It looks as though no one ever comes up here. Why is that?" Rebecca asked as she and the maid closed the massive doors behind them.

"It's never been open since I've been here. I think it was closed down not long after it was built. The attic is this way," the maid replied.

Rebecca wondered why the place had been designed so large if it went vastly unused. What had been Timothy's vision when he had built it?

The maid opened the heavy door at the end of a long hall and Rebecca ascended the dusty stairs. She left Rebecca to explore the attic, explaining to her that most of the old woman's belongings were stacked in the north corner.

Alone in the upper reaches of the enormous residence, Rebecca thought even the attic was beautiful, the massive beams rising above her head. The heat was not nearly as oppressive as she feared, though the area was close and warm.

In one corner stood an abandoned dress form, several trunks and a stack of wooden crates. Rebecca decided she would start with the boxes, curious as to what she might find. As promised, she did discover needlework and was astonished by the volume of lovely wool yarns in a vast collection of colors and stunning natural shades. There was a fine sewing machine marked *Remington* in a custom cabinet and Rebecca wondered if it were made by the same company who had manufactured David's rifle. There were dress patterns and notions galore and Rebecca was saddened that all of the beautiful and incredibly useful items were hidden away where they could not be appreciated and enjoyed. Oddly, she found stacks of pattern books filled with baby clothing, designs for lacy sweaters and tiny booties. She looked at the dates on the books and saw that many were just a few years old. Rebecca speculated that perhaps Timothy and Corissa had planned a family. Maybe that would explain why the house had been built with so many rooms.

The girl was finding that her excursion to the attic was not the exciting venture she had imagined when Timothy had first suggested it. Instead she felt emotionally overwhelmed by the history in the family's items. The sewing machine appeared to never have been used, the attachments still sealed inside of a box in the cabinet drawer. Had it been a misguided gift as the house had?

Feeling uncomfortable exploring items that were not her business, she selected a bundle of soft yarn and a few more knitting needles. She found a small oval basket, filled it with the yarn and prepared to go downstairs.

Rebecca struggled to shake off her feeling of uneasiness as she set the basket on the floor and closed the attic door.

Chapter Twenty-Five

Elgerson instructed Mark and the older Evens boy to gather as many of the chickens as possible and not to venture into the woods. He assured them that he and the other men would return as quickly as possible and checked both of the boys' rifles before unhitching the horse from the wagon.

A collection of riders, including the sheriff, rode directly up the hillside towards the abandoned shack.

When they emerged from the dense forest onto hard packed dirt Timothy circled with his horse in confusion. There was no structure of any kind. Elgerson slid from the Arabian's back and paced around the clearing uncertainly.

"This is the place, I'm sure." His voice was irate and agitated. "Damn it!" Elgerson slapped his thigh with his hat.

"You sure this was the place, Tim? There's nothing here, not even the remains of a shack."

Timothy looked up and glared at the man.

"Son of a bitch," Elgerson swore under his breath.

The riders dismounted and paced the area in disappointment.

"Look at this, Tim." The sheriff pointed to a large hole, smooth and round on the forest floor. "Looks to be some kind of a burrow. I've never seen an animal build this kind of a thing right out in the open like this. No grass or nothing."

The men gathered about, standing in a circle around the lair while Elgerson pushed a stick inside and then held it to his nose.

"Possum hole would be my guess."

"Doesn't seem right, Tim." The sheriff squatted down beside him. "There had to be something over this spot. The sky opens up to here, no possum would do this out in the open like this."

"We'll take a look around and see what else we can find," one of the men stated, and walked slowly into the woods.

All but Elgerson and the sheriff scouted out the surrounding area while the two of them checked out the clearing closely. Within several minutes one of the men called out.

When they reached the man the others joined as well. Lying against the knotted root of a tree were a bloodstained man's boot and a leather sole nailed to a broken piece of wood. Elgerson and the sheriff examined the evidence closely while attempting to understand how it fit into the information they already had.

"We know the girl was bleeding when Mark found her and he said she was dressed in men's clothing. This piece here isn't from the same type of boot. Can't say why it's nailed to the wood like this but it could be any number of reasons. I think we ought to take these back and see what the woman and your boy have to say about them."

The group met back at Elgerson's cabin and found that the two boys had collected and caged most of the chickens, but had given up their efforts in order to stay close to the building as they had been told. It had apparently been an accomplishment to gather what fowl they had, since both boys were angry and out of breath.

"Stupid chickens!" Mark was muttering under his breath.

"That's good enough, Mark," Elgerson decided. "Take a look at these things we found. What can you tell us about them?"

"Did you go to the shack?" the Evens boy asked excitedly.

"There's no shack there now," Elgerson scowled.

"What?" Mark wheezed. "What happened to it? I know there was a shack there! Pa, you saw it!"

"Don't know, boy, but it's not there now. Take a look at these things. Show him, Ben."

The boy examined the articles and was sure that the boot matched the one that Rebecca was wearing and thought that maybe the leather sole was nailed to the door.

"They took it down? Why did they take it down?" the boy asked, puzzled.

"I've got a few ideas about that," the sheriff remarked.

"I've got a few myself," Elgerson grunted. "It doesn't look good. Well, there's nothing left there now except the burrow in the clearing."

"Burrow?" Mark looked up excitedly. "Rebecca said that there was a rat in the shack with her. She tried to tell me that it was bigger than a cat. Did you see a giant rat, Pa?" The boy was sure Rebecca must have imagined the rodent, but if not, a giant rat would be something to trap up there.

"Looks like a possum hole, not a rat." Elgerson needed to talk to the girl.

"Maybe she never saw a possum before," the

Evens boy interjected. "Girls think they are giant rats."

"She was sure of it." Mark was disappointed.

"Mark," Elgerson addressed his son. "Exactly how bad was Rebecca's bleeding when you found her? The boot's soaked in dried blood and I thought she just had a bump on her forehead. Was she thinking clearly?"

"She was bleeding pretty badly when I found her," the boy replied. "Her shirt was covered in it and most of her pants. She looked really pale and shaky. She seemed alright while we were coming back here, except that her side was hurting, but she was kinda funny. I was afraid to let her sleep a long time like Mister Klehm. I remembered that you said if he slept too long after he got hit in the head he might never wake up. I kept waking her up for a while, she was pretty sleepy, but I think she was alright."

"I think that girl's lucky to be alive, Tim," Ben remarked. "Sounds like you did exactly the right thing, Mark."

The boy smiled at the sheriff, relieved that Rebecca hadn't died.

Elgerson hitched up the wagon filled with the caged chickens, and he and the sheriff rode back together while the boys rode the horses. Timothy wanted to discuss his thoughts with the man before returning home and talking to the girl.

"Why take down the shack, Tim? Whoever brought the girl up here had to know she got away somehow. Just doesn't make sense. Did they take it down because they knew we were riding up to have a look? I'm not fond of that idea. There's no one in town or at the train station or ticket office that has seen Finn Morgan in days. This just isn't right," the sheriff said.

"I'd had the same thoughts myself, Ben. If they were using the shack as a hideout for the robberies and the girl got free, of course sooner or later someone would want to find the place. I've got a bad feeling. Something just doesn't add up. I've got to say I'm concerned about Finn myself. He's not a bright man. I'd hate to think anything had happened to him as well."

"Tim," the man spoke cautiously. "I've been thinking. Since I know the girl's up at your place and all…" the sheriff paused.

"You think she had something to do with all this?" Elgerson stated flatly.

"I have to consider everything, Tim."

"It's alright, Ben. I had already thought of that. That's why I asked the boy to tell me more about her condition. I can't figure that they'd beat her up that way if she was in with them unless there was a problem." Elgerson shook his head unable to make sense of the girl's possible involvement.

"I just can't see it, Ben. She's puzzling, that's certainly true, but I think she's a victim. I did have another thought."

"What's that?"

"Maybe she saw something, possibly someone on the train? She might not have known who it was, but they could have gotten it in their minds she could identify them. I think we have to find out who this woman is who took her from the station."

"Never thought of someone being on the train,"

the sheriff replied.

Elgerson could not shake the image of the blood covered boot and Mark's description of Rebecca's condition. He hadn't been aware of how severe her injuries must have been. Then he'd wrestled with her himself, thinking the girl was a thief. He supposed she could have stayed with Mark, recuperating, and then tricked him into giving her money before leaving him at the cabin. He just didn't see it in her. The train robbers had kept horses tucked away for an escape. He knew Rebecca did not ride well. He just couldn't fit her in anywhere into the situation.

If she was a victim it made much more sense. The girl was terrified and her actions were what the man would expect. He imagined her lying in the dirt by the possum hole, bleeding for an unknown length of time. She had to be a victim.

He spent the remainder of the ride certain that he needed to find out more from the girl. He wondered if she really remembered anything all that well, but he would get what information he could from her.

The sheriff sat beside the big man and tried to fit Rebecca into the group of train robbers. He was not convinced that Rebecca was also just a random victim.

When the men parted at the lake the sheriff informed Elgerson that he'd be stopping by after supper to speak to the girl further.

Mark climbed into the wagon with his father and Timothy questioned him again about the girl's condition and how she came to have the money. Further convinced that she was an unfortunate victim and trying to understand why they had taken her to the shack and left her for dead, he began to worry about the girl. What if someone did believe she was a witness? Elgerson urged the horses to a quicker pace.

Rebecca returned to her room with the basket and considered starting a pair of woolen socks. If snow fell in this area maybe she'd make a pair for Mark and another for Timothy to thank them before she left. She hoped it would be something to keep them warm after she'd gone. The thought of leaving Stavewood depressed her deeply and her room was so warm she decided instead to take a walk outside and compose her letter to Emmy in her mind first before putting it to paper.

Chapter Twenty-Six

*A*s Rebecca reached the bottom of the stairs she heard horses at the front of the house and, thinking perhaps Timothy and the boy were returning, opened the front door.

An excessively embellished carriage opened to reveal Octavia, entirely clad in a dreary shade of gray, all pieces of her ensemble a perfectly matching shade. Even the feather on her fitted bonnet was dyed the same monotone shade.

Rebecca sighed deeply. Without Timothy at home she would be forced to entertain Octavia herself. Rebecca hoped that, with the man out, perhaps Octavia would not stay.

The big girl unashamedly displayed her ample bosom as she leaned to step out of the coach, leaving Rebecca to question if American women found it acceptable to go calling in such flaunting attire during the day. She had not recalled any of the women at the party being so openly displayed, and decided that this was something Octavia chose as her own style.

"Good morning, Octavia," Rebecca greeted her politely. "Please come in."

"Where's Timothy?" the woman asked and brushed past her into the foyer.

"I'm afraid he went up to the cabin with his son. Would you care for tea?" Rebecca felt as if it were her responsibility in Timothy's absence to entertain his friend as cordially as she could.

"What?" Octavia snapped, turning to Rebecca, peering at her as if having just noticed her beside the closed door.

"Timothy is out. Would you care for tea?"

"I need to speak to him now," Octavia stated, peering up the staircase and trying to see into the upper hall.

"I could give him a message if you like." Rebecca stepped up to the sizable woman. "I don't expect him to return until this evening."

Octavia faced Rebecca in obvious disappointment and scrutinized her carefully.

"Yes," she stated as she studied the petite girl. "Tea would be fine."

Rebecca escorted Octavia to the parlor and went to the kitchen. Finding no one around she set out biscuits on a tray and filled a china teapot she found in a low cupboard behind several pots.

When she returned with the tray Octavia was arranging the candlesticks on the mantle.

"I've always hated these things here," she continued to inspect the candlesticks.

"Please, have some tea." Rebecca poured the tea gracefully and the two women sat facing one another. "Is there something you would like me to relay to Timothy?"

"Relay? Oh, yes. I wondered if my mother had been out this way. I haven't seen her for several days, and, although Mother comes and goes as she pleases, I did expect she might come home earlier."

"I don't know about Timothy, but I have not seen her myself. Are you worried?" Rebecca sipped her tea.

"Not really, just curious. She can't be far I suppose. The bank said she made a deposit just yesterday." Octavia looked restlessly around the room and picked up a small silver box from the side table.

"I apologize that I never met your mother the night of the party. Perhaps another time," Rebecca remarked, watching the woman inspect the trinkets carefully beside her chair. "I'm sure Timothy will be sorry to have missed you." Rebecca hoped that Octavia would prepare to leave, not entirely sure how to address the woman's handling of the property in the house. She knew Timothy and the woman were close, but was unsure of their exact relationship.

"So, tell me, Rebecca, whatever color would you

call that dress? It's a very vivid shade after all." Octavia asked distractedly.

"Are you and Timothy very close?" Rebecca asked, deciding she ought to find out more about the woman and changed the subject to avoid becoming rude.

"Terribly!" Octavia responded, suddenly interested in Rebecca and the conversation. "I've known Timothy since we were children. We've always been so close. I was away, you know, when he married Corissa. I've always blamed myself for that, leaving the poor man alone to make such an awful mistake." Octavia punctuated her conversation by fanning herself with her handkerchief. "How long are you planning on being here? I thought you said you were leaving soon." She leaned slightly towards the smaller girl.

"I have some arrangements yet to make, but I don't expect it will be very much longer."

"A shame," Octavia rose from her chair and flipped her handkerchief. "Then you won't be able to attend the wedding."

"You're planning on being married?" Rebecca fidgeted slightly in her chair, not sure she wanted to hear the answer to her question.

"Of course. Tim and I will be married in the spring I expect." Octavia strolled away casually.

Rebecca caught her breath. She told herself she should not be surprised, she had suspected they might be close. Still the announcement startled her, hearing the words aloud.

"I'm sorry." Rebecca tried to appear composed. "I did not realize that you and Tim were engaged. I suppose I should congratulate you." Rebecca rose from her chair, not entirely comfortable with the woman towering over her. She found the sound of the woman's voice made her feel as on edge as the topic of conversation.

"Well, it's not common knowledge yet, but I'm sure everyone will know soon. I was hoping dear Tim would bring it up the night of the party, but as it was, we never got a moment alone."

Rebecca had no idea that Timothy planned a wedding announcement and wondered why it had not been made while the man was on the stage. He had seemed concerned with Octavia's late arrival and perhaps he had changed his mind for some reason.

"Congratulations, Octavia. Timothy seems to be a very fine man and I wish you happiness." Rebecca struggled to regulate her breathing and felt faint in the warm room.

"Yes, I'm very lucky to have him," Octavia continued. "When I think of all the couples I've known who have rushed off to the altar without thinking, well, I just can't imagine! Don't you agree?" She turned and faced Rebecca.

"Yes," Rebecca replied quietly.

"Why look at poor old Mister Freid at the party the other night! He ordered that girl, mail order you know, and then brought her right out in public to the party!"

Rebecca sat back down in the chair.

"I mean, I understand that when he lost that gambling bet at Rival's he agreed that as part of his debt he'd let the men order him a woman, but then to go ahead and marry her when she arrived! I just can't imagine!" Octavia ranted on completely unaware of Rebecca's acute discomfort.

"I mean, yes, maybe it was cruel of the men to send away for a woman as a joke, but then for the man to pity her so much as to actually marry her? Heavens! And the girl, what could she possibly have been thinking? Don't you agree, Rebecca, that the thought of putting yourself up for order like that is cheap and degrading? Why, the girl is no better than a common prostitute. Everyone around here agrees, I'm sure. I just fear that those horse-brained men might get it in their fool heads to order more of those women as a joke. I think it's ridiculous!"

Rebecca could not listen any longer. She made quick excuses and thanked Octavia for her visit, while promising to relay her concerns about her mother to Timothy as soon as he returned. She picked up Octavia's unfinished tea, set the cup on the tray hurriedly and stood in the entrance of the parlor gesturing towards the door.

As she stood on the porch and balanced herself against the open doorway she tried intensely to appear composed.

Octavia turned to her, standing in the hot sun beside her lavish coach.

"This was actually very nice, Rebecca. I hope you have a fine trip when you go away. Please make sure you leave an address where we can send you our wedding invitation. They will be so beautiful. I look forward to letting everyone know when I become Mrs. Timothy Elgerson."

Chapter Twenty-Seven

*R*ebecca staggered into the dark foyer, her eyes blinded by the bright sunlight reflected on the porch, and pushed closed the heavy door behind her. She grabbed at her waist, fighting off nausea and clung to the open doorway to the study. Her heart pounded inside of her chest and she struggled to remain on her feet.

"It cannot be possible!" her mind screamed. "I was upset about Octavia's conversation and I had to have heard her wrong."

Rebecca ran to the desk in the study and began to frantically shuffle through the envelopes she had seen there the evening before.

There it was. Plainly printed out before her, stark and obvious in black and white:

Timothy Elgerson
Stavewood Estate
Billington City, Minnesota

"No!" her mind screamed again. "How could I not have realized it? Mark. Mark must have said it. The hotel, they had checked into the hotel? The party? Someone must have said the name at the party.

Someone *must* have used his name!"

Rebecca screamed aloud and sank to the floor. All of it unraveled into horrifying place in her mind. The ad in the newspaper for the mail order bride, a joke! The limited information, carefully chosen, yes, because it was all a hideous joke! The terrible trip, nothing but the absolute necessities to get her here. All because it was set up. A joke! Timothy Elgerson had no need for such a wife. He was a man who would never consider such a thing! He had plans to marry a woman who was right here! Timothy Elgerson. The name cried out in her mind. Timothy Elgerson. Timothy Elgerson was young and intensely handsome and owned most of the territory around him. It was unthinkable that he would have any need to order a stranger for a wife. She had left her home and come all this way to a place where she had nothing and no one, because of a joke. Timothy Elgerson was here, he's the man whose home she is sitting in right now and he did not know! He didn't know she was brought here as a joke and was no better than a prostitute! What would he think of her now if he knew? She was no better than a prostitute.

Rebecca wanted to run, if only her legs would carry her. She hoped she would just stop breathing and die. If she could only just die. Shame began eating at her, wrenching her heart as she sat in the dark foyer, staring at nothing. Rebecca saw nothing. The big clock in the hall ticked slowly, a bird chirped on the porch railing just outside, but Rebecca heard none of it.

Alone in the dark hall of the beautiful Stavewood estate of Mr. Timothy Elgerson, Rebecca sat staring and felt as if her mind were slipping away. It didn't matter that something inside of her was dying and she sat alone and wanted it all to end. She rose slowly and stumbled through the house, seeing nothing. as if in a trance, and walked outside into the hot afternoon sun. Through the garden and across the gazebo she walked, not feeling the sunlight or the air or her own footsteps. She walked silently into the woods.

Time passed and she had to accept that she had not died. Her heart still beat and the day felt warm and the world still went on around her. Once the sobs began, they tore at her chest, and she knew that, however cruel life was to her, it nevertheless remained. She was still alive, she was still at Stavewood and her situation could not be changed, could not be wished away. It would cling to her and become part of who she was. She fell to the ground among the acorns and the ferns and let her pain wash into the earth, each tear disappearing silently into the rich soil beneath her. The land of Stavewood accepted Rebecca's agony with no remark, no opinion and no reprimand. It accepted Rebecca as she could not accept herself and silently swallowed her agony and her spirit. Rebecca surrendered and poured out the pain.

She arose as the shadows spread and she brushed the leaves from her skirt. She took a deep breath and stood listening. She felt as if something inside of her had changed, something elusive, as if strung tightly, but not quite snapped. Through the woodland she could hear the whisper of rushing water and she wandered through the trees following the sound.

Chapter Twenty-Eight

*T*imothy unhitched his horse from the buckboard, leaving Mark and his friend to dispatch the chickens into the coop. He rode his stallion at a quick clip to the main house and began to look for Rebecca.

"Birget, have you seen Rebecca?" he asked in the kitchen, unable to find the girl.

"No, sir. I know she was up to the attic today in search of some knitting things and I saw her in her room earlier, but I have not seen her since. It's awfully warm to be indoors. Perhaps she decided to go for a walk."

The man had been concerned since having the thought of someone returning to harm the girl and didn't care to hear that she might be wandering the grounds.

After checking the rose garden and stables, his apprehension for the girl's safety grew and he returned to the house to question the staff further.

"Birget, she has to be here somewhere. What time did you see her last?"

"It would have been late morning I suppose. It couldn't have been much later. The girls and I walked out to the barns near noon and only just returned."

Timothy grunted and shook his head and decided to try the path into the woods. As he reached the clearing he stopped and listened, unsure if he heard a voice in the distance. He cut into the woods toward the creek, and the area of the falls, and spotted Rebecca immediately as he emerged from the woods.

Perched on a flat rock, below the slow ripple of the falls, the girl sat gazing across the creek.

Her sweet clear voice was melancholy and soft and Timothy listened carefully, standing at the edge of the thick forest.

I want none of your petticoats and your fine silken shows.

I never was so poor as to marry for clothes,

But if you prove loyal and constant to me

I'll forsake my own true love and get married to thee.

The melody seemed familiar to him, though he could not recall ever having heard a lyric to the tune. The song was pleasing and Rebecca's voice beautiful and he began to step out to approach her.

Timothy quickly realized that Rebecca had removed her stockings and had hiked her frock up above her knees. Her bodice was partly unbuttoned and quite revealing and she leaned back, supporting herself with her arms, as she continued singing to herself.

The vision of her, glistening in the sunlight, her bright pink dress spread about her on the rock, revealed enough to show her soft beautiful complexion. Timothy came to an abrupt stop. Her hair tumbled free, tendrils softly damp against her face and neck, as her chest rose and fell in the warmth of the day.

Timothy was captive, watching the girl, and he felt himself stir with desire for her. Her head fell back, exposing her neck and shoulders and he felt compelled to rush to her and take her into his arms. It didn't matter what was proper, or what he did or didn't know about her. He felt he could no longer contain himself and he wanted her completely. He strode boldly up behind her and as Rebecca opened her eyes she saw the soaring man standing above her and nearly slipped into the water in an attempt to gather together her bodice.

Rebecca jumped to her feet.

"Timothy, you startled me."

He said nothing and looked hungrily into her eyes.

Rebecca felt her breath quicken as everything she knew about him now rushed through her mind. He looked at her so oddly… eagerly. Had her world been a different place she would be here, right now, passionately surrendering herself to the man and she would be fulfilled. In another world she could be his bride and live with him in happiness at Stavewood for the rest of her life. But this was not that world. In this world she was a joke, a common prostitute and, though every part of her wanted to throw herself into his arms and beg him to take her, she could not. Rebecca gathered her stockings and shoes and ran back to the house.

Timothy stood, his head bowed, and let her run back into the woods. He cursed under his breath, fighting off his overwhelming frustration. How dare he think he had any right to her, he asked himself. Timothy Elgerson started to think he'd gone too long without a woman and was beginning to take leave of his senses. With resolve he went back to the house to wash for supper and the sheriff's visit.

Birget watched Rebecca run though the kitchen, her dress nearly soaked and her shoes in her hand. When Timothy stomped in behind her she began to hope that there was something they might be trying to hide from her and giggled to herself.

Rebecca changed into a clean gown and gathered her ragged emotions in preparation to go downstairs and face the man. Whatever he had discovered on his trip to the shack had put him in a very strange mood. She'd seen it in his eyes before, and he had come upon her so suddenly she was sure something was very wrong. She dressed carefully and arranged her hair slowly, hoping that the more prepared she was, the more easily she could handle whatever the man had to say to her.

She checked her appearance quickly before leaving her room. Her hair was gathered loosely to the back of her head and cascaded over the shoulders of her fitted dress. She had chosen the royal blue for its serious tone and the neckline plunged slightly behind a sheer white lace above the bodice and featured a high, stiff collar trimmed in lace. Rebecca stood straight, gathering her resolve before leaving her room and descended the stairs.

When she reached the study she could see him, sitting in his leather chair, one leg across his knee, studying the fire. She swallowed hard and entered the room.

"Timothy," she stated a bit more loudly than she had planned.

He jumped to his feet and faced her, ashamed of his earlier behavior and faced her squarely.

"How was your trip?" her voice cracked slightly and she cleared her throat silently.

He sank back into the chair, unable to apologize, as he had promised himself he would. "Interesting," he replied.

"How so?" Rebecca felt that her response sounded cold. What had happened was not this dear man's fault. She attempted to try again. "I was worried."

Timothy couldn't be sure, but he thought that her eyes glistened with the threat of tears, yet she sat quietly and composed, as though with no emotion at all.

"Awful, Rebecca. It wasn't as I expected."

"I'm sorry," she whispered. She had to face whatever it was he had to say.

"Why?" He looked her in the eye and could sense… remorse? Why, he thought, what had she done?

"I am," she replied softly.

Timothy was certain this time that she was near tears. Had he been wrong all along?

"Rebecca, I need to know. Are you involved with the people who left you at the cabin?"

"What? Of course not!" She was completely confused and stood up before him. "Why would you even imagine that?"

"The shack was gone. Someone had dismantled it entirely. There are just some things that don't make sense. I had to know, I had to ask." He stood up to face her. "If you are involved we might be able to understand. Believe me I don't want to ask you this. I just have to know." He looked into her eyes pleading for the answer he wanted to hear.

"No, Timothy," she replied firmly. "I was taken by someone I know nothing about." Rebecca choked back a tear and met Timothy's eyes.

"Did you see anyone on the train? Anyone who may have been hiding something or behaving strangely? Why would they have taken you up there and left you to die? Did someone… did Finn…?" He could not form the words to ask the question. "Did anyone touch you…?"

"No, no that!" she gasped. "I wish I knew."

He had no doubt that she was answering his question honestly and that she knew nothing more about being taken. The pain and pleading in her eyes made him want to take the whole memory away. How could anyone not see how delicate and helpless she could be and just leave her there to die?

"We found a hole in the middle of the clearing," he continued. "And a boot and a leather sole. Nothing else."

"The rat!" Rebecca exclaimed. "There was a huge rat that left through a hole under the cot!"

Timothy decided that whether it was a giant rat or a possum didn't really matter. He could see clearly that it terrified her.

"The boot was completely covered in blood, Rebecca. How long were you there? What did they do to you exactly?"

"I remember being at the station, I thought I was going to…" she caught her breath. "I don't know. Then it was dark and I was inside the shack. There was a hood over my head, and my wrists and ankles were tied and I was bleeding. I had a pain in my side that has never gone away, I don't know why." The young woman exhaled deeply.

"I'll get the doctor up here tomorrow. I'm sorry, Rebecca. I should have taken you to see him straight away. I just had no idea." Timothy shook his head and studied the girl.

"Oh please. You shouldn't. It's fine. I want to just forget it all."

"Rebecca, we have to find these people. After dinner the sheriff will be up and you have to tell him everything. Do you understand me?" He took her by the arms wanting her to understand how important her information was.

Rebecca looked up at him and tried to compose herself. She would describe Bedra to the sheriff and tell him anything except the reason she had come here. By the time the sheriff found the woman, and Finn had told him the truth, she would be far away from here and would never have to see the look in Timothy's eyes and face the shame of what she was.

She looked at him and knew that if he ever knew the truth she could not bear it. His gaze was so loving and open now.

In a breath she fell into his arms and his lips were pressing against her own hotly. She felt his firm grip of her and she melted into his warmth and the safety of his strength. He pulled her hungrily into him and she felt his excitement firmly against her thigh. She wanted him, wanted his kisses, his hunger for her, as he pressed against her passionately, displaying his desire.

"Octavia!" she thought. "Oh, no!" Rebecca pulled away suddenly.

Timothy held her in his arms and looked at her. Why had she drawn away? He knew she wanted it too.

"Rebecca," he whispered hoarsely.

"Timothy…" She began to shake. "I can't. I don't belong here. You have no idea who I really am and you cannot belong to me. I can't."

The big man sank into the chair as Rebecca gathered herself and went to dinner.

Timothy composed himself and, tired of trying to understand her reasoning, joined Rebecca and the two boys in the main dining room. He watched her face, hoping for some understanding of why she would deny something he now believed they both wanted and feelings they both shared.

Chapter Twenty-Nine

$\mathcal{W}$hile the boys complained about their frustration handling the uncooperative chickens Rebecca sat upright in her chair and attempted to enjoy her meal, barely able to taste the tender beef, and consumed several glasses of cool lemonade. Timothy's appetite was no better, but his beverage of choice was a large goblet of brandy.

"Timothy," Rebecca addressed the man without looking up from her meal. "Octavia was here today looking for you. She mentioned that her mother had not been home in days, but she did not seem to be too terribly concerned. She wondered if we had seen her." Rebecca chose not to bring up the remainder of their conversation.

Timothy studied Rebecca carefully. He preferred not to have dealings with Octavia's mother if possible, and was not concerned himself over the woman's whereabouts. He began to wonder if Octavia had said something to Rebecca that had made her pull away from him while he held her. Timothy grunted and scowled. Octavia and her overpowering matron had long imagined that he had some kind of interest in the poor girl. He took a deep gulp of his brandy.

The boys were excused from the table and Elgerson informed Rebecca that they ought to wait for the sheriff in the study. She agreed and told him she would join him shortly.

Timothy refilled his generous glass and paced the study in aggravation, waiting for the woman to appear.

Rebecca remained at the table for several minutes preparing herself for the inquiry, avoiding the study for fear that the man's presence would cause her to forget herself once again. When she heard the knock at the front door she swallowed hard and joined the two men.

"Good evening, Rebecca," the sheriff greeted her formally, acutely aware of the tension between his long-time friend and the beautiful woman. "I'll make this as brief as possible."

Rebecca sat stiffly in the chair, afraid that if she remained on her feet her resolve would evaporate.

The sheriff wondered about the extent of her injuries. She answered his questions as clearly as she could and explained the arrival at the shack exactly as she had to Timothy earlier. He questioned her about her possible involvement with the people who had left her there. He was blunt and direct, and he seemed satisfied with her answers.

"Rebecca, I need you to describe the woman who left you at the shack as clearly as you can recall."

"She was a very large woman," Rebecca replied, struggling with her composure. "She had bright, red hair and an extremely gruff manner. She wore men's clothing and her face was weathered and freckled. I'm sure she knew Finn quite well. She spoke to him roughly, as though he were a child."

The two men stared at one another in disbelief and Rebecca was confused by their reaction. She had answered as honestly as she could, but they seemed perplexed by her description.

"Damn, Tim!" the sheriff blurted out, pacing before the fireplace.

"It's got to be Dianna Weintraub, but what the hell would she want Rebecca for?" Timothy was agitated as well.

The young woman was uneasy with their reaction, unable to understand the revelation, although she had a feeling that she ought to be able to.

"You know her?" she blurted out, her fear of discovery mounting.

"She's Octavia's mother, Rebecca. None of this makes any sense."

She sank in the chair.

"Rebecca, you said something earlier about Octavia being here? What happened?" Timothy spun to face her.

"She said her mother had not been home in a few days, but had made a bank deposit recently, yesterday. She didn't seem terribly concerned, but I believe it was the purpose of her visit. She did seem very disappointed to have missed you," she told both men.

"I'll bet," Elgerson muttered. "Nothing else, Rebecca? Was she threatening to you in any way?"

"No," Rebecca sighed. "I think she was being herself, but no threats."

"I don't know what the woman's up to, Tim, but I think it might be a good idea to get some of your men up here to keep an eye on the place until we find out what's going on. I'll get up to the Weintraub place and see what their story is up there."

Rebecca was sure the men did not believe her.

Maybe Bedra was someone else entirely.

"She told me her name was Bedra and she claimed she knew Timothy." She thought about the trip to the shack.

"You must be mistaken, Rebecca. 'Bedra' is a word the locals use. It's Scandinavian, I believe. It means 'idiot'," Timothy mumbled, shaking his head in confusion.

Rebecca pursed her lips in anger and humiliation and choked back her tears.

"Sounds more like Dianna Weintraub all the time," the sheriff remarked.

"Tim, I'm done here. Thank you, Rebecca. I know that this was difficult for you."

"Let me get my horse, Ben," Elgerson blinked to clear his head.

"Don't bother, Tim. I'll get the deputies to go up with me. I think it's best you stay here. I'm not sure why Dianna might be after the girl, but, until we find out, you had better keep an eye on her." Ben was aware that Tim had been drinking heavily. He bid Rebecca farewell as he was leaving.

Timothy refilled his glass and struggled with the information. Dianna Weintraub was an unpleasant woman, but he could imagine no reason why she would attack the girl.

"Rebecca," he barked as she rose from her chair to leave the room, puzzled and exhausted.

"Yes?" She turned to him, embarrassed and ashamed. "Idiot," she thought.

"You can't think of *any* reason why Octavia's mother would want to hurt you? Anything at all?

Even something outrageous?"

"No, I cannot," she whispered, wringing her hands.

"There has to be an explanation, Rebecca. What else did Octavia say to you today?" Elgerson swayed slightly.

"Nothing." She faced him squarely. "I suppose it's because I am an idiot." She fled from the study quickly, her tiny feet barely touching the stairs as she ran for the safety of her room and closed the door.

Timothy gulped his brandy and stormed out to the kitchen in search of his butler. He instructed the man to fetch a few of the farm employees and to post them around the property.

"I'm not sure why," he told the butler. "But there's something fishy going on with the Weintraub group and they're not to be anywhere around Rebecca until the sheriff gets to the bottom of it."

Elgerson stood in the kitchen staring up to the ceiling and, in his belief that Rebecca had more information than she was letting on, decided to question her further.

Chapter Thirty

$\mathcal{R}$ebecca finished changing from her dress into her nightgown and curled up on the bed. She pulled the sheet up to her face and cursed under her breath with words she would never imagine using out loud.

Timothy turned the polished brass knob to her room and found it locked. The blocked passage infuriated him. This was Corissa's general practice and he would not tolerate it again.

"Rebecca, unlock the door."

"Please, go away," she sobbed.

"Damn it, Rebecca, I will not! If you do not unlock this door now I swear I will break it in!" His face was red with anger.

Rebecca was terrified that he might actually do as he had threatened, and, fully aware of the man's physical strength, she scampered across the room, unlocking the door quickly and then stood behind the bed quivering.

He turned the knob slowly at the sound of the freed lock and entered into the darkness, closing the door behind him. Rebecca stood silhouetted against the window, her sheer gown invisible against the filtered moonlight.

"Please…" she whispered, concerned he might hurt her in his obviously drunken state. Having felt the sting of inebriated attacks in her dreadful marriage, she knew better than to instigate the man.

"Rebecca, why?" his toned softened.

"Timothy?" She had to reassure herself that this was not David swaying before her, but instead the kind and generous man that the last weeks had shown her.

"Why do you run from me? What is it that I've done to you? Am I so improper in my behavior that you find me repulsive?"

"Repulsive? Of course not," she replied quietly. How could he imagine that she felt that way? "I think you're wonderful," she admitted, crying quietly in her misery. She felt so charmed by the man and terrified to have him find out what she really was.

"Then why? You pull away. You run from me. Tell me, damn it, what have I done?"

"It's nothing you've done, Tim. It has nothing to do with you at all."

"What then?" She could hear his mood rising. "Damn it all, Rebecca, tell me!" he demanded.

"You know nothing about me. You know nothing about how I came to be here. Please, Timothy. I can't."

"You say that you can't and I don't believe you!" He stepped around the bed boldly, trapping her in the corner. "It's that you won't. You could tell me I disgust you and that would make sense, but you say you can't. Why?" He took her arm firmly and in terror she tried to crawl across the bed.

He caught her efficiently by the ankle, pulling her from the bed and standing her firmly in front of him. He recalled how effectively the petite woman had dispatched him the last time he tangled with her and he eased his grip.

Rebecca stood facing him and ceased her struggling.

Timothy peered down to her sweet face, the tears running down her cheeks and his anger melted away.

"Rebecca," he whispered hoarsely, "it doesn't matter who you are. I don't care. I never have. I don't care." His deep voice trailed off as he held her before him.

Rebecca touched his firm cheek softly and put her hands on his shoulders, as he pulled her to him. She knew him, felt his insisting need for her, and suddenly it didn't matter who she was.

For this moment there was nothing more in the world except his fevered kisses and his unrelenting arms holding her secure and safe from all of her fears. She was no better than a common street walker anyway and it didn't matter how she behaved, or what anyone else thought of her. The only thing that mattered, right now, was the way she felt in his hungry arms.

She felt him pull her tightly against him, his consuming desire pressing against her and she returned his greedy kisses with her own.

His hands were inside of her gown, hot and firm against her back. He kissed her on her neck, her shoulders, and she felt her gown slip from her body.

His lips tasted her, exploring her slowly, and she laid her head back in surrender.

Timothy drank in her sweet beauty, as warm and yielding as when he had seen her lounging on the rock in the sun. He sampled the soft rise of her breasts, taking what he had watched so enticingly the night she stood beside him, beguiling in her laced emerald gown.

He held her away from him unable to believe her compliant surrender in his arms, and looked into her usually unfathomable green eyes, yet there was nothing in her face he did not understand. Her look was inviting and filled with longing for him, and he kissed her firmly.

He whispered her name and she returned with his own.

She felt herself lifted gently and he laid her tenderly across the bed, placing his arms to either side of her, stopping to study her delicate face.

Timothy was sure he was in a dream and any moment reality would interrupt him and he'd awaken alone, or worse, in an instant she would pull away. Instead, she pulled him to her and rolled him gently beside her and she began to undress him slowly.

The enchanting ecstasy of her bold move was more exciting than any experience he'd ever had and she removed his clothing carefully, exposing his full desire for her.

He moved to kiss her and she reclined, her kisses hungry as she pulled him into her, and she arched her back beneath him as they connected in their intimacy.

Rebecca felt him move with her as perfectly as they had danced, each thrust of his desire fulfilling her own. As she felt his shudder she exploded with him in the warm thrill of perfect satisfaction. She moaned as she was overcome with a feeling of complete fulfillment she had never experienced before.

The soft moonlight spread across the two of them as she kissed him feverishly. He stepped out of the bed and wrapped himself in the sheet. He gathered her easily in the blanket and into his arms, taking her down the dark hall and carrying her swiftly to his room, pushing the door closed behind him.

He placed her tenderly on the bed.

"This is where you belong, Rebecca," he whispered and kissed her hungrily as he entered her again.

Chapter Thirty-One

$\mathcal{T}$he sheriff mounted the steps of the Weintraub house shortly after daybreak. He hadn't been by the residence in years and found it run down and sorely in need of a coat of paint. Finn was often about the place doing some fix-up job or another for Dianna, always her rather simple-minded brother forever at her command, but the house looked as though no one had made any sort of repair in several months. The family had never reported him missing, but his employer hadn't seen him in weeks. In a world where men went off to hunt, sometimes for weeks, a missing person could be lost for long stretches before the sheriff's office ever heard from the family. Ben hoped that's all Finn was up to.

He knocked on the door loudly and, after several minutes, Octavia appeared in her robe. Obviously none too happy to see the man, she tried to explain that she was not up to visiting at this particular moment.

"I need to speak to you, Octavia, and it cannot wait."

She led him into the parlor. The house was disheveled and dark.

"If this is about Mother you shouldn't have bothered. She stopped home last night and said her and Uncle Finn were riding out to look at some horses and wouldn't be back for several days."

"Your uncle was with her?"

"That's what she said." Octavia flopped down onto the settee and appeared annoyed.

"Do you know where they were headed?"

"No, I have no idea." Octavia rubbed her eyes, it was clear she wanted to return to her bed.

"Octavia, what do you know about that girl staying out at Timothy's place? Does Dianna know her?"

"Rebecca?" Octavia was suddenly awake.

"Yes." The sheriff found it curious that Octavia would be so interested in the girl.

"I was just out there talking to her. Strange girl, she acts as if she thinks she's the queen or something. I don't think it's proper that she's staying at Stavewood. It's not right that she's up there alone with Timothy."

"Had you or possibly your mother ever met her before?" The sheriff knew that Dianna had been pushing Octavia to marry Elgerson for years, but Octavia's jealously of Rebecca was harmless, he thought. The sheriff was sure she could not possibly imagine herself married to the man.

"No, I never have. I'm certain Mother never did either. She didn't make it to the party you know. Why would Mother have anything whatsoever to do with Rebecca?"

"That's what I'm trying to figure out. Rebecca is staying out at Tim's because she met with some trouble with the train and someone took her off into the woods. There's talk that your mother might know something about that."

Octavia rose suddenly and paced around the room.

"Trouble with the train? Where exactly?"

"Out at Hawk Bend a few weeks back." Sheriff Carson could see Octavia was behaving oddly and continued. "Why? Does that bring anything to mind?"

"Of course not. Don't be silly! I'm just on edge with the robberies and all. Maybe Rebecca was trying to rob the train and she got hurt or something. Mother certainly would have nothing to do with that. Perhaps Rebecca is a train robber!"

Ben Carson knew from experience, that when anyone he suspected started making suggestions as Octavia was now, something was wrong.

He finished questioning the woman, certain that something wasn't quite right, but unsure if she was involved or simply on the fringes of whatever Dianna and Finn were up to.

He informed Octavia that he would need to speak to both Finn and her mother and decided to inquire at some of the surrounding homes to ask if any of the neighboring families had seen anything lately. He left the Weintraub house certain he needed to find Dianna and Finn as quickly as possible.

Chapter Thirty-Two

Rebecca heard activity in the kitchen downstairs and thought it best that she return to her room to dress, having nothing to wear in Timothy's massive bedroom. She studied the room carefully, open and inviting in its magnificent warmth. Unsure of how she might explain her situation, she decided it best to do so fully clothed. If she remained they might never talk and she knew she must tell everything to Timothy. Even with his assurances that her circumstances didn't matter, the man at least had the right to know the whole story.

She slid his solid thigh from across her hip, wrapped herself in a sheet from the foot of the bed, tiptoed to the door, and peered out into the hall. Slipping out quickly, she reached her room, stepped silently inside, and closed the door behind her. Rebecca sighed. Timothy's staff was unlikely to see her at this hour and be aware of her indiscretion, but she feared that Mark and his overnight guest might discover her and she wished to avoid embarrassing explanations.

Rebecca sang in her morning bath, and dressed gaily. She giggled to herself, lost in the perfect memory of the previous night. She pushed her concerns away about divulging her true reasons for having found her way to Stavewood and decided that most certainly Octavia was no longer a part of the picture.

Timothy sat up suddenly in the bed and his head pounded mercilessly. He rubbed his forehead and struggled in confusion. Ben Carson had been there, that much he clearly recalled, and he knew he had drunk far too heavily and that he and Rebecca had fought.

He thought he remembered her running off to her room, but could not recall what had happened that had led up to that. Then he remembered seeing her in his bed, warm and compliant beneath him. Or was she? If she had actually been here and not part of his drunken imagination, where was she now? He searched the bed despite his raging headache and found nothing of hers. He did however find that the sheet was damp and cursed loudly.

It had been a dream. In his cups and frustration over the girl it had all been a dream. After being alone all this time, desire had freed itself from him physically, but not from his mind and he threw the pillow across the room, sending it tumbling into the corner.

"This is ridiculous!" he said loudly. That fool girl had been too much on his mind. If he could not drink away her torture of him, his obsession with her would become uncontrollable. He threw aside the wet sheet and sat painfully on the edge of the bed.

"Timothy Elgerson, you are a fool," he said, aloud, to himself. "If that woman thinks she can leave me to spend my nights dreaming of having her while she denies me at every turn, she is very wrong. She will bewitch me no longer!" He headed for his bath with determination.

At the breakfast table Rebecca was dressed and enjoying her breakfast, her cheeks glowing with pleasure. Elgerson stalked into the room and stared at her angrily.

"Timothy?" she asked, totally bewildered by his mood.

"Haven't you worn that dress once before?" he asked in a raspy voice.

"Yes," she replied, feeling a bit offended by his tone.

"If you need more things to wear I'll get them for you. Since you have decided to refuse me touching you, then at least perhaps you can accept that I dress you to please the eye!" He slammed the door behind him as he left the room.

Rebecca was stunned. Was he still drunk? Why ever would he make such a remark to her after their night together? Suddenly she gasped and her fork fell to the table.

He didn't remember. He had assured her that it didn't matter who she was and made love to her in a drunken state, too inebriated to even recall it.

"You stupid fool!" she called after him.

He heard her voice behind him and turned to have it out with the frustrating female once and for all. He'd show her who the fool was!

"Mister Elgerson!" One of the farm hands called to him, standing out in front of the open stable. "You ought to take a look at this!"

Timothy stood firmly in the doorway to the yard and decided that the impossible Rebecca could goad him no longer. She would not provoke him in any way. He stomped out to the stables.

Rebecca threw her napkin on the table and ran up to her room. "You are impossible, Timothy Elgerson, and I was a fool to imagine you might actually care about me." Rebecca paced the room cursing in her anger. "How dare you take me to your bed in your drunken state and use me like that and not even recall it! I might as well have been a prostitute. Then at least I would have cash and not just these dresses to please your eye!"

She threw open the window to shout out into the yard and saw Timothy standing with a group of men and closed the window quickly in frustration.

"Timothy Elgerson, you are a beast," she hissed through clenched teeth. She wished she had a broader vocabulary with which to curse the man.

She stormed down the hall with determination and found the butler arranging clothing in Timothy's room.

"I would like to post a letter as soon as possible,

could you please tell me how I might go about doing that?" she asked the man irately.

"I can take care of that for you, Miss," The girl always seemed so sweet, but it was apparent she was very perturbed.

"Fine," she stated. "I will prepare a letter immediately. Where might I find the paper to do so?"

In minutes he supplied her with writing materials. Rebecca closed the door to her room and wrote a letter to Emmy requesting that she wire her money at her earliest convenience. An explanation would be given once she had arrived at home. She knew Emma would gladly send her fare and she could leave the impossible Timothy Elgerson behind.

She sealed the envelope and set it upon the writing desk before her.

Overwhelmed with emotion, she began to sob pitilessly. Her anger spilled forth, making her feel frazzled and the night's previous experiences continually came into her mind.

"I did exactly what I promised myself I would not do," she said to herself. "I let myself go to him and what have I got for it? He will go ahead and marry Octavia, although honestly, I can't imagine why. I will go home and have to explain everything to Emmy. I will still have nothing, except debts to her and, of course, you, Timothy Elgerson. I hate you!" She threw herself on the bed, knowing that although she said it out loud, her heart said something else to her. Yet, she could not stay and the thought of the trip home alone terrified her even more, knowing what possibilities it might hold.

Mark passed Rebecca's room trying to see why

the men had gathered outside and tapped quietly.

"Rebecca, is everything okay?"

"I'm fine, Mark. Thank you," she replied, upset that the boy had heard her.

He opened the door slightly and was overcome with concern.

"Rebecca, why are you crying? Please, don't cry. It'll be okay." Mark was so fond of the woman he would do anything to make her happy.

"I'm just sad." She dried her eyes and pulled a shawl about her shoulders.

"Whatever's wrong, we'll fix it. Pa and me. We can fix anything!"

"No, Mark, it's not that simple. As soon as I can make arrangements I will be going home, back to England. I'm sorry."

The boy was devastated. Since Rebecca had arrived, the house was happy again, possibly happier than he ever remembered. His father had shaved, not just for the party, but every day since and he ate regular meals with them. Pa looked happy for the first time. The staff was content with the family home and he believed that if she should go he'd be back out at the cabin, with Stavewood closed up again, and his father rarely around.

"No!" The boy shouted. "You can't leave! I need you to stay!"

Rebecca took the boy by the shoulders and faced him squarely, sighing deeply.

"Mark, I cannot stay. I have to go home. This is your home, but not mine. I don't belong here and I will have to leave. Please try to understand."

"But you do belong here! Since you came here

everyone is happy now. Please, Rebecca, please stay!" He pleaded with her and began to cry, hugging her fiercely and clinging to her pitifully.

"Mark, please." She tried to soothe the boy and stroked his face.

"You're going to leave me just like Mom did, and you'll go away and never come back, just like she did. I heard you and Pa this morning! I know he's mad at you like he was with her. That's why you want to go away. He's making you want to leave like he did with her!" He sobbed violently.

She made the boy look at her and continued.

"Mark, that is not true. Your father did not make her leave. They may have been angry with one another, but what happened to her was an accident. You can't blame your father for that. He loves you and I know your mother did as well!"

The boy pulled away from her and ran down the stairs. Rebecca followed him quickly, wanting desperately to make him understand.

When Mark reached the yard Timothy intercepted him and caught him mid-step, he didn't want the boy anywhere near the stables. It was nothing he wanted the boy to see.

Rebecca ran up behind him and looked at Timothy, who was obviously upset.

"Take him inside, Rebecca," Timothy commanded, and Rebecca knew something was terribly wrong.

'Pa, she's going to leave!" the boy blurted out. "Please Pa, don't make her leave!"

"Mark." The man squatted down to face the boy eye to eye. "We'll talk about it later."

Timothy Elgerson looked up at Rebecca seriously. With the commotion in the barn his mood had changed and he felt his remarks in the morning light had been an overreaction to something the woman knew nothing about. Rebecca stood facing him obviously emotional and concerned, but he had no time to address the problem now.

Rebecca took the hysterical child to his room and sat reading to him until he had dozed off.

Once the boy was sleeping soundly, she slipped quietly from his room and swiftly went out to the barn. A group of men were loading the chestnut onto the back of a wagon. The lifeless animal's throat had been cut and exposed.

Rebecca covered her face in horror and Timothy heard her gasp. He directed the men to cover the animal, put his arm across her shoulders and led her into the yard.

"What happened?" she looked up at him in shock.

"Not sure. Someone went after the horses last night," he replied, looking at Rebecca frankly.

"Where's the other horse?" Rebecca knew that the stable closest to the house held only the chestnut and the huge Arabian.

"I don't know. Both stalls were open and the chestnut was left in the stall. I'm hoping he ran off. He's not easy for anyone, including myself, to handle. It's possible he just broke free. A couple of men are off getting the sheriff. I expect him anyway with news of Octavia and her mother.

"Rebecca, I need you to stay as close to the house as possible, and I don't want you anywhere outside unless one of the men is with you. I'm sorry for my mood this morning. I had a bad night and I guess I wasn't myself."

Rebecca looked at him searchingly. He clearly had no memory of them together and she suddenly felt less infuriated and something more tragic. As she watched his worried face and the concern in his eyes and listened to his genuine apology with no memory of their night together, her face grew serious. Rebecca admitted to herself, clearly for the first time, that she was in love with the man and she felt her heart breaking.

"I'm sorry. I don't want to trap you here. Mark said you wanted to leave and you are free to do that when this has all blown over if you like." He stopped mid-sentence and looked into her eyes. Timothy struggled to continue. "But, right now I think it's best you wait. Whoever went after those horses may have meant it for a message and I'm afraid they may be after you."

What was it he saw in her eyes? Disappointment, because she felt trapped? No, it was something else. He found himself wanting her again and struggled to clear his head. His stomach lurched and his head pounded and, if he wasn't mistaken, the woman looked at him as though she felt something for him. "No. That's impossible," the man thought. She turned him down at every advance. When this was all straightened out he'd let her go and, in time, the torment would cease.

"I understand, Tim," she replied without hesitation. "You have enough to think about without worrying about me." She gathered her skirt and walked back to the house slowly.

He watched her delicate steps as she crossed the lawn, wondering why she wouldn't let him care for her. Why did she keep him away? More pieces of his dream floated back to him, as they had forced their way in all morning, despite the horse, and he wanted more than anything that the dream had been reality, but it was not.

Sheriff Carson and two deputies arrived to witness Timothy Elgerson observing the girl cross the lawn and dismounted from their horses. The entire county was buzzing with gossip about the handsome Timothy Elgerson and his beautiful visitor, the lawmen's wives included. They waited for the man to notice them and he turned and strode towards them with obvious concern on his face.

"Your men told us about the horse. What the hell is happening here, Tim?" the sheriff asked.

"Someone got to them during the night I suspect. The Arabian is missing and they cut the chestnut's throat." Elgerson's voice cracked. It was widely known what the horse had meant to him.

"I'm sorry, Tim. It was a fine and beautiful animal." Carson struggled for the right words.

"What happened at Weintraub's?" Timothy could not think of the chestnut right now.

"Let's take a look at that horse first." Ben Carson was still going over Octavia's possible involvement in his mind. He just didn't think the woman had anything directly to do with Rebecca's kidnapping, but he felt that she knew more than she had let on.

The two men walked back out into the yard and Carson related his conversation with Octavia to Timothy.

"I just don't think she had any idea what I was talking about until I mentioned the station at Hawk Bend, and then I knew something was not right, Tim. I have to figure she knew somehow that the girl was out there. Maybe someone mentioned seeing Rebecca out there. I'm just not sure. It was plain to me that if she had any information she didn't know it involved Rebecca until I talked to her."

"So you are thinking that Dianna and Finn were involved?" Elgerson wasn't sure he was comfortable with the fact that Ben had possibly given information to Octavia. He liked and admired the sheriff immensely, but didn't always agree with his methods.

"Hardly seems possible. But I have to say I'm leaning more that way all the time. It looks as if Dianna was around last night and had Finn with her, although Octavia never actually saw him. She told her they were riding out to take a look at some horses."

Timothy looked hard at the sheriff, uncomfortable with the implication of the remark.

"I had the same thought, Tim," Carson replied, as if reading Elgerson's mind.

"I'm taking a ride back over that way now to see if any of the neighbors saw Dianna and Finn. I'll let you know what I turn up."

Ben Carson rode away from Stavewood at a quick gallop and Elgerson stood watching the man in exhaustion, and then went into the stable to dispose of the horse.

$\mathcal{R}$ebecca sat in her room staring at the letter to Emmy, struggling in indecision. If she stayed at Stavewood until the mystery of her kidnapping was solved, as Timothy requested, she would then be here when they discovered the truth about her. Although her frustration with the man had not been resolved, she tried to put it aside and look at the situation clearly.

If she left Stavewood now, as quickly as possible, perhaps the threat they all faced would simply go away. She decided not to post the letter, and write another. In the evening she would approach Timothy and ask to borrow passage from him. She would ask only what she required to make the trip. She reasoned with herself that she had survived the trip from England with little more than the cost of the tickets, and therefore could return in a similar fashion. She would ask for as little as possible. If she could make him understand that her remaining at Stavewood was a threat, he might agree and she would travel back to England.

Rebecca was overcome with a hollow feeling at the thought of leaving the beautiful home she had grown to love. She decided to check on Mark and perhaps try to make him understand before she approached Timothy.

She gathered up her feelings of hopelessness and walked along the hall, listening to the disconsolate sound of her own footsteps and entered the boy's room.

Mark was no longer sleeping on the bed and, thinking he might have gotten hungry, Rebecca went down to the kitchen to find him, checking Timothy's room and the study on the way. Unable to locate the boy, she looked out into the yard and then returned to the upper floor by the back stairs and called to him. She did not receive an answer so she called throughout the main floor. When he did not reply she became concerned that he may have gone out to the stables in search of his father, but as she crossed the yard she was overcome with a feeling of dread and quickened her pace.

Reaching the barn, breathing rapidly, she found Timothy tying a tarp over the chestnut on the wagon and tried to calm herself, not wanting to sound panicked.

He looked up and could see her concern.

"What's wrong?" He stood up and studied her face.

"I took Mark inside after he was so upset and waited until he had fallen asleep. I went to check on him but I can't find him anywhere."

As Timothy raced across the yard to the house, Rebecca struggled to follow him, explaining that she had called throughout the house and he hadn't replied.

Elgerson bellowed for the boy, stopping the cook in the kitchen and questioning the maids he found dusting the upstairs rooms. When Mark did not answer he ran out of the front door and began to call the boy's name loudly from every direction surrounding the house. Rebecca checked every closet and hiding place in the main areas of the home that she thought he might have hidden away in, while listening to Timothy's unanswered calls. She tried to put away the vision of the slain chestnut and fear gripped her tightly.

Timothy ran back into the house, checking with her before sprinting out into the barn. With the stallion missing and the mare dead, he yelled back to Rebecca that he was going out to the stables to look for the boy there and would return with horses.

Rebecca stood in the yard and tried to imagine where Mark might have gotten to, preferring to think that he had simply gone off somewhere to hide, disappointed with her talk about leaving.

She dashed back into the house and instructed the staff to continue to search anywhere the boy might have hidden himself again and hurried to the creek where she had gone when she wanted to think.

As she searched the banks and frantically called him she began to blame herself for his disappearance. Whether he was hiding or had run away, or the terrifying possibility that someone had taken him, it all came back to her. Whoever might be after her may have taken the boy. Her thoughts were overwhelming.

When she heard horses in the direction of the house she ran through the brush towards the house where Timothy had returned with Ben Carson and his men, but not Mark.

Elgerson wondered if the boy may have headed

for the cabin and the sheriff and deputies decided to scout the woods since it was likely he was traveling on foot.

"What if he's not on foot, Tim? What if he's not left on his own?" Rebecca stood beside the stomping horses and looked up to him, her face pale with worry.

Timothy looked down at her, terrified at the thought and the men decided that only one man should check close to the house while the others widened their range. Rebecca stood wringing her hands frantically beside the horses.

"We'll find him," Timothy tried to assure himself as well as the anxious, young woman.

Rebecca rushed back to the house and changed from her inhibiting dress into the clothing she had arrived in. She returned to the woods surrounding Stavewood, calling for the boy until her throat was raw. She could hear the deputy call out Mark's name occasionally in the distance and the sound of Birget's frantic cries for the child kept her from losing her bearings in the deepening shadows of the thick woods. It occurred to her that the decision had been made that she stay close to the house, but thought that perhaps if someone had taken Mark and found her instead, they may let him go.

When she was no longer able to see into the thick woodland she made her way back to the house, stopping along the way to catch her breath and hoarsely call out for Mark.

Lacking any more ideas of how she could possibly find him, she returned to the house and inspected every room and under every piece of furniture again. She spoke to Mark throughout her search, begging him to appear, pleading that, if he were merely hiding, he might emerge.

Birget stood at the bottom of the stairs, listening to Rebecca's wretched pleas and crying into her apron, sick with worry.

Hours passed as Rebecca went between calling raspingly out into the yard and beseeching the boy all through the house until the staff thought they could no longer bear her desolate calls. Rebecca collapsed in the hall, begging for him to show himself, but no answer came from the missing child.

Birget begged her to try to eat something, but Rebecca refused and went out to search the stables again.

As morning dawned, a jagged chill in the air, Rebecca drug herself back to the house, having searched every crevice and building surrounding Stavewood. She collapsed into the kitchen chair.

Birget stood behind the devastated girl and held her shoulders while Rebecca wept with worry and exhaustion. The cook put a plate of steaming soup before her, but she only looked past it, trying to think of someplace she had overlooked.

Regular knocks could be heard at the main door, right after sunrise, as news of the missing boy spread throughout the territory and volunteers arrived to help search for Mark. At noon Octavia arrived, nervous and behaving oddly and wanted only to see Timothy. The butler sent her to the parlor in the rush of the arrival of concerned neighbors and friends.

Rebecca busied herself in the kitchen where she

found it easier to be distracted working with the swarm of concerned neighbors. She retrieved a large map from the wall in the study and spread it out over the kitchen table, examining it carefully and marking out the surrounding property. It had become apparent to her that it would be pointless for all of the volunteers to search for the boy without direction, possibly missing him in the confusion, and she began dispatching each group to cover a particular area.

In the chaotic kitchen Rebecca made sure Birget prepared gallons of coffee to warm the returning search parties and saw to it that each departing group knew exactly which area had not yet been searched.

Each time a band of men returned with no news her heart fell, and, as the covered areas began to expand on the map, her fear increased.

The sun set too quickly, allowing the temperature to fall still further and whispers of concern over the threat of frost began among the men gathered outside.

When Timothy arrived he passed the neighbors in the yard shaking his head in silent despair. He stood in the kitchen doorway, watching Rebecca, her face filthy and exhausted, as she directed the next search party to an area to cover.

She looked up as she was dispatching the men and met his tortured gaze. His face was pale and ragged and his shoulders were slumped in pain. He approached her and studied the map beside her, leaning to support himself on the counter at the realization of how massive an area had been covered with no results.

Rebecca grasped his arm firmly, directing a man beside her to take over and led Elgerson, senseless with exhaustion, to the study. She poured a liberal amount of brandy in a large goblet and handed it to him.

"Drink it, Timothy," she instructed him firmly. "You have a lot of friends doing everything that can be done. They'll find him, I'm sure."

He looked up at her, deep circles beneath his tortured eyes and his cheeks hollow and ashen.

"Rebecca," he whispered huskily. He drained the brandy in one deep gulp and buried his head in his hands.

She stood in front of him, her heart breaking, and took the glass from him. Silently she refilled it and set it beside him.

Octavia entered the room from across the foyer, impatient with being left alone in the parlor, and stood in the doorway watching them.

Timothy grabbed Rebecca by her hips and began to sob violently and the girl bent and wrapped her arms around his shoulders, silently sharing his fear.

Octavia Weintraub turned abruptly and strode out to her carriage, whipping her horses to a swift gallop. She had a suspicion where her mother might be and rushed to find the woman.

Chapter Thirty-Four

*A*fter delicate prodding and a bit more brandy, Rebecca was able to direct Timothy up the stairs and laid him out on the bed, removing his heavy boots and riding clothes. In the dark of the previous night together she had never seen the man disrobed and could not help noticing his muscular, rugged physique. She covered him warmly and, after checking the procedures in the kitchen, instructed the butler to add wood to the fireplace in Timothy's room.

She returned to her own room, bathed quickly and changed into a clean dress. She hoped the bath would revive her, and that a break might supply her with a new plan. Back in the kitchen, a volunteer's knock was unheard by the busy staff and Rebecca pulled open the entry.

A brightly dressed woman, her bonnet flushing with feathers stood nervously on the porch.

"I was wondering if there was something I could do. I heard about the boy disappearing and thought that if I could help in any way at all." The woman, however striking, was obviously quite uneasy, and she looked from side to side past Rebecca apprehensively before addressing her directly.

"Please excuse me." She offered a silken-gloved hand as Rebecca invited her in.

"I know you may not want me here, but I just felt that I had to try."

Rebecca appreciated anyone who was kind

enough to help them locate Mark. She thanked the woman, grasping her hand warmly.

"Hello, I'm Rebecca. Timothy is finally getting a moment of rest and I'm sure there's something you can do."

"Oh, thank you. I want so badly to do something to help. My name is Bess Rival. It certainly is a pleasure to meet you!" Bess shook Rebecca's hand vigorously.

Rebecca led Bess to the kitchen, thinking that the woman certainly looked capable enough to take over the coffee preparation so that Birget might have a break.

As the kitchen door swung open and she led Bess Rival into the room all conversations fell silent. A few of the men cleared their throats and Birget gasped loudly.

Rebecca directed Bess through the hushed kitchen, unsure of exactly how to address the obviously concerned crowd. She instructed Birget to allow Miss Rival to take over, and then to take a much needed break.

Birget grabbed Rebecca by the hand and pulled her to the pantry.

"What on earth is going on here?" Rebecca had no patience for the indifferent greeting Birget had given the woman.

"Rebecca, how dare you bring that woman into the house!" Birget was frantic.

"Who is she?" Rebecca asked impatiently.

"Why she's the Madam!" Birget gasped.

"The Madam? Whatever are you talking about?"

"The Madam. She runs the saloon in Billington."

"Well then I expect if she runs a saloon she certainly is capable of making coffee."

"No, no." Birget looked back over her shoulder. "It's got whores!"

Enlightened, Rebecca understood the group's behavior, but suspected the men's reaction meant something very different than Birget's had, especially since Bess Rival was a very stunning woman. She didn't know much about the woman's profession but decided that Bess had seemed genuine in her offer to help and any offer of assistance should be accepted.

"I understand your concern, Birget, and perhaps at any other time this might be a problem, but this is not the time. If Bess Rival wants to help us find Mark, I will not refuse her kindness. If there's even a chance that one thing can help us find the boy, how can I refuse her offer? We're all exhausted with worry. Birget please help the woman find what she needs and try to get a little rest."

The plump woman listened and reluctantly agreed, although uncomfortable with the situation. She returned to the kitchen and instructed the Madam before making her way quietly upstairs.

Bess Rival's presence in the kitchen seemed much more easily accepted by the men once they saw Rebecca's practical approach to the Madam and the serving of coffee resumed.

Bess watched Rebecca move with command among the turmoil, directing men easily twice her size, despite her obvious fatigue and worry. Bess had heard talk of Rebecca's presence at Timothy's and the rumors of her beauty. Rebecca certainly was stunning, and Bess admitted to herself, probably perfect for Timothy Elgerson. Rebecca's attempts to stop at nothing to find Timothy's boy only illustrated further that she belonged here. Bess Rival sighed in resignation, her bright gown behind a white apron, in the kitchen at Stavewood, filling cups. There was no question in her mind that, however it had come about, Timothy Elgerson had the woman he had long needed right under his nose.

Chapter Thirty-Five

ℛebecca checked the progress on the map once again, finding that the man she had left in charge was quite competent and she climbed the stairs in exhaustion to check on Timothy.

She found him sitting on the bed, head in his hands when she walked into the room.

"Any news?" He looked up at her, his face drawn and haggard and overcome with fatigue.

"Not yet," she whispered, as he pulled a sheet across his bare lap.

"Who undressed me?" He looked at her with one brow lifted.

"You needed some sleep."

Rebecca searched the room for clean clothing and

prepared a bath.

"This will help you feel better." She led him to the room and helped him lower his tortured body into the steaming water.

"I don't know where he could have gone," he choked as she rinsed his limp arm. "Where could he possibly be?"

"They'll find him, Tim. I'm sure. He ran off. Boys do that sometimes. They'll find him just fine." Her reassurances did nothing to help her alleviate her own fears, but seemed to calm Timothy's agony somewhat.

"Lay your head back," she whispered and lathered his thick mane thoroughly.

He felt her gentle, kind touch and thanked her softly as she rinsed him carefully and began to dry him slowly.

"I'm alright," he said taking the towel from her and Rebecca left him to dress.

Bathing the distraught man left her feeling drained and weak and she went to her room, but could not bring herself to lie on the bed. Too exhausted to pace any longer she sat beside the window and looked around the room. She heard his heavy footsteps as Timothy passed her door and descended the stairs. She absently reached to move the basket of yarn that she had left too close to the rocker, spilling the skeins of yarn, a small puff of dust landing on her shoe.

She leapt to her feet suddenly.

"The attic!"

She ran from her room to the back staircase and scrambled up the stairs frantically.

Racing down the hall she threw open the door to

the attic and stopped immediately. Her footsteps from her previous visit remained, faint in the pale dust, and another pair lie beside them.

She called out, but decided it was best to check the attic before going for help. The footprints were everywhere and she spun frantically, trying to discern where they led, calling the boy hysterically.

A single set of footsteps ended beside a massive trunk and Rebecca rushed to it and fought open the heavy lid.

There, amid the soft folds of stored clothing, the boy lay in a tight ball. His face was bright red and Rebecca found that the lid would not stay open without her support. Terrified that closing the lid might worsen his obviously poor condition, she struggled out of her shoe and, using one foot, pushed it into the trunk's hinge. She tested to see that it had propped up one side, wriggled out of the other shoe wildly and shoved it into the other side.

It was impossible for her to lift the boy from the trunk. She reached inside and felt his face, his body temperature was perilously high, and she ran down the hall, calling for help and throwing open rooms until she found one with an adjoining bath and turned on the faucet.

For a moment she heard only air and prayed that the faucet was connected as it spat a rush of cold water. She soaked the linens, carried them dripping to the trunk and placed them around the boy, under his limp arms and across his forehead. She pulled his boots and stockings off hastily and slapped the soles of his feet.

When she saw him stir she patted his cheek

firmly, calling his name and begging him to respond.

"Rebecca?" he whispered, barely opening his eyes.

She held him to her, flooded with relief, and pushed the wet hair from his face. She continued in vain to call for help, afraid to leave the boy in the precariously propped trunk as tears ran down her cheeks.

Chapter Thirty-Six

$\mathcal{T}$imothy reached the foot of the immense staircase and stood outside the kitchen door listening. He could hear the men discussing the search and was overcome with grief. They had searched what they agreed was a large area. Beginning to fear the worst, he turned and walked to the study.

He wracked his brain, trying to imagine what else he could possibly do. They had searched everywhere, and yet had not found the boy. He had known there was a threat and it had never considered to him that Mark was in any danger. But, if he had run away it had to be because of his conversation with Rebecca about her leaving. Either way, Timothy felt he was responsible.

He climbed the stairs to go over the conversation she had had with the boy, but found her room vacant.

On the floor, in a perfectly orderly room, the yarn lay spilled out beside the overturned basket.

Timothy Elgerson sprinted for the third floor.

As he reached the top of the stairs he heard her cries, begging frantically for help and he dashed toward the open attic doorway. Rebecca recognized his approaching steps and called louder.

Timothy bounded up the stairs and rushed to the chest, lifting the boy out quickly and squatting to the floor, the boy sagging in his arms.

Mark opened his eyes and whispered, "I wanted to be near Mom."

Timothy and Rebecca sat speechless, and Elgerson carried the boy, dripping wet, but alive, down the back stairs to the kitchen. As he entered the room through the most direct route in the house, the crowd in the kitchen rushed to help. Rebecca sent two men to get the doctor as Timothy took the boy up the main staircase to the second floor.

Several men rode out to gather the search parties and Rebecca grabbed a pitcher of cool water on her way to follow Timothy.

As the boy's temperature began to normalize he became more coherent and Timothy and Rebecca changed the boy into dry pajamas. When he complained that Rebecca was in the room as he was being changed, both Timothy and Rebecca laughed in relief.

Rebecca dried her tears and covered her eyes while Timothy finished helping the boy change.

"Were you looking?" Mark asked weakly.

"If you are so concerned that I was peeking," she remarked, "then you must be fine."

Timothy Elgerson walked out into the hall as Birget arrived, hugging the boy ferociously. Rebecca followed Timothy silently, and stood beside him. He turned to her solemnly and pulled her to him, clinging to her fiercely.

Chapter Thirty-Seven

*W*ith a clean bill of health from the doctor, and Rebecca's discovery of the large mouse hole in the attic trunk that had allowed air into the big chest and spared the boy's life, Stavewood settled down that evening.

Rebecca thanked each volunteer profusely while Timothy talked to the men in the yard. She noticed through the large front windows that he thanked Bess Rival genuinely and walked her to her carriage. Although the boy had been in the house all along, Rebecca felt that the support Timothy had received from his friends and neighbors made the search for the boy bearable, and she marveled at how well he must be liked for everyone to show such profound concern.

When David had died the circumstances were terrible, yet only Emmy had come to share Rebecca's grief. She was glad that Timothy had such a large group to support him. Rebecca wondered however, what had become of Octavia.

After Rebecca and Birget had fed Mark a hearty supper, Ben Carson arrived, and Timothy and the sheriff met in the study. They closed the door behind them, leaving Rebecca concerned over their conversation and she went up to her room for a hot bath.

She dressed for bed and shook the dust from the yarn out the window into the night air and began to cast stitches rhythmically onto the needles. Too overwrought to consider sleeping just yet, and worried about the reason for Timothy's meeting with Ben, she hoped a few rows would relax her so that she could get some needed rest.

Timothy had turned to her, without reservation, to pour out his relief once the boy was found, and Rebecca could not ignore the feelings from the emotional exchange.

Her conscience nagged at her and she realized that, had she been honest with the man and admitted her reason for coming to the territory, none of this might have happened. If they had all known who she was, instead of being here now she would have returned straight away to England and perhaps the boy would have been less distraught. It was her presence here that had caused so much heartbreak. Timothy and Mark deserved to know the truth.

After knitting several rows, working steadily in the round, she decided that, first thing in the morning, she would tell Timothy the truth, unless, of course, he was finding it out right now.

"I hate to bring this to you after the day you've had Tim, but it just can't wait." The sheriff stood facing the fireplace.

Timothy sat exhausted in the leather chair hearing the man out, certain that sleep would elude him even if he were to try to rest.

"While we were out looking for your boy today we came across Finn Morgan." Ben Carson cleared his throat.

"What did he say about Rebecca?" Elgerson rose from his chair and approached the man.

"Finn won't be saying much anymore, Tim. We found him up past the old mills with his throat cut from ear to ear."

Timothy stepped back in shock and disbelief.

"Who would do such a thing? First the horse and then this? But why?" His nerves frazzled, Timothy paced the room running his hands through his hair.

"That's not all, Tim. I think you ought to have a look at this. Maybe you can help me sort this out."

He handed Timothy a crumpled bundle of papers and Elgerson spread them on the desk and braced himself against the desktop.

There were receipts for train tickets, ship's passage, and one for the coach from St. Paul. There were first class tickets that were stamped *returned*, with receipts for third class tickets bearing the same time and date. The more costly tickets were purchased by T. Elgerson. The cheaper tickets had been purchased by F. Morgan. All of them were issued to R. Fagan.

"Tim, where did you send these tickets? It looks like Morgan cashed them in for cheaper ones and pocketed the difference, I guess."

Elgerson's shoulders sank.

"I posted an ad for a mail order bride, Ben," Timothy admitted. "I got it in my head that, if I could get a woman out here to take care of Mark, it'd make him happier somehow. I thought that the women who answered those types of ads might be down on their luck. I can easily take care of someone, and she could possibly be a mother to the boy. It seemed like a reasonable idea at the time. I bought the tickets at the Hawk Bend Station from Finn."

Ben Carson sighed. The thought had crossed his mind that his friend had sent for someone, possibly a woman, but he could not fathom any reason Tim would do such a thing.

"What became of her, Tim?"

"I have no idea, Ben. I haven't heard from her," he said, running his fingers through his hair. "I checked the stop in Billington, but she never arrived. I suppose she might have been late, and I sent an awful lot of cash with those tickets. Maybe Finn took that as well. For all I know she never left. That's a hell of a long trip to make without plenty of money."

Ben Carson stroked his jaw, considering what fate might have befallen a woman traveling alone, especially in light of the recent developments. "It just doesn't sit right with me that Morgan would exchange these tickets, Tim. I've known that fella since he was just a kid. Sure, he wasn't the brightest of men but, I don't think he was a thief."

Timothy gathered himself and faced the sheriff.

"I do have an idea who might have exchanged the tickets and maybe a reason why," Ben continued. "You know, Tim, that Dianna had been pushing that girl of hers on you for years. Maybe she got it in her fool head that she'd exchange the tickets, hold back the travel money, and maybe keep the woman from coming. I was out at the house the other day and the place looks mighty run down. Maybe she could have used the money too. Do you think it's possible that somehow she was up at Hawk Bend the night Rebecca got off the train and figured that Rebecca was your mail order bride because of her accent?"

Timothy looked at the man's face and considered the possibility. Dianna Weintraub was a rough woman, and she liked control of anything and everyone around her. There was only one thing she wanted above everything else, and that was to marry off her spoiled daughter.

The woman honestly believed that Octavia, though as big as a farm mule, was a rare beauty and would make a great catch someday. Octavia had put on a massive amount of weight, and was quickly passing marrying age. Maybe Dianna was feeling desperate. Timothy found it hard to accept she would attack Rebecca so brutally, but it would explain many things.

"I know she wanted to marry Octavia off pretty badly, but this sounds pretty desperate, even for Dianna. I know she never had any patience with her brother, but to kill him? It seems outrageous." Timothy didn't much like the woman, but this was an awful lot to suppose.

"Does it, Tim? You've seen Octavia the last year. I'd think marrying her off might be near impossible these days. Dianna's one of the most bull-headed people I've ever met. The more I think about it, the more it makes sense. It's the only reason I can come up with that she'd go after the girl that way."

"Ben, she left her for dead. I'm certain of that. Do you really think that Dianna is capable of doing all these things, just to marry off Octavia?" Timothy could not accept the horrifying theory.

"Well, there's something funny there too. When I talked to Octavia she seemed fine, you know, bored like she can be with everything. But, as soon as the subject of the Hawk Bend station came up, she showed an awful lot of interest. I think that Octavia knew something had happened up there. I don't think she knew it was Rebecca though, until I brought it up."

"Why kill the horse, Ben?"

"Well, Tim, I'm still working on that one. I know that you've had dealings with Dianna and have known her for years. One of the things I've learned while being sheriff around here is that folks you'd never imagine are sometimes capable of unpredictable things. It'd explain an awful lot, Tim. Just think about it.

"Listen, you've had a hell of a day. Get yourself some rest and I'll stop by tomorrow. I just didn't want you to hear about Finn before we talked. You take care, and keep that boy and Rebecca close, until we figure all this out."

Ben Carson gathered up his hat and, concerned with his friend's haggard appearance, patted Timothy on the shoulder and then let himself out.

Chapter Thirty-Eight

$\mathcal{T}$imothy Elgerson stood beside the open fireplace in his immense study trying to make sense of Ben's theories and the recent events in his life. Fighting exhaustion and feeling drained, he pulled out the bottle of fine brandy and sat it on the mantle. Deciding that the powerful liquor might help him sleep, but not bring him clarity, he set the bottle back on the tray and walked to the kitchen to survey the yard and take a look at the stables.

If he were to agree with the sheriff's speculations, much of what had gone on seemed to fall into place. Not all of it, but more than he was ready to accept. He had to admit to himself that there was always something about Dianna Weintraub that had left him uneasy around the woman, but he had continually attributed his feelings to the woman's incessant pressure to convince him to have some attraction to Octavia.

He often felt pity for the girl. Since childhood she had been an awkward, sloppy girl, never seen as attractive by anyone of the opposite sex. Dianna's obsessive love of her daughter had driven her to push the girl into situations that only made Octavia open for further rejection and ridicule. Dianna wanted her to sing, and had invested heavily in lessons for the girl. She enrolled Octavia in charm schools and art lessons, and at one time arranged for the girl to travel overseas to study ballet.

Octavia accepted her mother's opinions without any of her own, remaining uninterested and untalented throughout the endless exposure to the best education. An uninspired child, Octavia went through life accepting her mother's ambitions for her and never developing into the cultured beauty Dianna struggled to create.

Over time, as the girl showed no promise of improvement and began to gain weight, it was as if Dianna began to panic and reasoned that, if she could only find Octavia a successful husband, the girl would be cared for. Dianna began shifting her ambitions from educating the girl, to pushing her into provocative necklines and attending social events throughout the territory. She introduced Octavia to every unmarried landowner, regardless of his age or appearance.

After the death of Corissa, Octavia formed the one opinion she had developed on her own and decided that Timothy Elgerson was the man for her. Unable to deny the girl anything, and frantic to find her a suitable mate, Dianna became determined to give her daughter what she wanted.

Had she become so obsessed that she would kill poor Finn and abduct a complete stranger, leaving her for dead? Timothy shuddered at the terrifying thought.

All his reasoning brought him back to the same conclusion. Every event surrounding Rebecca's kidnapping seemed to fall into place, with the exception of the slain chestnut and Finn's murder. If Dianna had gone after Rebecca because of her daughter and if she had discovered he had ordered a bride, then he was responsible for what had happened to Rebecca.

He reasoned that, by being too blind to see the ramifications, Dianna had become dangerous in her obsession and the woman he had sent for had become a target. Rebecca then was an innocent victim of mistaken identity, taken and abused, and nearly killed due to his carelessness.

He stood staring into the night, realizing that he had brought Rebecca to Stavewood as well. Instead of sensibly sending her on to continue her travels, he had brought her here to unimaginable danger. He felt responsible for the girl. He had attacked her himself, believing she was a thief. He had considered that she had something to do with the robberies of the train. Then he had become enamored with her. He cursed himself for his selfishness. No wonder the girl was less than receptive to his advances.

Timothy blamed himself for all of it. Every step of the way he never really considered Rebecca's real situation.

"Always the fool, eh?" he muttered to himself.

Timothy Elgerson knew he had to tell Rebecca the truth.

Chapter Thirty-Nine

*R*ebecca listened for Timothy's footsteps on the stairs, and, as the minutes ticked by and the sock took shape in her agile hands, she became more concerned.

She wanted to have the opportunity to explain the situation to Timothy herself. If Timothy found out from Ben why she had come here he might not allow her to tell him from her point of view.

"I suppose it doesn't matter," she stated quietly to herself. "When he knows it won't matter how he found out."

Emotional and anxious, she abruptly set her knitting aside and stood at the window to stare out into the blackness of the night. Seeing only her own tortured reflection she began to pace the room.

She battled with how she might explain herself, should she have the opportunity. How would she justify the fact that she never admitted she was simply a fool who had answered a deceptive advertisement and traveled halfway around the world only to find a man who had no need for her?

Instead of disclosing from the beginning why she had been on the train and accepting her situation, she had carried on a charade that only compounded her lie at every turn. If she had explained why she came, even to Mark when he found her, the boy probably knew about that man's bet and would have told her long ago. If she had paid any attention to the train stops, the cryptic ad, had even heard the Elgerson name at some earlier time while with the man, if she had not been such a fool, she would not be here now.

Now, she had taken so much from this man, and had never been forthright with him. She had accepted his home and his clothing, and most important his kindness. She had driven his son to the brink of death. She had even made love to the man. It was no excuse that he did not recall their night together because she did, and quite vividly. How could she imagine she had the right to love him when everything was a lie?

If Timothy already knew he would certainly put her out, or worse, allow her to remain in her shame. The thought that he might be finding out who she really was at this moment was more than she could bear.

Not caring that her nightgown and robe were not appropriate attire, Rebecca stumbled into the hall and sped down the main stairs.

The study doors stood open, the room unoccupied. Rebecca froze. She took a deep breath and went to find Timothy to face her situation once and for all.

Chapter Forty

$\mathcal{R}$ebecca walked through the kitchen door, finding Timothy racked with fatigue and staring out into the night.

He was in no shape to be confronted by her, or, if he did not already know, to accept her explanations, but she knew her lie could not go on any longer.

"Timothy," she whispered timidly, her eyes brimming with tears. He did not turn and face her.

She filled the teapot and searched the pantry for tea. When she had gathered her ingredients she set out two cups in anticipation to begin.

"Rebecca, you should get some sleep." His tone was distant.

"I cannot sleep. Timothy I..." her words caught in her throat.

"The search parties found Finn Morgan today." The big man fought with his resolve, staring at nothing.

"Then the sheriff spoke to him." Rebecca was certain he knew.

"The man was dead, Rebecca." He turned and faced her.

Rebecca exhaled and her hands flew to her face. Finn was dead! They all had to know, and now! It didn't matter where he heard it, he had to know now.

"Oh, Timothy, I am so terribly sorry." Rebecca was beyond tears.

"It's not your fault, Rebecca. Please sit down."

"But it is. Oh, Timothy. I'm so sorry. The man was kind to me. You have been so kind. I'm so, so sorry what happened with Mark. It's entirely my fault. I don't even know how to explain, but I need to make you understand! If I'd never have come here none of this would have happened this way!"

"Rebecca!" he cut her off firmly. "Listen to me, please. I know how all of it happened. I need you to listen to me now." His voice was clear and unwavering.

Rebecca braced herself against the table, trying to prepare herself for whatever he decided to do with her. She would not interrupt, she could not apologize. Whatever he had decided she would have to accept.

"I suppose I should begin with this," he pulled the ticket receipts from his shirt pocket and set them on the counter before her.

Rebecca took a deep breath and studied the documents, going back and forth between the copies of the tickets, familiar to her, yet something was very wrong.

After several moments she looked up in confusion. They were receipts of her travel tickets, but there were two. One set was duplicates of what she carried, but the other was first class. She had never received first class tickets. Was he trying to tell her that the joke of the gambling bet was intended somehow to be less cruel? That when the pranksters had originally set out their pretense they had purchased better tickets? It was plain now that Timothy knew she was a picture bride, that was evident, but why two sets of tickets?

Rebecca stammered in shame and uncertainty. Did he want an explanation? Dare she ask why there were two sets? Her hands began to shake and she stared at him in fear and confusion.

Elgerson began to pace, running his hands through his hair and trying to find the right words.

He leaned across the high table and faced her squarely.

"When Corissa died the world seemed to end, Rebecca." He was addressing her in an intense, serious tone and Rebecca fought the overwhelming desire to run.

"I could not face her death, but Mark fared even worse. The boy hardly ate. He cried constantly. I could find no way to appease him. She was his mother, and I was simply the man she had married." Timothy leaned back slightly.

Rebecca stood transfixed, knowing it was all her fault that the boy had become attached to her, and awaited her fate.

"I tried to find a way, any way to care for him," the exasperated man continued. "I decided that if he had a woman around, someone to take care of him, it might be better for him." He began to pace back and forth in the room.

Rebecca was lost. What was he saying? She stood completely still.

"I arranged a mail order bride, Rebecca, for the boy. I thought I could help her out and find someone to care for him. Heaven knows that I was not able to do the job!"

Rebecca was dumbfounded. He *had* sent for her, perhaps not for the reasons she imagined, but he had sent for her himself! Her mind raced, trying to make sense of what he was saying.

"It's my fault you were abducted, Rebecca!" he shouted, facing her. "They must have taken you from the train station because of your accent, thinking you were the woman I ordered. Dianna found out, I assume through Finn, that I had ordered a bride. In her attempt to intercept her, Dianna must have heard your voice somehow and decided you were the woman I had sent for and taken you. Don't you see, Rebecca that everything that has happened is because of me?"

"Timothy, no!" she screamed. "No! It's not because of you! No!" Her face flushed with frustration and it all began to make sense.

"Yes, Rebecca! Don't you see? I set her up. I set you up with my fool plan to help the boy. It was me, Rebecca! I might as well have been the one who left you up there to die myself!" He rounded the corner of the table and stood face to face with her, trying to make her understand and knowing she might run before he could make himself clear.

"Timothy, you are dead wrong!" She met him with equal demand.

He stepped back and softened his tone. "I'm sorry Rebecca, please stay and hear me out."

"No Timothy! I have heard enough and now you have to listen to me!" Her heart pounded and her mind raced. She was not afraid any longer and she had to make him see that he was wrong.

"Timothy there was no mistake on the woman's part. You ordered a bride to help you take care of your son. You ordered her yourself and apparently bought expensive tickets for her travel? It was no joke? Not a mail ordered bride over a bet?" Rebecca held her breath.

"A bet? What on earth are you talking about? Freid's bride? That was something else entirely. I don't gamble, Rebecca. I may be a fool but it was no bet. I ordered a bride. It's as simple as that. I have admitted it and I'm sorry! It nearly cost you your life and I cannot change that, but trust me, that is exactly what I did!" His frustration with her unwillingness to accept the facts and his admission was draining his patience and he stared at her angrily.

"I understand that!" she replied. "I believe you ordered a bride!"

"Then what, Rebecca? Do you want me to reach back and change the past? Do you think I should beg for forgiveness? I don't know what to do! I can't make it up to you. I did it. I admit it. I ordered a bride and as a result I have trapped you here. I cannot change that." He buried his face in his hands, his elbows on the table, in total frustration and humiliation.

"Timothy," Rebecca took a very deep breath and steadied herself against the table. "I know you ordered a bride because it was me. I am R. Fagan." Rebecca felt faint.

He lifted his face from his hands and stared at her.

"What?" he choked.

"R. Fagan, Rebecca Fagan. I am the woman you ordered to care for your son. There was no mistake. I got the tickets. I answered the ad. I was on the train to St. Peter. I am the one who brought this all about."

"Rebecca, no. How is that possible?" Timothy studied her weary face.

"Timothy," the young woman sighed. "My husband was murdered. I had nothing and the servants had the missive with the ads. Your ad was so clear, so absent of empty promises. I was, I am destitute. I'm ashamed enough of the fact that I answered your ad, but I told no one. I never told Mark, and I did not tell you. As time went on I was more mortified. When Octavia pointed out that man, and his 'picture bride' at the party, I fainted."

Timothy Elgerson stared at the girl in shock.

"You were so kind to me," she swallowed hard. "Stavewood is so perfect, so beautiful. I couldn't admit my shame to the sheriff or to you. I didn't want anyone to know about me.

"The day Octavia visited, you were away. She told me about the bet the man had lost, and the men who ordered him a wife. I was sure that was what had happened for me. For the life of me I never heard your full name. I never heard 'Elgerson' until Octavia said it that afternoon. When I realized it was you I became even more ashamed. I thought someone had sent for me as a joke and I couldn't tell you. How could I? What would you think of me? She said that the women who answered those ads were not thought of as anything more than common prostitutes and I believed her.

"Then Mark was lost, the horse was killed and now Finn is dead. All because I was too proud to say anything. This is not your fault, Timothy."

He studied her pale face and saw the pain in her deep, emerald eyes. He could not conceive of any reason she would even consider answering such an ad. Rebecca was unmistakably the most beautiful woman he had ever seen. She was intelligent and refined and there was not a man alive with two eyes in his head that could miss that. He could not believe that she would ever imagine herself unable to find any number of men who would do anything she pleased.

Why would she admit to answering his ad when it was so apparent to him she'd have no need for such a thing? Yet, everything she said fit the truth perfectly. In fact, it should have occurred to him before. If she had said something earlier, so many things would have gone differently. He understood her reasoning perfectly. He was embarrassed himself when he placed the ad, giving it all to Finn because he thought the man too simple to understand what it meant.

Rebecca stood terrified, waiting for the man to respond to her admission, but he just stared at her strangely. If only he would say something. Even if he were to hit her as David would have done, it would be some reaction. She begged him silently to say or do anything at all.

He continued to look at her, piecing everything together. He recalled every look, and all the times she had made no sense, and every time he had looked at her and tried to understand.

It all made perfect sense. She had been telling him the truth. She had not invented some story to make him feel less responsible. If anything, the blame had become worse. Instead of a stranger, she was exactly the woman he had sent for and the danger remained the same. It had become so complicated and overwhelming he could not put together a response.

Timothy sighed and walked heavily to the chair and slumped down, his head in his hands.

"Oh, Rebecca," he finally moaned.

She turned to him and cried softly. "Timothy, I'm so sorry. I tried to bring myself to say something, but every time I refrained it got worse. And with each terrible turn it became more impossible to tell you. I never wanted to hurt anyone. I hoped that you would never know who I really was, what I really am. I kept hoping that, if you never found out what a desperate and shameless thing I had done answering the ad, believing after time it was only a joke, and thinking about what everyone here thought about picture brides, you'd accept me somehow. It made sense to me that it was a joke. I could never imagine anyone like you would order a bride. You are rich and handsome and so very dear." Rebecca sat down before him.

"You had Octavia," she continued. "Why on earth would you possibly want me? Even that night we spent together..." Rebecca stopped short and Timothy looked up suddenly.

"That night? The night I got so drunk?" He stood up, overturning the chair.

Rebecca hid her face in her hands, too overwrought to have thought about what she was saying.

He pulled her up and stood her upright to face him.

"What happened that night, Rebecca?"

She began to shake violently.

"It wasn't a dream! What happened, Rebecca?"

"It doesn't matter," she cried, pulling from him. "I let it happen because of how I felt about you. I never meant to trick you into being with me, I didn't. I just wanted you."

She fled to the stairs and he followed her close behind. As she turned to slam the door he burst in and demanded she describe what he had come to believe was only a dream.

"I can't," she cried as he grabbed her arms and forced her to face him.

"Rebecca, tell me! Did I force you that night? I have to know!"

"Force me? No, you forced me to do nothing."

Timothy relaxed his grip.

"Then, what?"

"There was no pressure on your part," Rebecca turned from him in complete embarrassment.

He sat on the bed, as Rebecca closed the door quietly. "I thought it was all a dream. All day I thought about it, that it was the most incredible dream. But it was not a dream. You were in my bed that night, and here. It was here too, right here in this room."

"Yes," she whispered. "Right here."

"But you never said anything."

"The next morning you were so angry, and you didn't remember." She sobbed quietly.

Timothy groaned, "Oh, God…"

"It's alright, Tim. It happened. I wanted it to happen. You were drinking and I did nothing to stop it. It happened and you should not be sorry."

"Are you?" He looked up at her breathing hard and tried to swallow the lump in his throat.

"Sorry? That I mislead you? Yes, terribly. Sorry that you were so perfectly wonderful? Never!" She looked into his tormented eyes wishing everything had been different.

"If I had told the truth all along then there might have been hope that everything was as perfect as that night. But I didn't. I kept the truth from you and everyone else. I had no right to be with you that night. I am sorrier for that than anything." She stood before him crying softly, hoping with all of her being that he could just forget it all. Forget she had come, forgive her lie and, if possible, in some way forget what she was.

"I'll leave immediately, Tim. I can't undo any of it, but I will never forget that night."

"Leave? Is that what you want, Rebecca? Do you want to leave Stavewood?"

"No," she cried hard. "More than anything I want to stay, but I know I cannot."

"Rebecca, tell me." He held her shoulders powerfully and stared into her eyes. "If this could all be resolved, if none of it mattered, Rebecca, what would you want?"

"You," she whispered.

Chapter Forty-One

*T*imothy Elgerson whisked Rebecca swiftly up into his arms and carried her through the hall. She clung to him, afraid that none of what was happening existed, and just as quickly as it happened it would all disappear again.

He expected, in his state of exhaustion, there would be little performance on his part, but he wanted her close to him, safe in his bed.

He placed her gently onto the bed, covering her carefully with the downy quilts. Then he walked around, undressed and climbed in next to her.

He propped himself up on one elbow and looked down at her face seriously.

"Stay right here!" he commanded her and fell back onto the bed.

Rebecca lay listening to his breathing. In a few seconds she heard a soft sigh and smiled. Snuggling beside his safe warmth, she drifted off to sleep.

Timothy Elgerson lay awake in the soft light of early morning with Rebecca Fagan beside him, breathing softly, close to his side.

Her slender leg was thrown across his bare thigh and he knew instantly that a good night's sleep had done wonders as he stirred beneath her.

He turned to face her and found her smiling at him invitingly.

"Mister Elgerson, it appears that at least part of you has decided to begin the day," Rebecca giggled.

Timothy chuckled deeply and pulled her towards him, smothering her with his kisses and leaving her panting for breath.

"Rebecca," he whispered as she slipped away from him. She stood beside the bed, allowing her gown to fall from her shoulders into soft folds about her ankles.

Her body was perfectly shaped, her shoulders pale and silken in the soft morning light. He felt her warmth, enticing and compliant as she slid back in beside him and he struggled for control. He had foggy memories of their first time and he feared had performed badly. He did not want that to happen again.

He touched her slowly and carefully and in his hunger for her he struggled to take his time. He kissed her softly on the nape of her neck and he felt her shudder, begging for more. As his warm lips touched her breast she arched her back and pulled him closer.

Her trim waist encircled in his firm hands, he lifted her gently while kissing her belly softly and Rebecca feared she could stand no more. As he lowered his kisses, she caught her breath, unsure of how she should behave, but her craving for whatever he had planned for her overcame her apprehension and she allowed herself to accept his advances.

As his kisses reached their destination Rebecca gasped and lifted herself to him without restraint, the warmth of more pleasure than she had imagined washing over her. She pulled his broad muscular shoulders up to face her and as he entered her, the pleasure engulfed her even more.

Timothy held back, watching her panting, immersed in fulfillment, feeling every vibration of her soft moans. His name escaped her lips in a soft whisper as every inch of her flawless body blended perfectly with his own.

"Rebecca, I was such a fool," his voice deep and low, as in ragged breaths he whispered heavily against her lips. He drew her to him suddenly, thrusting deeply and pulling her powerfully against him, fiercely trembling as she rose to meet his passion.

Rebecca's fingers felt the immense strength of his muscles rising against her as she seized the firm flesh in his straining release, the imposing tightness of his broad powerful shoulders exploding as they expanded against her craving grasp.

The depth of his passion filled her entirely as they joined together in a perfect bond, the unreserved fulfillment of desire they could both no longer deny.

He moved slowly as he shifted his weight from her, and pulled her to him, and she buried her flushed face against this throat.

"Rebecca," he whispered, her tender face pressed

against him. He looked down, her soft eyes met his own and he knew instantly what he had seen in the depths of her passionate gaze for so long, afraid to acknowledge.

"Marry me, Rebecca."

She choked and her eyes filled with tears.

"Nothing else matters, none of it ever has. Marry me and I will stop at nothing to make you happy. I promise."

"You already have," she whispered. "Yes, Timothy. I will marry you."

Chapter Forty-Two

As she rose from the bed, gathering her robe in one hand and trailing it behind her, she smiled provocatively and walked towards the bath.

"If you continue in that manner, woman, I fear you will find yourself back in my bed!" He scowled and made a move to get up after her.

Rebecca giggled and scampered into the adjoining room, closing the door behind her.

Timothy lay back in the bed. The pleasure of the

morning and Rebecca's return of his love had changed his world, but he knew there were problems he would have to address.

He would have to explain this amazing turn of events to Ben and many others as well. He decided he ought to speak to Rebecca about it before revealing the full story to just anyone and worried that word of their relationship might make some things worse. If Dianna was pursuing Rebecca, this could provoke her and the thought worried him.

When she returned, clothed in her robe, he sat up on the bed and approached the subject.

"This changes everything you know." He studied her face, awaiting her reaction.

"Does it really matter, Timothy?" she asked, curling her feet beneath her robe on the bed beside him. "If you want me, no matter what, then no other opinions really matter. I was ashamed of answering your ad. I was so ashamed that I kept it hidden. But I never have been ashamed of what I feel for you."

"When word gets out it might make you more vulnerable to Dianna and Octavia. I'm worried about that risk."

"Is that your worry?" Rebecca was afraid there might be something more.

"Yes." He pulled her to face him, looking openly into her eyes. "Rebecca, I love you. I think I have since that day I pulled you from the mare in the woods. Through all of this that hasn't changed. I only worry that something might happen to you."

"You deserved that kick in the woods," she smiled through her welling tears, and put her head against his wide chest.

"It was Stavewood," she whispered, tracing a delicate finger along his ribs.

"Stavewood?"

"The day I arrived, I saw the look in your eyes that day. I knew then, it was as if I had always belonged here. I knew then."

"You have always belonged here, Rebecca. I built Stavewood for a dream I thought I had found. But I was mistaken. The day we arrived and I looked at you I knew I had built it for you."

He held her close to him, their thoughts and fears intertwined until they heard activity downstairs and Rebecca's head shot up.

"How will I get back to my room like this without anyone seeing me?"

"This is your room now. Stay here."

"Timothy," she scolded. "If Mark knew I was sleeping in here what would he think?"

"He'd probably be thrilled! Anyway I think after the sounds that have been coming from this room, the whole household probably knows!" He smiled devilishly.

"Oh!" she huffed. "You're just as impossible as you were before I told you that I love you."

"No, you said you loved Stavewood."

"I was wrong," she pouted. "You're even more impossible! Now how am I going to get back to my room?"

"Alright, I'll be a lookout. How would that be?"

She smiled at him sweetly, "I love you, Timothy," and gave him a shove with her tiny foot.

"Ach!" He fell back on the bed.

Before he could execute his furtive plan Birget

appeared at the door, unable to find Rebecca and flustered with worry.

"Rebecca's here," he informed the cook, after jumping into his pants and answering the door, unable to have the poor woman worried about the girl.

Rebecca stood behind the door glaring at him as he smiled.

"Ah," the cook replied. "Then she is safe."

"I suppose that would be a matter of opinion, Birget."

Rebecca was stomping her feet silently behind the door, showing claws and mouthing threats.

"Very well, sir. I will serve breakfast." Birget turned away puzzled as Timothy closed the door.

"You!" Rebecca dashed at him, beating him soundly on the chest, her frustrated voice a rushed whisper. "How dare you, you shameless rogue!"

"See Rebecca?" he announced proudly as she battered his solid chest. "I don't care who knows!"

"Stop tormenting me and see if I can get back to my room!"

He peered out into the hall, making an exaggerated display of looking up and down the corridor several times and pushed Rebecca out, his big hand on her soft backside.

Forgetting to mention the sheriff's arrival, Birget turned on the stairs in time to see Rebecca being thrust playfully into the hall and scolding Timothy. Birget waited until she heard Rebecca's door softly close, and climbed the stairs to make her notice to her employer, smiling broadly.

Timothy appeared in the dining room, carefully shaved and smartly dressed. He had checked Mark, and, finding the boy was chipper and eager to be out of bed, told him to come down for breakfast.

The boy felt that something had changed, but when Rebecca arrived in his room, her cheeks rosy and smiling broadly, he was certain something was going on.

"Rebecca?" he asked as she combed the boy's hair. "Are you still going to leave?"

"No, Mark, I think not. Things are different now. Your father and I will explain it to you soon."

She turned him to face her and to check his appearance.

"Is it because you're in love?"

Rebecca nearly choked. "What?"

"I know you are both in love. I can tell." He announced devilishly.

"But, how?" Rebecca was terrified that her and Timothy's love making may actually have been heard all through the house. Rebecca blushed deeply.

"I dunno, I just can. I see how you look at each other. I watched you dance and stuff. I think you and my father are in love, but you're both chicken." He smiled proudly.

"Chicken? How dare you!"

Mark grinned, and walked slowly from the room, looking back at the woman, smiling knowingly.

Rebecca groaned in embarrassment.

It was shocking how bitterly cold Rebecca's room felt to her, as she entered to dress for breakfast.

She hurried through her hot bath, the warmth of the steaming water unable to chase the chill from her shivering body. Selecting the warmest of her dresses, she decided that the weather in her new home was frustratingly unpredictable, and hoped it would stabilize quickly before she either melted away or froze to death.

Donning her only wrap, a soft and lacy shawl, she draped it around her trembling shoulders and descended the massive main staircase. Surprised to find the family dining room was vacant, she hastened to the larger dining room while trying to chase off her chill in the warm hall.

"There you are!" Timothy rose from his chair at the head of the table, and walking to Rebecca, pulled out the chair at the opposite end.

Rebecca looked around the room as Mark and Ben Carson rose from their places, the boy's face dark with concern and the sheriff appearing confused. She lowered herself into the chair, bewildered that it was not the place at the table she ordinarily used, and frowned, concerned with Timothy's odd behavior. He returned to his seat, a peculiar, serious look upon his face.

Immediately the staff filed into the room silently, worried looks on their faces, and lined themselves in an orderly fashion along the wall.

Mark recalled that the last time his father called the staff in such a way was before he released many of them shortly after his mother's death, and closed down Stavewood to relocate to the hunting cabin.

Both his father and Rebecca had seemed so cheerful, but suddenly his father's demeanor had changed and he had left the family room and directed them to wait in the formal dining room. The boy fought back tears in confusion and waited, dreading his father's announcement.

Timothy stood and began.

"Since you all seem to be expecting the worst, I suppose I should explain why I have gathered all of you, including you as well, Ben, together this morning."

The occupants in the room avoided looking at the man, with the exception of Rebecca who was dumbfounded at what she began to suspect the man was up to.

"No," he began. "Contrary to what I'm sure you are all thinking I am not closing Stavewood."

Rebecca could feel confusion and relief flood through the room.

"I merely wanted to inform all of you collectively, lest there be gossip or misunderstand among any of you, since you are all a part of my household, and you a very close friend, Ben," Timothy continued seriously.

Ben Carson lifted his eyes from the table and felt he should be embarrassed somehow.

"I suppose I have tormented you all enough, and so, my reason why you are all here."

Every face in the room watched Timothy Elgerson silently, Rebecca drawing in a deep breath.

"To my unbelievably good fortune, Rebecca has

agreed to remain at Stavewood. She has also agreed to marry me."

The room exploded in a collective gasp as Mark rushed to Rebecca's side in tears and threw his arms around her slender shoulders. Ben Carson, although overcome with curiosity over the turn of events, shook Timothy's hand vigorously as the staff chuckled and Birget wiped her tears on her generous apron.

"Well, it's about damn time!" The cook bellowed above the chattering and, overcome with emotion, walked out of the room.

The staff filed out behind her, smiling to Rebecca with warm congratulations, Mark beside them, hopping about and whooping loudly.

Rebecca blushed from the warmth of the compliments and shook her head as the boy danced around, sure that he was perfectly healthy, regardless of his recent ordeal.

"Well, Tim," Ben sat back in his chair. "I have to admit that this is no surprise. My Missus has been carrying on about the two of you since your party, as well as most of the territory I suspect. I'm sure myself that this is a wonderful match for the both of you, and I'm certain you will be quite happy together." Ben smiled to Rebecca and nodded appreciatively. "However I have my concerns over your announcement, Tim. I'm sure you must have considered the ramifications this might have."

"I have." Timothy smiled reassuringly at Rebecca.

"Well, before we even discuss any of that, I'm all ears man. What happened after I left last night?"

Rebecca cleared her throat and excused herself.

Although it had not occurred to him to relate anything to the sheriff that in any way involved their intimate lovemaking following their conversation in the kitchen, he could see embarrassment plainly in her eyes.

He recalled how he had felt at Ben's discovery that he had, in fact, ordered a mail order bride himself and understood her concerns.

"Please, excuse me one moment," he nodded to Ben and crossed the room as Rebecca lifted herself from her chair. Gently he directed her out into the central corridor.

"Rebecca!" he exclaimed. "Why are you shaking?" He had thought his announcement an amusing surprise but now became concerned.

"I'm sorry," she whispered, kissing him softly on the cheek and grasping the warmth of his wrist. "You are so endearing to make your announcement. Although I suspect you took years off Birget's life." Rebecca smiled, shaking her head.

"Your hand is freezing!" Timothy wrapped his arms around her and felt that her entire body was chilled.

"My room was so cold when I went back to bathe. I have to say your weather here is quite unpredictable."

He went to the kitchen after instructing her to wait by the fire in the study and returned with a woolen cape that seemed large enough to cover every inch of the woman and wrapped it lovingly around her shoulders.

"The maids will bring your breakfast in here and they are going up to warm your room now. I'll come up as soon as Ben and I have finished talking." He kissed her, drawing her close to him and enfolding her in his powerful arms.

Rebecca wished she could remain there, basking in his love and radiating warmth. She could not possibly tell him that she had chosen her heaviest dress, and nodded quietly.

He kissed her passionately, still fighting the feeling that everything he was experiencing seemed unreal and she looked lovingly into his eyes. He looked into the depths of her emerald eyes and felt her desire for him and he pulled himself away.

"If I linger here any longer, madam, you will no longer be chilled, I'm quite sure, and I may never return to speak to the sheriff. Cease your torment of me and stay here beside the fire."

Rebecca giggled softly and kissed his firm cheek.

Chapter Forty-Three

*E*lgerson returned to the dining room contemplating that the girl had only a limited and temporary wardrobe, certainly not what she would require for a Minnesota winter. He tried to resolve how he could possibly take Rebecca safely to town, wishing he was instead driving the chill from her, unclothed beside him in a warm bed.

"Please, forgive me." Timothy returned to his chair.

"Understandable." In his absence, Ben had been presented with a generous and delectable breakfast and had enjoyed a moment alone with the feast while Timothy spoke to the girl. "I have to say, Tim that this is the finest food I've eaten in years, with the exception of course of that wonderful spread you put out at the gathering."

"It's odd that you should say that, Ben." Timothy plunged his fork into a gravy smothered steak, temptingly tender beside fresh, fried eggs and mounds of perfectly browned potatoes and golden onions. "It seems since that party most of the meals here have been unusually delicious. I suppose Birget must have improved her skills while I was away." Elgerson looked toward the kitchen thoughtfully.

Both men enjoyed their meal and sat back satisfied with steaming mugs of richly brewed coffee before commencing with their conversation, deciding not to interrupt their fine meal with the business at hand.

"I believe we have resolved a large part, if not all of our mystery, Ben," Timothy began.

"Any answers would help, Tim." Carson knew that, based on Tim's announcement of marriage, there had to be some very interesting information indeed.

"We were completely mistaken about Rebecca." Timothy struggled for the right approach. "Rebecca is, in fact, the bride I ordered."

The sheriff gasped, choking on his coffee.

Timothy allowed the man to digest the information and collect himself as he himself had done since the discovery.

"Are you sure?" Carson shook his head bewildered.

"I was a fool not to see it myself. R. Fagan is indeed her name. She was on the train headed for St. Paul to meet with the coach to Billington. She got ill on the train, got off at Hawk Bend, and explained to Finn that she was a mail order bride. She was on the exact train she should have been on, with a very British accent as well. Had she remained on the train perhaps Dianna would never have intercepted her, but she left the train. She disembarked right under the noses of Finn and Dianna. When I showed her those tickets last night there was no question in my mind whatsoever that she recognized them. She knew those tickets, Ben. I had trouble believing it all myself."

Ben Carson could see that Timothy was making perfect sense.

"Dianna took her up to that shack because it was the closest place she could hold her near Hawk Bend Station," Elgerson continued. "I'm still not sure if she intended to return for her, or if she left her there to die.

"Finn was not terribly bright, Ben, but he was never a violent man as far as I know. He must have found out what Dianna, and possibly Octavia were up to with the girl and at least one of them killed him. Dianna I expect. Rebecca said Finn was kind to her. He may have been a bit taken with her."

"Why didn't she say anything? It's beyond me why she just didn't tell anyone who she was from the beginning. I knew all along she was withholding something, but I can't see why."

"Somewhere along the line she got it in her head that answering the ad was something she ought to be ashamed of, maybe somewhere in her travels." Timothy stopped abruptly.

"What is it?" Ben saw obvious concern on the man's face.

"Damn it, Ben. I hadn't thought of it before right now. The tickets Rebecca got were the lowest class in almost every instance. How the hell did she ever make the trip? That was months of travel in the worst possible conditions." Timothy sighed deeply and rubbed his cheek.

"There must have been something that got her here, Tim." Carson shook his head slowly.

Timothy tried to imagine her lengthy and incredibly uncomfortable trip, only to find herself abducted and left for dead by a madwoman and rescued by a child he himself had left to his own devices. She had never said a word about it. By keeping her secret entirely to herself no one could ever know what she had been through or understand her. It had not occurred to anyone, not even him, what she had gone through to be here. He stared at the door to the room and felt his chest tighten, a lump rising in his chest.

"This brings up my point, Tim. Like I said, everyone who'd laid eyes on the two of you together knew there was something there, long before either of you would admit it to yourselves. From what you're telling me, that girl had a hell of a trip. But she had an idea in her head she shouldn't tell anyone? Even after all that happened?"

"Well, Ben, it was more than one idea. The night of the party, that first night I brought her here, Octavia was carrying on about old Freid and his wife there. That's what sent Rebecca into a faint. A few days later, while Octavia was here, she told Rebecca about the bet the men put together to get Freid's wife here. I suspect that she neglected to mention that Freid won that bet. I'm sure Octavia let her believe that everyone felt the woman should be ashamed. Rebecca had no idea I was the one who had ordered her. Somehow she never heard my last name."

"Tim, I doubt that Octavia knew who Rebecca was at that point. Just the same, it's certainly like her to carry on about Freid. Makes sense she'd never notice that she was upsetting the girl. Octavia has a real talent for insensitivity. We all know that."

"I believe it will take a lifetime to get this all sorted out, Ben." Timothy cleared his throat.

"Things are bad with Dianna and Octavia now, Tim. What do you expect could happen to Rebecca when they find out that, even after abducting her and killing poor Finn, you plan to marry her? Announcing it to your staff here and all, I'm sure it'll be known throughout the territory by nightfall. I'm not sure it was a good plan.

"Don't get me wrong in saying this, Tim. Obviously that girl's been through hell and back. My wife would say that the two of you are 'meant to be'. I've known you a long time, what with all the women in half the county tripping over themselves ever since you were a kid. I know you are not a man to take marriage lightly. But I know what you went through after Corissa, and, if my suspicions are right, Rebecca's probably a lot more right for you. It's risky is all. I'd hate to see anything happen to her. Or to you either."

"Then maybe it's time everyone stops tripping over themselves, Ben. I have found Rebecca, and I will marry her. I want the world to know it. Maybe Dianna and Octavia need to move on." Timothy Elgerson set down his coffee cup with determination.

Rebecca found her room warmer and draped the cape across a chair before settling down to her knitting while she waited for Timothy. She thought that his room was most likely warmer, but knew that until their marriage she would have to keep to her own room.

Her mind was still overcome with the direction her life had taken. She sat quietly, rhythmically counting off her stitches. Warm tears ran unnoticed down her fair cheeks, wetting her dark lashes. All of her dreams of building a new life had been more difficult than she had ever imagined, yet, as unrealistic as they all had been, she had found so much more.

Had she known that, through the wretched sickness on the ship, the tortured miles on the stifling train, even lying in the dirt of the shack, she'd find herself here at Stavewood loved by such an amazing man she would have still set her slender foot on that first step.

Rebecca sat peacefully alone in her room, as she carefully turned her needles to shape the heel on her first gift to her soon-to-be husband.

Chapter Forty-Four

$\mathcal{R}$ebecca's handiwork flew from her hands and dropped to the thick oriental carpet beside her and she leapt to her feet as the sounds of horrified cries filled the yard. She took to the stairs, her chest pounding, reaching the door of the dining room as Timothy and Ben Carson burst from the room ahead of her. Timothy turned to her suddenly and instructed her to stay inside and Rebecca followed them to the kitchen, and then stood terrified with the women at the window.

Several of the men Timothy employed were gathered around the frantic Arabian, as the huge, panic stricken beast tore at the reins. While four of the men struggled to keep the animal under control, several other men, upon much smaller horses, pulled at ropes tied to the big black beast.

A panicked rider clung to the animal's immense

back as the horse kicked and reared violently.

When Rebecca saw Timothy rushing suddenly into the path of the maddened stallion she could not contain herself and ran out into the yard.

"We caught him riding up the east path, Tim," one of the men yelled over the screams of the steed.

Elgerson ran toward the horse and shouted in a loud, commanding voice that made Rebecca stop dead in her tracks. The animal ceased his fighting and circled, agitated and enraged, stomping loudly in the dust. Rebecca felt the vibration of every hoof from several feet away.

Timothy pulled the rider from the massive horse's back and pushed him upright against the boards of the stable as the other men stepped away. The huge Arabian snorted loudly and paced the yard, free of the rider and the imprisonment of the men.

Rebecca ventured slightly closer and recognized that the man Timothy held against the rough boards was Jude Thomas, the man who had been so forward with her the night of the party.

"You better have a damn good reason to have been riding that animal, Thomas, and you'd better have it fast, because it will be the last thing you'll ever say."

Elgerson held the smaller man fast against the wall, Jude's feet barely touching the ground. Rebecca could see the large veins pulsing on Timothy's neck, his face red with anger.

"Go to hell, Elgerson!" Jude hissed. "You can go to hell and take that whore with you!"

Elgerson lifted his massive fist and struck the man violently, the long fingers of his left hand curling around Jude's throat as the man continued to infuriate him.

"You think you can keep me away from her like you tried with Corissa? This one will come to my bed just as quickly as the last. Now, get your hands off me!"

The men in the open yard stepped back, as if they all silently agreed that what they were witnessing was justified. Ben Carson stood without a word beside the house, watching an event long in coming that no man would be able to stop.

Elgerson struck him again even more violently, and raised his fist for another blow when Rebecca could stand it no more. She ran to his side and grabbed his arm with all of her strength and began shouting.

"Timothy, stop! You'll kill him!"

"That's exactly what I have in mind," he growled, breathing hard.

"No!" Rebecca screamed. "He's not worth it! He's just a drunken fool. He's wrong, Tim. Let him go!"

Elgerson spat against the wall, inches from the man's face and flung him violently onto the hard packed dirt.

"Ben, get him the hell out of here. He's nothing but a horse thief! Get him off my property before I give him what he deserves!"

The men gathered the broken man, pulling him roughly up from the ground and carrying him around the house to the sheriff's buggy.

Elgerson leaned, his arms out straight in front of him, stretched and taut against the stable wall, cursing under his breath.

"It's true, Rebecca," his voice graveled and strained.

"Timothy," she whispered quietly. "It doesn't matter. Remember? None of anything that happened before matters now. I love you and it's the only thing that matters to me. I don't care about him, I love you."

He turned to her and searched her delicate features, his face twisted in pain.

Rebecca threw her arms around his sturdy chest, burying her face against his shoulder and he gathered her into his arms. They stood together silently beside the rough building. Ben Carson pulled his buggy around with Jude Thomas unconscious inside, and disappeared into the trees along the lane.

A snowflake swayed gently on the wind and settled at their feet, melting into the firm ground.

Chapter Forty-Five

$\mathcal{T}$imothy whispered to her as the massive black horse snorted loudly and walked hurriedly towards his stall in the open stable. "Rebecca, you are going to freeze out here."

"Is he alright?" She cautiously followed the huge stallion, trying to inspect him, but afraid to get too close.

"You're afraid of that horse? Funny you weren't afraid of me a little while ago." Timothy shook his head and followed her into the stable.

"I never slept with the horse." She peered around the stall at the huge dark animal.

"I don't believe I want to imagine what you mean by that, Rebecca."

"The horse is just an animal, you have different feelings."

"You think his feelings are different?" Elgerson passed his hands over the horse's flanks and along his towering neck.

"The only horses I've ever seen were carriage horses in the park, and Mark's, of course, but she was quiet, not like this one. I've never seen one like him, with a temper and such, I mean." Rebecca stood in the stall adjoining the huge beast and peered at him curiously.

The monstrous Arabian nodded his head and snorted loudly. Rebecca stepped back.

"He feels a lot of the same things you do, Rebecca." Elgerson gently examined the horse and spoke to him softly. "Haven't you ever had a pet?"

"No," she whispered. "My family said they were too dirty. I never thought about it much I guess."

"Come around here."

"Oh Timothy, I couldn't. He's so huge. I'm really afraid."

"I'm huge. You're not in the least afraid of me."

"Not as huge as he is!" Rebecca blushed, realizing her remark about not having slept with the horse could mean something she never intended.

Timothy noticed her expression and chuckled softly.

"Never mind," she scowled.

"Come around. He won't hurt you and I think he should get to know you."

"You're going to introduce me to your horse? You really do want everyone to know," she giggled.

Rebecca ventured into the stall and stepped up beside Timothy, terrified of the animal. Elgerson took her by the shoulders, led her beside the horse, and, standing close behind her, lifted her hand slowly and spread open her palm.

The big Arabian rubbed his wide muzzle into Rebecca's hand, lifting its broad head, flattening its ears and nickering softly.

Rebecca gasped and held perfectly still, Timothy's safe, solid body pressed firmly against her back.

"He can tell you're afraid. That's liable to make him nervous. You have to let him know you're not going to hurt him," Timothy bent and spoke close to her ear.

"Hurt him?" Rebecca spoke barely above a whisper. "How on earth could such a huge beast ever think I could hurt him?" She looked up at the man, her eyes wide.

"You'd be surprised at how many thoughts he has. Try petting him, like this." He took her delicate hand in his own and ran it along the horse's back and neck.

Rebecca could feel the powerful shoulders moving, strong and alive as Timothy pressed her open hand slowly along the stallion's powerful body. The man pulled his own hand away gently assuring her that she needed to pet the animal so he could learn her touch.

"Horses communicate very strongly through touch. He can feel if your hand is steady, or if you fear him. He'll learn to trust you by the way you speak to him and the way you touch him. He'll learn to recognize and respect you and he'll learn what you expect from him and he'll let you know how he feels."

"I expect he might eat me," Rebecca laughed. The warm strength of the animal was exhilarating beneath her hand. "Respect me?" She ran her hand up to the horse's ear and along his nose. "Is that why you could yell like you did when those men were fighting him and he stopped jumping in the air?"

"He was afraid and confused. When he recognized my voice he felt safe. That's what calmed him down."

"I still don't understand how anything so big could be afraid of anything."

"I do," he remarked distractedly. "Rebecca, tell me about the giant rat."

"In the shack?"

"Yes." His deep timbre was soothing and affectionate in her ear.

"It was huge!" She shuddered slightly and Timothy placed his hands protectively on her slender shoulders as she continued stroking and exploring the horse. "In England there is a rat. Sometimes you see it late at night beside the sewers, but it's not as big, perhaps the size of my foot.

"The rat in the shack was quite different. It had red eyes and sharp teeth like needles, and it was the biggest rat ever!"

"That's because it wasn't a rat." Timothy chuckled slightly to himself and she felt his amusement against her back.

"It certainly *looked* like a rat." She looked around and met his smiling eyes.

"It was a possum."

"What's that?" She watched his face curiously.

"It's an animal that mostly comes out at night. They eat bugs. They might even eat a small rat. Have you ever heard of someone 'playing possum'?"

"Yes, I believe so." Rebecca listened to Timothy's firm voice and found herself scratching the Arabian without realizing it.

"That's because when you scare one badly enough he'll lie right down and pretend he's dead. Doesn't sound like a very threatening animal, though they can certainly give you a nasty bite."

"Play dead? This one most definitely did not play dead. I screamed quite loudly, and it simply stole away down the hole."

Timothy laughed at her delightful way of describing things and pressed up closer to her.

"Timothy?"

"Yes?" he sighed, feeling her safe within his grasp.

"Does he have a name?"

"The possum?" Timothy watched Rebecca

finding the horse's favorite places to be scratched as she gently dug her nails into his tough hide.

"No, the horse. Does he have a name?"

"Cannonball. He's enjoying that, Rebecca. It appears you've made a friend."

The Arabian neighed loudly and Rebecca's eyes flew open in surprise as she pulled her hand away. The big animal butted her with his muzzle, apparently wanting her to continue.

"Of course, you will have to keep scratching him until he's had enough now. You could be out here all day." Timothy laughed heartily.

Rebecca looked at him concerned and scratched Cannonball vigorously.

Mark ventured around the open door of the stable and watched Rebecca scratching the horse and smiled. He knew she had been terrified of the good natured chestnut. He watched Timothy looking down at her affectionately and giggled aloud, both adults turning suddenly to catch him spying.

"What are you doing there, boy?" Timothy called out.

"Watching two chickens fall in love."

"Chickens?" Timothy led Rebecca from the Arabian's stall, pulling the gate closed behind them.

"He says we are chickens, Tim. He called me that this morning as well." Rebecca crossed her arms and scowled at the boy.

"Why on earth would you call us chickens?" Timothy looked at the boy disgustedly.

"Because it took you so long to hug and stuff."

Mark kicked at the stall and smiled impishly.

"Off with you!" Timothy made a sudden move towards the boy and he scampered across the yard and back into the house.

"Rebecca, you must be frozen clear through. Let's get inside."

"Tim, look!" A soft flurry of flakes drifted across a graying sky.

"I was afraid of that," Timothy frowned.

"Afraid? Look how beautiful and delicate they are!" Rebecca tried to capture a flake on her hand.

"Until they begin to pile up around the door and you can't leave the house."

"Oh, my!" Rebecca gasped as Timothy hurried her into the house.

Rebecca shuddered, suddenly feeling the cold and stepped into the warm kitchen.

"I can see I will need to dress you properly, and quickly. I don't expect this snow will amount to much, by the look of the sky. If it's not too cold tomorrow we'll see about taking care of that." Timothy rubbed her arms and led her to the study and the crackling fireplace. Running up to her room he returned with the heavy cape and her knitting balanced in his open hand like a tiny bird.

"What are you making here?" He peered at the needles poking out of a large ball of yarn, the unfinished ribbing sitting up slightly.

"It's a sock." Rebecca took the items from his hand and shook her head at his odd expression.

"It looks nothing like a sock, you know."

"It will by the time it's finished," she huffed. "I thought if it gets cold enough, like now, you and

Mark might enjoy warm wool socks."

"Like now?" Timothy laughed loudly. "Woman, trust me, this is not cold!" He continued to laugh as he stirred the fire.

Rebecca was concerned. She didn't think it could get too much colder. She wrapped the cape around her lap.

Birget toddled into the room, announcing lunch.

"Birget, wait." The cook turned to face her handsome employer. "What's going on in that kitchen of yours?" he asked with a puzzled look on his face.

"Nothing, sir. Why do you ask?" Birget took an offended stance.

"It seems that, since you filled Octavia's menu for the party, the food emerging from that room has been unusually delicious."

Birget stomped her foot and scowled at Rebecca, pursing her lips tightly.

Rebecca shook her head almost imperceptibly and fussed with her knitting.

"I'll not hold my tongue long, Miss," Birget huffed loudly and stomped out of the room.

"Rebecca?" Timothy faced her, his voice demanding.

"Yes?" she gazed up at him innocently.

"What's going on?"

"With what, dear?" she asked sweetly.

"Octavia had nothing to do with the food at the party, did she? That's what all the fuss was about when we first arrived! That kitchen was in chaos. You took over that day in the kitchen, didn't you?"

"It's not important really, Tim. She simply had not given them a menu and Birget and I planned it ourselves," she replied softly, a bit uncomfortable with his demanding tone.

"You had to have heard everyone complementing the food profusely, and you certainly cannot have missed my recent comments at meals. But you never said anything. Why?"

"It really didn't matter that much, Tim. I thought you and Octavia were close and you had a houseful of very upset servants and a large gathering planned."

"You walked into Stavewood, took over the staff, the menu and the food and pulled off that huge party in one afternoon?"

"Certainly not alone." Rebecca was very irritated at his attitude. "The staff worked feverishly. Even Mark rearranged the tables per my instruction and your party went well enough I thought. I'm fully aware that this is your home. I only did what had to be done." She peered at him indignantly.

Timothy laughed loudly, his resounding voice filling the room.

"Why on earth are you laughing?" Rebecca set her knitting aside and faced him.

"You are something else, you know that, Rebecca?" He could barely contain himself.

'Well, I'm sorry," she huffed.

"Sorry?" He turned to her and her face was flushed.

"Rebecca, do not be sorry! Don't you know how amazing you are?"

Rebecca was entirely confused.

"You came into this massive house, in that outlandish outfit I might add, and managed to get my entirely stubborn staff to prepare that feast yourself in one afternoon. Rebecca, my dear, I cannot wait until our wedding day!"

Rebecca's tightening shoulders dropped and she laughed with relief.

"For heaven's sake, Timothy, why must you terrify me like that? I thought you were angry with me!"

"For filling me with that incredible food and throwing that magnificent party? How could you imagine I would be anything less than completely beguiled by you?" He shook his head at her, studying her fragile face and concluding that the delicate woman sitting in confusion before him most definitely deserved better than she most likely had ever had.

"Rebecca, I have to ask you something. Believe me, I am not in any way angry with you."

"I understand now, Timothy, I just thought…"

He faced her and held her petite frame, gazing into her bewildered, emerald eyes.

"Those tickets I showed you, those were the tickets you used to travel here? Not the first class ones I sent. The other set, right?"

"Yes," she looked openly into his handsome face.

"You came here on the ship's third class? And the train as well?"

"Yes, uh hum," she replied, a captive in his gaze.

"Why? The trip must have been unbearable the entire distance. You could have exchanged the tickets and returned home, anywhere along the way. Why did you continue?"

Her eyes filled with tears and he watched her

intensely.

"There was nothing to go back for. My husband was murdered, everything I owned and all the money had been gambled away. I had no family, only a cousin. I don't know, Tim. I had nothing there and your ad…" she choked on her tears and he pulled her to his chest.

"My ad? Rebecca, the ad said nothing," he whispered softly, his face close to her ear.

"Not to me. It said everything to me." Rebecca sobbed deeply.

"You are amazing, Rebecca. I sat here doing nothing. I didn't even care if I lived or died and you came all this way. I can see that it's time someone learned to appreciate you."

He pulled her to him and kissed her deeply and she fell easily into his arms.

Birget cleared her throat loudly.

"Yes, Birget, we're coming now," Timothy responded, standing upright beside Rebecca.

"Very well," Birget replied and turned, rolling her eyes.

"Birget?" he called to her.

"Yes, sir?" she turned.

"The food has been quite delicious. In the future when you and Rebecca do this sort of thing again you must promise me you will not hold your tongue."

"Definitely not, sir." The woman smiled devilishly.

"Thank you."

Rebecca pushed Timothy away. "You, sir, are quite impossible!"

Timothy followed her into the dining room,

entirely enchanted by the soft sway of her hips.

Chapter Forty-Six

Octavia paced in the confines of the small lodge and watched a snowflake drifting outside of the tiny window. "Mother, I can't possibly remain here another minute! I'm going back down to the house before we get snowed in here and I lose my mind!"

"I wish you wouldn't, child." Dianna tried to reason with the girl.

"We've been here for hours and I still haven't seen Uncle Finn. I can't stand it any longer and I'm tired of waiting. I just don't see how hiding away in this godforsaken cabin is doing anything to stop that girl from stealing my beau from right under my nose!" Octavia whined.

"I told you, leave the girl up to me. I'll take care of it, just be patient."

"Patient? For heaven's sake, Mother. First orders that maid order bride, now she's living right under his roof with no chaperone and I can't stand it any longer! I saw them together, him holding her in that way! It's indecent, Mother, and they were right there in the middle of the house with dozens of people around!"

"Octavia," Dianna sighed. "His son was missing. The man was distracted. If you had made yourself known to everyone there he would have turned to you just as easily. He wasn't thinking clearly and that bitch is taking every opportunity."

"That's exactly what I mean!" Octavia turned to face the older woman and stomped her foot indignantly. "She is right there flaunting herself now, and I am not." The big girl could see the memory of Timothy clinging to Rebecca and she got a very uneasy feeling. There was more there than just the girl being so beautiful, but she quickly blocked it from her mind.

"Be patient, Octavia." Dianna's tone was kind and pleading. Her eyes darted around the room distractedly, as she tried to devise her new plan, despite the constant complaining.

With Octavia's restless impatience, Dianna wasn't sure she would be able to keep the young woman at the hunting lodge for very long. She considered that it might be best to let her ride out now, before the snow began to lie. It would be difficult to discover where Octavia was coming from. Dianna did not believe the snow would accumulate, but if she should be wrong, her own whereabouts would be easily discovered if she left tracks.

Again she considered reminding Octavia to take care who she talked to and exactly what she said. She felt sure that her daughter would say too little to be a threat, except, perhaps, for Dianna's present whereabouts. Even though she felt confident that Octavia knew only about Rebecca, and nothing regarding Jude or the trains, she did not want to risk any confrontations.

"You're sure no one asked you any questions that day you were last out at Stavewood?" Dianna had to ask one last time.

"No!" Octavia shouted, inches from her mother's face. "I told you! That foolish girl was running all over the place telling everyone what to do and the place was packed with people. I sat alone forever in the parlor and Timothy did not even greet me or pay any attention to the fact that I was there!" Octavia buried her face in her hands and wailed loudly.

Dianna held the bawling young woman by her broad shoulders and tried frantically to soothe the sobbing girl.

"Alright," Dianna sighed. "You go ahead and get back home. Take care that no one sees you at the junction. I'll fix everything, I promise."

"Fine!" Octavia grunted, her eyes suddenly dry. She began roughly pushing her gloves down onto her plump fingers. "If I see Uncle Finn I'll send him straight up. Goodbye, Mother." Octavia threw her cape haphazardly over her shoulders and rushed out to her carriage.

Dianna Weintraub watched the carriage bound along the narrow path, disappearing into the dense forest, and swore under her breath.

"Damn that Finn," she cursed aloud.

If the fool man hadn't gotten in the middle of things, all of this would be so much simpler, she thought. Of all the rotten luck, after watching that train for days, waiting for that damn bride.

"If I had not left him at Hawk Bend just for those few hours he would never have laid eyes on the girl and been so taken with her," Dianna spat. "What the hell were you thinking, Finn?" she shouted towards the sky. "Why the hell did you set her free for Elgerson to find, and why did you try to hide that damn shack?"

Dianna leaned in the doorway, struggling to push her illogical younger brother out of her mind. He had insisted he hadn't set her free, and he took apart the shack so she wouldn't come back. He made no sense at all. He was gone now, it had to be done. Dianna Weintraub returned to the warmth of the lodge and pulled the door closed behind her.

Confident that Rebecca was too afraid to tell anyone about her, Dianna believed that, should anyone question Octavia, she had little to tell. She was not entirely comfortable that Octavia had remembered the rarely used hunting lodge, but the woman assured herself that her dear daughter had everything to gain by getting the man she wanted, and would not tell anyone of her whereabouts.

She assured herself that it was probably a better idea to let her daughter go home. Jude was due back at any time, and had he showed up while Octavia was there, it would have been difficult to explain. Dianna went back to studying the train schedules.

By midnight she began to curse the man. He still had not arrived as they had planned. Considering the fact that he was not much brighter than her fool brother, Dianna began to wonder if she would be forced to seek him out as well. Without him her plans for the next train hold-up would have to wait. As it was, they were being forced to travel far out of the area.

Octavia hurried down the mountain towards home. She wanted to change into a more provocative outfit and pay Timothy a friendly visit. Once he saw her in her revealing new dress she was sure she could distract him from that British bitch.

By mid-afternoon she had stuffed herself into the gown. She had traveled miles to find a dressmaker that would finally listen to her about how a decent dress ought to fit. She rouged her cheeks brightly before lumbering into her carriage and heading west.

Chapter Forty-Seven

*A*s he pierced the crust of his steaming chicken pie Mark exclaimed, "I remember last year when it piled up so high we couldn't even see the stables!"

"I think you're upsetting Rebecca with your stories, Mark." Timothy looked up at the boy sternly as he saw the woman frown with concern over massive amounts of snow.

"But, it's true Pa! You remember. We had to tie a

rope to the house just to find our way back!"

Rebecca gasped. "Oh, Timothy, is that really true?"

Elgerson glared at the boy.

"Rebecca, have you given any thought to your wedding gown?" Timothy thought he had better change the subject as Rebecca's face was consumed with worry.

"Yes!" Her face lit up.

"I thought maybe you had," he chuckled.

"Timothy, I'd like to ask you something." She swallowed, unsure of how to bring up the topic.

Timothy lowered his fork and watched her face seriously.

"In the attic, there are a few sewing things. I wondered if perhaps I might…if no one is using them and if they aren't too personal or anything…" Rebecca lowered her eyes unsure if she might be approaching a sensitive subject.

Timothy sat back in his chair.

"You mean the sewing machine?" Mark swallowed his mouthful of food.

"Yes," Rebecca replied, watching Timothy's face darken.

"I bought that machine for Corissa." Timothy cleared his throat and looked at the young woman.

"I'm so sorry. I shouldn't have said anything." Rebecca returned to her hot lunch.

"Rebecca?" She looked up at the man, ashamed for having mentioned the machine. "I could have the men bring it down this afternoon. Would you like to use it?" He studied her fair face.

"I didn't know exactly what it meant. It's not

important."

"Do you know how to use it? Could you teach me?" The boy squirmed in his chair.

"What did you think it meant when you saw it up there?" Timothy continued to watch her closely, and Rebecca became increasingly uncomfortable.

"I don't know." She faced him, looking into his eyes. "It's quite beautiful and I thought it a waste to have such a lovely machine put away like that when someone could be enjoying it."

"Amazing," he smiled, his eyes never leaving hers. "Then I give it to you. What do you plan to do with it?"

Rebecca caught her breath. "Sew, of course!" She grinned and resumed her lunch happily. Timothy Elgerson was an unusual man indeed, she thought to herself.

"Rebecca, I have some things I must deal with this afternoon. I have paperwork I've been putting off for far too long. When Mark comes back with the men why don't you have them rearrange the room you've been using and bring whatever you like from the attic." They walked towards the study.

Rebecca kissed his cheek. "Thank you," she whispered.

"Stavewood is yours, Rebecca, and everything in it, including me. You were right, what you said earlier. What happened before shouldn't matter. That sewing machine did mean something when I ordered it. But, like many other things around here, I didn't know it at the time. I'm beginning to think that I did several things for you, Rebecca, without ever realizing." He stood studying her delicate face. "I hope you enjoy it.

"Besides," he continued. "You can change that bedroom into a sewing room since you won't need it as a bedroom any longer."

Rebecca gasped. A change in the sleeping arrangements was a topic she had avoided. Timothy watched her as she bit her lip thoughtfully.

"Timothy, I can't just move into your room!"

"Why not?" He smiled at her devilishly.

"We're only just engaged. Maybe in America couples sleep together before they are married, but not in England."

"It didn't seem to matter before." He watched her seriously.

"I'd be so embarrassed. Everyone would know. What would we tell Mark? He can't think that's how people behave." Rebecca was uncomfortable. She wanted nothing more than to spend every night with him, warm and safe beside him in the huge bed.

"What was it you said you wanted, Rebecca?" He pulled her to him suddenly.

"You," she whispered.

"Then you had better plan a wedding very quickly, my dear, because I will not wait long." He kissed her eagerly.

Chapter Forty-Eight

$\mathcal{T}$he resounding knocker echoed suddenly in the foyer and made Rebecca jump. She smoothed her hair as Timothy growled and pulled open the front door.

"Octavia!"

Rebecca heard Timothy's startled exclamation and caught her breath.

The big woman bounded into the house, handing Timothy her cape casually. She exposed her wide cleavage, almost enough to show her areolas, and she threw herself into Timothy's arms, greeting him with a brash kiss.

Rebecca gasped and held her fingertips to her face.

Elgerson grabbed Octavia by her substantial shoulders and stood solidly facing her.

"Octavia," he glared at her angrily.

"Oh, Tim." She fanned her face with her glove. "I've been so worried about Mick. I came here while you were searching for him, but no one told you I was here and I wanted so badly to see you." Octavia stared angrily past the towering man and frowned towards Rebecca.

"Mark is just fine," Elgerson grunted.

"Oh how wonderful." Octavia brushed past the man and faced Rebecca squarely. "I see that you are still here."

Timothy stepped beside Rebecca and spoke firmly to Octavia.

"Rebecca has decided to stay at Stavewood, Octavia."

The woman's thickset face turned white.

"Oh. But there's hardly any snow out there just yet." Octavia began fussing with her sleeve and pressed her hand against her bodice. The garment shifted slightly and Timothy lifted an eye brow in anticipation of the view he feared might present itself with a 'pop' at any moment.

Rebecca lowered her gaze and touched her forehead, equally afraid of what she might witness.

"Come in, Octavia." Timothy gestured towards the parlor, hoping that, if the big girl would sit down, all three of them might be spared the certainty of great embarrassment. Besides, he wanted to speak to her regarding her mother's whereabouts.

"Perhaps you would care for tea?" Rebecca asked politely, as Timothy smiled briefly towards her and she struggled with her composure. She was not entirely sure what the man was up to, but accepted his lead curiously. Something about Octavia made her uneasy, even before she knew the kind of person she was.

"Actually I am quite famished. I had no chance to eat anything this morning." Octavia settled into the chair as it creaked in loud protest.

"I'll see to correcting that." Rebecca nodded to Timothy and left to prepare a tray in the kitchen.

"How is your mother these days, Octavia?" Timothy sat across from her, his elbows on his knees facing the girl squarely and doing his utmost to ignore her display.

Octavia studied his fine face. He was carefully shaven, his cheekbones high and smooth. His hair was pulled back neatly and gathered at his nape, exposing his long, elegant neck, tanned a golden brown. His expression was serious and she could have swooned as she looked into his soft brown eyes.

"Mother?" Octavia struggled to recall how she was supposed to respond. "Oh, she's well. She and Uncle Finn have gone off again. You know how Mother is. She decided she wanted some new horses, although I can't imagine why. We have many you know." She avoided the man's unwavering look and fanned herself clumsily.

"There are several people who would like very much to talk to her. When did you see your uncle last, Octavia?"

"Not in a while, actually. He's such a simpleton and you know how Mother has to watch him all the time. I'm sure that's why she took him along. It certainly would not be because she wanted his help."

The big woman grew uncomfortable with the man's intense stare and tried to rise from the chair. The confining seat did not free her as easily as she had hoped so she settled back and began to arrange her skirt.

Timothy stood up suddenly. There was no question in his mind that Octavia was unaware of her uncle's murder and he wrestled with the decision of informing her or letting the terrible news pass for the time being. Octavia was an ordinary, spoiled girl, he thought, without much common sense. However misguided she may be in her intentions he believed she was undoubtedly ignorant of Dianna's activities. The news of Finn's murder was something he decided to leave out of their conversation. He knew the girl would not take the news well and it would make it impossible to question her further.

"Octavia, do you know where you mother is now?"

"Not a clue!" she blurted out assuredly. "I have no idea." Octavia squirmed in the chair and avoided Timothy's questioning look.

Rebecca returned with the maid who placed a gleaming silver tray on the cocktail table, brimming with pastries and a tall china teapot.

"Ah!" Octavia's face brightened as she wiggled forward in the chair and filled a napkin with the delicate cakes. She popped a tidbit into her mouth and rolled her eyes in appreciation.

Elgerson admired the appealing arrangement of flaky treats and sampled one himself. Octavia's groans of delight were not exaggerated, he thought, and he nodded approvingly to Rebecca.

His fiancé smiled knowingly. She had noticed that the man had particular tastes and she was thrilled that he enjoyed her latest attempt to satisfy him. The rich, freshly whipped cream that Birget had prepared, added the perfect touch to her pastries.

Octavia looked up from the delicacies long enough to witness the pair's private exchange and began brushing the morsels hurriedly from her crumb filled lap.

"Rebecca, I would like to speak to Timothy privately," she announced, grasping the arms of the straining chair and pushing herself to her feet.

"I'm sure that whatever you have to say can be said with Rebecca here, Octavia." Timothy walked to the window and gazed out at the last of the day's flurries.

Octavia was insulted by the man's remark and turned to face Rebecca openly.

Rebecca smiled kindly at the flustered girl and stood unfaltering, her hands clasped at her waist.

Octavia, certain that the girl did not want to hear what she had to say anyway, crossed the room to Timothy and tried to insert her hand into his arm. He lifted his arm slowly and walked away from her.

"Timothy," she began, squaring her shoulders. "I think it is inappropriate for Rebecca to remain here any longer. It's very improper that she stays here, without even as much as a chaperone. I'm certain that the entire territory is whispering about how reprehensible it is!"

Timothy turned and watched Rebecca from across the room as she stood modestly, her clear emerald eyes watching him closely as she lifted a fine brow questioningly.

"Reprehensible," he repeated and nodded to her knowingly.

"And frankly," Octavia continued, unaware of the exchange, "I feel that in light of our relationship I cannot let it happen any longer!"

"Our relationship?" Elgerson turned and faced Octavia, cocking his head to one side. "We've known one another for a very long time, Octavia, but I doubt that allows you to decide who I marry."

Octavia fell back, grasping the back of the chair

as she stared at Rebecca in shock.

"What?" She spun to face Timothy, her color rising and stomped to face him. "Do you have any idea who she is? She's nothing more than a common tart. How dare you, after all these months of leading me on, allowing me to think you loved *me*?"

"Octavia!" Timothy's voice was bold and uncompromising. "I will not allow you to insult my future wife. Furthermore, I never gave you any indication that we were ever anything more than friends. Tell me, Octavia, whatever gave you any idea that Rebecca was common at anything? Do you know something about her you think I should know about?" He leaned close to Octavia's face, his own unwavering and demanding.

"I know you ordered her like a piece of equipment from a catalog!" Octavia tapped her foot arrogantly.

"Where exactly did you get that idea?" Elgerson's jaw tightened as he clenched his teeth and faced Octavia angrily.

"From Mother, of course. But I'm sure everyone knows!" She folded her arms across her chest and pursed her lips.

"I'd like to ask your mother about that myself, Octavia. Where exactly might I find her?" Elgerson stood inches from the spoiled girl and glared at her threateningly.

Octavia burst into tears and tried to run from the room.

"Octavia, don't you dare leave this house! Where is your mother now?" Timothy stood with his fists clenched and his bellowing voice filled the sizeable room.

Rebecca stood silently, nearly holding her breath, witnessing Octavia's tantrum as the big woman turned and glared at her.

"Future wife?" she spat. "You're nothing but a common whore!" Octavia turned in Timothy's direction and glowered threateningly. "You'll not find my mother, you fool, not if she finds both of you first!" Octavia stormed out, slamming the front door and hurrying to her carriage, Timothy behind her onto the porch steps as she sped away.

Rebecca caught her breath. Octavia's tone and her use of words gnawed at her memory. Something in the way she said the word 'mother' caused her stomach to turn and brought a pain to her side.

Chapter Forty-Nine

$\mathcal{R}$ebecca spoke quietly. "Let her go, Timothy."

He stood watching Octavia's carriage careen across the lawn.

"Damn it all!" he swore. "She knows. She probably knew it all along. Damn her. That stupid girl is liable to get herself killed. She's probably running to her mother right now!"

"Timothy." Rebecca led him inside and closed the

big oak door.

He looked at her fair face and he could see she was pale with fear. He took her arm and led her to a chair in the study near the fire, kneeling beside her.

"I'm sorry," he said. "You have nothing to worry about. I swear I will never allow anything to happen to you." He rubbed her cool hand briskly, a worried expression on his handsome face.

"Timothy," Rebecca sighed. "Octavia was at the Hawk Bend Station."

"What? You saw here there? Then she did know!" He was more infuriated than ever.

"No, she never saw me there. Octavia arrived at the station while I was in the back room. I never saw her face, I only heard her voice." Rebecca swallowed hard.

"She and Dianna went outside and I stayed in the back room, I don't know what they talked about, but it was Octavia, I'm certain. Something about her made me uneasy from the time I met her. It was her voice just now. I recognized her voice! But, the way she was at the party, and the day she was out here to see you, I'm certain she did not know who I was. Octavia knew all along that her mother was up to something, but I don't think she knew it was me, at least until after that day she came calling for you."

"I was a fool to say anything to her!" he growled. "It will only aggravate the situation, and who knows what Dianna will do to her? I'm sorry. I hoped if they knew it would just pass and both of them would just give it all up." He began thinking aloud.

"No," he considered. "Dianna would never do anything to hurt her. Whatever Octavia may or may not be, everything that woman does is for that girl. She would never do anything to her daughter." He turned to Rebecca. "It's you I'm worried about. Dianna will be infuriated to hear we plan to marry. I see that now."

Rebecca considered Timothy's face, dark with anger and worry. She saw a strong, muscular, robust man with incredible physical strength. He'd watched his marriage fail and seen his intense love cast away. In his own way, to defend his happiness, his anger and his strength were his weapons. He had not simply told Octavia about their engagement to boast, he had to announce it, to let everyone know, perhaps especially those whom he saw as a threat. He had found love and used his strength to defend his happiness. She also understood that he used his temper as well. But Rebecca had experienced Dianna's terrible wrath and she knew her capabilities were immeasurable.

After seeing his anger with Jude Thomas that morning, and now again with Octavia, she remembered what he had told her about the Arabian. Cannonball had been angry, but, in spite of his terror, had listened to the man. Not because he was afraid of him, but because he trusted him. Rebecca began to feel that Timothy needed someone he could trust. She needed to be stronger than the man's fears.

"You have to understand that I love you, Timothy, and nothing anyone says or does could possibly change that. Both Dianna and Octavia would have known sooner or later anyway."

Timothy sighed deeply and laid his head against her knees and she felt his anger begin to dissipate.

"I'll tell you something, Rebecca." She could feel the depth of his voice as she placed her hand on his shoulder. "If this madness does not cease it will be the death of me. Are you alright?"

"I'm fine really. I just was so terrified when I finally recognized her voice. Really, let's try to put this away for today." The man rose and pulled her to him.

"Timothy," she whispered, captive in the warmth of his arms.

"Yes?" He kissed the top of her forehead.

"Is Stavewood always so filled with excitement?"

"No, Rebecca. I believe you brought that with you."

She kissed him softly and teased a long tendril of his hair.

Chapter Fifty

Rebecca directed the men to relocate the dressing table elsewhere in the room, while the maid dusted behind them hastily. She then followed them to the attic and sent them down with the sewing machine.

She stayed behind in the loft and pulled away dusty sheets covering a large cabinet in the far end. Bolts of fine fabrics filled the cupboard, as large as the wall and higher than her head. Silks and taffetas and numerous calicos in every imaginable color had been stored neatly. Recalling Timothy's words that she was welcome to anything she liked, she began sorting through the stacks. Fine wools and brushed flannels, many still wrapped in brown paper, caught her attention. She decided that she could devise patterns with the paper and make more clothing than she would ever need to wear. Considering the possibility that perhaps the staff might own some of the fabric, she assembled the notions and a large basket of trims and set them near the door for the men to bring down upon their return. She chose a bolt of exceptionally soft, black wool, carrying it down the back stairs to the kitchen.

"Birget!" Rebecca called to the cook as she struggled to balance the heavy fabric through the kitchen doorway.

"Heavens, Miss. What on earth have you got there?" The cook dropped her ladle and rushed to help the tiny girl with the huge bolt.

"Thank you," Rebecca panted softly. "There are piles of fabric up there, in the attic. Are they yours, or perhaps someone else's? Timothy told me I could take what I like, but I wanted to be sure."

The rotund cook laughed soundly. "Ah, no. You know Timothy. He bought that huge machine one year and of course it had to have all the fixings. He said you were bringing the machine down. Whatever are you going to do with this?"

"It's so cold now, and my dresses seem light. I thought I might make myself a lovely dress."

"Well, child," the cook laughed. "If you can sew half as well as you can cook, I'm sure it will be very lovely indeed!"

Birget instructed the maid to take the bolt up to Rebecca's room as she noticed the petite woman favoring her side. She had seen her hold herself in a similar fashion before and decided at her next opportunity she would mention it to Timothy.

Rebecca found the machine placed carefully in her room, the surface gleaming and dusted. She thanked the maids and the men profusely as they left. She sorted through the threads and trims carefully, selecting a wide, white lace, and then another, somewhat narrower, and laid the paper from the bolt out on the thick rug to begin her pattern.

Timothy set aside his work briefly and went to the kitchen in search of Mark and found Birget and the maids discussing Rebecca and laughing enthusiastically.

"What about my beautiful fiancé has all of you so entertained?"

"Ah!" the cook giggled. "That tiny girl came down in here with a bolt of fabric near as tall as herself! Her eyes were sparkling like a child on Christmas morning. I think you've set her loose now, sir, and there'll be no turning back!" The women burst out giggling. "I wouldn't be the least bit surprised to see her with a whole new wardrobe before I've finished preparing supper here!"

Timothy shook his head, pleased that someone was enjoying his Christmas gifts after all, and thoughtfully went out to the yard in search of the boy.

After sending Mark on an errand to the barns he went up the back stairs to check on his bride-to-be, curious to see for himself what the fuss was about.

Rebecca's door stood ajar a few inches and Timothy peered in silently, slowly opening the door for a clearer view. He stood listening and holding his breath as her soft voice delicately filled the room.

Rebecca had moved the smaller pieces of furniture into one corner and unfurled fabric across the floor. She crawled on her hands and knees, arranging her pattern on the fabric. Her mouth was filled with long pins and her hair slipped from her high bun, curling in soft wisps around her tiny face. The inviting presentation of her trim backside, as she stretched and reached across the floor to smooth the paper, stirred Timothy and he had to fight to keep his composure.

Singing softly to herself, she rose to her knees, and tilted her head back wistfully. Her tune was clear and soft as she pushed aside a wayward tendril:

The pale moon is rising above the green mountain.
The sun is declining beneath the blue sea.
When I strayed my love to the pure crystal fountain
That stands in the beautiful vale of Tralee.
She was lovely and fair as the rose of the summer
Yet t'was not her beauty alone that won me
Oh, no! T'was the truth in her eyes ever dawning
That made me love Mary, the Rose of Tralee.

She bowed very properly and giggled, then turned quickly on one knee to get a different angle on her pattern and gasped loudly.

"Timothy! What on earth are you doing? You frightened me!" The devilish hunger in his eyes gave evidence that he had been watching her and had not just arrived.

"I had never imagined before this moment, that watching someone crawling around on the floor could be so stimulating," he grinned wickedly.

"I thought you were busy working. Why ever would you want to spy on me?" She stood up self-consciously and tried to smooth her disheveled hair.

"What was that you were singing, and who is your invisible suitor? Is he anyone I might know?"

"Oh!" she huffed. "You shouldn't be spying on me! I sang quietly enough that I was disturbing no one." She smoothed her skirts demurely.

"Well, I am sorely disturbed, my dear woman, but certainly not by your singing." He strode into the room.

"Oh, Timothy! Not on the fabric! Here, come around here. Look at what I've found!"

She began to tell him how the fabrics upstairs were so magnificent and she made him feel the lace and fondle the wool. Her face was flushed with excitement and he understood why the kitchen staff had been so entertained by her enthusiasm.

"Do whatever you like with it. If it saves me a trip to the dressmakers I definitely encourage you!" He put the lace back in her hand and studied her elegant features, the picture of her on the floor still in his mind.

"Do you think your singing is disturbing, Rebecca?" He watched her sticking pins firmly into a fat cushion.

"My mother sang beautifully, but David thought my voice weak and squeaky. He asked that I not sing where I might be heard." Rebecca scowled and set the pin cushion beside the sewing machine.

"Then he was a fool." Timothy stepped around the fabric carefully. "Let's do this then. I think you should sing everywhere, every day, so that everyone can listen to your sweet voice. If I'm to be your husband now, then that's the new rule!" He grinned at her, curling his long fingers around the lapel of his jacket, and bowing before leaving the room. From the corridor he heard her sweet giggle and descended the stairs lest he be captivated by her crawling about on the floor again.

Mark returned from his mission, as was evidenced by the squeals of the women in the kitchen. Timothy swung open the kitchen door, hushing them soundly, and took the gift from Birget's plump hands.

The small kitten, its tiny ears poking from the sides of a fluffy face, mewled softly in the man's warm hands.

"Is it for the Miss?" the young maid inquired as she cooed at the tiny creature.

"It most certainly is." Timothy held the velvety kitten up and inspected it carefully.

"I'm sure she'll be thrilled!" Birget smiled as she

stirred her soup.

"Rebecca told me she has never had a pet. I thought I'd surprise her." Timothy believed the kitten would suit the girl just fine.

"She told me that, too. She was terrified of the chickens," Mark interjected.

"Then it's time she had a pet, don't you think?" Timothy handed the fuzzy feline to the boy. "Take it down to the cellar and find a box or something to keep it in. After supper you can fetch it for her."

"It's the best one, Pa! The others are kind of wild and they're spitting already and everything. This one likes to be held. I don't think Rebecca will be afraid of this."

"Let's hope not!" Timothy chuckled as he rubbed a long finger about on the furry head and returned to the study to finish his work. The kitchen smelled wonderful and he was eager to set his work aside and enjoy a hearty meal. He was also looking forward to seeing Rebecca's face when she received the tiny pet.

Chapter Fifty-One

Rebecca finished cutting the pieces for her new

dress, rolled the remaining fabric onto the bolt carefully, and set the room back in order before attempting to thread the sewing machine.

Birget appeared at the door, announcing supper, a very odd look on her face.

"Is something wrong?" Rebecca asked the cook, who looked as though she were about to cry.

"No, nothing at all." Birget replied, her lips tight, as she quickly went downstairs.

Rebecca brushed her hair back into place and pulled several bits of black fabric from her skirt before heading down for dinner.

Timothy and Mark had assembled in the family dining room, smiling broadly, and Rebecca was sure something was most definitely strange at Stavewood.

"All of you are up to something." She slipped into her chair, looking mystified as Timothy pushed her close to the table.

Mark giggled and Timothy glared at him and returned to his place at the table.

"Did you sew on the machine yet?" the boy asked as Birget appeared with a platter of lean roast beef.

"Not yet, but I'm getting ready to thread it now." Rebecca peered at him from across the table suspiciously.

"When you figure it out can you show me how it works?"

"No new dress yet, Miss?" Birget asked, smiling as she filled Rebecca's plate.

"Birget believes you were going to turn out a new wardrobe before she finished dinner tonight." Timothy poured the rich gravy over a mountain of fluffy potatoes, smiling slyly.

Birget laughed and returned to the kitchen.

"Is that why you are all behaving so strangely, because I can sew? Is there something especially amusing about that?" She tasted the beef, and was pleased with the hearty flavor.

"Not at all! I told you, I thought it was wonderful!" Timothy hummed as he sampled the tender beef. "Rebecca, this is superb. I don't know what you and Birget have been plotting in that kitchen, but I fear it will have me two sizes larger before spring."

"If you get too much bigger I'll feel like I am sleeping with Cannonball!" Rebecca scolded.

Mark laughed quietly, delighted that she felt comfortable enough to tease the man so easily.

"I have not an inch of fat on me!" Timothy looked sidelong at the boy.

"I was not referring to your being fat in any way, sir," Rebecca smiled.

"Ah, so the 'big' was intended to refer to something else." He smiled at the woman knowingly.

Mark was not sure why Rebecca blushed so profusely.

The woman glowered at the man, and put away her teasing.

After a light dessert of chopped and sugared almonds, between flakey layers of paper thin buttery pastry, Timothy sent Mark to get him some papers from the study and then excused himself briefly.

"I'm sorry, Rebecca, there's a paper I forgot to ask the boy to bring. Don't get up. I'll be right back to share coffee with you."

Rebecca was enjoying her dessert too immensely to leave her place and sighed with pleasure at how sweet the confection tasted.

Mark ran back into the dining room and plopped into his chair.

Rebecca heard a tiny cry, as if from an infant, and turned to Timothy standing behind her with an odd smile on his face.

"Go ahead, Pa!" Mark bounced excitedly.

Timothy opened his massive hands to reveal the tiny kitten, a fluffy ball of pure black with wide, deep, blue eyes, mewing softly and squirming restlessly.

"Timothy!" Rebecca exclaimed. "Wherever did you find this little sweetheart?"

She gathered up the tiny creature and enclosed it in her fine hands, studying the feline lovingly and producing soft kissing sounds that made the kitten purr loudly as it began rub against her thumb.

"So this is what you were all up to! You're a bunch of scoundrels!" She kissed the tiny kitten's head and smiled at Timothy fondly.

"You told everybody you had never had a pet," Mark explained. "Pa thought of it and I picked it out!" Mark happily dove back into his dessert.

"How sweet of both of you!" Rebecca nuzzled the kitten close to her face.

"It's good practice, Rebecca," Timothy commented as he returned to his chair and sipped his steaming coffee.

"Practice? For what?"

"Babies!" Timothy chuckled as Rebecca studied the helpless creature and wondered to herself what kind of a mother she'd make.

Chapter Fifty-Two

*T*imothy growled, dropped the deeds onto the table next to him and studied the young woman beside him before the den fire. "I swear these documents get more impossible to make sense of every day."

Rebecca was contemplating her knitting and looked up at him thoughtfully. The kitten was curled contentedly in her lap.

"What kind of papers are they?" She set her knitting aside and rubbed the kitten's head with one finger.

"Nothing you'd find interesting, I'm sure." Timothy watched her fondling the animal and considered addressing the problem that had been interrupting his concentration.

"Perhaps I could help. My father was a rather successful barrister and I often assisted him at his office."

"It doesn't matter right now, Rebecca." He rose from his chair and pulled the brandy bottle from the shelf.

"Timothy, what's wrong?" She lifted the kitten gently and set the sleeping pet into the basket of yarn at her side. She studied Timothy's troubled face.

"I'm worried, Rebecca." He filled the snifter and gazed into the fire.

"About Dianna?" As much as she had enjoyed her afternoon and the delightful gift, she herself had been unable to rid her mind of the situation.

"There's no question in my mind that Jude killed the chestnut, and took the Arabian, possibly for his own. Did you know that Jude is a cousin of Octavia's?" He sipped the brandy slowly.

"You mentioned that before. Why would he come after the horses?" Whatever the man's reason, Rebecca was uneasy.

"Jude Thomas and I go way back, Rebecca. I'm sure you've figured out by now that there was something going on between him and Corissa." Timothy turned to her seriously.

"There is nothing whatsoever that I myself find attractive about the man. Is that what you're concerned about?" Rebecca felt him scrutinizing her closely.

"Not really, but there are other things. Mark was not exaggerating about the snow. I worry that you don't realize a lot of things about me, Rebecca. Or about what life will be like here for you." He turned from her, a faraway look in his eyes. "I'm not sure you'd be happy at Stavewood in time."

"What would make you even imagine that?" Rebecca impatiently awaited his reply, leaning forward in her chair and hoping he would look at her.

"Once the snow does fly it won't stop, not for months. Then there's the cold. Dressed properly we could get into Billington occasionally, but it will become an excursion, and you'll find you probably don't want to spend much time outdoors. If there had been less commotion going on here I would have taken you out riding several times before now, just to get you out before winter."

Rebecca watched the side of his face closely as he gazed into his brandy, swirling the dark liquid in the large glass.

"There's the house to run," he continued seriously, "And if you enjoy your knitting and that sewing machine over time as you seem to now, maybe you'd be happy here."

"Timothy, are you afraid that I decided to start sewing because you didn't take me shopping when I was cold?" Rebecca never meant to make him feel she was not being well cared for.

"I can probably buy you anything you desire, Rebecca. But, however fortunate I have been in my business dealings, the fact remains that I'm not much more than a glorified logger who lives in the middle of nowhere. With Dianna around you'll even be more confined at Stavewood than ever. Yet, even once that situation is resolved, some isolation will always be a factor."

He turned to her, his face solemn and unsmiling.

"Timothy, whatever gave you any idea that I could possibly be anything less than completely contented here? I love to sew, that has nothing to do with whether or not you can buy me things. Yes, I was cold, but I've found that fine wool. That wool comes from you. Stavewood is a very large house, with a full staff and I am sure I will have more than enough to keep myself busy. Please do not imagine that I could ever feel restless here with you."

"Oh, Madam," he shook his head. "Trust me, you will get restless!"

"Firstly, my dear sir, let me tell you that I am nothing less than perfectly contented here. Do you imagine that if I were to get bored, confined by some snow, I would love you any less?" Rebecca rose from her chair and stood to face him.

"It's happened." Timothy looked at her openly.

"Well, it won't happen to me, Timothy!" Her tone was unwavering and she looked frankly into his eyes. "I am more in love with you than I ever imagined possible. I came here for you, for Stavewood, because it's where I have always belonged. If I were to find myself in England again, with or without the means to care for myself and, even if the world seemed perfect, were anyone to ask me if I would set foot on that train again, I would not hesitate for a moment."

He studied her face closely, her eyes welling up with tears and a fierce determination in the emerald depths. He took her gently by the shoulders.

"Rebecca," he whispered passionately. "It seems that everything imaginable has stood in your way to keep you from being here now, yet none of it stopped you. How can I possibly meet the expectations you must have after all of that?"

"Timothy, don't you see you already have? We have many things to be worried about, but my feelings for you and the happiness I have found here should never be one of them. You must believe in that and put at least that worry aside."

He pulled her to him intensely, holding her so tight against him that she began to ache. She listened to the deep timbre of his heartbeat and cursed everyone around him who had not appreciated the generosity and love he was so eager to give.

"If there's anyone who is undeserving, Timothy, it would be me," she whispered. "You are a wonderful man, and I plan to spend the rest of my life appreciating your love."

He held her in front of him and stood looking at her face, the soft warmth in her loving eyes and the perfect delicate features of her astonishing beauty. He kissed her ravenously.

Rebecca felt totally complete in his strong arms as they stood embracing. For a time now they were quiet and safe from the threat that surrounded them both.

"You cannot imagine sleeping in that cold, empty bed alone tonight," he whispered.

"I'd rather not, but I think it would be best. I don't care what anyone thinks, but I do care about Mark and what he is learning and it simply seems unacceptable." She stood with her hands resting against his chest.

"Then we'll sleep in *your* room tonight," he stated, pleased with his alternative.

Rebecca giggled. "You think it's about which room we sleep in?"

"Then we'll stay awake all night while I make love to you and not sleep at all." He looked down into her eyes, his own eager and smiling.

"You would have me sneaking around every morning until we're married? I don't think it matters which room we're in, or whether or not we actually sleep. We will be discovered," she scolded.

"I'll go for the reverend now, and it will be done." He could see that Rebecca believed he was teasing her.

"At this hour? I think not!"

"Then at daybreak. It's settled!" He kissed her warmly and she fought with her resolve.

"Timothy," she whispered and he lifted her lightly in his arms.

"This is kidnapping!" Rebecca giggled.

"Even better!" He chuckled deeply as he climbed the stairs two at a time.

Chapter Fifty-Three

Timothy laughed as Rebecca wrapped herself in the twisted, white sheet, scolding him soundly for having lured her once again to his bed.

"I think that would be a perfect wedding gown."

"I think not," she gasped. "Why, it's not even decent!"

"I noticed that! Well, if not a wedding gown then perfectly acceptable for coming back to bed." Timothy lie on his side, reclining on a high stack of pillows, watching her pace the room in the revealing sheet.

"Please, I have to get to my room before the entire household is up!" Rebecca leaned toward him, whispering loudly, offering the man an inviting glimpse of her barely covered breasts.

"Alright," he sighed as the girl wrapped herself more decently. "Sew up the thing if you must, but be quick about it so we can hurry up and get married."

"You're not serious," she gasped.

"Perfectly!" He smiled smugly and brushed a lock of hair from his face, his broad shoulders bare and bronzed against the white sheets. "We'll go into Billington straight away this morning and be back here having a honeymoon before nightfall. You did agree to marry me!"

"But, what about a wedding?" Rebecca was sure he was most certainly joking.

"We'll have a wedding in the spring with flowers, relatives, the works. Whatever you please, Rebecca. We'll invite the entire county if that makes you happy, but we'll marry today." He sat up on the bed, not bothering to pull the blanket across himself, shaking back his mane of hair.

Rebecca blushed and smiled at the clear view she was afforded of his bare thighs and exposed position.

"Oh, pardon me. I'll be more careful for the rest of the day," he smiled, gallantly covering himself. "But, after today you'll have to get used to it."

"Stop teasing me and get me back to my room!" she demanded in a hushed tone.

"I'm dead serious, Rebecca." His demeanor became suddenly subdued.

"You can't be!" She sat in the chair, tucking the sheet around her bare legs.

"Why not? Of course you want a wedding, a gown, a celebration. I would never imagine denying you any of that. We will have it all, all of it and more, but I don't want to wait." He faced her, his forearms on his thighs as he leaned toward her earnestly.

"You really are serious. You want to elope?" She could not believe he was ready to marry her this instant. "Just so that I don't sleep in my own room?"

"Partly, but that certainly is not the main reason. It's rather obvious, you have to admit, that having you in my bed has not been all that difficult, at least the last few nights."

"Oh, stop!" She began to pace the room, trailing the sheet carelessly behind her. "It seems so rushed, so sudden, to just run off."

"Are you unsure in any way that you want to marry me?" His voice was questioning.

"No, of course not!" She turned to face him. "That's not it at all!"

"Then, why not? If you are ready, and trust me, I am much more than ready. Why not?"

"I'm not sure why not. It just seems reckless, I suppose."

"Rebecca, you got on a train and traveled halfway around the world for about ten words in an ad, and you think marrying me today is reckless?" He laughed heartily.

"Oh, stop, Timothy. You're twisting it all around." She resumed her pacing.

Timothy set his foot firmly on the trailing sheet as Rebecca paced past him and she lost her grip on the fabric and he deftly gathered it into his lap.

She faced him, entirely bare, and frowned.

"Marry me, Rebecca," he said softly, as she wrapped her arms around herself. "Not in a week, or a season, or a year. Marry me today. I have spent far too long without you. We'll dress and tell Mark and the staff. We'll go to Billington today. I'll buy you the biggest ring that money can buy and bring you back here as my wife. Back to Stavewood. Here, the way it should have been the day I finished it." He looked clearly into her eyes, never wavering as she listened quietly.

"A ring?" Rebecca choked.

"Of course!" Timothy burst into laughter. "The biggest we can find. Say yes!"

"But what will I wear, and what will we tell everyone and-and…" she stammered. "Yes!"

The air was crisp and clear as Rebecca snuggled into the furs in the coach, warmly dressed in a smart black wool dress Timothy had borrowed from one of the maids. Although the dress was designed to be covered with a large apron, and might look severe on anyone else, on Rebecca it was stunning.

Her hair carefully arranged, and her cheeks glowing with excitement, Timothy climbed in beside her and shouted for the driver to go ahead.

"Are you excited?" he whispered close to her ear and put his strong arm around her, pulling her warmly to his side,

"Yes," she giggled. "Very!"

"You're sure you want to do this today?" he asked.

"You!" she huffed. "Two hours ago it seemed like I had no choice, and now you ask me if I am sure? You are incorrigible, Timothy Elgerson!"

"Not nearly as much as I expect to be tonight."

Rebecca could feel the deep vibration of his laughter as she nestled close to him.

"Is it too cold to open the window?" Rebecca felt so closed in, within the confines of the coach, while the air seemed so sweet and fresh outside.

"Not if you're warm enough. I'll open the window if you like."

Timothy pulled back the heavy curtains, opening up the view to a startling blue sky, and he slid open the window.

Rebecca looked out at the leaves, drifting by the hundreds down around them and she inhaled the crisp air. With the trees having lost so many leaves, the panorama opened up and Rebecca could see for miles as the carriage rolled gently down the hillside from Stavewood.

"The air smells different today," she mused aloud.

"That would be from the snow yesterday. When

the snow falls enough to cover the ground the air can be so clear it nearly hurts to breathe it sometimes." He spoke softly as he reclined in the carriage.

"Timothy, why is the third floor closed at Stavewood?"

"What makes you ask, Rebecca?" He looked down at her sweet face, the soft furs gathered around her fetchingly.

"The turret. When I was up there the day I first went up to look for knitting things, we opened the door and stepped out on it. It was so beautiful. I'd never seen anything like it. I thought, perhaps when everything was covered with snow, it might be beautiful as well."

"What possessed you to go out into the turret at all?" He watched her and listened seriously.

"I don't know," she replied wistfully. "It felt as if the house wanted the door open. It was funny because the door was heavy. When it came free it was as if the house sighed." Rebecca mused at the memory.

"When I built the house there was something inside me that could not be stopped." His voice was quiet and quaking. "My father used to joke about how many cubits high it should be, and asked if God had commanded me to build it, like Noah and his ark.

"At the time I wasn't sure myself why I felt I had to build Stavewood and, contrary to what everyone thought, I had begun the house and milled most of the lumber even before I met Corissa."

"I thought you built it for her?" Rebecca looked up and saw his serious, faraway look.

"No, not originally. After I met her, she was lost and restless. I thought if I brought her to the house it might make her happy somehow. Since it was strong and sound, I thought it would make her feel more secure. I was very wrong.

"Corissa thought it was confining, and the day I took her up to the turret she remarked that it was like a prison tower. Originally there were windows up there, my thoughts being that you could go up there on any day, even the coldest of days when the skies were most vivid and the stars their most brilliant, and admire it all. All of Stavewood, and much more.

"One winter, in a very bad blizzard, one of the windows cracked and I took them all out. After that I sealed off the third floor. Once, I thought we'd have guests in the house, and a family." Timothy sighed deeply.

"It's interesting, Rebecca that you would be moved to go out into the turret and I believe you heard it sigh. The day I closed the door I heard it myself."

Rebecca let a tear fall onto the soft furs and it slid down slowly and dropped onto Timothy's sturdy hand.

"Would you like windows back in the turret again?" he asked.

"No, because it's so beautiful outside here, even in the cold. I think the bracing weather is part of the beauty of the view."

"Maybe that's why the window cracked." Timothy considered Rebecca's unerring observations about the house.

"But, I would like to open the third floor one day," she sighed. "For a family."

Timothy held her close, one part of him listening for any sign of danger and the other feeling her perfect in his arms. He had two riders following, discreetly and at some distance, as the couple left Stavewood. Taking Rebecca into the city had other advantages than just eloping.

They rode in silence while she watched the landscape pass and choked back tears at the beauty of the lake, just beginning to freeze.

As they approached Billington, the road filled with coaches, buggies and riders and Rebecca sat up and peered out of the window excitedly.

"Last chance," Timothy announced loudly. "Speak now or forever hold your peace!"

Rebecca laughed gaily as they pulled up before the jeweler's.

Chapter Fifty-Four

*I*nside the shop she was like a child, pointing at the rings and commenting at each one. The jeweler, taken by her exceptional beauty and engaging enthusiasm, pulled out his sizing tools eagerly to measure her finger.

He frowned and cleared his throat. Unable to break the news to the girl, he looked up at Elgerson.

"I'm afraid I have a limited collection in the Miss' size, sir."

Rebecca, having not laid eyes on a ring she liked, smiled to get his attention.

"There is a ring here, I just know it, sir," she stated confidently. "Could you show me what you do have?"

"I do have a very petite ring, but only the one." The clerk frowned earnestly.

"I only came to purchase one," Rebecca replied softly.

The jeweler hurried to the back of the shop, disappointed that the one ring he had was not the new and lavish piece he was sure Timothy could easily afford for the petite bride. The ring was only an old estate piece he had just purchased on a recent trip overseas and he was sure it would not be to the girl's liking.

"We'll wait and look at the ring, Rebecca, but I have no problem going on to St. Paul. We can marry there tomorrow just as well." Timothy watched her eagerly awaiting the return of the salesman, and braced himself for her eventual disappointment.

The jeweler took a moment to clean and polish the piece, and was astounded to discover that, once taken from its surroundings among costume pieces, the ring was quite unusual.

"No," she whispered calmly. "Trust me Timothy. If this is to be, the ring is here."

He stood behind her and adjusted his stiff dress collar, uncomfortable with her declaration.

The clerk returned, somewhat flustered, and handed the tiny wooden box to Elgerson.

Timothy opened the box slowly as Rebecca stood on her tiptoes and peered inside. She held her breath as he pulled the delicate ring from the box and placed it in her palm.

The ring featured a warm gold setting, sweeping in two lacy swirls of tiny diamonds, enclosing a perfect oval emerald, the exact shade of the enchanting eyes of the beautiful bride-to-be.

Timothy was astounded. Where he had expected to purchase a massive diamond to encumber Rebecca's tiny hand, instead, miraculously, the only one that would fit her was perfect indeed.

She gazed into his eyes and smiled, "This is my ring."

Rebecca browsed the shop, and soon found a man's ring, quite heavy, and set with two emeralds of the same shade. It fit Timothy perfectly and looked quite elegant on his fine, broad hand.

As they stepped out into the street, he turned her to him, overcome with questions and looked into her eyes.

"How did you know that he had your ring? It's perfect, Rebecca. I would have chosen it for you myself had I not thought you'd prefer something much larger."

"I don't know, maybe it was what you said about Stavewood and the window cracking. It just seemed that it was meant to be."

He stared into her deep green eyes and agreed that it indeed was meant to be.

"Timothy and Rebecca! What a stunning pair you make!"

They looked up to see the elderly couple Rebecca had met at Timothy's party, and were a bit flustered at having been caught in their public display of affection.

"How wonderful to see you both!" Rebecca took the woman's hand and smiled sweetly at the gentleman. "I must admit my shame. I met you both at the party and was so rude to have never gotten your names. Please forgive me!"

The woman was strikingly attractive, and smartly dressed, her silvering hair upswept into a stylish hat. The gentleman was nearly as tall as Timothy, with a rugged and stately manner.

The couple laughed, admitting that they had never been properly introduced, and the gentleman turned to Timothy, instructing him to do so now.

"Rebecca Fagan, may I introduce Phillip and Isabel Elgerson, my parents." Timothy bowed as Rebecca gasped loudly.

"Oh, heavens! Please forgive me, I had no idea!" Rebecca was obviously flustered and thrilled.

"Rebecca and I are to be married," Timothy announced.

"So we heard, so nice of you to have told us," his mother scolded.

"Today," he continued.

"Today?" The Elgersons looked at each other and smiled at the surprise.

"We'll be having a ceremony in the future, but today we are eloping. Is that what you called it, Rebecca?" Timothy turned to her and smiled broadly.

"Oh, please come with us!" Rebecca pleaded, her intentions genuine.

"Is it traditional, dear, to have the groom's family present when one elopes, Isabel?" Timothy's father turned to his wife.

"Since when has Timothy, or you for that matter, ever done anything traditionally?"

Rebecca laughed with delight, her wedding day becoming more perfect.

"You have, of course, bought this dear girl a ring, Timothy?" Isabel asked.

"The most astonishing ring, as a matter of fact!" Timothy boasted.

"Then I believe we ought to wait to eat, Isabel, and attend our son's wedding first!" Phillip announced, as Rebecca and Isabel whispered in appreciation over the emerald ring. He gathered Isabel's hand, placing it in the crook of his arm.

The woman pulled her husband aside and they slipped into a florist's briefly, reappearing excitedly with a large bouquet of white flowers.

In the private office of the magistrate, Rebecca repeated her vows in a sweet clear voice as Timothy smiled and looked into her eyes. She studied his firm, strong face and contemplated his resolute, muscular jaw line as he watched her solemnly. She hesitated, looking away once, for a moment, his want-ad appearing in her mind. She marveled at how many places she had been and all that she had been through to be where she was standing right now.

Isabel Elgerson smiled at her with quiet understanding as Rebecca looked back to Timothy and continued, "I do."

Timothy Elgerson stated his vows, unwavering as he gazed into her clear emerald eyes, her beautiful face flawless with serious composure. He knew that every moment of his life he had looked for her loving gaze and he swallowed hard before responding in his deep resounding voice, "I do."

Chapter Fifty-Five

*T*he elegant dining room was warm with candlelight and the hearty congratulations of friends and acquaintances, as a steady stream of patrons recognized the couples and stopped by their table to say hello.

"Timothy, you really should consider the cottage!" Isabel exclaimed as she and Phillip treated their son and his new bride to a lavish dinner.

"She just spent months redecorating the place, Tim. I have to say myself that it would make a rather nice place to honeymoon," Phillip admitted.

"I suppose I should let my wife decide." Timothy smiled broadly to Rebecca. "I had hoped to be back at Stavewood tonight, but at this hour we may be staying in town as it is. What do you think, Rebecca?"

"Oh, please do!" Isabel urged. "You'll have all the privacy you please," she smiled knowingly at her son. "It's so cozy and since we have had no chance to get to know you we could spend some time together."

"Mother, it seems to me that, if you want us there so that you can get to know Rebecca better, there won't be much privacy at all." Timothy sipped his wine, raising an eyebrow towards his father.

"That is so kind of you. I don't know what to say." Rebecca looked at the friendly faces surrounding the table. She felt warm and relaxed and sat studying her wedding ring thoughtfully. The wine was leaving her with a deep glowing feeling and she didn't really want to make a decision in either direction.

"You'll have plenty of time at Stavewood once the snow flies," Isabel continued her persuasion. "Bring her, Timothy. We would enjoy it so much!"

Timothy looked concerned. "There are other things we have to consider, Mother. Rebecca ran into some problems on her journey and I have some men watching Stavewood, there is a situation I think you should be aware of."

Phillip removed his napkin from his lap and placed it on the table.

"We heard some things, Tim," he studied his

son's face seriously. "I can assure you that if you are in any way concerned, I can put a few of the men around the cottage during your visit. We'll be right there at the main house ourselves should either of you need anything. You know our place is not nearly as isolated as Stavewood. It might be safer in fact."

"Rebecca," Timothy turned to his bride, watching her eyes. "I think it might be a better idea than staying in town tonight. And, since Mother seems so determined, how would you feel about staying at the cottage for a night or two, then we'll go home?"

"It might be fun," Rebecca smiled. She was unsure how disappointed Timothy might be over not returning to Stavewood. She knew she was a bit disappointed herself.

"Then it's decided!" Isabel exclaimed.

Timothy gathered her beside him in the furs, as the carriage turned towards his childhood home, and Rebecca giggled.

"What has you so amused, Mrs. Elgerson?" He watched her face, her cheeks flushed and rosy.

"I'm not sure. The wine perhaps?" Rebecca giggled again.

"Ah!" Timothy smiled. "Well then, my dear, I can hardly wait until we reach our destination."

"And why would that be?" Rebecca snuggled into his sturdy chest.

"Because, Rebecca, if you are drunk it will be easier to have my way with you." Timothy felt the excitement of his approaching honeymoon as his beautiful bride's delicate hand slid provocatively along his thigh.

"How far a ride is it?" she asked teasingly.

"A fair ride, I expect. Why do you ask?" he examined her face suspiciously as she wrapped her arms around his neck.

Rebecca kissed him passionately and Timothy displayed no resistance as she slipped her slender hand inside of his jacket, stroking his chest boldly through his shirt.

She began unbuttoning him slowly as he reached to secure the curtains in the enclosed carriage.

He found her kisses along his chest maddening, and, as she placed her hand unashamedly over the hard ridge against his thigh, Rebecca felt him stiffen from her touch. Having never approached a man so shamelessly, she hesitated for a moment, before moving her fingers slowly and firmly along him and it was clear he was not offended by her boldness.

He turned her to face him as his excitement built and Rebecca's desire for him matched his own. He unfastened her bodice, fondling her warm breasts above her corset, his touch sending spasms of excitement through her.

Rebecca, unbridled in her curiosity, slid her slender leg across his thigh, straddled his knees, and unbuttoned his trousers. As he pulled her towards him in his desire, she placed a gentle hand against his chest, holding him in check. She found that part of him that she wanted to know more intimately and grasped him firmly. He swallowed hard, watching her face, fighting to concentrate, the warmth of her hand consuming him with desire.

Rebecca gasped softly in surprise as she felt his

stiff firmness in her hand, more exciting than she ever imagined and explored the length of him with her fingertips.

"Rebecca," he groaned.

"Do you mind?" she asked softly. "I just wondered."

He watched her face, fighting for control and swallowed hard.

"What do you want to know?" His breathing was hoarse and labored.

"What you feel like," she panted softly.

"And?" He closed his eyes and moaned deeply.

"Very nice," she whispered slowly and her grip tightened.

He pulled her to him, kissing her fiercely. Her touch was unbearably seductive.

He placed his fingertips on her hand, his self-control becoming impossible. His breathing halted. Rebecca slipped brazenly from her lacy bloomers and sat across his lap.

He lifted her onto him and she arched her back in sudden ecstasy and moaned, her head tilting back and her lips parting in a soft moan of pleasure. Captured in her passion, she looked into his eyes, fierce with desire for him, and he surrendered in release to her unmistakable sensuality.

"I ought to give you wine more often, Madam," he sighed and gazed into her eyes, consumed with love for her.

Suddenly, a bit embarrassed at her boldness, she blushed and buttoned her bodice carefully.

"You're blushing, Rebecca. Why?"

"I was overcome, I suppose," she whispered. "I

just wondered what it would be like to touch you. I never have, and I was curious."

"Rebecca," he lifted her chin with is finger gently, looking into her eyes. "You are my wife. I would hope you would do anything you'd like. Don't be afraid, Rebecca. There is nothing you could ever do in our lovemaking that you should ever be embarrassed about. I certainly am not." He smiled devilishly. "As far as I'm concerned, you are welcome to be curious like that any time you like."

The young bride blushed again, and Timothy chuckled.

"I'm not sure exactly how far we are from my family home, but I guarantee that if we arrive in such a state you may have much more to blush about."

He set Rebecca on the seat beside him. He gathered himself, watching her beside him trying to dress, flustered and self-conscious, and Timothy shook his head.

"I think in the future there might be a few more things you could be curious about."

She scowled at him, smiling, and smoothed her skirt carefully.

He studied her flustered face, wondering what kind of a marriage she must have had to be so anxious about her natural curiosity.

Chapter Fifty-Six

$\mathcal{R}$ebecca stood before the cottage as Isabel had requested before running inside to light the lamps. The leaded windows began to fill with a warm glow and Rebecca felt enchanted.

The tiny, Victorian home was painted a soft yellow and adorned with a pure white gingerbread trim, featuring steep angled roofs and a large oval window in the front door.

"It looks like a fairy tale!" she observed aloud.

"Wait until you see what she has done inside." Phillip laughed and rolled his eyes. "I swear the woman feels denied at never having had daughters and always wanted dollhouses all about the place! She actually comes out here by herself and has tea."

"Tonight it is a honeymoon cottage!" Isabel announced as she returned to the porch.

Phillip checked inside the coach, and then turned to his son as Timothy released the driver to return to Stavewood. "Tim, didn't you and Rebecca bring any luggage at all?"

"Rebecca and I had not planned to stay the night in Billington, Dad. We never packed any luggage." He draped a soft fur around Rebecca's shoulders.

"I have the perfect thing at the house for you, Rebecca!" Isabel exclaimed. "And I'm sure Phillip has something Timothy can use for the night."

"You don't need to bother tonight, Mother."

"Nonsense! How often is there a new bride staying at my honeymoon cottage? Both of you ride up to the house and we'll set you up for the night while the place warms up and you can come back here straight away. You're worse than your father in your lack of patience!" Isabel smiled at Rebecca, as she turned away fearing she might blush.

Timothy sighed and then helped Rebecca into the family coach and they reached the main house quickly.

Isabel led Rebecca through the grand home, solidly built and elegant in its modern straight lines.

"This is very different from the cottage," Rebecca mused, as she examined the portraits lining the upstairs hall.

"That's why I wanted the cottage built. I love this home, but I always longed for some ruffles and lace and they never seemed to fit into this household. Timothy's father built the house during our engagement, and, although I love its solid elegance, I wanted a home of a different type as well.

"I always hoped one of the boys would have a family and the grandmother lurking inside of me wanted a cottage perfect for reading fairy tales." Isabel watched Rebecca's face, looking for her reaction. She led the girl into a massive bedroom with soaring ceilings and substantial, carved furniture.

"This is like a cathedral!" Rebecca whispered in awe.

"The Elgerson men do not hold back when they build," Isabel shook her head, a fond smile on her lips.

"Enough of my babbling. There's plenty of time to talk about families. I doubt my son's patience will hold out long."

Isabel sorted through a large armoire, finally emerging with a carefully bundled parcel.

"I wore this on my honeymoon. Perhaps you would like it for yourself."

Rebecca unfolded the wrapping carefully, uncovering a delicate negligée, a trail of tiny embroidered flowers flowing the length of the gown. She looked at Isabel speechless and tears glistened in her eyes.

"I expect it might be a bit large for your petite size, Rebecca, but, if Timothy is anything like his dear father, I expect he won't notice," Isabel smiled wistfully. "This is your wedding night and you should feel more beautiful than any night in your life. The night I married Phillip I felt like a vision in this."

Isabel took Rebecca's hand gently, and looked into her eyes. She held the girl warmly as she cried.

"Thank you," Rebecca whispered softly. "This is all like a dream I fear I will wake from. I am so in love with your son."

Taking the girl by the shoulders, the older woman looked seriously into her face.

"Rebecca, you are my daughter now. I have never seen Timothy so happy, so comfortable with anyone. He is my only living child and the pleasure you have put on his face says to me that you are something very special. I wish you all the happiness in the world, and I hope you will always look at Phillip and me as family."

Timothy stopped in the doorway, listening quietly, having grown impatient waiting for the women to return.

"Timothy!" Isabel caught him as he listened. "I

see you have not given up your talent for spying! You look out for him, Rebecca. He has an unerring talent for watching you when you have no idea that he's there!"

"I know!" Rebecca giggled.

Chapter Fifty-Seven

$\mathcal{R}$ebecca dressed unhurriedly, brushing her hair to a soft shine, leaving it loose, and lowered the delicate gown carefully over her head. The gossamer fabric fell against her slender body and she smiled with satisfaction. Rebecca did indeed feel more beautiful than she ever had in her life.

She set her brush down and sighed deeply, before leaving the bath.

Timothy paced the room impatiently, oddly nervous as he waited for her to emerge.

The light from the open doorway silhouetted her perfect figure as she stood demurely and met his appreciative gaze.

He lifted her easily and carried her slowly, lowering her softly onto the ruffled bed.

"Rebecca," he whispered. "You are absolutely the most breathtakingly beautiful woman I have ever seen in all of my life."

"And I am entirely yours," she whispered, kissing him softly.

His kisses inflamed her and he made love to her with gentle passion. Rebecca felt more complete than she ever imagined possible.

She lay beside him in the warmth of his love and the aftermath of their perfect union. She listened with complete contentment to the strong beat of his heart.

He lifted himself to face her, his soft brown eyes searching her own, his handsome face tanned and rugged.

"Are you happy, Rebecca?" he whispered.

"Blissfully," she replied softly.

He pulled her to him, and tucked the warm, down coverlet around her and she drifted off, certain that she now believed in fairy tales.

Chapter Fifty-Eight

$\mathcal{T}$wo weeks flew past them in a flash, filled with delightful visits to Timothy's family home and perfect nights when they slipped ecstatically away in each other's arms. Timothy shopped with her and they dined in all of Billington's finest restaurants. Rebecca felt as if she were living a dream, and, as much as she missed Stavewood and everyone there, she regretted that the honeymoon would eventually have to come to an end.

"We'll go back tomorrow," Timothy agreed, as they lounged over brunch in the sunny breakfast room of the cottage.

"I miss Mark and Stavewood," she admitted, rising from her chair to kiss the man on the cheek. She felt a stab in her side, and winced.

"Is something wrong? Would you rather not go home?" Timothy watched her with concern.

"No, I want to go back, really. I miss Stavewood very much. It is home," she assured him.

"Then something else is wrong. What is it?"

Rebecca moved slightly and winced again.

"It's nothing, really. I've got a stitch in my side."

The third spasm was harder to ignore and Timothy scooped her up and carried her to the bed, despite her protests.

"Timothy. Honestly, it's nothing. It will pass. It always does."

"Always does? How long has this been going on?" He stood over her, his face dark with worry as she lay on the bed.

"A while. Timothy, please don't make such a fuss. I'm fine."

"Since the shack? Is that when? Birget told me she noticed you favoring your side. Mark said you may have been kicked. Is that it?"

"It's fine, really." Rebecca knew her time of the month had come and gone and supposed she might be expecting, but did not want to speak before she was certain.

"Has it been the same pain since then? The truth, Rebecca."

"It's the same place, yes," she whispered. "But it might be something else."

"Something else?" he looked at her questioningly.

"I missed my time, but I didn't want to say anything until I was sure." She lowered her eyes self-consciously and sat up on the bed.

"A baby?" He sat down beside her and watched her closely.

"I'm not sure though. I've never had this happen before," she replied tentatively.

"Are you unhappy that you might be expecting, Rebecca?" He touched her cheek.

"No, not at all, it would be wonderful!" She looked into his worried eyes. "I just wanted to be sure before I got too excited."

Timothy kissed her face eagerly, overcome with relief.

"Timothy," she asked with surprise and worry. "Why are you crying?" She put her slender hands on either side of his face and turned him to her, his eyes meeting her own.

"It doesn't matter, Rebecca, remember? What happened before, it doesn't matter." His face was dark and serious.

"No, it doesn't. Corissa was expecting once, wasn't she?" She had suspected it before, recalling her trip up to the attic at Stavewood. Now she wanted to hear it from him.

"Yes," he whispered, "but she didn't want another child and she had been with Jude. She found a doctor in St. Peter. Are you sure this is what you want?"

"More than anything in the world, Timothy. I would be overjoyed."

Rebecca felt another stitch and Timothy walked up to the main house to get his mother, despite Rebecca's quiet protests.

Isabel sat beside the girl on the bed and talked to her softly, while Timothy paced the parlor impatiently.

"I'm not a doctor, Rebecca, but I've carried four children and you should not be having these pains. You can't think of yourself as being a burden. If you are carrying a child then you must think about your baby and let a doctor examine you. Phillip has gone to fetch him now and if there's nothing wrong then we'll all be assured and you'll know."

Rebecca sighed, she was so concerned about the fuss everyone was making and thought that, since the pain had lingered for so long, she could just continue to live with it. But if she was expecting it was different. She agreed to let the doctor examine her.

Isabel held Rebecca's hand beside her as the doctor completed his examination. He confirmed that she was indeed expecting, but expressed concern. Timothy's parents excused themselves, retiring to the parlor so the doctor could talk to them privately.

"There's no question in my mind that you are going to be a father, Tim," the doctor began, as he stood at the foot of the bed.

Timothy kissed Rebecca's hand and she smiled up at him sweetly.

"From what Rebecca has explained to me, and the nature of her discomfort, I suspect she's had some damage to her rib cage. Her condition is causing some pressure and may become much worse as her situation progresses. Any other time I would consider binding her ribs, but in this circumstance it is out of the question."

Timothy ran his fingers through his hair.

"Tim, listen to me," the doctor spoke sternly. "Rebecca is in perfect health otherwise and her confinement appears quite normal in every other way. The damage is not too severe and there appears to be a fair amount of healing. There is no reason to think your wife and child are facing any serious risk.

"Rebecca will experience some discomfort. In fact, she may be quite uncomfortable from time to time, and she is to avoid any strenuous activities until the baby is born. You keep her fairly quiet and I expect you'll be bouncing your first-born on your knee before you know it."

He shook the doctor's hand, thanking him as he left the room, and then knelt beside the bed.

"I'm so sorry, Timothy." Rebecca whispered.

"If I ever find Dianna, I swear I'll kill her!" He ground his teeth.

"Timothy, stop it. The doctor said I'll be fine. I feel fine now, and for all of the time we've been here

I've been feeling wonderful." She smiled at him reassuringly. "You told me yourself that I'll be trapped by the snow soon. Now I have something to do. I'll work on a new baby!"

Timothy looked into her eyes and swallowed hard.

"Like the doctor said, you'll be bouncing our baby soon. Please stop your worrying. We're going to have a baby!"

Chapter Fifty-Nine

$\mathcal{T}$imothy paced the parlor of the cottage angrily.

"Rebecca, it's out of the question. We'll stay here until the baby comes and I think it's safe to make the trip, not a minute before."

"It's just a few feet of snow. I'm feeling fine today, I'm sure the ride would be alright. I can't imagine making you stay here for months." Rebecca was disappointed not to be returning to Stavewood, but she was sure Timothy was devastated.

"You're not making me stay. I just think it's the only way. Why risk it? If something went wrong neither of us would forgive ourselves." He sat down beside her at the table, taking both of her hands and looked at her openly.

"I'll be back first thing in the morning with everything you need and we'll just stay here. You loved this cottage when we first came. It's just a much longer honeymoon than we ever imagined." He smiled and kissed her hands.

"Not much of a honeymoon now, I suppose," she sighed.

"We can continue to satisfy your curiosities in no time, it's always a honeymoon to me." Rebecca had to smile at the twinkle in the man's eye.

"I will enjoy that very much," Rebecca blushed. "I'm anxious for that myself."

Isabel walked onto the porch and held Rebecca by the shoulders, standing behind her on the cottage porch, as Timothy pulled away in the carriage.

Rebecca turned, unable to watch the man leave, and cried onto the older woman's shoulder.

"He'll be back soon, Rebecca. It's not good for you to make yourself so upset. Come inside out of the cold and we'll have something naughty and delicious to eat."

Rebecca allowed the woman to lead her inside and sat at the table, a faraway look in her eye.

"He wanted so badly to return to Stavewood right away, right after we were married, he even stated it as we were leaving there. Oh, Isabel, I feel so terrible." Rebecca fought back her tears. "He was so worried I would feel trapped at Stavewood like Corissa did, and now I have trapped him here away from home. I feel fine really, a little twinge sometimes, but not much more than before."

"Before now you didn't have your baby to consider. Think about it, Rebecca. Inside of you a part of both of you is growing, depending on you to take care of yourself so it can come into the world healthy and strong. Timothy is a grown man and he knows he can't just do as he pleases. He has a family now and he understands that. He loves you so much. Trust him to make the right choice. I assure you, he does not feel trapped any more than you did at Stavewood."

Rebecca smiled. She accepted Isabel's perspective and tried to understand. She sighed and decided that something to eat sounded wonderful.

"I have to admit to you, Rebecca," Isabel opened the basket she had brought down from the main house and revealed a collection of delectable pastries. "I'm rather pleased you'll be here to have your baby."

"Are you excited about becoming a grandmother at last?" Rebecca pulled one of the chairs closer, arranging the pale yellow gingham cushion and propping up her feet.

"You can't imagine! I'm also quite happy that you convinced Timothy to bring Mark back with him. Phillip and I have never had the chance to get to know him, though we certainly have wanted to. Corissa would have none of it.

"When you told me about being up at the cabin for so long I could have killed Timothy for leaving the boy there while he was away. We would have loved to have had him here. It's a good thing he'll have you to teach him to be a more responsible parent. He never cared much for our methods." Isabel chuckled, tasted the pastry, and rolled her eyes.

"I don't know anything about it myself. I don't know how well I might teach him." Rebecca tasted the pastry and agreed with Isabel's' appreciative expressions. "Timothy gave me a kitten, for practice he said, right before we left to be married."

"See, Rebecca. There's a perfect example! Timothy is thrilled that you're expecting."

"Yes, you're right," Rebecca sighed. "I just feel as if everything has gone badly and I can't stop wanting to cry about every little thing."

"That's part of how you learn to be a mother." Isabel placed her hand upon Rebecca's on the table. "You cry over everything. Sad, happy, sweet, silly. When your baby comes you understand how important every little emotion can be and you understand so much more. You'll feel your baby's every sensation and know how to communicate and care for him.

"That however, does not apply to men. With men you understand less and less."

The two women laughed and Rebecca began to understand that Isabel was the perfect person to help her prepare for her baby.

In the morning Timothy returned as promised, grinning broadly, with Mark beside him, holding the mewling kitten in a basket. He began unloading the carriage, taking out a boxful of yarn in every shade of blue.

Rebecca hugged him fervently and ruffled Mark's hair as she accepted the kitten.

"Pa said you need more practice." Mark's eyes

were twinkling and Rebecca was sure they must have had some interesting conversations about the baby.

"He said I was getting a brother or a sister in the spring and I needed some practice, too." The boy was visibly pleased.

"I see you expect me to spend much of my time knitting. But only in blue?" Rebecca smiled at the two males, lifting her eyebrows and examining the bundles in the box.

"Well," Tim said devilishly. "If not blue, you could use these!" He reached inside the vehicle and pulled out an equally large box filled with pinks.

Rebecca laughed, and, taking Mark by the shoulder, led him inside.

Later, Phillip and Isabel took Mark up to the main house with promises of wonderful books and toys, threatening to tell stories of how badly Timothy had behaved as a child. Their son and Rebecca were left to enjoy their evening alone.

"You thought you might be expecting before we came to town, didn't you?" Timothy was lying on the bed, Rebecca's head on his chest as he played with her hair.

"Yes," she whispered, drowsy with the pleasure of his fondling.

"Why didn't you say anything?"

"I didn't want you to marry me just because I was expecting."

"Afraid you'd be trapping me?"

"Yes, rather. I talked to your mother after you left. Do you remember when you asked me if I would feel trapped in the winter at Stavewood?" She moved slightly to free her hair from beneath her, allowing him more to play with.

"Yes, vividly. Why?" He let a long strand fall from his fingers.

"She told me that it was the same thing, my thinking I had trapped you here. Is that true?"

"My mother is a very wise woman, Rebecca. She's exactly right."

Rebecca ran her slender hand along his thigh, stopping short of being too intimate.

"I'm not sure that's such a good idea." He held his breath.

"It's fine. I asked the doctor when he stopped by yesterday."

"You asked him what?" He lifted his head and looked into her eyes.

"If it would hurt me if we made love."

Timothy cleared his throat, embarrassed to imagine what the conversation must have sounded like to the doctor. "What did he tell you?"

"No swinging from the chandeliers and no standing me on my head. He suggested that there were ways we might enjoy one another I hadn't thought of before." Rebecca smiled up at him, a twinkle in her eye.

"What? I don't want to envision that conversation at all." He blushed.

"That's what he said," she grinned at the memory. She was nervous about asking, but the doctor was open and frank with her, professional, yet understanding.

Timothy groaned, still uncertain and terrified that

he might hurt the girl or her baby in some way.

"You're afraid, aren't you?" She asked, laying her head back against his chest.

"Very," he responded softly.

"Then why don't you just let me satisfy my curiosity and you just lie back?" She began to stroke his thigh a bit more boldly.

"Possibly," he whispered cautiously. "Just exactly what are you curious about?"

"I'll show you," she whispered as she turned and crawled up to face him.

Chapter Sixty

$\mathcal{P}$atches of the rich soil had begun to show through melting snow in the woodland surrounding the cottage and the spring day was unusually warm. A bright collection of crocus was beginning to bloom along the pathway.

Mark was seated beside Rebecca as she read aloud on the porch swing. "Grandmother Isabel told me that if I asked you might let me feel the baby pushing. She said to ask very nicely so you wouldn't be uncomfortable."

"Grandmother?" Rebecca asked, watching the boy's face.

"Sure, she's going to be the baby's grandmother, so that makes her my grandmother too, right?"

"Yes, you're exactly right!" Rebecca watched the sleek black cat chase her yarn on the porch and then rub affectionately against her leg.

"So, does the baby really push?"

"Yes, quite well in fact." Rebecca took the boy's hand and pressed it to her rounded belly where the baby had kicked soundly just moments before.

As her unborn infant pushed a tiny foot firmly against her Mark nearly leapt from the chair.

"I felt it!" he exclaimed and held his hand carefully against her. "There it goes again! What's it doing in there?" Mark was clearly amazed.

"Getting crowded, I expect." Timothy walked out onto the porch, having listened to their conversation from inside the doorway.

"You should feel it, Pa! It's pushing really hard!"

"I have. It pushes me all night." Timothy placed his hand lovingly on Rebecca's shoulder.

Rebecca shifted her position slightly.

"Mark, let Rebecca be now. Why don't you take the cat for a walk up to the house so Rebecca can get her nap?"

The boy patted Rebecca's belly softly, leaned close and whispered. "It's spring now, you can come out pretty soon." He jumped from the porch, calling the cat, which followed him as he ran up the path.

Rebecca laughed and Timothy shook his head.

"I guess he's getting excited," Timothy chuckled.

"I'm just getting uncomfortable," Rebecca sighed.

Timothy helped her from the chair and took her arm, leading her inside. They both knew that the baby was becoming difficult for Rebecca to carry now, but her pregnancy had gone well and her date was not far away.

"I feel like a human pumpkin," Rebecca remarked as Timothy helped her into the bed.

"The most stunning pumpkin I've ever seen."

Rebecca settled against the soft, propped pillows and studied her husband's fine face.

"Something happened while you were up at Stavewood. I know it, please don't deny it."

"You have enough to worry about. Let it be and I'll sit with you if you like." Timothy lifted her legs easily and placed her feet on his lap.

"If you don't tell me I will continue to worry and might imagine something far worse than the truth. I'm only expecting, Timothy. I'm not an invalid."

He rubbed her slender foot slowly, wishing she had not seen the concern on his face and hoping she would abandon her questioning.

"I'll only keep asking. Tell me please. You don't need to worry alone."

Timothy sighed and looked her in the eye.

"There's talk that Dianna is back in the area. Someone may have seen her in the woods surrounding Stavewood."

"Oh, Timothy!" Rebecca tried to sit upright in the bed.

"Sit back. I told you, you have enough to worry about. It's fine. Nothing has happened for months. They could have been mistaken." He sat her back and covered her legs with a light quilt.

"Timothy," she scolded. "Dianna is not a woman you tend to mistake for anyone else."

"Maybe it was just a huge moose," he smiled.

"Oh, you!" Rebecca smirked. "You're just trying to keep me from worrying."

"Most definitely, woman. You let me worry and you sleep." He tucked her in and sat carefully on the bed beside her.

"I'm not in the least bit tired." She took his hand gently.

"Because you are going to lie here and worry now."

"No, that's not it. I've felt rather energetic all day I just don't move quickly enough for anyone to notice." She giggled.

"It may be all that fresh air you have gotten today. Here, come closer." Timothy pulled her to him and Rebecca snuggled into his shoulder.

"I'm nervous, Timothy," she moaned.

"About Dianna? Don't be."

"No, about the baby coming." She rubbed his hand absentmindedly.

"Do you feel alright?" he looked down at her, concerned.

"It's not that," she sighed. "What if I scream or something?"

Timothy chuckled deeply. "I've heard you scream before. I'm sure everyone will survive."

"Me? Scream? Never!" she gasped.

"Close enough." Timothy cleared his throat.

Chapter Sixty-One

*T*imothy heard his voice being called from somewhere in the fog. He could see into the mist and Rebecca was standing there, tears running down her cheeks. He could not move his legs to go to her. "Timothy," she called to him again and he sat upright in the bed.

Rebecca was not in the bed beside him. He pulled on his trousers hurriedly and heard her voice again.

She was standing in the bathroom, an odd look on her face.

"Oh, I'm glad you heard me. I think it's time." She gathered up the hem of her nightgown and blushed. "I think my water has broken."

Timothy Elgerson had practiced this moment in his mind a thousand times, yet none of what he had carefully planned came to him as he stood there in complete confusion.

"Alright." He shook his head and ran his fingers through his hair trying to think.

"You need to go up to the house and get your mother, Tim. It's time for the baby to come." She spoke to him slowly, carefully.

"Yes!" He turned to follow her instruction. "Wait, what about you?"

"I'll wait here." She smiled.

"Where's Mark?" he looked around the hall where he stood as if he expected to see the boy.

"He's sleeping. I'm fine. Just go up and get your mother."

Before she could stop him he ran and woke the boy, instructing him to dress quickly and watch Rebecca and not let anything happen while he was gone. He threw on a shirt and ran up the hill to the main house.

"Rebecca!" the boy gasped. "Are you okay?" He ran to her, flustered, and he saw her standing in her crumpled gown. "How did you get all wet?"

"It's almost time for the baby to come. Remember how we talked about it floating?" Mark took her arm and tried to sit her in the chair in the hall.

"Yes," he replied, his eyes wide with fear.

"Well, before the baby comes the water that's it's been floating in comes out. It's perfectly normal." She cursed Timothy for waking the boy, leaving her with such an awkward explanation.

"Oh, yeah," he nodded. "Cows do that, too." Rebecca sighed.

Rebecca was overcome with a powerful contraction and suddenly appreciated that Mark had put her in the chair.

"What can I do?" The boy frantically wanted to help.

Rebecca panted softly as the contraction passed.

"It's fine, Mark. It's just the baby's time to come and it's very hard work."

"It looks like it. Does it hurt?"

"Oh, yes," she laughed.

"Do you want something to bite down on?"

"What?" She looked at the boy questioningly.

"One of the men at the mill got a big splinter of wood in his leg once and they let him bite his belt while they pulled it out. I can look for Pa's belt."

"No, thank you. I think I'll be fine."

"Okay." He watched the young woman closely.

"Whiskey maybe? Sometimes people drink whiskey. They said it's good if something really hurts."

Rebecca gasped and grasped the arms of the chair tightly.

Mark watched her straining and remembered how helpless she had been the day he found her in the shack and how he had cared for her. Everyone told him he had done a good job of helping her and he wanted to do well now. Isabel had talked to him about how to not upset Rebecca in any way. His father had given him honest information on how babies were born, and how they came to be, but no one had told him how to get them born. He had witnessed many births of cows and horses at Stavewood, but he was certain a person having a baby had to be very different.

He stood beside the woman, holding her wrist while she gripped the chair, and felt the strain in her arm. As soon as she began to relax he pulled a blanket from the bed and wrapped it gently around her shoulders and asked her if she wanted dry clothes so she didn't catch a chill.

"Thank you, Mark. No," she whispered and began

again to pant softly.

"Does it feel like when you were hurt at the cabin?" He hoped that maybe if she kept talking she might not notice the pain so much.

"No." Rebecca looked up to his worried face. "It's like a very, very tight squeeze. It's very tight and then it stops for a minute. You just stay with me until the next one comes and your father brings Grandmother Isabel. That would be a great help."

She grasped his hand tightly as her next contraction began and Mark was shocked at how forcefully her tiny hand grasped his. He was taller than her now and he never realized she was so strong.

As she relaxed again he heard the carriage pull up in front of the cottage, but he stayed by her side until Isabel and his father hurried in.

Timothy rushed to Rebecca, still in his bare feet, his face taut with worry.

"Rebecca," Isabel squatted down to face the laboring woman as she panted softly. "The pains, are they close?"

"Very!" Rebecca tried to force a smile as her contraction intensified.

Isabel placed her hands gently on Rebecca's abdomen and felt the intensity of her pain.

"Mark," she rose and faced the boy. "I want you to go with Grandfather Phillip to get the doctor. He's waiting in the carriage. Do not let him drive like a crazy man. Do you understand? We'll be fine until the doctor comes. Just make sure he doesn't go too fast. Alright?"

The boy nodded vigorously in agreement, looked at Rebecca worriedly and ran out to the carriage.

"Timothy, I want you to strip the bed and make it up with those things I prepared, then come back here and help me get Rebecca into the bed."

He was relieved to have something to do and rushed to change the bed.

"Tell me about the pains, Rebecca. Are they stronger in the front or against your back?"

Rebecca whispered. "The back."

Timothy returned and helped Isabel, carrying his laboring wife into the bedroom where they situated her on the bed.

"I want you to wait outside while I examine her, Tim." Isabel's voice was clear and controlled. "I'll call if I need you."

Chapter Sixty-Two

$\mathcal{T}$imothy walked from the room, feeling helpless at the sight of his petite wife straining on the bed. Isabel closed the door behind him. He sat on a chair with his head in his hands and sighed nervously.

Isabel examined Rebecca carefully, running her hands along the woman's abdomen as another contraction began and checked for the presentation of the infant's head. Since losing babies of her own in childbirth, she had studied everything she could get her hands on and now she often assisted women in the area with their deliveries. Isabel examined Rebecca again and the young woman begged not to be touched. She was certain the baby was breech. If she could not turn the child it would not go well for Rebecca or the baby, and this was such a slight girl. Isabel became very concerned.

Rebecca moaned and gritted her teeth, gripping the sheets tightly, her face contorted in pain.

"Timothy, get in here!" Isabel called.

The man rushed into the room, panting hard as he watched his wife struggling on the bed.

"Timothy, I need you to help me turn her over. Do exactly as I say. You must help me to get her over onto her and knees and as soon as I tell you, then we must turn her back over onto her back and then get her upright. It is imperative that you do exactly as I say."

"Something's wrong," he groaned quietly.

"We need to turn that baby, now do as I say!" Isabel's commands were clear and concise and Timothy rushed to the bedside.

"Yes, like that. Lift her and set her up on her knees with her hips elevated. Carefully, take her by the hips and lift. Yes, like that!"

Timothy was alarmed, afraid that the rough handling of his wife would only hurt her further. He was unsure of how he could manipulate Rebecca as his mother instructed, without injuring his wife.

Rebecca screamed out in pain, begging the man to let her be and she felt her baby shift inside her. Terrified, she begged him to stop.

"Now, turn her over quickly!" Isabel directed him and he deftly turned Rebecca's tiny body, slipping her on her back onto the bed. Isabel examined Rebecca again quickly. She was confident that the baby had turned and she felt Rebecca surrender to another contraction.

"Timothy," Isabel looked seriously at her strapping son. "I'm going to need you to help me hold her up. You can do it. You have to hold her exactly as I say and do not let her slip away. Get on the bed behind her." Timothy stepped up on the bed, lifting Rebecca from behind, his face dark with fear.

"You need to put your arms around her chest here." Isabel grabbed Timothy's arms firmly and crossed them beneath Rebecca's breasts. "Lift her up so she is squatting over the bed. We need to keep that baby facing the right way and this will help Rebecca deliver more quickly." Timothy was intensely afraid he would break the girl's ribs, and struggled to hold her firmly, but do no damage.

Rebecca screamed out as Timothy lifted her upright and then got on his knees behind her. He held her, squatting over the bed and the girl pushed, struggling against his broad chest.

"Rebecca, listen to me!" Isabel took Rebecca's face in her hands and spoke to her firmly, calling her name until she was sure Rebecca heard her.

The girl moaned, trying to focus on the woman's face through her pain and terror. She knew something was very wrong. Timothy's grip on her was keeping her upright when all she wanted to do was collapse on the bed.

"When I tell you to push, you must push,

Rebecca. Even if you think the pain is going to pass for a moment, you cannot let it. You have to push."

Rebecca whimpered and begged them to let her be.

"No, Rebecca. It's time for your baby to come and you must do as I say."

"Timothy, please," she begged through clenched teeth. "Put me down, please!" She tossed her head against his shoulder, crying and begging in pain.

"Keep her up, Timothy. Do not let her slide down."

Timothy fought against his wife's straining as she pushed with amazing strength against his expansive chest and he struggled to keep her lifted over the bed without crushing her. Rebecca's body was slick with perspiration, and she pleaded again for him to release her.

With his hands and arms across the top of her abdomen he could feel the strength of her contractions, and for a moment he opened his fingers against her straining pressure. He could feel the miracle of her body's force as the muscles within her pushed to bring forth their baby.

"Now! Push! Push as hard as you can!" Rebecca strained violently, groaning with effort, her back solidly against Timothy as she pushed into his unyielding strength and her contraction overcame her. As the pressure began to ease, Isabel shouted to her through the fog of her labor.

"Keep pushing, Rebecca. Push! It's almost here. Honey, you must push! Timothy, tell her!" Isabel shouted.

"Push, Rebecca! Please, push now!" His voice

was deep and his words were hot in her ear. She grimaced with pain, put her chin on her chest and pushed with all of her might to free her baby.

She fell back against him as she felt the release, shaking and begging for it to be over.

"Again, Rebecca. Push again! The baby's head is here, honey. You need to push once more!"

"No, no more," Rebecca cried pitifully.

"Our baby is here, Rebecca! Push one more time!" Timothy whispered to her as he felt another contraction compress her slender body.

Timothy and Rebecca's baby slipped into Isabel's waiting hands and the infant let out a lusty wail.

"It's a girl! You have a baby girl!" Isabel inspected the baby quickly, setting her on the bed for a moment while she pressed Rebecca's belly firmly to finish the delivery.

Rebecca screamed in agony and collapsed back into her husband, trembling and in tears.

"You can lie her down now." Isabel dried the infant quickly and swaddled her tightly once she had tied off the cord.

Timothy let his wife fall against him and cradled her in his arms. Her face was pale and beautiful and she tried to whisper his name as tears streamed from the corners of her eyes. He gathered her exhausted body and kissed her cheek. Stepping off of the bed, he lifted her gently, her body quivering with exhaustion, and placed her tenderly on the bed.

"Timothy," she looked into his fatigued eyes. "The baby, is the baby alright?"

"She's perfect and beautiful, Rebecca!" Isabel answered. She walked to the bed and lay the tiny bundle in Rebecca's arms as Timothy lifted her up to sit upright, holding her as she accepted the newborn from Isabel's loving hands.

Rebecca looked down at the tiny infant and gasped. "Oh, my," she whispered. Placing the baby on her lap, she unwrapped her carefully and studied her daughter. She touched the baby's solid chest and stroked her little bowed legs.

"She is so small!" Rebecca caught her breath as the dainty infant squeaked. She swathed the baby carefully and lifted her gently, turning to her husband and looking into his astonished eyes.

"Timothy, I need you to take the baby into the other room while I examine Rebecca and clean her up." Isabel watched the couple with her new granddaughter, pride swelling in her chest.

Timothy took his newborn daughter into his immense hands and held her before him reverently, carrying the child out of the room as though she might break at any moment.

Isabel could not contain her amusement and laughed aloud as she closed the door to the room.

She pressed Rebecca's belly firmly, while the petite woman squirmed, and assured her that everything was perfectly normal. She helped her to a chair and quickly changed the bed. After putting her into a fresh gown, she situated Rebecca as comfortably as possible in the bed.

Chapter Sixty-Three

Timothy Elgerson sat alone in the cottage parlor, his daughter placed uncertainly on his lap. The baby rubbed her tiny fist against a pink cheek and pursed her lips, frowning. He touched her small hand with his finger, feeling larger than he ever had in his life. The baby opened her fist and grasped his forefinger firmly.

Timothy caught his breath, and the newborn struggled to focus on her father's face, as he leaned close to her and whispered.

"Hello, little miss. Allow me to introduce myself. I am Timothy Elgerson, your father." Timothy could barely contain his wonder as the baby wrinkled her nose and squeaked softly.

The carriages arrived outside and Mark ran into the house. He froze at the sight of his father bent over the tiny bundle.

"Is that the baby?" he gasped.

"Mark, come here and meet your little sister."

The boy tiptoed to his father awkwardly as Phillip and the doctor stood in the doorway, quietly watching the boy kneeling beside his father and studying the new baby.

"She looks just like Rebecca," he whispered, "But really small. Look, Pa! She even has hair!"

Timothy chuckled as he rose from the chair and

handed the infant to his father. "Grandfather Phillip, meet your new granddaughter." The baby squirmed in the arms of the family patriarch and cooed softly.

The doctor tapped on the bedroom door and entered quietly as Isabel finished settling Rebecca against the pillows.

"Well, my dear. You are looking quite well!"

Rebecca smiled weakly and pulled the warm blankets close to her. "You never told me I would have to be spun around to have that baby," she smiled gingerly.

"Spun around?" The doctor looked at Isabel puzzled.

"The baby had to be turned. It went quite well actually." Isabel smiled proudly.

"I see," the doctor frowned. "Well, Rebecca, you appear to have come out of it just fine." He examined her briefly and nodded approvingly to Isabel.

"What I didn't tell you is that you have the best midwife in the territory beside you." He nodded and gathered his bag from the bed.

"I'm sure I have the best mother-in-law," Rebecca replied.

Timothy returned with the baby, and Mark rushed to Rebecca's side, patting her hand protectively.

"Rebecca, the baby looks just like you!" he informed her excitedly. "Are you better now?"

"Yes, Mark, much better." She rubbed his arm affectionately.

"I wanted to stay and help you, but I had to make sure Grandpa Phillip didn't get hurt driving the buggy too fast."

Timothy smiled and winked.

"Thank you, Mark. Your father and Grandmother Isabel did just fine."

"That's good, because I was really worried."

Timothy laughed heartily and turned to his mother to grip her hand.

"Everyone out!" Isabel scolded. "Let's leave Rebecca to feed that baby. I think you fellows can all go off and celebrate."

Isabel took the infant from Phillip's proud arms and handed her to her mother, closing the door as Mark and the men left the room.

Sitting beside Rebecca, Isabel helped her put her new daughter to her breast and, once the baby was nursing happily, gathered up the linens and straightened the room.

"What have you decided to name her?" she asked as she sat down in the chair beside the bed, enjoying the sight of her beautiful daughter-in-law feeding her new baby.

"Louisa Elizabeth Elgerson." The young mother whispered as she watched her baby blissfully, feeling quite exhausted. "They were my grandmother's names."

"Very pretty," Isabel replied quietly as she took the sleeping infant from Rebecca and set her in the waiting bassinet.

"To Louisa Elizabeth Elgerson!" Phillip toasted as the men touched their brandy snifters, dipping in the butt ends of cigars, even allowing the boy a taste in a snifter of his own.

The long-legged men lounged on the porch in the

late morning sun. Isabel came out onto the porch and noticed Mark with his brandy. She shot the men a glaring look and they raised their glasses to her, grinning broadly.

"You two are beyond belief!" She smiled and shook her head.

Chapter Sixty-Four

*T*imothy sat restless and fidgeted in the tiny kitchen, watching Mark from across the room. He was trying desperately to make Louisa laugh despite her loud wails.

"I think she's really mad, Pa." The boy sighed and dropped into a chair.

"What do you imagine she could possibly have to be that angry about?" Timothy set aside his paperwork and crossed the room to pick up the fretting child.

"I think she wants to eat again. She looks pretty darned mad to me."

Rebecca stepped sleepily from the bedroom and gathered up the now wailing infant, who began to root against her breast violently. She returned to the room without a word and in moment the house returned to a peaceful bliss and Timothy sighed.

For several days Rebecca felt as if she could not sleep enough. Timothy often paced the floor, softly whispering to the persistent infant, and Mark learned to change diapers while singing *Skip to My Lou* all hours of the day and night. All of their lives revolved almost entirely around tiny Louisa.

The baby settled into a routine as the days warmed and her demands for constant feeding subsided, to the relief of everyone in the household. Her tiny form began to fill out and one afternoon Timothy was certain she smiled at him.

"I guess it's too early to think about the next baby," Timothy speculated aloud as he cradled his daughter in his powerful arm.

"Another one?" Rebecca looked up from her knitting and observed him watching Louisa fondly.

"Another baby!" He smiled at her handsomely.

"I would think you had been up enough nights singing to the one you have already." Rebecca shook her head, smiling.

"This one is much too small to fill the entire third floor of Stavewood. I believe we'll need several just like her before we can load the place up. Don't you agree, Loo?" he cooed.

"She'll grow in time." Rebecca sighed, grinning.

Rebecca had nearly regained her strength and, as the seasons changed, she approached Timothy on the porch.

"I think it's time," she placed her hand lovingly on his shoulder.

"Time?" he replied absently, his face serious as he stared into the trees.

"I think your sentence should be over now, sir." Rebecca moved to the chair beside him.

"Is that a proposition, madam?" He looked up at her curiously.

"Yes," she smiled at him mischievously. "And more."

"After all these weeks of waiting, I can't imagine anything I would enjoy more." He looked at her lovingly and smiled.

"It's time to return to Stavewood." Her face was serious.

"Are you sure?" He fought to contain his excitement.

"We need to go home. I miss the place terribly and I can no longer bear to watch you suffer in this tiny cottage." She smiled and touched his arm. "Take me home, Timothy. Take me back to Stavewood the way we planned on our wedding day."

Timothy stood and pulled her close to him, kissing her fervently.

He looked down into her emerald eyes and whispered to her. "I would enjoy that almost as much as our wedding night."

The man had made regular trips to Stavewood, always returning with piles of gifts for Rebecca and the baby, clothing and yarn and silver rattles. Rebecca could knit for every minute of the rest of her life and never make a dent in the mounds of yarn he had carted back. He made several trips to the dressmaker, once bringing back a girl to take Rebecca's measurements, and supplied her with an astounding wardrobe with which to dress her returning figure.

He struggled to keep himself from his beautiful wife, her figure fuller and more inviting. He could barely contain himself until Louisa was settled in the nursery at Stavewood.

He now spent several days riding back home to bring as much as he could to the big house. The last day he stopped at the home of his parents, so that Mark could kiss them goodbye. The boy rattled on in excitement, as he always did, happy to be returning home again while soothing the big cat captive in the box on his lap.

"Don't you worry, son," Phillip had placed his hand on the boy's shoulder. "Your Grandmother and I are coming up next week. I'll bring those good poles and we'll hit the lake and bring in some of those walleye."

After bringing Mark back to Stavewood, Timothy returned to the cottage to find Rebecca finishing a thorough cleaning in anticipation of returning home the following day.

With no one about the place except her and the infant, Rebecca selected a lightweight green gown that fit her waist. She was nearly as thin as before her pregnancy, and she left a few buttons unfastened at the bodice, in the heat of the afternoon. With her hair piled loosely upon her head, Timothy found her kneeling on the floor trying to retrieve a tiny stocking from under a chair.

"Let me get that," he whispered, unable to take his eyes from her generously displayed cleavage.

"There is something about you crawling about on the floor that I find quite unnerving, woman."

Rebecca sat back on her ankles, her hair tumbling in soft tendrils around her shoulders and framing her delicate face. "Tell me all about it," she smiled provocatively. She could see the hunger in his eyes and was eager for him to find her beautiful once again. "Do I still spark your interest?"

"More than ever." His heart pounded in his chest as he watched her regarding him eagerly.

"Where might that daughter of ours be?" he looked into the sultry depths of Rebecca's emerald eyes.

Rebecca smiled mischievously. "I moved her bassinet into the other room."

Timothy accepted her invitation openly and pulled her to him.

Rebecca fell into his arms impatiently and he kissed her feverishly. She felt the remaining buttons of her bodice fall free as he cupped his hand against her full breast and she caught her breath, the pleasure of his touch filling her with an equal hunger for him.

"Woman," he whispered hoarsely, "you have no idea how nearly impossible it has been to keep myself away from this."

He pressed his lips between her breasts, now completely fulfilled with her progression into womanhood. Rebecca arched her back with pleasure.

He continued to unfasten her dress and she pressed herself against him, moaning with desire.

When she felt his firm hunger against her thigh she could stand no more. She stood up beside him and let her dress fall free to the floor.

Timothy caught his breath, having been denied the vision of her for so long. Her waist was still slender and firm, her hips now fuller with curves, and her breasts full and firm. Where Rebecca had been beautifully petite and delicate, her body now was that of a woman, possessing provocative fullness and Timothy could contain himself no longer.

Rebecca walked slowly to the bedroom and the bold view of her curved backside had him struggling to his feet to follow her.

She lay on the bed, her hair pulled free to tumble around her, open desire in the depths of her eyes.

He disrobed slowly, his white shirt falling from his broad shoulders, exposing his powerful chest, his trim waist, his firm and taut stomach. As he removed his trousers from his powerful legs, Rebecca gasped at the sight of his openly displayed desire for her and she lifted herself from the bed and pulled him to her hungrily.

He filled her to perfection, satisfying the craving Rebecca hungered for as she rose to meet him and he drew her to him, whispering her name softly and fulfilling his own hunger for her.

Rebecca lay beside him, the warm afternoon sun streaming across the bed, Timothy's muscular body stretched beside her.

He watched her face as she ran her fingers through his hair, pushing it back from his face and searching his warm brown eyes.

"Are you happy?" he asked her, his voice smooth and deep.

"Perfectly," she whispered in reply.

"Tomorrow we will go back to Stavewood." He turned onto his side to face her. "Tomorrow I'll be bringing my family home."

"Tomorrow," she whispered.

Chapter Sixty-Five

$\mathcal{R}$ebecca called from the cottage. "Are you certain we have everything?" She checked the house one last time as Timothy assured her that the carriage was fully prepared. The driver waited patiently as Phillip and Isabel tucked Louise inside, kissing and fussing over her.

"I've had that route checked and rechecked, Dad," Timothy assured him. "I'm sure we'll be fine. There's been no trouble."

Rebecca stopped in the doorway of the cottage and, although it was lovely, imagined that Stavewood was whispering on the afternoon breeze, calling her home.

She kissed Phillip and Isabel warmly and Timothy lifted her into the carriage eagerly and they began their journey home.

"Excited?" Timothy gathered the baby into his lap and the young wife snuggled into his shoulder.

"Very. I'll miss your parents so much, but I feel as if I belong at Stavewood." Rebecca sighed.

"As you always have." Timothy looked into her glistening eyes.

"So much has changed since I've been there," she thought aloud. "I'm a wife and a mother now. I feel as if I'm a different person since we've been there."

"We both are, I suppose. I never really thought about it all that much on my trips back, but for you I guess, many things have changed. I'm glad we're going home. I need you there, and Louise should be there." Timothy watched his daughter sleeping in his arm. "Stavewood is missing something since you've been gone. Maybe it always was. It's as if it were always there, waiting for you."

"And I was waiting for Stavewood, and you." Rebecca took his hand and stroked her baby's sweet face.

"We'll be taking the back ridge road. We'll get there that much faster." Timothy laid his head back against the seat as Rebecca dozed in the strength of his arm.

Chapter Sixty-Six

Rebecca heard a loud crack shatter the quiet of the ride and woke suddenly as the carriage shifted to one side.

"Timothy!" she screamed, watching him pull the baby to his chest as the vehicle tilted violently.

"Get down!" he shouted, pushing her onto the floor of the carriage. Rebecca doubled over as the coach began to overturn.

Timothy heard a gunshot and tried to gather his feet beneath him. He found himself outside of the carriage, the baby pulled close to his chest. He felt the searing crease of the next bullet graze his shoulder and scrambled to the cover of a nearby tree trunk.

His feet gave way beneath him as he stumbled too close to a slick embankment and he began to roll. He held the infant to him, supporting her with the strength of his arms as they tumbled.

Splinters of bark exploded over his head as he lay in a deep ravine at the bottom of the long hill, the child silently studying his face. He heard the scuffle of feet above him and felt the warmth of his own blood wetting his shoulder.

"Philip! You must tell me what route they've taken to Stavewood!"

Octavia was reining in her horse brutally, in front of the cottage, frantic and breathing hard.

"I believe my mother has gone completely mad!

You have to tell me! She's going to kill them both if someone doesn't stop her. Please!" Octavia was screaming hysterically and pleading with the man.

"They took the back ridge road. I'll get my men together!" Phillip replied, but before he could finish, Octavia turned her horse and rode swiftly towards the ridge.

Timothy looked into the dark eyes of his softly breathing daughter and prayed that she didn't utter a sound. She was the perfect image of her mother and the man held his breath, his mind racing. He tried to devise a way to get to Rebecca and still protect the child.

"Rot in hell, Elgerson!" He heard Dianna's voice echo through the ravine. "You could have had Octavia, but you lusted after that bitch instead! Well, now you can just rot in hell!"

Timothy heard her stomp away on the hard packed road.

"She thinks I'm dead," he whispered, holding perfectly still. The baby smiled innocently.

He waited several seconds until the footsteps had completely died away and silently made his way up the hillside, the child against him in one arm. Part way up he heard Rebecca scream out his name and he stopped, listening and hoping with every inch of his being that he could rush to her. He heard her cry out again, indignation in her voice, and he continued to scramble up the hill.

As he reached the rise to the road, he heard a horse galloping off swiftly, and the angered cry of his own animal, still fastened to the carriage. Rebecca was nowhere in sight.

He leapt up onto the road and set the child in a soft pile of clothing near the carriage. He struggled to unhitch Cannonball from the carriage, the horse finally scrambling to its feet and stomping in circles angrily. Commanding the horse firmly he pulled the animal clear of the carriage. The dead body of the driver lay motionless beneath the broken wheel.

He held his daughter, frantic with indecision, while the horse snorted hotly at his shoulder. He could not leave the infant alone in the wilderness, and he knew that if he could not reach Rebecca, Dianna would surely kill her.

He tried to devise a way to carry the baby and still travel on horseback, but the Arabian bore no saddle and, even without the child, Timothy would have a hard ride. He pulled a piece of leather luggage from the carriage hoping to attach it across the animal's back. He tried stuffing the bag with a shirt, and pulled the flap closed loosely to allow for air. He drew his rifle from the broken carriage and tried to find a way to hold the child and mount the animal. Timothy heard a fast approaching horse.

Believing he recognized Dianna racing towards him, he sighted the muzzle of his gun, targeting the approaching rider.

"Timothy!" Octavia shouted.

He held onto the trigger and began to squeeze it slowly.

"Timothy! Stop! I know where Mother may have gone!"

He lowered the rifle, his breathing rapid and hoarse.

"Where? She has Rebecca. Where is she?" he

yelled.

Octavia jumped from her horse, running frantically to face the infuriated giant.

"Have you come to claim your prize, Octavia?" Timothy snarled at her through clenched teeth.

"Mother's gone mad! You have to believe me, Tim. I had no idea of all the things she's been doing!"

"Get out of my way, Octavia. I have no time to listen to your lies. Tell me where she's taken my wife!" He lunged at her, grabbing her by the shoulders.

"I was a stupid fool!' Octavia cried. "She told me that she would take care of things. I let her do everything for me. I never cared as long as I had everything I wanted! She killed Uncle Finn, she admitted it all! She cut that poor sweet man's throat and left him dying, she wants to kill Rebecca too!" Octavia did not fight as Timothy growled fiercely into her face and held her in his painful grip.

"I thought I was in love with you until that day your son was missing. It all made sense the day you told me you were to be married. I was so angered not to get what I wanted. But you weren't in love with me. You belonged to Rebecca. Tim, I was a fool and Mother has her now. Please listen to me. She's heading for the clearing behind Hawk Bend Station. You have to go after her. She's crazy, Tim! She'll kill her!"

Timothy pushed her from him and turned to mount his horse as Louisa let out a clear squeal.

"Damn," he cursed. He opened the bag and lifted out the child, his hands shaking with fear and indecision.

"Timothy?" Octavia gasped. "Where on earth did you get a baby?"

"She's my daughter, Octavia."

"Give her to me, Tim. You can't go after Rebecca with a baby! Don't be a fool. Leave her with me. Go get your wife!"

Timothy looked at her, his face dark and infuriated.

"Damn it all, Octavia!"

"Tim, I would never hurt her. Please, go get your wife before this poor baby loses her mother. Now!" Octavia screamed at him, her body shaking with fear.

Timothy looked down at his daughter's tiny face and quivered in dread as he handed her to Octavia, choking back tears. He took his rifle and leapt onto the Arabians back.

"I swear Octavia. If anything happens to that child I will hunt you down until my dying day."

"I know," Octavia whispered as the man rode off.

He picked up Dianna's trail quickly, quaking with terror as he rode. His eyes spilling over with tears, he drove his horse, clinging to the animal's mane with fear and hatred.

Timothy Elgerson rode on, crazed, until he found evidence that two people had left a horse and scuffled in the dirt.

The Arabian was frantic, sensing his master's panic as Timothy lay against the big stallion's back studying the jumble of footsteps in the dust.

He heard a shout not far in the distance and urged the horse forward, easing out his rifle. Through the tangle of trees he could make out the broad back of

Dianna, her feet planted beneath her and could hear her bellows.

"I will find you and kill you, bitch!" she screamed. "Elgerson is dead and I swear you will rot in hell beside him!"

Timothy slid from the horse's back, and circled around on foot through the undergrowth. He found a bushy thicket and hunkered down to sight his rifle when suddenly Rebecca reached out from under the bushes and grabbed his arm.

"The baby?" she whispered, in a barely audible rush.

Timothy nodded and held his finger to his lips.

He stepped through the woodland and heard a sharp click.

"There you are bitch!" Dianna stood over Rebecca, her gun cocked.

Timothy lifted his rifle and fired. The bullet found its target and Dianna Weintraub fell to the ground dead.

He hung his head and swallowed hard. Timothy tried to call to his wife. His chest was tightly fixed and he felt strangled, his breathing too constricted to utter a sound.

He saw her move in the thicket. "Rebecca," he uttered.

"Timothy?" She scrambled to him, her face choked with tears. She threw herself to him violently as they held one another on the damp forest floor.

"The baby. Timothy, where's the baby?" She shook uncontrollably and clung to his arm.

He pulled her to her feet without a word, nearly dragging her to the horse and flung her onto the

Arabian's back. Jumping up behind her he kicked the horse to a fast run.

"Is she alright?" Rebecca cried, her voice trailing off in their speed.

The huge animal carried his frantic riders swiftly along the narrow road, Rebecca clinging to the horses' mane, the big hard man against her back.

Chapter Sixty-Seven

*T*imothy reined the horse to a sudden halt, and leapt from the animal's back. He began to search the area around the overturned carriage.

"Where is she?" Rebecca screamed as she slid from the horse and stumbled hysterically in the road.

Octavia emerged from the woods, her face streaming with tears. Rebecca gasped in terror.

The big woman walked to Rebecca and handed her the baby, sobbing deeply.

Rebecca took her daughter carefully, her face pale with fear and moved aside the blanket to see her infant daughter looking up at her calmly. Her arms began to tremble violently and she held the baby close to her.

"I never wanted it to be this way," Octavia wept.

Timothy strode to Rebecca's side and laid his arm across her shoulder protectively, his heart pounding thunderously in his chest.

"Your baby, she's so beautiful." Octavia choked. "I thought I was in love. I only wanted you to love me."

Timothy looked at the big woman, and Rebecca held her baby close as they watched Octavia standing wretchedly in the road.

"She killed him for me, you know? She did it all for me. She said it was because she loved me!" Her cries turned to anger and she snarled.

"She didn't love me, she only loved herself. The farm is in foreclosure. She needed money. She told me I was in love with you. It was easy for her to convince me because I had no idea what love was." She wiped her eyes with the back of her hand.

"It's right here, though, isn't it? You see! It's right there in the baby's innocent face. I was looking at her and I heard the shot. I know what happened. I know what Mother has done. I knew it had to happen. Your baby smiled at me, and I knew. It was not about love. It was never about love."

"I'm sorry, Octavia." Timothy hung his head.

"Don't be, Tim. You can't change any of it. You can't bring back Uncle Finn. You can't undo what Jude did to that poor horse. No one can do anything more about what Mother did to both of you. What I tried to do." Octavia doubled over, consumed with grief. After several wrenching sobs she stood up and looked at them both.

"Timothy Elgerson, you were my friend once, and I was never really grateful for that. You take Rebecca home now. You take her and your baby home to Stavewood where they belong.

"I'm going to my mother. Mother thought you could capture love by hating. I don't hate either of you. I never want to hate like she did.

"Rebecca, you love that baby. Teach her what love really means. She is the most perfect thing I have ever seen."

Octavia gathered her skirt up around her feet and started up the road, turning into the woodland.

Rebecca buried her face into the strong shoulder of her husband, sobbing softly as she stood with her family in the road and heard the shot from Octavia's pistol echo through the woods.

"It's all over, Rebecca." Timothy Elgerson whispered to his wife.

Chapter Sixty-Eight

The magnificent Queen Anne stood proudly on

the hilltop, her majestic turret piercing the dazzling blue sky. Leaded glass windows glittered brilliantly, each facet reflecting the surrounding white pine and deciduous forest, as if the glorious spectacle existed entirely to frame the regal home.

"Welcome home, Rebecca." Timothy smiled lovingly to his wife and daughter beside him as he pulled the carriage from the road into Stavewood.

The End

South of Stavewood

In book two of the *Stavewood* saga, at the

wedding of Timothy and Rebecca Elgerson, the adventure of the family of *Stavewood* continues. Emma Harris arrives, Rebecca's cousin from England, having followed the mail-order-bride on her own adventure. On that day Emma Harris becomes more than a guest and begins a new life in beautiful northern Minnesota.

Roland Vancouver, once a successful foreman at the Elgerson mill, attends the ceremony as well. Less than optimistic for a happy future, he can only hope for a miracle. That glimmer of faith puts him in the path of Emma and the promise of love that takes them both on a journey of a lifetime.

Follow the lives of the families of *Stavewood* in *South of Stavewood* and book three, *Home to Stavewood*, coming soon!

If you enjoyed reading *Stavewood* I would be very thankful if you would post a positive review online. Your support is invaluable and I read all reviews. Your opinion will help me to continue the *Stavewood* series, as well as to write other books. To leave a review, please visit the page for this book at Amazon or Barnes and Noble. Select "Write a customer review".

Thank you so much for your support!
Sincerely,
    Nanette